# AFTER THE CROWN

"Majesty, I'm hearing gunfire outside my offices. Where's your *Ekam*?"

"In the hallway, I assume," I said.

"I'm not sure what's going on. I recommend you get back onto the *Vajra* with Admiral Hassan now. I'll touch base with you as soon as I can."

"Gods go with you." My voice sounded strange in my ears. Caspel gave me a fleeting smile and disconnected.

"Majesty, I second Caspel's suggestion. We can better protect you—" Admiral Hassan broke off, her eyes flying wide. "Incoming. I've got multiple bogies of unknown origin coming out of warp. Majesty, you need to—"

And then the building exploded around me.

Praise for

# BEHIND THE THRONE

"This debut ranks among the best political SF novels in years, largely because of the indomitable, prickly Hail... [a] fast-paced, twisty space opera"

*Library Journal* (starred review)

"Taut suspense, strong characterization, and dark, rapid-fire humor are the highlights of this excellent SF adventure debut"

*Publishers Weekly* (starred review)

"Full of fast-paced action and brutal palace intrigue, starring the fiercest princess this side of Westeros"

*B&N*

"Promising science-fiction series... for fans of stories with plenty of action and political maneuvering"

*Booklist*

By K. B. Wagers

*The Indranan War*
Behind the Throne
After the Crown

# AFTER THE CROWN

## THE INDRANAN WAR: BOOK 2

# K. B. WAGERS

orbit

www.orbitbooks.net

ORBIT

First published in Great Britain in 2016 by Orbit

1 3 5 7 9 10 8 6 4 2

A CIP catalogue record for this book
is available from the British Library.

ISBN 978-0-356-50802-3

Printed and bound by CPI Group (UK) Ltd, Croydon CR0 4YY

Papers used by Orbit are from well-managed forests
and other responsible sources.

MIX
Paper from
responsible sources
FSC® C104740

Orbit
An imprint of
Little, Brown Book Group
Carmelite House
50 Victoria Embankment
London EC4Y 0DZ

An Hachette UK Company
www.hachette.co.uk

www.orbitbooks.net

*To: Mom & Dad,*
*Tracy, Sara & Jeffrey*
*I love you.*

1

The execution site was an unremarkable building in the government sector across town. The room went quiet and the rolling murmurs on the air vanished when I walked in with my BodyGuards around me. We were a week out from the coup attempt that had taken the lives of too many of my Guards, and my teams were still in disarray. So both my *Ekam* and *Dve*, Emmory and Cas, stood at my sides. Zin, Willimet, and Kisah were behind us.

I was dressed in a black, military-style uniform—no sari, no mourning powder streaked across my face. It was a deliberate statement about the traitors whose deaths I'd come to witness: my cousin Ganda and my former nephew Laabh.

"Your Majesty."

Everyone in the room either dropped into a curtsy or bowed low.

"Everyone up, please." I moved across the room, exchanging greetings with the judge, the lawyers, and the police.

"Majesty." Prime Minister Eha Phanin executed his perfect bow and held a palm out to me in greeting. "We are glad to see you well."

"You also, Eha; I was relieved to hear you weren't injured in the chaos."

Phanin waved a long-fingered hand in the air. "I was in my offices when the incident occurred. Thankfully we went into lockdown and I don't think I was on their list of targets, given how unimportant my position is."

I didn't have a good reply for that. Technically he was the head of the General Assembly, but the political body was more for show than anything. Phanin had no real power in the governing of Indrana. He was there to placate the masses.

Even if I was going to change that, it wasn't something I was going to say out loud.

"Your Majesty." Two naval officers approached, saving me from the awkward situation. Phanin murmured his good-bye and stepped away.

"Commander Timu Stravinski." The commander was a man with graying hair at his temples and clear gray eyes. He saluted me and nodded to Emmory.

"Commander."

The young woman with him was barely eighteen. Her eyes were dark blue and her blond hair was twisted up into a smart knot off the collar of her naval uniform. I knew who she was before she said her name. My cousin. A member of my family—same as the woman I was about to kill.

"First Lieutenant Jaya Naidu, ma'am." She saluted me.

"Lieutenant." Ganda's little sister wasn't the spitting image of her treacherous sibling, but I could see the resemblance and I felt Emmory brace for a scene.

"I volunteered to witness, Your Majesty. To spare my parents further pain. They have removed the traitor's name from the family tree. I am not here for sympathy or to ease her passing. I'm only here to see justice done." Jaya bowed sharply.

"Give your parents my condolences," I said. I had seen my aunt several times during matriarch council meetings, but hadn't spoken to her. I hadn't seen my uncle since before I left home. I remembered my mother's only brother as a kind man with a gentle face.

"My family is loyal to you, Majesty."

"Of course. Thank you." I murmured the reply because I couldn't think of anything better to say. Lieutenant Naidu nodded again and left me alone.

There was no one here for Laabh except his lawyer, who bowed low in front of me. My nephew's father was gone, fled to the Saxons. His mother and sister lay dead from a bomb he helped radical *Upjas* plant. Leena's family had already washed their hands of him, lest the displeasure of the throne splash back on them. There was no one left for quiet denunciations and murmured declarations of loyalty. I was the only family he had left, and just this morning I'd issued the order to wipe his name from our records forever.

I spotted Leena Surakesh when she slipped in through the door, already dressed in widow's white. There were circles under my niece-in-law's eyes, and she gripped her sari so tightly that her knuckles stood out in stark relief against her skin. What had been a social coup for her was now a nightmare.

Murmuring my apology to Laabh's lawyer, I crossed to the door and pulled Leena into a hug before she curtsied. She froze, startled, and then clung for a moment.

"I left Taran at home," she said as she stepped away. "I didn't think it was appropriate. He doesn't understand what's happening."

"That was a wise choice. Leena, he's still my family. Whatever he did, it was because of his brother. We don't hold Taran accountable."

3

We'd retrieved some of the data from Dr. Satir's *smati* and it corroborated Laabh's story that the *Amanita virosa indus* had been slipped to Mother in the weekly gift of *lokum* Taran brought her. I had to contend with the idea that Dr. Satir might have known about the drug, though that secret died with her. There were no records of the treat being scanned when it was brought, and my suspicions over Mother's still-missing *Ekam*'s involvement in this whole mess ran high. Bial was a puzzle for another day. He'd fled Pashati the day of the attempted coup after saving my life.

"Please don't take him, Majesty. I've come to care for Taran."

"I have no plans for that, Leena. I received your mother's petition and I concur that the best place for him is out of the public eye. Taran will stay with you."

"Thank you."

Leena's eyes strayed over my shoulder toward the chamber on the far side of the room. "I loved my husband once. I'd thought he could be so much more."

"That's not a crime," I replied, watching as the bailiff escorted Laabh and Ganda into the chamber. "You've never seen anyone die, have you?"

"No, I—no, Majesty."

I took her gently by the shoulders. "There's no shame in looking away. This way is quieter than most, but you're still watching someone's life vanish in front of you. It changes a person to witness it."

"You've seen it."

I felt the smile flicker to life at the corner of my mouth. "More times than a person should."

"Then I will be strong like you, Majesty."

I didn't know how to tell her that strength had nothing to do with it. That even the strongest woke up in the middle of the night covered in sweat—remembering. So I let her go and looked at Willimet. "If she needs to leave, go with her."

"Yes, ma'am."

"Your Imperial Majesty and the others in attendance." The judge was a tall, slender woman named Sita Claremont. She addressed the small crowd as the technicians strapped Ganda and Laabh onto the tables in the chamber. The sound of their work was muffled by the glass partition separating us. "We're here today to see justice done in the matter of the Empire of Indrana versus Ganda Rhonwen Naidu and Laabh Albin."

Laabh was calm, his dark eyes still burning with fanatical hatred when they met mine. Ganda was less calm, her eyes darting around the room and her breath coming high and fast in her chest as the table was tilted slightly up so we could see her face.

Judge Claremont turned to look at the prisoners behind the glass. "You have both been found guilty, through evidence and your own confessions, of waging war against the state, direct participation in regicide, attempted regicide, and treason. Your right to trial was dismissed at the empress's pleasure. It is the empress's wish that on this day you take your last breaths and let the Dark Mother have her justice over you."

Ganda flinched. Laabh remained perfectly still.

"Your Imperial Majesty, is there any mercy in you for these two traitors?"

I'd known the judge's question was coming. The palace had been inundated with calls and messages about the execution. I'd read most of them and answered several of the calls personally. The one from Amnesty Galactic had been the most interesting.

In the end, I couldn't let it influence my decision. We had written confessions from each of them about their involvement in the deaths, and no matter my personal feelings on the matter, that was enough to condemn them.

Plus I knew better than to leave a living enemy behind me. I'd learned that lesson the hard way from Po-Sin, the gunrunning gang leader and my former employer.

"There is not."

"Very well." Judge Claremont nodded. "Do the condemned have anything to say?"

"I did what I had to for the good of the empire." Ganda's voice didn't ring with the same conviction as my mother's *Ekam* when he'd claimed the same thing. "The empress turned us belly-up to the Saxons and drove this empire into the ground. Now you'll all allow that trash upon the throne. A criminal, a self-admitted gunrunner! She's not worthy of your respect or your loyalty!"

I kept my face blank as she railed. I wasn't ashamed of the things I'd done after I left home.

"If you didn't want me to come back, Ganda, you shouldn't have killed my sisters. Cire should have been empress, or her daughter, or even Pace. All of them would have been a better choice than I am. It's your conspiracy, your treachery that put me here."

"No." Ganda shook her head, tears rolling down her face, but she didn't have any argument to make that would have swayed anyone's sympathy.

Laabh lifted his chin, the haughty look unable to fully hide the fear in his eyes. "You will all regret this," he said. "We see farther than you can imagine, and our plans are far more glorious than this piddling empire. You won't live through the next spin of the planet around the sun, you gunrunning whore."

There were gasps of outrage in the room. I crossed my arms over my chest and met Laabh's glare with a cold smile. "You won't live to see them fail," I replied.

Whatever he shouted in reply was cut off by Judge Claremont's quick gesture. The com system was deactivated and the two technicians in the room donned their helmets as the tables were lowered once more.

Nitrogen asphyxiation had been the preferred method of execution in the empire for thousands of years. It was a quick and painless method, but as I'd pointed out to Leena, it was still taking another human life.

The lights on the wall of the chamber flashed, and at Judge Claremont's nod the technicians threw the switch. The air circulators in the chamber sucked the oxygen out, replacing it with pure nitrogen.

Laabh was unconscious in under a minute with Ganda quickly following suit as the oxygen in their lungs and then their blood was replaced with nitrogen. The hypoxia that followed would cause brain death in a matter of moments.

I'd seen messier deaths and been directly involved in more than a few of them myself. This wasn't even the first time I'd stood on the other side of a glass window and watched people die, but there was undoubtedly something cold about these quick and silent deaths. It felt weird, clinical. It made me uneasy.

I watched their chests rise and fall, breaths growing shallower as the heartbeats on the monitors above the tables slowed. Laabh convulsed, and Leena's choked sob echoed through the room.

"*Uie Maa*. Take her outside, Will," I murmured without looking away from the people dying in front of me.

The shrill tone of the flatline indicating brain activity had ceased sounded through the speakers after Willimet ushered Leena out the door, as first Laabh's and then Ganda's brain shut down. The masked techs moved around the tables, efficiently checking their patients and passing the information along to Judge Claremont.

"Brain death confirmed," she announced. "Heart death to follow in approximately three minutes."

The flatline tone had been turned off with the confirmation, so we all stood in silence again as we waited for the final words from the techs. The one at Laabh's side turned and nodded once, but I didn't release the breath I was holding until Ganda's tech nodded also.

"Heart death confirmed. Execution sentence carried out at 2253 Capital Standard Time. Let the record reflect that justice has been served."

"Majesty." Emmory's voice held a hint of warning when I stepped up to the glass.

"There is ash on the air. Spiraling higher. We are cut down by sunlight. Mother Destroyer finds mercy in the taste of our skin." The words of the poem spilled from my lips in a whisper.

"Cas, we're moving, have them bring the car around." Emmory put a hand on my back. "Majesty, it's time to go."

I turned away from the glass, not in the mood to argue with him. With a final nod at the people assembled, I let my Body-Guards whisk me away from that place of death and back to the palace.

I made a beeline for the liquor cabinet by the fireplace and poured from the first bottle I grabbed. Fire blossomed in my chest, melting some of the ice lodged there, so I poured another shot and tossed it back.

"Majesty—"

"Not the time to chastise me, Zin."

"Actually, I'm kind of wishing I weren't on duty," my *Ekam*'s husband replied with a smile. "You probably want to be careful though. You didn't eat much at dinner."

I paused in the act of pouring a third glass and gave him

a look. "Is that part of your job now? Monitoring my food intake?"

"That's always been part of my job. I'm just mentioning it now because a third shot of Calasian whiskey on an empty stomach will probably put you on your ass—Majesty."

Snorting with laughter, I took my glass and sat down on the couch. "I could drink you under the table, Tracker."

"Don't even think about it, Zin," Emmory said. "First off, you're not having a drinking contest with the empress. Secondly, she probably *can* outdrink you. You're good but you're not in the same league as someone who drank a squad of Hyperion Royal Marines unconscious."

"I thought that story wasn't true." Zin raised an eyebrow at me.

"Partially." I saluted him with my glass and winked. "Two. There were only two and it was a close call. And don't think I don't realize what you're up to."

"Who, us?" Zin grinned at me.

"I have to do that again tomorrow. Shiva, that was cold." My good humor abruptly vanished and I stared into the swirl of golden-brown liquor in my glass. At least my former Body-Guard's execution would be less public.

"Yes, you do. It's necessary, Majesty."

"Doesn't make it any easier."

"I'd worry about you if it were easy." Emmory sat down across from me with his hands braced on his knees. "That's not the only thing that's bothering you though, is it?"

"They deserved it," I said, unblinking.

He nodded.

"They killed my mother, my sisters, Jet, Ramani. Too many others, Emmory. I'm not sorry for what just happened. I swore I'd find the people responsible for this and make them pay."

The whiskey disappeared in a swallow and I set the glass down with the careful precision of someone who'd had just a little too much to drink.

"Bugger me." I muttered the curse under my breath. "Not a word." I held up a hand in Zin's direction as I got to my feet and swayed a little. "Not a single word."

"What upsets you, ma'am?" Emmory prompted. "The fact that you're sorry for the necessity of killing or that you're not sorry?"

"Next time I'm just pulling the trigger myself. It's easier than standing there and letting someone else do my dirty work."

"Answer the question." The snap of command in his voice did the trick, and I whirled on my *Ekam*.

"Damn you! I don't know!" I shouted. "I'm supposed to be sorry, aren't I? Isn't that what civilized people feel when they watch someone die right in front of them? Especially like that, all trussed up and helpless? I could have granted clemency. We had the information we needed from them. I had the power of forgiveness in my hands and I could have just let them live out their days in a cell. I've spent the whole gods-damned week talking to people who thought I should.

"But standing there, all I could think of was how I'd promised my sisters I'd find the people responsible and make them pay. All I could remember was Po-Sin breaking my leg after I turned my back on a Yakuza who was still alive." A curious amusement swelled as I remembered. "He shot the man first, then taught me a lesson I've never forgotten about turning my back on my enemies. I don't leave living enemies behind me, Emmy. Ever."

Zin made a noise that sounded like I'd punched him. Emmory, in contrast, went still. He never broke eye contact with me, but I'd gotten better at seeing the signs of their background conversations.

Our *smati*, the array of five microscopic chips inserted into key areas of the brain, used our own neurons and pathways as power and conduits to create a permanent interface. It allowed for communication, visual and audio recordings, even photography with the right tech installed in one's fingertips or palm. The device had a massive storage capacity, and for the right price a host of other handy applications.

The range had improved over the years, going from just a few meters to over a hundred on the military models. Anything past that required access to a communication array.

For Emmory and Zin, it improved upon a relationship already honed by years of working together.

I let it drag on for a minute or so. "Are you two finished talking about me?"

"Zin objects to Po-Sin's teaching methods, ma'am."

"He wouldn't be the first," I replied, and sank back down on the arm of the rose-colored couch. "Hao was furious and I thought for sure Portis was going to kill him. The pain was—" I fumbled for words to describe it. "I'd screwed up though and almost got killed because of it. It was a good lesson to learn. I've never made that mistake again. I'm a gods-awful noble, Emmory, more comfortable in drinking contests and tavern brawls than I am at court."

"You are the Empress of Indrana," he said quietly.

"More's the pity," I shot back. "Right now I'd rather go back to being a gunrunner."

"No, you wouldn't." And just like that, the man I'd known for less than an Indranan month read me so easily and so completely that all I could do was stare at him.

I'd made my choice to stay, and whatever liquor-fueled words came off my tongue didn't change that. "Fine. I wouldn't." It was the closest I'd come to admitting he was right. Getting to my feet, I debated the wisdom of having another drink before deciding I really didn't want to be hungover tomorrow. "I'm going to bed."

"I'll send Stasia in, Majesty."

"I don't need her," I replied. My maid was too kind and the thought of exposing her to my sharpness didn't sit well with me. I closed my bedroom door, stripped out of my clothes, and crawled into bed. Within moments I was asleep, but my dreams were filled with death and pain and I woke in a pool of moonlight and sweat.

I got out of bed, wrapping myself in my robe, and leaned against the windowsill. The moon was high in the sky, beaming through the stained-glass windows.

"Come in," I said to the expected knock on my door.

"Majesty?" Zin, as usual, was the one to check on me, and I didn't look away from the moon as I waved him into the room. "Are you all right?"

"Just another dream. I'm getting used to them," I lied.

"You shouldn't have to, ma'am. We could see if Dr. Ganjen can give you something to help you sleep."

"I'm fine, Zin." I turned from the window with a smile.

"Do you want me to send Stasia in with something to drink?"

"I want to know what Laabh was talking about when he said 'our plans.'" I grabbed the poker and jabbed at the coals before throwing another log on them and sitting in my chair. The flames crawled along the edge of the wood, gaining strength as they found more fuel. "This isn't over, Zin. It might never be over."

"We all signed on for the long haul, Majesty, if that's what you're worried about."

I laughed but didn't look away from the fire. "I'm not worried about you, or Emmory, or any of the BodyGuards who survived." Thoughts of Jet and the others brought a sharp pain in my chest and fisted a hand against my stomach. "I don't know who to trust, Zin. If this spreads as far as Laabh claimed, who can we trust?"

"I don't know, Majesty. I promise we're looking into it. Every contact he had, every meeting and com link, every single person who came within two meters of the man is on our radar." Zin knelt next to my chair. "If they truly do have a plan, they'll have to move on it and we'll be ready for them."

"I need something to do."

"Right now? Sleep, Majesty. You need the rest." He got to his feet and offered me his hand.

"*Dhatt.* You're as much a bully as Emmory." I sighed but took it and let him usher me back to bed.

"Good night, Majesty. I'll see you in the morning."

# 2

The biggest problem, Your Majesty, has been the distance. Given the importance of the mission, my operative obviously—"

"Caspel, if you don't get to the point I'm going to shoot you," I warned with a raised eyebrow.

Caspel Ganej, Director of Galactic Imperial Security for the Empire of Indrana, didn't flinch at my words. A smile curved under his beaklike nose. "Your pardon, Your Majesty, but you are unarmed."

I kept my eyebrow up as I glanced over my shoulder. "I'm sure Emmory will let me borrow his gun. Won't you, Emmory?"

"Of course, Majesty."

Caspel grinned at me. "Your Majesty, the area is unstable and we cannot trust Admiral Shul. All I know at present is that Governor Ashwari made it off the planet. I am sure my operative is bringing her back here with all haste."

"Thank you, Caspel. Was that so hard to say?"

"No, ma'am."

"I want to know immediately if you hear from your operative."

"Yes, ma'am." Caspel nodded as he rose. *"Majesty, I will need to speak to you in private about Admiral Shul."* Caspel's stride toward the door didn't slow and I had to stop myself from turning around to stare at his retreating back.

*"Our usual meeting place?"* I replied over the dedicated line of my *smati.*

*"Yes, ma'am."*

"Who's next, Alba?" I reached for my cup. *"I'll see you at first song then, Caspel, and you owe me. I'm going to be dead tired tomorrow."*

*"I wouldn't ask if it weren't important, Majesty. And we both know you haven't been sleeping anyway."*

I wasn't going to ask how he knew that.

"We've got half an hour before you need to head for Shivan's. Matriarch Desai needs five minutes, and Matriarchs Gohil and Khatri have asked for a moment of your time if you can spare it."

"Really?" I paused with the cup at my lips. "I'm interested enough to squeeze them in, Alba. Tell them they have fifteen minutes, so I hope they're nearby. Have Clara come in while I'm waiting." Taking a sip of my blue chai, I shared a look with Emmory.

"I have no idea, Highness," he said in answer to my unasked question.

Matriarch Clara Desai had terrified me when I was a child. She was one of the few people besides my father who could get me to behave. Now I counted the older woman as one of my closest allies in the palace.

She entered the room, a woman my height following on her heels. A person would have to be blind not to see the family resemblance. Clara dropped into a curtsy, while the woman in the gray uniform bowed low.

"Good evening, Majesty. May I present my daughter—Major Gita Desai."

"Majesty." The woman bowed again.

"A pleasure, Major. You're with the army?"

"At present, Majesty, yes."

I eyed Clara's daughter. "Well, my curiosity has been piqued. What does that mean, Major?"

Major Desai dropped to a knee. "Your Imperial Majesty, I know you are in need of BodyGuards. I would offer my life to that end, should you desire it."

Matriarch Desai's face was perfectly neutral, betraying nothing about her personal feelings on her daughter's decision. I raised an eyebrow at Emmory. He responded with the barest shrug of his shoulder.

"A very generous offer, Major Desai." Getting up off the couch, I grabbed her shoulders and lifted her to her feet. The memory of doing the very same thing to Jet rushed through me, and I had to close my eyes for a moment before I drowned in my grief. "One I will gladly entertain, but with the reminder that my *Ekam* has the final say on replacements and I wouldn't think to countermand his judgment where my safety is concerned."

"Of course, Majesty."

"Major, if you'll go with Alba, she'll take you to Cas and he can get you started with in-processing. Have you spoken to your commanding officer about this?" Emmory asked.

"I have, sir. She is in full support."

I watched Matriarch Desai watching her daughter as she left the room. Some of her sadness slipped through the mask and I laid my hand on her arm. "Clara, I could tell Emmory to—"

"Please don't, Majesty. She's no safer in the army than she would be at your side, and it would devastate her if she knew

16

she missed her chance to be your BodyGuard because I wanted to keep her safe."

"It would," I murmured. "It took me twenty years to forgive my mother for it."

Matriarch Desai curtsied again. "With your leave, Majesty. I know Alice and Zaran are anxious to speak with you and your schedule is full."

I waved a hand and shook out the deep blue skirt I was wearing. Taking the heavy white sari from the back of the couch, I wandered to the bank of windows in my reception room. I'd worn my customary uniform to Nal's execution this morning, but afterward I'd felt the need to change into something with a bit more protection from the cold. I wrapped the sari around myself, understanding a little better the struggle my mother must have experienced—knowing I'd wanted so fiercely to join the military, but wanting so desperately to keep me safe, especially after my father's death.

The sun was setting behind the waters of Balhim Bay, throwing streaks of gold across the rippling sheet of navy that stretched in an arc to the south of Krishan. The white caps of the waves were the only other break in the darkness. Frost crawled across the panes of glass as the temperature continued to drop with the setting sun. Magh was a bitterly cold month, the short days still struggling to grow longer in the wake of Pratimas.

It suited the mood. I'd been home barely four weeks now and had seen more death here than my whole time away. This was saying something, considering gunrunners dealt out an awful lot of violence.

The door opened and I heard Emmory's murmured greeting but didn't turn around even though I was extremely curious about the requested meeting. Whatever it was, it was important enough the pair had hung around the palace hoping I'd say yes.

After a sufficient number of heartbeats had passed, I faced them and both women dropped into curtsies. "Your Majesty."

Alice Gohil had been one of the first matriarchs after Clara to acknowledge my claim to the throne and offer her support. And her companion was the newly appointed Matriarch Zaran Khatri, whose testimony would likely convict her mother of treason in absentia.

"Alice. Zaran." I nodded at them as they rose, noting with quiet amusement they both wore the *salwar kameez* that was coming back into style. It was as close as the noble families were willing to get to my own simple style of dress.

"Majesty." Zaran dipped her blond head again when I didn't say anything else. "Thank you for seeing us." She was a good head taller than her darker companion, and apparently the reason they were there at all, judging from Alice's silence. "I understand you are meeting with Abraham Suda, and I realize I have no right to ask you for a favor—"

"Who told you that?" I softened my raised eyebrow with a smile when she blanched. "Not the information about the meeting, but the idea that you have no right to a favor. If not for you, Zaran, it would have taken us a lot longer to figure out who was involved in the conspiracy, who was responsible for the murder of my family. A lot more people could have died. We owe you a great deal."

"Yes, Majesty. I know, but my mother is—" She stopped, swallowed, and then straightened her spine as she looked at me with a strength that surprised me. "A traitor, Majesty."

"You are not."

"I am not. I love Indrana. I am loyal to the throne and to you. I want to make this empire better."

18

"You want to be there when I meet with Abraham and the *Upjas*. Granted." I grinned at the shocked look on her face.

"Majesty, I—"

"Were you expecting a debate on the subject, Zaran? You've been in contact with them. More recently than I have, I'll add, and likely are more in tune with their actual plans. It would be helpful to have you there. Alice, too, I think, even though I know she only came with you for moral support."

An idea had already taken root in my brain and I waved a hand at them with a smile. "I'll have Alba message you tomorrow with the time and location of the meeting. Good night."

"Good night, Majesty."

I braced myself against the back of the couch as the room spun. Emmory was at my side in an instant, his arm around my waist holding me up.

"I'm fine." I pressed a hand to my forehead. "Just dizzy."

"You're exhausted. We should cancel dinner."

"I can't. I need to see Taran. I wouldn't sleep anyway." I leaned against him as we moved around the couch and then dropped onto it with a curse. "I'll be fine, I just need to get my breath." I closed my eyes, opening them when Emmory crouched beside me.

"Here," he said, holding up his gloved hand. I leaned in and inhaled the mist that spiraled upward.

My head cleared as the Phrine hit my system and everything around me sharpened like it was cut from crystal.

"Better?" he asked.

I nodded and smiled, hoping it would ease the frown on my *Ekam*'s face. Phrine was bad news. The adrenaline-based drug had its uses during battle and things like hostage situations, but long-term use was asking for heart failure and other less fatal but still nasty complications. Emmory and I both knew we couldn't keep using it, but I also couldn't seem to get a decent night's sleep and there was just too much to get done.

I blew out a frustrated breath. "Do you have a list of younger nobles who are involved with the *Upjas*?"

My *Ekam* waited a beat before responding. "Possibly, Majesty. May I ask why you'd like to know?"

"Curious, mostly. I'm too close to this to really be involved. We all know it. Abraham and I can meet and exchange pleasantries, but if we want any actual discussion to happen it's going to have to be out of our earshot."

"You're talking about negotiations?"

"I am." I nodded, tapping a finger on the window. "Alice doesn't believe in the *Upjas*' cause and would provide a critical eye in counterpoint to Zaran's youthful idealism."

"It could work, Majesty. You really don't have the time in your schedule to personally oversee negotiations with what's still technically a terrorist group," Alba said, handing me my chai. It was hot again, and I sipped at it as Emmory mulled over my idea.

"I have a list, Majesty," he said finally, his dark eyes thoughtful.

"Fantastic. Message Abraham then, and tell him to come to the palace and see me." Smiling brightly when my BodyGuard gave me the Look, I handed my empty cup back to Alba. "We'd better get going, or we're going to be late and Leena will fret."

I was surrounded by familiar faces as we headed up the steps into Shivan's. I was trying to keep my outside appearances to a minimum since I knew Emmory hadn't approved more than a handful of new BodyGuards and didn't want any of them on duty when we were out in the open.

*Funny, Hail, you make it sound like you've been coming here forever.* I'd only been once since I'd been home, back when Jet had still been alive. Rama had worn a look of nervous concentration as he'd ushered me past the clamoring media, and Adail's face had been blank as he waited inside the door of the restaurant. Now they were both dead, too. Adail turned traitor on me and killed Rama, and Emmory killed him in turn.

"How does a week and a half feel like a lifetime?"

"Grief stretches out our hearts, Majesty." Zin pushed the door open for me. His gray-green eyes were gentle with shared pain. We'd all lost and grieved as we counted the dead from the failed coup. I missed them all, but Jet's absence was a painful hole I knew Zin felt. He had grown close with the BodyGuard who'd sacrificed himself for me in Garuda Square during their short time together. I'd survived and stayed on my throne, but some days the cost didn't feel like it was worth it.

Offering up a halfhearted smile, I went through the doorway of the gray brick building and left the noise of the outside world behind.

"Majesty." Avan Shivan took my hands and pressed kisses to my cheeks. The rotund owner of the restaurant had remained a dear friend despite my time away. I'd spent many hours hidden away in the kitchen in the days after my father's death. This restaurant was still a haven, free from media surveillance and anyone whom Avan deemed unsuitable. "Your nephew and sister-in-law are waiting for you."

"Thank you. It's busy tonight."

"We're out to a six-month waiting list, Majesty." He smiled. "Everyone wants to eat here on the off-chance you'll stop by."

I laughed. "I'm glad I'm good for business."

"Elevator, Majesty?"

"You mean I have a choice, *Ekam*?" I teased.

The last time I'd been in Shivan's, Emmory had been so paranoid I'd had to take the stairs. Granted, people were trying to kill me at the time, so it wasn't wholly unfounded. Stairs sucked regardless, so I headed for the elevator before Emmory changed his mind.

I had no way of knowing what Taran's reaction would be. He'd loved his brother, idolized him, and he was old enough to understand what was going on despite Leena's attempts to shield him from the worst of it.

I'd ordered everyone to silence about the fact that it had been Taran's weekly visits to my mother that had allowed the traitors to poison her. We'd gone to great lengths to keep that information secret. There were things an eight-year-old boy didn't need to know, and if I could protect him from the worst of the fallout it was worth the lies.

"Nervous, Majesty?"

I shot him a sideways look. "I don't know anything about kids, Zin. What am I supposed to say?"

"My aunts always started with 'Hello, so good to see you.'"

I punched him in the shoulder as we exited the elevator. "I hate you."

"Yes, ma'am." He exchanged a nod with Indula and Willimet, the latter opening the door for me with a smile. For whatever reason, Indula had passed Emmory's test and was out in public with us. He was the only one of the new recruits I'd seen with us outside the palace—possibly because he'd been my mother's BodyGuard and had proved his loyalty when he'd turned Bial over to us during the fighting.

As I'd learned in the last month, Zin was frequently right. I worried about Taran for nothing.

"Aunt Hail!" My nephew would have rushed me but for Leena grabbing him by the collar. Taran jerked to an unwilling stop. "Your Majesty." Throwing his guardian a look over his shoulder, he gave an awkward bow.

At the insistence of Matriarch Desai and Matriarch Surakesh, I'd agreed to strip Taran of his princely status and allow him to be formally adopted into the Surakesh clan. He was officially just a noble now and not a member of the royal family.

"In private there's little need to be so formal," I said with a smile. "Either of you."

Leena's answering smile was cautious. "I'm trying to teach him some respect for the throne, Majesty. Given the circumstances I thought it would be best."

"True." I crouched down and held out my arms to my nephew. "But we are family and that is also important."

I pressed my cheek to Taran's curly hair as he hugged me. He was the only family I had left, the only Bristol offspring from my mother's line besides me to survive. The tragedy was that the traitors had managed to wipe out my mother's direct line in the end. There were distant second cousins, the offspring of my grandmother's siblings and their children, but Taran would never take the throne, and I couldn't have children of my own.

Not that I'd shared *that* secret with anyone. An ambush on a backwater planet had destroyed any hope of an heir from me, but the only man who'd known about it was dead and I wasn't about to announce it after narrowly surviving a coup attempt by my cousin and nephew.

Besides, with Indrana hovering on the verge of a renewed war with the Saxon Alliance and my own grip on the throne still tenuous, it was the last pot of oil I needed to throw on the fire.

"Mr. Joshi says I have a real talent for quantum mechanics." Taran babbled on about his day as he released me and sat down. I shook off the chill and forced my attention back to him, and before I knew it dinner was over.

"Young man, let me show you a puzzle. If you can figure it

23

out I'll believe your tutor's high praise," Zin said, gesturing for Taran to follow him to the window so that Leena and I could talk in private.

"Have you had any luck?"

"Nothing, Majesty." Leena glanced over her shoulder at where Taran was happily chattering at Zin. "I've looked through all Laabh's communications that I could access. He was smart enough to keep it off the house servers."

I kicked myself again for listening to everyone who'd told me I couldn't violate Laabh's privacy and forcibly download his *smati* before he'd had a chance to delete all his files. There'd been very little information after his death, and all that we'd gotten from Ganda's computer was proof that she hadn't known any of what Laabh and Wilson were planning.

"I'll keep digging, Majesty. We did get some leads on his repeat visitors, and my security is following up on that now."

"Do that, Leena. I don't want to be blindsided by whatever he claims is coming."

"Absolutely, Majesty."

We said our good-byes, Taran too busy trying to figure out Zin's puzzle to notice that the adults were equally preoccupied.

I boarded my aircar behind a privacy screen, my Body-Guards splitting into the decoy cars Emmory insisted upon. Given that Mother's first *Ekam* had died in an aircar crash, I couldn't blame him for the precaution.

"Pity we can't just meet with Caspel now," I muttered, staring out the window at the night sky. "It wouldn't surprise me if he just appears if you say his name three times."

My *Ekam* shook his head and laughed. "He's neither demon nor wizard, Majesty."

"Neither are our enemies, and yet they seem to have vanished like it." I picked at the stitching on my skirt for a moment and then looked up at Emmory again. "Sometimes it feels like we've done this for a lifetime."

We hadn't though. Over a month ago my *Ekam* had been a Tracker, sent by my older sister to bring me home. I'd been determined to stay as far away from Indrana as I could, the thought of returning to the confines of the palace unbearable. But the deaths of my sisters and my mother's decline into what we'd thought was Shakti dementia hadn't given me much of a choice once I'd returned home.

"Sometimes it does."

I wasn't sure if him agreeing with me was a good thing, so I looked back out the window, keeping my thoughts to myself.

# 3

"M ajesty?"

I turned from the bedroom window at Emmory's call and wiped the angry tears from my cheeks with the heel of my hand. "We should go; you know how nervous Caspel gets when we're late."

"You didn't sleep."

"I did."

"Liar." My *Ekam* gifted me with a rare smile. "You dozed. Same as you have for the past week. You can't keep staying out of dreams, Majesty. It's not good for you, and neither is the Phrine."

"Neither are the nightmares." I crossed to the closet. Emmory would stand there all night and lecture me rather than get moving. Pushing aside the clothing, I tapped the code into the hidden doorway and looked over my shoulder at him. "I'm tired, Emmory, but it's more exhausting to have to watch Portis die or Jet get blown up than it is to go without sleep for a bit."

Emmory didn't counter me, but I could feel his disapproval boring into my back.

I crawled into the confines of the tunnel, and thankfully Emmory didn't pursue the conversation as we headed out of the palace. I could wrestle with my claustrophobia or argue with my BodyGuard—but not both.

"Bugger me." The cold hit like a knife in the kidney, and I huddled deeper into the hood of my dark coat as I pulled my SColt 45 free. I grabbed Emmory's hand and helped him to his feet. After a quick nod at me, he put a hand on my back and we started off down the alleyway.

The night was dark. The sky above filled with stars winking through the thin veil of scattered clouds. Cold air stung my lungs, a sharpness I could only counter with shallow breaths. The streets were empty; only one other figure in the distance hurried to their destination without the slightest glance toward Emmory and me.

Half an hour later we were down by the docks. The sound of the waves was loud in the early-morning air and the chill sank past all the layers of clothing, biting deep.

Emmory stepped in front of me when a shadow separated from one of the buildings.

"It's just me, *Ekam*," Caspel said, his hands up.

"It is flat-out ridiculous that I have to sneak around just to be able to meet with the head of my spy agency in private. We could be in my rooms, Caspel. Warm."

"My apologies, Majesty. It is the nature of the game. Walk with me. There's a fire around the corner."

True to his word there was a vacated heating coil that spat blue flame in an alcove off to our left. I stuck my hands as close as I dared while Emmory turned his back on us, scanning the darkness with unforgiving eyes.

"What is so damned important, then? Or do I have to stand out here and freeze before you tell me?"

"I was finally able to get in touch with my operative aboard Admiral Shul's vessel." Caspel's grim look accompanied his words and made my stomach twist.

"How bad is it?" The fire forgotten, I wrapped my arms around my waist and tried not to shiver.

"Bad, Majesty. The admiral is behaving as though everything is fine for the sake of the rank and file. However, most of his command crew and a significant portion of the ship's crew have voiced displeasure over your ascension to the throne."

"That's not really a new thing."

"True," Caspel said without a hint of irony. "Admiral Shul has a higher-than-normal percentage of males on his command ship and in the 2nd Fleet as a whole. Also, my asset hasn't confirmed yet, but they suspect Major Bristol is still on board the ship."

"He doesn't deserve that name. He only got it when he married my sister."

"My apologies, Majesty. I was using it out of expediency and to avoid confusion."

I nodded only because it was too cold to argue, but I had formally revoked Albin Maxwell Bristol's standing from the Bristol ranks at the same time I'd removed Laabh, and I didn't want to hear that name in conjunction with mine again. "Can they confirm without blowing their cover?" I asked.

Caspel wiggled a gloved hand. "Possibly. Given what we know, Majesty, my first thought is that my operative have an exit strategy ready for themselves and as many loyal subjects as they can gather should—"

"The proverbial shit hit the fan?" I returned Caspel's nod of agreement. "Yes, absolutely. And I want an idea of how many other loyal subjects I have in the fleet entire. Let's not allow Shul to run off with any more of my ships than we have to."

"Absolutely, Majesty."

"We're out then; I'm freezing and Emmory is no doubt getting antsy."

"Of course, Majesty. We'll speak again when I know more."

"Somewhere warmer."

"Of course, Majesty." Caspel bowed and vanished into the shadows like a ghost.

Rolling my eyes, I looped my arm through my BodyGuard's and headed back out into the light. *"Thoughts on that?"* I asked through our *smati* link. *"We can trust him, right?"*

*"As much as I trust anyone, Majesty."*

*"That's not at all reassuring."*

*"Being reassuring isn't part of my job, Majesty."*

The image of Jet, reminding me that his job wasn't to keep me happy, lanced through me. It was followed by the memory of my demand that he not die and his smartass comment that that was in his job description.

"Majesty?" Emmory stopped, his gloved fingers closing on my wrist. I must have gasped out loud.

"Memories," I managed, and forced out a smile. "I'm not going to cry here, Emmy, my face will freeze."

I met the sun the next morning with bleary eyes and an edgy temper that carried itself into the daily briefing in my mother's office. I hated this room; the decorations were all wrong and I swore I could feel my mother's judgment raining down on me from the painting on the far wall. I didn't belong here.

"Majesty?"

I looked up at Clara and blinked. She raised an eyebrow, glancing at my desk where my fingers were drumming. I stopped them. "Sorry, what?"

"We are still clearing the rubble of the Imperial Tactical

Squad headquarters. For the moment General Vandi and the remains of the ITS command staff are using offices generously provided by Matriarch Tobin, but we need to discuss the long-term plan for rebuilding the site."

"And the cost," Phanin murmured. "Apologies, Majesty, but our budget is stretched tight as it is."

I nodded. I'd seen the numbers myself and even though I didn't understand half of what they meant, I could understand the big red mark of an ever-increasing debt.

We were stuck in the eternal struggle of being rich in resources but poor in available credits.

"Is there any reason they can't stay where they are for now? I'd prefer to not rush a reconstruction; that's how mistakes get made."

"I can't see why not," Admiral Hassan replied with a shrug.

Clara nodded in agreement. "Matriarch Tobin has said the ITS is welcome rent-free for as long as it takes to get the new buildings up, though we should probably discuss paying her something if it takes longer than a year."

"Okay, get someone on reconstruction plans and keep me in the loop. I don't really need to sign off on any of it. I trust you'll find someone competent enough."

Clara smiled slightly and swiped her finger through the air, scrolling down the list of meeting minutes on her *smati*. "You are meeting with the *Upjas* this afternoon, Majesty."

"Yes. Abraham and Tazerion are coming to the palace. Alice and Zaran will be in attendance." I arched an eyebrow at Phanin's poorly concealed frown. "Something to say, Prime Minister?"

"With apologies, Majesty, I believe this is a bad idea."

"You've said that the last several mornings. I get it. You don't want me to meet with them, but you're not in charge here."

Phanin bowed his head. "With ap—"

"If you say that again, I'm going to get out of this chair and punch you in the throat."

Phanin paled. Clara blinked at me. And the others around the room froze. I hadn't raised my voice at all, but my reputation still held the floor. I wondered if I'd still be able to command so much fear in twenty years or if I would have to actually punch someone in the throat occasionally to make sure it stuck.

"The *Upjas* are not the problem, and the throne will listen to their words. Then we will make up our minds. Indrana has enough enemies. I'd rather start looking to make some allies, and there is no better place to start than with our own people.

"If you don't like it, Phanin, that's fine. But I don't want to hear another word about it, and that includes talking to the press. Are we clear?"

"Perfectly, Majesty." He bowed his gray head.

"Bugger me, you people make me need a drink." I got up and crossed to the bar and poured myself a single shot of whiskey. Everyone found other things to look at as I tossed it back and returned to my seat.

Admiral Hassan cleared her throat after a minute. "Unless you have something else, Your Majesty, we have a meeting with the rest of the Raksha in half an hour and I'd like to go over the recent information on Canafey before that."

"No. I think we're done here. Clara?" I stood, everyone else following me.

"That was everything, Majesty." She dropped me a curtsy. "With your leave."

"I'll see you later." I watched Phanin leave the room, wrestling with my annoyance. I hadn't liked the man from the first moment I met him, but I couldn't put my finger on why.

"Politicians make my teeth hurt, too, Majesty," Hassan said

softly once we were alone. "But they have their uses and Phanin is very popular. Your sister listened to his advice."

I wasn't entirely sure why Cire had listened to his advice; the man set my teeth on edge. But she always had been more patient than me.

"So have I. I just don't agree with him." I rubbed at my forehead and hissed an exhale. "I'm also very irritable right now, Inana. I'll try to refrain from being—" I groped for the right word.

"Yourself, Majesty?"

I shot her a glare. "Ha. But yes, I guess so. Let's go look at the map before the others show up."

"Majesty, the *Upjas* are here."

I dragged myself out of the dreamless doze with a groan and shot Alba a dirty look I knew she didn't deserve. My chamberlain didn't flinch, which was one of the reasons I'd hired her in the first place.

She handed me a metal tube, and the bright burst of orange hit my nose with the cold water that misted over my face. It helped some, but I still looked in Emmory's direction.

My *Ekam* met my eyebrow with the Look. "You need actual sleep, Majesty."

"Until I can get it, this is going to have to do. I could just get the Phrine myself, Emmy. It says something that I'm asking you instead so you can keep track of how much I'm using."

His look clearly told me he wasn't sure just what it said, and to be honest I didn't know myself. What I did know was that I couldn't go into this meeting with my head full of sand.

I mustered up a smile. "Please?"

Emmory let out an almost imperceptible sigh before holding his gloved hand out. I inhaled, my head clearing instantly and my eyes losing their gritty feeling.

With Alba's help I brushed the wrinkles out of my black pants and readjusted the white silk top with its dark red flowers chasing down the sleeves. Then we headed out of my quarters and down the hallway to the smaller meeting room off the throne room. It was normally used for visiting heads of state, but the location meant that Abraham and Taz would have to go through the throne room, and I thought a reminder of who I was would be helpful.

The location for the first official meeting between the Empress of Indrana and the leadership of the *Upjas* had been hotly contested in the press for the better part of three days. Many people thought it was foolishness to allow them into the palace. I knew it was the best way to get Emmory to agree to the whole thing in the first place.

"Your Majesty." Alice curtsied as we arrived. "Everyone else is already inside."

None of us in the chamber would be armed—not even my BodyGuards. It was how I'd been able to convince Abraham to come to the palace, despite my promise of clemency. Emmory had fought me on it and the only way I'd won was to allow him a full contingent of Marines in the room next door.

"The mood?"

"Nervous, Majesty," she replied without hesitation. "Abraham is better at hiding it than Zaran. Tazerion seems quite at ease."

I wasn't going to admit that I was nervous, even though my stomach was doing a strange little dance. My childhood best friend, Tazerion Benton Shivan, was behind that door. I hadn't spoken to him since the day I left home.

Cas and Zin were at my back and I shared a look with Emmory before nodding to Alice, who reached out and pushed the door open.

"Her Imperial Majesty, Empress Hailimi Mercedes Jaya Bristol." Alba had a good pair of lungs on her, a fact that most people missed due to her soft tone.

Abraham and Taz bowed in unison.

"Thank you for coming." I forced myself to keep looking past Tazerion's brown eyes to Abraham as I held my hand out to him with a smile. "We look forward to these conversations and hope they'll be the first of many as we forge a new path for Indrana."

"Your Imperial Majesty. We thank you for agreeing to see us." He pressed his palm to mine, though his smile was guarded and he stepped aside for Tazerion far more quickly than he should have.

"Your Majesty." There was a teasing note in Taz's voice I was surprised my *Ekam* didn't take exception to as my childhood friend held his hand out.

I pressed my palm to his. The years had added even more size to him. My long fingers still only came to his first knuckle and he towered over me—a rare feat given my height.

A whole wealth of emotions went to war in my chest and I had to settle for smiling awkwardly instead of saying hello until I could be sure my voice was under control.

"It is good to see you again," I said.

"I did not think the Dark Mother would be so kind." Taz smiled.

"She rarely is."

"We are grateful, Majesty, for this chance to speak with you."

"I know it took a lot of trust for you to come here," I said. "Demanding no weapons was a risky move."

"I suspect that you still have the upper hand even without weapons, Majesty."

"I have been told that fistfights at negotiations are frowned upon."

Tazerion laughed, causing everyone else to stare, and I covered my mouth with a hand in a poor attempt to hide my smile.

Rather than joining me, Abraham struck up a conversation with my chamberlain. Taz folded his hands together and bowed again. "Do you mind if we sit, Majesty?"

"Not at all." I took a chair and gestured at the seat next to me, feeling stupid and awkward. "Abraham is content to speak with Alice and Zaran?"

Taz nodded and looked over his shoulder, sending his black hair shifting over his neck. It was long, brushing the collar of his black shirt. "This is the easy part. It will be much harder after we leave here."

"Trouble in paradise?"

He laughed. "More like human nature, Majesty. Tell me when more than three people have been able to easily come to a consensus about important issues. The moderates have always supported Abraham's vision for the *Upjas*, but don't let that fool you into thinking everyone does."

"Point." I leaned back against the sturdy gray cushion of the chair and crossed my legs. "You all appear to have come to some kind of agreement as to how to proceed."

"Some kind," Taz replied with a shrug of his shoulder. "Christoph's faction was just the most vocal and willing to split. There are plenty still with us who think that only violence will get people's attention—it's really just a matter of degree."

"Words versus fist versus hammer."

"Versus tactical sonic device."

I grinned at him, then sobered and studied my old friend.

Taz sat calmly under the scrutiny. He'd always been good at that. A still mountain to my raging storm.

He hadn't changed much, adulthood filling out his face in some places and chiseling it to sharp planes around his jawline and eyes.

"Did you ever marry?" I hadn't meant to ask the question out loud. "Bugger me. Sorry—you don't have to answer that."

"I didn't, Majesty. I wasn't interested in raising children in a society that tells half of them they're not as good simply for the way they were born."

I raised an eyebrow at the snap in his voice and deliberately didn't look at my three BodyGuards, all of whom had given up the pretense of not listening to our conversation.

"How do we fix it, Taz?" I leaned forward, resting my forearms on my knees. "Things were wrong when I left; I can only assume they're worse now. But my assumptions won't go a long way to offering up useful solutions. I need some solid details and even more solid ideas for fixing this."

His relief was visible and for a second I thought the tears in his eyes were going to spill over. Then he blinked, cleared his throat, and smiled. "How soon do you want it, Majesty?"

"Tomorrow if you think you can manage it. Changing people's minds is going to take a lot longer, but I can implement actual procedural changes whenever I feel like it." I winked. "It's apparently one of the perks of this job."

"I'll send it to Alba tomorrow, then."

"Bring it by in person, Taz," I said. "I'd like the chance to talk more." Exhaustion slammed into me as the Phrine ran out and I barely kept myself from tipping over onto the floor.

"Hail, what's wrong?" Taz reached for my hand, stopping short at Emmory's warning snarl.

"It has been a long month," I managed, knowing my weak smile didn't ease anyone's worry. "I'm just tired."

"Get her out of here; you can't let Abraham see her like this," Taz said.

"You'll have to carry me if you try to get me on my feet right this second," I murmured, intrigued by Taz's concern not only for my well-being but for how the *Upjas* would perceive any sign of weakness from me. "Just give me a moment. Emmory, I'm sure you have a distraction up your sleeve that doesn't involve hurting anyone?"

He gave me the Look and I saw Alba shift out of the corner of my eye to block me from Abraham's view. "It's not unreasonable that Your Majesty would have another commitment," Emmory said softly. "Can you make it to the door?"

"Should be able to." I took a few deep breaths and then stood just as Alba brought Abraham over. I held out my hand with a smile. "I'm sorry to have to leave, though I'm sure you'll all get more work done here without worrying about me."

"Majesty," Abraham said with a quick bow over our pressed-together hands. "Thank you again for this. It means more than you know."

"It will benefit the people of the empire." I nodded. "We will speak later." I smiled at Taz, nodded at Alice and Zaran, and somehow made it out of the room before my knees gave out.

Zin caught me around the waist. "Majesty?"

"Just pick me up," I said with a sigh. "I don't have the energy to argue with you about carrying me."

He muffled his laugh but I still felt it rumble in his chest as he carried me down the hallway.

Leaning my head on the back of the couch, I fought against the blackness that was trying to drag me under.

"Ma'am, just sleep. We'll be right here." Caspian Yuri Kreskin had been silent up to this point. My baby-faced Guard had started out as a shy, hesitant member of my BodyGuards; now he was my *Dve*, Emmory's second-in-command. Of all of us I think he'd changed the most in the past few weeks.

"There are things in the dark, Cas." My reply was slurred.

"I know." He closed a hand around mine. "We'll be right here."

I gave up and slid under the surface of consciousness.

# 4

I woke to stillness. No panicked flailing or tears. A quick glance at the time on my *smati* showed I'd been asleep for close to sixteen hours and the first of Pashati's suns was starting to rise. The light from the primary star, Nasatya, would drown out any coming from Dasra. The secondary sun's orbit had taken it away from us to the edges of the system. It would be another ten years before it swung back around, bringing with it an eerie twilight during the winter months and oppressive heat in the summer. Right now though it would appear as little more than a dim star following behind the sun—when you could see it at all.

I felt much the same. Adrift and yet following some path I couldn't quite see. "Bugger me," I muttered, rubbing both hands over my face as I rolled from my bed. I was still dressed in my clothes from yesterday—a small blessing—and padded over to the window in stocking feet.

I'd made the choice to stay in the chaos of the weeks prior, knowing even now it was the right decision. For all my outward calm I felt like I was lurching wildly from one decision to the next with nothing but a desperate hope the people around me wouldn't let me fuck up too badly.

*You're being a ridiculous drama queen, Hail.* Portis's voice was low and amused in my head. I didn't mind it, even if he was making fun of me. He was dead and gone, so in my head was the only place I'd ever hear his voice again. Portis had been my best friend, my love, and the man my childhood BodyGuards had sent after me when I left home.

While I'd been away he'd tried to keep me safe. The whole time he'd been reporting on my exploits back home, albeit heavily editing things at times.

"I miss you, ass."

*This isn't any different from running a ship and you know it. Stop second-guessing yourself and get on with it.*

"There aren't enough hours in the day." I hated the whine in my throat and turned from the window with a hiss. There were as many hours as there had always been, and other people managed just fine.

Emmory stood by the window in the main room, staring out at the sea. His lips moved, low voice rolling across the room as he had a conversation via his *smati*. He half turned toward me with a smile.

My *smati* blared a jarring warning of an incoming rocket, but before I could scream the window disintegrated, flame eating the air. Emmory vanished through the gaping hole in my quarters.

I woke so violently from the nightmare that I fell from the bed. The floor bruised my knees and as I dragged in gasping lungfuls of air I could taste the smoke and fire. I pressed my forehead to the smooth wood, feeling the tears drip from my eyes.

"Dream. It was just a Shiva-damned dream, Hail. Pull yourself together." But the time showing in the corner of my vision said I'd been asleep for sixteen hours. The similarity to my nightmare had me lurching to my feet and out of my bedroom.

Emmory stood by the window, but unlike my dream he cut his conversation short the moment I came through the door. "I'll call you back. Majesty?"

"Get away from the window." Knowing it was stupid, I grabbed him by the arm and dragged him back toward my bedroom door. "There was a—I had a—you died." I sank to the floor and Emmory followed me down.

"It was a dream, Majesty. One of the side effects of Phrine is the nightmares. You know this."

"It was so real." I buried my face in my hands, hating the tears but unable to stop them. "How stupid. I shouldn't let it—"

"You have been going since our boots hit planet. You have been nearly stabbed, shot at, poisoned, and damn near blown up. Hail, any one of those things would have put a lesser person on their knees."

It sounded so strange to hear him say my name. The last time had been right after the explosion in Garuda Square. I looked up at him, rubbing the tears from my face.

"How do you know what to say?"

That rare smile peeked at the corner of his mouth. "It's a gift, Majesty."

"It doesn't feel like I slept at all."

Emmory helped me to my feet. "You did and soundly. At least up until a few minutes ago. I'll have Stasia bring some food while you get a shower. That should help."

"I'll hurry, I'm sure we're behind—"

"I canceled all your meetings for today, Majesty. Alba rescheduled what she could; the others will manage fine without you there for one day." He grabbed my shoulders and stared me down. "You're done, Majesty. No more Phrine. We've pushed it past the breaking point here."

"I'm fine—"

41

"Your heart almost stopped."

I blinked at Emmory's clipped tone and then nodded. "Okay. We're done." Laughing at his surprised expression, I tapped him on the chest and slid out of his grip. "Did you expect me to argue? We've gone to great lengths to keep me alive, Emmy. It'd be stupid if I went and did myself in just trying to run the empire. If I'm in this for the long haul we'll have to figure out a better way to get things done."

"I've instructed Alba to pare down your schedule to start. We'll revisit things after you've rested up and see where we can adjust permanently."

"Maybe I should just let you run the empire, Emmy."

"Not in a million years, Majesty."

The laughter helped chase away the fear as I headed into the bathroom. One shower and change of clothes later and the last vestiges of the dream faded away.

"Who were you talking to?" I asked Emmory before taking a bite out of a biscuit.

"General Saito has a call-in scheduled with Trackers Winston and Peche in two days and wanted to know if I'd be free to join her."

"Do they have news about Bial?"

"I have no way of knowing that, Majesty."

Bialriarn Malik had been my mother's *Ekam*. His involvement in the plot to murder my whole family was as yet unknown because he'd fled just after saving my life.

Only after he'd vanished did my own *Ekam* inform me that Bial had been chosen for the Tracker Corps. An accident that killed Bial's sister just after they were paired put him into a coma. The coma kept him from succumbing to the madness that usually befell severed Tracker pairs.

"What did you tell her?"

"That it depended on how Your Majesty felt."

"I don't need a babysitter, Emmory," I replied, holding up my glass and wiggling it at him. "I'm of legal drinking age and everything."

It was more fun to try to make him laugh than it should have been. Emmory's chuckle was accompanied by a resigned shake of his head. "Majesty—"

"Seriously, I'd rather you go hear what they have to say so that you can report back to me. I'm not going anywhere and I'm assuming we have enough Guards on duty?"

"I've approved Iza, Gita, and Indula for full duty. Unless Your Majesty has objections."

"You know I don't. I like Iza and Indula. I'll know better when I spend more time with Gita, but I trust your judgment on it."

Iza Hajuman was a policewoman who'd stumbled upon us after the explosion in Garuda Square. Cool under fire, she'd stayed with us the whole way through the assault on the palace. I was pleased she'd accepted Emmory's offer of a job.

I'd had six other offers of BodyGuards from major houses since news broke about Gita, but she was the only one Emmory had accepted so far.

Indula was an enigma. He'd clearly done something to earn Emmory's trust. I'm sure it had to do not only with the fact that he'd been one of my mother's BodyGuards but also that he was instrumental in preventing Bial from taking me prisoner when we'd returned to the palace to confront my cousin.

"I'm putting Gita on Team One with Zin and Kisah. Iza and Indula will be on Two with Will. There's still a decent pool of Guards to choose the rest of your teams from, but I need the time to really vet them."

"Take whatever time you need. I trust you."

Emmory smiled. "That's nice to hear, Majesty."

"Well, you haven't tried to kill me yet, is all I'm saying." I stuck my tongue out at him. "You know what we need in terms of security and I'm pretty sure I promised you at one point that I'd keep my nose out of that arena. Besides, we've got all the time in the world," I said with a shrug.

# 5

It was more than strange to spend the rest of the day doing nothing. Emmory had been right about my schedule, and the Phrine. The withdrawal headache hit several hours later and I realized how off I'd been on my own dosage estimates.

I managed to nap for a few hours but shook myself awake when the nightmare started and spent some time catching up on Hansi and the other social media networks, and reading through an endless stream of emails.

It was after lunch when the news reports started rolling in and I sat up on the couch. "Alba, turn the news on the wall."

A young male reporter was standing in front of a park I recognized as the one within a few kilometers of the palace. "... the protesters clashed at about 17:00 standard time. Though the majority of either side seemed to stay out of the fighting and it is unclear just who initiated the conflict, Indranan Police Force riot control swept in and intervened in the fighting. Those responsible for the violence have been arrested, but no word yet from the IPF as to what the charges will be."

"Bugger me," I muttered. "What happened?"

"From what I can see, Majesty, there was a group of *Upjas*

supporters engaged in a demonstration at Indranan Lights Park. A group of counterprotesters showed up and things got violent."

"Do we know who started it?"

"We don't, ma'am. I've requested a list of those who were arrested from the IPF; we'll see how long it takes for me to get a response."

"If you don't have one in an hour, let me know."

"Yes, ma'am." Alba tried unsuccessfully to hide her frown behind her tablet.

I raised an eyebrow at my chamberlain. "What?"

"Nothing, Majesty."

"Cowshit, Alba, what is it?"

"It would perhaps be better to just let the police handle this."

"Oh?" I glanced over her shoulder at Emmory.

He shrugged. "It is their jurisdiction, ma'am. It would be better for the crown to remain unbiased."

Laughing, I got to my feet. "Depending on who you ask, that's already an issue, Emmory. I've read the news articles. I'm either being far too lenient on the *Upjas* or not listening to their reasonable requests."

"Be that as it may, Majesty, there are laws in place for these situations. If the crown starts interfering in them without good reason it could cause more problems than it will solve."

I glanced back at the screen, where footage of the violence replayed. Pulling a face, I waved my hand and turned it off. "All right, I'll stay out of it for now. I want a regular update on the situation."

Alba nodded. "Of course, ma'am."

I survived the rest of the day and into the next morning before the restlessness took hold. After lunch, Stasia and I undertook the task of cleaning out my father's office. She'd offered to do it without me, but I felt like I needed to be there.

"I had it aired out and we shut down the screens, Majesty."

I nodded, stepping through the door straight into the past. "Mother shut up his office the day after he died. Nothing has been touched in here for twenty years."

The desk and shelves were pristine, protected from the dust that coated the floor by the screens. That dust was marred by footprints.

Father's desk was a massive thing, pale wood streaked with stains, and my breath caught as a memory surfaced.

"I sat here." I touched the edge of the desk just to the left of the heavy leather chair. "And recited the planets in the empire to him while he worked. I got them all right, so he took me to the beach." My voice felt thick in my throat. I sank down into his chair and reached for the old-fashioned photo in a solid wooden frame.

My father, younger than I was now, smiled back at me with his arms looped around two men. His best friends—they'd all gone to the Academy together. I frowned, unable to remember their names. Both had been killed in a shipboard accident just before the start of the war.

"The day before he died, I sat here and studied for the naval entrance exam," I continued, setting the frame back on the desk. "He always preferred the chairs by the fireplace. We were going to talk Mother into letting me go early."

"Haili, baby. Go on." *Dad's voice was weak over our* smati *link and his blood was all over my hands.*

*"I won't leave you." I gripped my father's hand tighter at the sound of his voice in my head.*

"I don't want you to see this. Go on. I love you."

"I love you, too." *I replied in my head because I didn't trust my voice to say the words as I let my BodyGuards drag me away.*

"Majesty, are you all right?"

I wiped the tears away and forced a smile. "*Uff.* We'll keep the furniture and the books, Stasia. Pack up everything else and put it in storage."

"Yes, ma'am."

We got the office cleaned out, and I settled into the desk to read briefings. But the late afternoon found me restless again, and I paced the confines of the office while Zin stood quietly by the door.

The news was playing on the wall, the endless replay of the riots interrupted by a story about General Prajapati's trial. The trial room itself was media locked, but that didn't stop them from speculating on the events of the day. There was little question of the general's guilt; she'd admitted as much in my throne room. However, she was popular and good at her job. The calls for a royal pardon had already started.

"Damned if I'm going to be able to execute her," I muttered.

"Majesty?"

"Prajapati." I made a face and poked my finger at the images on the wall. "I'm not going to be able to execute her. I need her. Plus her lawyer's argument is solid. She was supporting what she thought was the better choice for the throne. We have zero proof they included her in any of the other plans."

"This isn't a democracy, ma'am." Zin actually sounded offended and I covered my mouth with a hand to hold in the laugh.

"And thank Shiva for it," I managed. "Things are messy enough as it is."

"What did you mean when you said you need her?"

I replaced the stream of the news with General Prajapati's file. "She was first in her class at Mumbai. She set records in the annual war games at the Royal Military Academy that haven't been broken in fifty years. She defeated the Saxons on the ground on four separate planets during the war.

"I can't throw all that skill away, even if she's a traitor. Even if she hates my guts. It'd be foolish. Unless a miracle happens we'll be at war with the Saxons again before the end of next year."

"You won't be able to trust her."

"I know. I have to hope she hates the Saxons more than me, or is telling the truth in her claims that she was doing what was best for the empire and prove to her I am what's best." I shrugged. "In the meantime, I'll put someone on her with orders to shoot her in the head if she looks like she's going to commit treason again."

Zin didn't comment with anything more than a raised eyebrow.

"I need to get out of here." I spun in a circle. "I'm calling Stasia for my coat."

"Majesty, we're not prepared for you to leave the palace."

*"Dhatt."* I threw my hands in the air. "I have to go somewhere. I've been cooped up here for too long, Zin. Are we really expecting someone to take another shot at me so soon?"

"We're always expecting it," he replied.

I made a face at him. "You sound like Emmory. Can I go to the library? I'm reasonably sure we can manage to keep me alive for that trip."

Zin nodded.

I grabbed the gray woolen sari from where I'd discarded it hours earlier and draped it over my green pants and top.

My three BodyGuards were in quiet conference in the hallway when I emerged, and Kisah and Gita both bowed. "Majesty."

I nodded in reply.

*Don't rush out of your meeting. I promise I won't leave the palace. We'll be in the library when you're done.* I sent Emmory the note even though I was fairly sure Zin had messaged him the moment I'd left my office.

The palace bustled with activity as we moved through the hallways. People curtsied or bowed as I passed, and I stopped occasionally to chat with those whose faces were growing more familiar by the day.

I waited with Zin at the doors of the library while my Body-Guards cleared the room. It wasn't open to the public, but authorized personnel were allowed access to the specialized material within.

In a digital world, print books still thrived, but most records were kept electronically. It was a rare collection of printed work housed here.

Mother had added extensively, if a bit randomly, to the collection, buying books from all over the empire as well as the Solarian Conglomerate and other places. I'd asked Father about it once and he said it made her happy.

I inhaled the familiar and comforting smell of old paper and crossed to the wide leather chairs by the massive fireplace. Besides Father's office, the palace library had been my favorite childhood hideout, curled up in a chair with a paper book or something on my *smati*, hiding from the world and from Mother.

The wave of nostalgia swamped me and I swayed for a moment. Zin closed a hand on my elbow.

"Majesty?"

"I'm all right. Just remembering."

Logs were stacked in the fireplace. As I grabbed the lighter from the mantel and knelt, Gita moved to intercept me.

"Majesty, let me—"

I cut her off with a look. "I'm the empress, Gita, not an invalid."

"Yes, ma'am. I'm sorry."

"You'll learn," I said, and lit the fire. It took a few moments of fussing to get the logs to catch, and the air-recyclers kicked in the moment their sensors detected a change in the $CO_2$ levels along with the rising smoke.

I rocked back on my heels and got to my feet. "Zin, have we heard from Taz?"

"He arrived back at the palace this morning, Majesty. Alba arranged a room for Shivan in the guest quarters until we could work him into the new schedule."

"Are you going to kick up a huge fuss if I message him and ask him to join me?" I gave Zin my best innocent expression in response to his very exasperated look.

"Majesty, he's the second ranking member of the *Upjas*."

"Who's here at my request. I'm sure he's been screened several times since he arrived. You can even do it again when Alba gets here with him." There was a knock at the library doors, and I beamed at Zin.

Gita was staring at us with wide brown eyes. Kisah grinned and headed for the door after Zin. "You'll learn," she said to the older woman as she passed, patting her on the arm.

I settled into the chair, wrapping the gray fabric around myself and tucking my feet up underneath me. The flames popped and crackled in the grate over the voices across the room.

"Your Majesty."

I smiled up at Taz, but it wasn't returned. "Have a seat. Do you want something to drink?"

"If it's no trouble. Tea would be fine."

"Alba?"

"Yes, Majesty." She left the room.

Taz settled into the other chair. He was dressed in a navy blue Nehru jacket, and his cream pants were loose except where they cuffed at the ankle.

"I'm sorry for my informal attire, Majesty. Your summons caught me by surprise."

"You look fine. And 'Would you like to talk?' is hardly a summons."

"It is when it comes from the empress."

"What's with the hostility?" I raised an eyebrow at him as I sat up straighter. Alba's heels clacked efficiently on the hardwood as she came back into the library with a tray. She set it on the little table nearby. I nodded my thanks and took the cup of chai she handed me.

I studied Taz over the rim of the mug. I'd thought after our first meeting we were going to slide back into friendship as though the last twenty years hadn't happened. However, the bruised wariness in his eyes told me I'd been an idiot to even consider it.

"Many thanks." Taz smiled at my chamberlain as she handed him a cup of tea.

Swallowing back the urge to ask the question a second time, I let Taz fix his tea. After he'd put enough sugar and milk into it to set a schoolyard full of children into spasms and drunk more than half the cup, he finally looked back at me.

"You've learned patience, Majesty," he said with a half smile.

"I had it beaten into me."

He still was as easy to read as ever, surprise flickering across his face while he tried to decide if I was joking or not.

"You arrested some of my people," he said finally.

"I haven't arrested anyone."

"Fine, the police arrested my people. What are you going to do about it?"

I didn't have to look around to know what my BodyGuards' reactions were. Gita's inhale wasn't quiet enough and I could feel Zin's glare like a laser blast slicing through the air. I set my cup down and stared at Taz.

The silence drew itself out into a single thread before he lowered his eyes to the floor and murmured, "Apologies, Your Majesty, I was out of line."

"Don't do it again. There are laws in place for what happened the other day, Tazerion." His full name felt awkward in my mouth. "We are not going to interfere and make things worse."

"I am sorry, Majesty. Your mother would have had them shot."

"I'm not my mother." I pushed out of my chair and set my cup on the mantel before resting both hands on the warm stone. The flames danced over the logs, curling around edges and blackening the wood as they flared brighter. A log collapsed, sending up a burst of sparks.

"That is very obvious." Taz had stood when I did. Setting aside his tea, he looked to Zin for approval before moving to the fire. "Things are changing. Sometimes it's a little much for any of us to handle."

"You don't say." I looked away from the fire at him. A tentative smile flickered in his eyes. "Why didn't you come with me?"

"I remember very clearly you saying you needed to do this on your own. That I shouldn't waste my life on your pursuit of vengeance, Majesty."

"It's just as well," I murmured. "You probably would have died out there. Everyone else did."

"I know. I'm sorry for your losses."

"It is over and done." I grabbed the fire iron to poke at the logs. "I am more concerned with Indrana's future than shedding tears about my past. Emmory says Abraham has left the capital."

"As I said the other day, the *Upjas* are fractured." He glanced over his shoulder at my BodyGuards again. "There's more to it than just that. Princess Cire's death hit Abraham hard. He has not recovered and I do not think he will. He loved your sister."

"I know." I smiled sadly.

*"Taz, was Atmikha their daughter?"* I asked the question over my *smati* because saying it out loud would have been a ridiculous risk.

*"Abraham has not spoken of it, but I believe it to be true."*

"So you're taking over leadership?"

"With his blessing, Majesty," Taz replied. "We think it would be best." His brown eyes reflected his earnest words. "There is hope that I can rally them enough to work toward the peace we all want. I am hoping you are willing to——"

One of the library doors banged open and Emmory strode in. He said something sharp to Zin, making his partner flinch, but Emmory's face was expressionless when he stopped and nodded to me. "Majesty."

"That was an entrance, *Ekam*." I picked up my cup and took a drink. "What is it?"

"Shivan, step back from the empress."

I raised an eyebrow at Emmory's tone. Taz took a step back but met my *Ekam*'s look with an easy smile.

"The empress requested me."

"The empress you wish to depose," Emmory said.

"I wish for equality, *Ekam*, nothing more. Despite the circumstances that put her there, I am happy to see her on the throne."

"Majesty, it is an unwise decision to meet with this man without more security."

"Excuse me?"

Everyone froze. The crackling of the fire was the only sound in the room and I could barely hear it over the pounding of my heart. I set my mug down carefully on the mantelpiece and rolled through my possible responses.

"Tazerion, it was a pleasure. Thank you for speaking with me. I'll see you tomorrow. Alba will take you back to your room."

"Your Majesty. *Ekam*." Taz executed a perfect bow and left the room.

"The rest of you get out of here. Except for you," I said, because Emmory actually turned to leave. The door closed behind Zin and I crossed my arms over my chest. "The next time you have something to say to me, either do it in private or over the com link. Don't you ever question my judgment in front of someone like that again. Are we clear?"

"I am concerned for your safety."

"Cowshit. You're questioning my competence, Emmory. That's two different things. I'm not an idiot, but treating me like that in front of a rebel sure makes me look like one."

"You met with a rebel leader with only three guards, none of whom were close enough to actually protect you from danger."

I took a step closer to him. "I could kick Taz's ass twenty years ago and I'm a whole lot meaner now than I was back then."

"Your confidence is admirable, Majesty, but it's my job to keep you safe. What if he'd been carrying a bomb like Ramani?"

My stomach clenched at the little girl's name. "I really want to punch you in the face right now," I said, and turned away so that I wouldn't give in to temptation.

"He's a member of the *Upjas*. His group is at least partially responsible for everything that has happened."

"The *Upjas* are fracturing. Christoph's break was just the start. Abraham can't keep them together, but he's hoping that Taz will be able to, or at least convince the majority to stick with them. That's the kind of thing I get from a meeting like this because there's no way in Naraka Taz will say that tomorrow with all the recorders and people who will be present."

"Majesty—"

"I'm not finished." I whipped back around with my hand held up. "I don't know what your problem is. I know what I'm doing here, whether I choose to share it with you or not. I'm going to follow my gut on certain things because it has never, ever lied to me. You are always welcome to disagree—in private—but in front of others you'll keep your mouth shut. Is that understood?"

Emmory snapped to attention, his shoulders and back perfectly straight. "Yes, Your Majesty."

"Get out of here, I don't want to see your face right now." I was still furious and as his footsteps echoed out of the room I sank down to the floor, staring at the fire until my vision blurred.

"Majesty?"

I stood to look at Zin. There was worry on his face but otherwise not a hint of how he might be feeling. I exhaled and rubbed at my forehead. "I wasn't being reckless, you get that, right? There was a reason for it."

"Emmory can be very focused at times, Majesty."

"Like a laser-guided missile."

A smile cracked through Zin's careful expression. "Yes, ma'am."

"I realize you didn't answer my question." I shot him a look and tapped my fingers on the tabletop as I passed. Glancing out the window at the sun hanging low in the sky, I shuddered. The tremor at the sudden thought of the night descending surprised and then infuriated me.

"*Hai Ram.* Am I really terrified of going to sleep?"

"Majesty?"

"Was there a story in my file about Rastinghowl?"

Zin frowned, his gray-green eyes unfocusing for a moment as he searched for the information. "No, ma'am."

"Interesting. Though I guess I'm not surprised Portis didn't share it. Someone would have ordered him to bring me home right then if they'd known."

"What happened there?"

"Rastinghowl isn't a place. He's a person. Was a person." I moved back to the fire and knelt in front of it. "He was wholly convinced that the world was ending and that his God would save him and his followers. I'm still not sure what he needed the guns for, but that's the logic of madmen, I guess.

"Hao shouldn't have done the deal in the first place. I told him not to, begged even. The whole thing felt wrong. But the money was too good to pass up. It went sideways, like those things always do, and we all ended up captive." I looked over my shoulder at Zin. "Rastinghowl and his followers took that whole 'body of Christ' thing literally. They ate Hamish before we managed to escape."

The shudder slid up my spine and I stuck my hands closer to the fire as Zin knelt at my side.

"I stabbed that man with his own knife and slept like a baby after. Hao never doubted my gut again. All the shit I've seen, why is it that now I can't stop the nightmares?"

"Everyone has a breaking point, Majesty. You're safe, at least for the moment. It's natural to lose it a little." Zin grabbed the poker and fiddled with the fire for several moments. "It's the same reason Emmory is wound so tight right now. In his experience things always go to shit right after the big events die down."

"That's what his problem is? He thinks I'm going to mess something up because I've let my guard down?"

Zin didn't answer me right away, and when he did, his eyes were on the fire, not on me. "*Dhatt*," he muttered. "He's not worried about you letting your guard down. He's afraid *he* will."

"What?"

"He dreams you died. Every night since the explosion, that's all he sees."

# 6

I didn't know what to say to Zin's revelation, and he refused to elaborate further, so I curled up in one of the library chairs and read a book until the flames died out.

The walk back to my rooms was silent and my *Ekam* was nowhere to be found. I ate dinner alone and went to bed early, hoping that the gods would be kind enough to grace me with another night of dreamless sleep.

Why I thought that, when the gods have never been kind to me, was the real question. I woke, gasping in the dark, and sobbed as the nightmare faded.

It took some coaxing, but I eventually fell back asleep. There was no more death, though my dreams were still chaotic and stressful enough that I woke in a foul mood.

My mood only worsened when I saw the report from Emmory about his meeting yesterday with General Saito. It was perfect and detailed, and likely would answer any questions I had.

It was so he wouldn't have to talk to me.

I closed it without reading it and slid out of bed. My

breakfast was laid on a tray and I picked at it while staring out the window.

"Are you not hungry, Majesty?" asked Bene, one of the newer maids, a young girl with large brown eyes and short brown curls.

"No." I waved a hand, snatching my chai off the tray before she could take it. Stasia didn't say a word when I put on my customary uniform, nor did my maid attempt to do much more than braid my hair back out of my face before I left the room for my first briefing.

Cas was at my shoulder. Normally his presence wouldn't have bothered me, but today all it did was highlight Emmory's absence. Zin had also gone off duty overnight and so I was surrounded by the members of Team Two as we headed through the palace.

Alba picked up on my mood as if we'd been working together for years, and no one bothered me when I passed through the hallways. I sat silently near the back of the room while the Raksha—Indrana's military council—discussed the latest Saxon fleet movements.

"The three *Vajrayana* ships that were out on maneuvers when the Saxons hit us arrived in system yesterday. I'm working on integrating them into Home Fleet. Since the hit on Canafey, we haven't seen any overt movement in that direction from the bulk of their forces," Admiral Hassan said, pointing at the worlds floating above the table in the War Room. "What we have seen is some movement closer to the heart of the Saxon territory since our last briefing, but nothing unusually large."

"Word on the ground in Canafey is they're still fighting pitched battles with forces they claim are Saxon Shock Corps Marines, but no one can give me a verified image." Caspel leaned on the table and frowned. "I also can't get a total on how many ships might be in the area. Initial reports said it was less than a dozen."

"We need to get reinforcements in there." Lieutenant General Aganey Triskan, Prajapati's replacement for the council, was a lean man with a sour face who'd come highly recommended by not only Admiral Hassan but General Saito as well. I was expecting some fallout for the decision—not only because he was a man, but because he was barely older than I was. "Our troops have to be running low on supplies."

"We can't send Admiral Shul in until we know what the situation is," Caspel replied. "Canafey isn't worth the entire 2nd Fleet, even with the *Vajrayana* ships. We're better off closing up the gap behind them and starving them out."

"There are people down there! Women, men, and children. How can you—"

"I am fully aware of who is on Canafey, Aganey."

"But not who's in the space above it? What good are you?"

"Enough, both of you." General Vandi slammed a hand down on the table after a glance in my direction. "Aganey, I know you are worried for your daughters, but let's keep a clear head, yes? Director Ganej is doing what he can with the limited information he has."

*"His daughters are on Canafey?"* I asked Admiral Hassan over our com link.

*"Yes, ma'am. One is stationed with the army on Minor. The other is Navy; she was working on the* Vajrayana *project."*

"My apologies, Director. I was out of line." Aganey folded his hands and bowed to Caspel, who waved him off.

"I understand your concerns, General. We're doing what we can. I promise you."

"Caspel, I'd like a plan from you by this evening to get intelligence on how many Saxon ships are in the system so we can decide how to proceed," Admiral Hassan said. "Until we have that information we are rather stuck. I, for one, am not interested in sitting around waiting for the Saxons to make their next move before we respond."

Heads nodded around the table. I got to my feet as the meeting wrapped up and headed for the door.

"Majesty, I'd like to apologize for our lack of progress with Bial." General Saito met me at the door, folded her hands together, and bowed. "Given that the accident occurred so soon after the pairing, there was no formal training for him. But he seems to have an innate talent. My Trackers are finding it challenging to follow his trail."

"You lost him?"

"I'm sorry, Majesty. I thought Emmory briefed you."

"He sent me a report. I haven't had a chance to read it."

"Oh, I assumed you two would talk."

"The morning was chaotic. If you'll excuse me, I have a meeting with the matriarchs." That answer sounded forced even to me, but I ignored the general's concerned frown and left the room.

I was dreading this meeting; however, dragging my feet wasn't an option since I was fairly certain Clara would just wait to start until I was there.

Better to be in my seat anyway. I hadn't officially met with the Matriarch Council since the coup attempt, and I was curious to see just how the ones who'd supported Matriarch Khatri would react.

"Cas, Iza's coming in there with me," I said as we hit the door. I turned to the young woman without waiting for a confirmation from my *Dve*. "I want you watching for any reactions that seem out of place."

"Yes, ma'am." Iza had been swept up in my wake during the coup attempt but didn't seem to mind her new job at all.

Matriarch Desai was already in the room and did little more than raise an eyebrow when Iza followed me inside and settled into parade rest behind my chair. The late-morning light filtered in through the stained-glass windows, throwing blue across the far wall.

I watched the door, carefully cataloging the entrance of each matriarch. Alice and Zaran were in deep discussion as they entered, but both curtsied in my direction and their smiles were genuine.

Matriarch Waybly, by contrast, couldn't meet my eyes and hurried to her seat. The dark-haired woman had voiced her agreement with Elsa Khatri's objections over my legitimacy for the throne, though she hadn't been involved in the loud debate that had followed. I made a note to investigate her further.

Ganda's mother, Loka Naidu, had dark circles under her eyes. I held a hand up to stop Iza before she could intercept the matriarch. My aunt came straight to me and dropped to her knees.

"Your Imperial Majesty. I offer my family's most sincere apologies and beg your forgiveness."

"*Mai* Loka." I held a hand out as I shifted to the edge of my seat. "Your other daughter already spoke with me. Ganda's actions were her own. I don't hold you accountable."

"I raised her better, Majesty. I don't know where she went wrong." Eyes dark with grief, she looked back at the floor. "I should have known what she was planning."

"Children are good at hiding things from their parents. My mother could have told you that. Get up. The floor is cold and you are forgiven."

"Thank you, Majesty." She smiled in relief, bowing again as she got to her feet and then moved off to take her seat.

I'd missed the entrance of the other matriarchs, one of the reasons I'd wanted Iza in the room. There were a handful I wasn't too sure of, and as I scanned the faces at the table, it was easy to take note of who met my eyes and who didn't.

Clara tapped her fist on the tabletop and all the side chatter stopped. "For obvious reasons there is a BodyGuard in the room. I expect this will continue until we can be certain we've cut all the rot out from this traitorous infection that plagues us."

Matriarch Prajapati shifted uncomfortably at Desai's words, knotting her slender fingers together until her knuckles were almost white. Her sister's betrayal had been no fault of her own, but I noticed how the space between her and those around her was a little wider than normal.

"I'd like to take this opportunity to welcome Matriarch Zaran Khatri to the council chambers." Clara smiled warmly. "Though the circumstances are unpleasant, we are looking forward to her wisdom."

I stomped my left foot on the floor in acknowledgment, the sound echoed by the others in the room for a few seconds before we returned to silence. Zaran nodded, slightly embarrassed by the attention.

"Zaran, if you would fill us in on the meeting with the *Upjas*?" Clara continued.

Zaran nodded, her short curls bouncing with the movement, and folded her pale hands together on the tabletop. "Three days ago, Alice and I went with the empress to meet with the two ranking members of the *Upjas*—Abraham Suda and Tazerion Benton Shivan. I believe there is another meeting scheduled today with Tazerion and two new representatives that is open to matriarchs and members of the Ancillary Council to further outline just what they would like to see from the government.

"During our meeting earlier, Alice and I had the opportunity to talk with both men. Abraham was very pleasant and polite. Not at all what one might expect from a rebel leader." She smiled briefly. "Since then I have spoken with several other members of the group. They are also all quite articulate and presented a united front in their desire to see what they referred to as 'true equality of the sexes' within the empire."

"You find something amusing about that, Matriarch Zellin?" I asked when the woman snorted.

"I find several things amusing, Your Majesty. Starting with the fact that we're even talking to a known terrorist group openly involved in seditious acts against the throne and ending with the idea that there isn't already equality for men. There's a male prime minister, for Shiva's sake; more than half your BodyGuards are men; and you just appointed a man to the Raksha. What more do they want?"

"If I could, Your Majesty." Alice spoke up with a raised hand. At my nod she looked across the table. "They want more than tokens, Tare. They want to not be passed over for promotions when they are more than qualified simply because their boss would rather put a woman in the spot. They want to be paid the same for the same work, not nearly half a *ravga* less."

"That's preposterous. I don't pay my male workers any less."

"Detailed studies across the empire say otherwise," Alice replied, but the murmuring agreement with Tare Zellin rolled over her words.

"Your Majesty, I'm very sorry, but I cannot in good conscience attend this meeting," Matriarch Surakesh said. "Good people were killed by this group not long ago. This empire has never negotiated with terrorists, and starting now when we are on the brink of war is not something your mother would have condoned."

I blinked at her, the refusal to attend the meeting so unexpected I was at a loss for words. Even worse, more than half the heads around the table were nodding in agreement.

And my mother. I kept my mouth closed even though I wanted to scream. If people didn't stop throwing her rule in my face I was likely to lose it.

*"Majesty, your blood pressure is a bit high."* Iza's voice was soft over the com link.

*"I know,"* I replied. *"You get used to it with this bunch."* I turned off the warning flashing in the corner of my vision and took a deep breath that didn't go unnoticed by the women at the table.

"Ladies," I said, resting my hands on the table and pushing to my feet. "I will say this only once, so I suggest you listen closely. Times are changing. You can like that or not, because no one—not even I—can force you to choose something that is not in your heart.

"Times are changing," I repeated. "Indrana must change with them or fall into the rubbish heap with so many relics of the past. I am not my mother, and the Indrana of the future is not my mother's empire. There is a wealth of untapped potential in our citizenry, and it is long past time our laws reflected a recognition of that potential."

I looked around the table. "I could force each and every one of you to show up to that meeting today, but I can't force you to hear Tazerion's words and I can't force you to open your hearts."

Alice stood also. "Her Majesty is right. I was skeptical and unsupportive of the *Upjas*, but I have come to realize that it is time to let go of the arrogance of our past. I encourage you all to actually listen today. Not with the intent to speak back, but simply to hear their message. I encourage you to talk with your own sons. You'll likely be surprised when you do."

A stunned silence followed Alice's words. I bit my lip to keep my smile in. Less than a month ago she'd told me she didn't believe in the *Upjas'* cause, but it seemed something had turned her around.

"Well, thank you for that, Your Majesty. Alice." Clara cleared her throat with a smile and tapped her fingers on the tabletop as we both sat down. "Zaran and Alice have prepared a full report on the meeting. I recommend everyone read it before this afternoon."

Matriarch Hassan knocked her knuckles onto the table. "As fascinating as this pet project is, can we discuss a more pressing matter? The empress needs to produce an heir and needs to name someone in the interim to make sure there's no confusion in the line of succession. War is looming. The populace is nervous. This would go a long way to calming them down."

I crossed my arms over my chest and tried not to glare at Admiral Hassan's mother. "Me having a baby is more important than the million other problems this empire has right now?"

Clara shook her head. "You do need an heir, Majesty. Matriarch Hassan has a point. Indrana cannot afford to be leaderless, especially with things being so volatile at the moment."

"For obvious reasons, anyone from my father's line is no longer eligible for the throne." I gave Loka a small nod. "Any other distant relations are only children and too far removed from the direct maternal line to be considered. Taran and myself are all who remain of Mother's line."

"You cannot name Taran, Majesty. The law—"

"I am fully aware of the law," I snapped, cutting off Matriarch Tobin's protest, and the elderly woman blinked at me in shock. "I am merely pointing out the impossibility in front of us. I have no family left."

"All the more reason for you to get cracking, child." Matriarch Maxwell thumped her fist on the table with a wheezing laugh. "Find a nice-looking and reasonably intelligent young man."

I dropped my face into my hands with a groan. Now was definitely not the time to let the council in on my barrenness. All Naraka would break loose.

Alice thumped her own knuckles on the table. "What Matriarch Maxwell is saying, admittedly without much tact—"

"Pfft, when you hit my age, child, you'll see tact is a waste of time."

Alice smiled sympathetically at me. "I understand there is a lot going on right now, but it is important you start interviewing candidates, Majesty."

"Fine," I said, leaning back in my chair and thumping a fist on the tabletop. "In the meantime, I'm naming Alice as my heir."

The room exploded into chaos.

Alice gaped at me, her cheeks going pale. "Majesty, no. I don't want—"

"And that's exactly why I chose you." I pointed across the table, ignoring the din. "You all pushed for this—don't protest now."

"Majesty, you can't make such an important decision without—"

"This is ridiculous."

"Majesty, this is something you should consider carefully—"

"Are you suggesting I'm acting impulsively?" I asked Clara with a raised eyebrow.

"Majesty—"

"No, seriously. I've been watching Alice since I got here. You all act like I haven't given the issue of who's running this empire after me—or if something happens to me—any thought at all. I am neither an idiot nor taking this lightly. Alice is highly capable. I trust her to have the empire's best interests at heart."

"Your Majesty, this is highly irregular."

*"Dhatt."* I ran my tongue over my teeth. "Matriarch Acharya, I am still in the mood for executions. I know for a fact that you were in agreement with the old Matriarch Khatri, and I have reports of you meeting with her outside the palace on more than one occasion, so I would advise you not to cross me right this second."

"Are you threatening me?" She gaped. "Matriarch Khatri was an old friend of mine; are we now under suspicion for any interactions we had?"

"Have you been paying attention? I don't threaten," I replied. "We're done here. Alice is my heir; if anyone would like to formally dispute that, let Matriarch Desai know." I waved a hand. "Now get out."

Everyone left except Alice and Clara.

"I'm going to be sick," Alice murmured.

"Not on the carpet." I grinned at her. "Don't worry—you'll get used to the idea."

"Majesty, the fallout from this—"

"We'll handle it, Clara. Alice can do the job if something happens to me. That's the important part of this, if I recall."

"At least until Your Majesty has a child."

I cleared my throat and forced a smile in Clara's direction. "Of course."

*You are going to have to tell someone about that one of these days, Hail,* the voice in my head cheerfully reminded me.

I snarled silently at it as I left the room.

# 7

The public meeting with Taz felt entirely different from the quiet of the library. I sat at the head of a ridiculously huge table in a room I was fairly certain hadn't been used for at least a decade. The windows arched to the ceiling and provided a view of the palace gardens, gardens that were currently covered in ice and snow.

I was tired and the pounding headache that had developed sometime after lunch kicked itself into high gear as the room flooded with people. Matriarch Surakesh was true to her word and didn't show; however, her eldest daughter, Mina, came through the door and gave me an elegant nod.

"Your Majesty."

"It's nice to see you. I wasn't expecting your family today."

"My mother and I are not in complete agreement about some of the issues this empire faces," she replied.

"Thank you for coming," I said, and she nodded again before moving to her seat.

Taz and two young men entered and the buzzing chatter went mercifully silent. "Your Imperial Majesty," he said with an elegant bow. He was dressed in a well-cut, dark gray Nehru jacket and pants of the same color.

"Tazerion. Garhi. Salham." It hurt more than a little that the youngest member of their group had the same name as one of my dead BodyGuards, but it was a popular name and there was no avoiding it.

I relaxed in my chair as the introductions commenced. Given the number of people in the room, it was going to take a while before everyone was settled again. Half the matriarchs weren't in attendance, though Matriarch Zellin surprised me with a curtsy before she took her seat. All the eldest daughters were here and I took that as a good sign. Prime Minister Phanin and several carefully selected members of the media were also in the room.

The security for the nobles and my two teams of Body-Guards shrank the space even further. Emmory was conspicuously absent, considering the fuss he'd kicked up about me being around Taz last night.

I pushed the thoughts of my *Ekam* out of my head as Clara welcomed everyone and graciously turned the floor over to Tazerion.

He cleared his throat as he stood, smoothing his hands down the front of his jacket. His nervous habit hadn't changed over the years.

"Your Majesty. Ladies. Prime Minister and distinguished members of the media. Thank you all for coming today and thank you for giving us an opportunity to have our voices heard.

"The *Upjas* have never been against the empire. What we want is simply to be a part of the empire, an equal part. We believe that excluding half the population from the ability to inherit titles, from helping to make the laws we must obey, from the basic respect afforded to women simply by the accident of their birth, is wrong."

I pulled my eyes away from Taz with some difficulty so I could scan the faces of the women at the table. The older matriarchs who did come were clenching their jaws and glared through unforgiving eyes—though Matriarch Tobin, ever the wild card, was smiling.

The younger women at the table were split. Some looked at their hands and shifted in their seats. Others shared the stone faces of the opposition. A small segment were smiling, clearly captivated by Taz and his message.

"Men fought alongside women to win our independence from the Solarians. You seemed happy at our support then and continue to accept it within all branches of the military. But we are more than just machines to be ordered about. We can think rationally. We are not controlled by our anger or ruled by our instincts.

"In this, the thirty-first century, do we not want to bring Indrana into the light? You are the ones who hold the power, but your power is not lessened by allowing us to determine our own fates, to feed our families, raise our children, go to school, and hold public office. Your power is not lessened by treating us as equals."

"You seek to bring an end to the monarchy." Matriarch Desai's voice was quiet in the stillness of the room.

Taz looked at me rather than Clara. "Is it not an antiquated system of government? It suited us in the early days, perhaps, when things were dangerous and the whole existence of our world needed a single voice to keep it moving in the right direction. Now with our people spread across so many worlds, with so many lives in the balance, is it right for them all to be beholden to one person?"

He waved a hand through the air. "We've seen the danger that leads to over the last two decades, how close our empire was brought to the brink of war. One upon which we still totter because everything hinges on one person's decisions."

*You're pushing it too hard, Taz,* I thought, wishing there weren't com jammers in place around the room. The muttering was low, but it wouldn't stay that way for long.

"Young man." Matriarch Maxwell raised a slender hand. "You are—"

Chastisement or compliment, her words were cut off by the seething rumble that shook the table. I looked to Cas, whose com system was unaffected by the jammer, and he stiffened.

"Up, Majesty," he said in a voice I'd never heard from my baby-faced Guard, but I had already pushed to my feet.

"Detain those three. Don't harm them." I had time to meet Taz's eyes as my BodyGuards hustled me from the room. He was standing in front of the other two *Upjas*, his hands raised and a resigned look on his face.

Cas kept a hold of my arm as we strode down the hallway. The other BodyGuards formed up around us, eyes hard at whatever the threat was. I was dying to ask, but I didn't want to distract him.

We weren't heading back to my rooms. Instead Cas took a sharp right down a narrow corridor. My *Dve* stopped outside a blank metal door, pressing his hand to the panel next to it.

I balked when the door slid open to reveal a tiny lift. "Where does that go?"

"Under the palace. Your mother had it built several years ago."

I resisted when he tried to pull me forward. My heart was pounding in my ears.

"Majesty, we have to."

"Didn't Emmory tell you—" I wasn't going to have this conversation out in the hallway, but my legs wouldn't move me toward the yawning steel coffin in front of us. "I can't—I can't go in there."

"Majesty." Cas now wore a look of panic that was probably the same as mine. "Please don't make me carry you. I have orders."

"I don't care about your fucking orders—"

"Majesty." Emmory appeared around the corner. "Everyone stand down. The threat here has been contained." The Body-Guards around us relaxed and Cas quietly shooed them down the hallway until Emmory and I were alone.

I closed my eyes. "What happened?"

"Two men drove a truck into the front gate of the palace and detonated it. I'm getting scattered reports that other places in the capital have been hit but nothing more than preliminary details at the moment."

"Dark Mother. How many?"

"The two women on duty at the gate were killed along with several civilians waiting to be admitted. A handful of others were injured." Emmory rubbed a hand over his head. "I don't have numbers yet on the other attacks. We weren't sure if there would be a force trying to breach the gate. I wanted you somewhere safer than your rooms. I'm sorry. I should have briefed you on this plan and reminded Cas about your claustrophobia."

"We probably should have done a dry run...or eight hundred." Swallowing hard, I cursed under my breath and took a step toward the lift. "In fact, we're here, we may as well see what happens while there's no urgency."

"Majesty—"

"Don't argue with me, please, it'll just give me an excuse to run." I was thankful for the lack of a skirt, which I'm not sure would have fit inside the tiny space. The lift was barely over two meters square—four people could have fit if they liked each other. Holding my breath, I stepped inside, and the floor shifted when Emmory followed me. I squeezed my eyes shut, knowing if I turned around and saw him blocking the doorway I'd lose it.

The door made no sound when it closed, but the light shifted behind my eyelids and my heart jumped in response. I opened them, studying my blurry reflection in the poly-steel wall.

"General Saito said the Trackers lost Bial."

"Majesty?"

"Just talk to me, Emmory. Give me something to think about besides the fact that we're in a box." I grabbed for the bar on the wall when the lift started moving and gave what I'm sure was a hysterical laugh.

"You didn't read my report?"

"There wasn't time this morning." I pressed my head to the cool metal. "And I was still mad at you."

"You were right, Majesty." He sighed. "I'm sorry for questioning your judgment. Cas said you ordered the *Upjas* detained."

"I think it's far more likely Christoph orchestrated these attacks, but it's safer for everyone this way."

Emmory leaned against the wall next to me and I turned my head so I could see his face. "Tu Winston is one of the best Trackers I know. They lost Bial's trail at Wasteland Station, but they were backtracking and she was confident she could find the trail she missed."

"You've been looking into his activities here, haven't you?"

Emmory nodded.

"I want a full report. We'll go over it from this end and

hopefully be able to find something that will help the Trackers when we talk to them again."

"We, Majesty?"

I shrugged a shoulder, trying to ignore the way the lift shuddered to a stop. "I want to know if he was involved in the plot against my family." The door slid open and I bolted out of the lift into the dubious safety of the underground chamber. "Or if he just had a misguided sense of honor and we should cut him loose. Send these Trackers after our mystery man, Wilson, instead."

"His trail is even colder than Bial's."

"I know, but he's more important. Bial's a puzzle, to be sure, but you and I both know if he'd wanted to bring this empire to her knees he could have done it long before I got home."

The underground room Mother had built showed no signs of wear. I couldn't help but wonder if it was paranoia or prudence that sparked the construction of what could only be called a war bunker.

There was a small hologram table in the far corner and several banks of screens on the wall. Tables and chairs along the other wall. I pointed at the two doors with a raised eyebrow.

"Sleeping quarters in the one on the right. The left one leads to a secondary exit."

Most of the tension left my shoulders at those words, even though I knew it was likely the exit in question was a tunnel of some kind. It at least meant that there was another way out besides that hideous metal box.

"Zin told me about the dreams."

"He told me about Rastinghowl." A small smile flickered to life on his face. "And that he was done being the go-between for us."

"That didn't even last a full day."

"He doesn't care for strife, Majesty."

"Who does?" I lifted a shoulder and then leaned against the hologram table. "What did you say to him when you came into the library?"

"I asked him how his leg was." Emmory actually looked ashamed. "I was angry. It was uncalled-for."

"But obviously pertinent. How did he hurt it? How did you get the Star?"

The Imperial Star was an award of great prestige. It wasn't issued for just any act of valor, but something above and beyond the call of duty that caused the recipient to walk the road to temple—usually they didn't return to the living.

Emmory wore his on his face for all the universe to see. I doubted it was from pride that the intricate diamond pattern, the four spikes turned slightly widdershins, rested in so prominent a location.

"I got it on my face so I would remember whenever I looked in the mirror that letting my guard down will get the people I love killed," he said as if I'd asked the question out loud. "Zin's leg isn't injured, Majesty. He lost it. Just below the knee." Emmory tapped at his own, his eyes clouding with memories and grief.

"We'd been in the field for several years, but we were still rookies. The case was an ugly one. You probably don't remember it; you would have only been nine or ten. We were tracking a serial killer who'd managed to escape off-world before his sentence could be carried out."

"I do remember—you're talking about the Fourteen Roses killer." I nodded, shuddering a little. "I remember Ofa and Tefiz being completely on edge the year before he was caught. We were barely allowed out of the palace before, and even after they caught him, Tefiz kept a hand on her gun when we went outside."

"It was just as well she did. His followers killed more people after he was caught than he did during his whole spree." Emmory shook his head. "Zin and I caught up with him outside of Solarian territory. He died in the shoot-out." My *Ekam* didn't blink when he told me the lie, even though we both knew his orders were probably not to bring Howell Tajman home alive.

"We'd shot one of the women with him and didn't check to make sure she was dead. She took Zin's leg off with a machete, and I got shot twice by another man who was hiding in a crawlspace."

I flinched.

"I let my guard down when I thought the job was done, and we both almost died. As it was, Zin lost his leg, and I can't ever forgive myself for that."

"He doesn't blame you," I said after touching my hand to my lips. I'd come close to losing these two before I'd even met them, and I wondered how things would have played out if they'd died in a run-down warehouse on some fringe Solarian world.

I'd likely be dead.

"He doesn't have to, Majesty. I was in charge and I messed up."

"You're afraid the same thing will happen here?" Taking a deep breath, I headed back toward the lift.

Emmory shook his head slowly. "It's not about being afraid, Majesty. I can't let it happen here. I swore an oath to protect you and the empire. I won't forsake it."

I wasn't about to tell my *Ekam* he was wrong. His penance was his own business. If I had learned anything about Emmory in the short time we'd been together, it was that once he swore an oath, not even the gods themselves could get him to turn his back on it.

We rode up to the surface in silence. The doors slid open and only the fact that I knew the rest of my Guards were still standing in the corridor kept me from doing anything but strolling out of the lift as if my heart weren't about to jump out of my ears.

"You're going to want to take a breath," Emmory murmured. "I'll unmute your vitals from the others once your heart has slowed down."

*"I'm working on it, Emmy,"* I said over the com without looking in his direction, and smiled at Alba as she approached. "Let's go talk to Tazerion. I really want to know if he was in on this plot or just a victim of circumstance."

# 8

"Where do you want to speak with him, Majesty?" Emmory asked.

"The throne room?"

Emmory and I shook our heads in unison at Alba's suggestion. "It's too formal," I said.

"Too exposed. They're confined to their rooms right now, but we could get an interrogation room cleared," he said.

"I'm not treating them like criminals, Emmory."

"They technically are, ma'am," Alba offered. "Only your temporary clemency keeps them from being considered as such."

"What about the room we were just in? It's been swept and cleared and swept again. I can't imagine things have gone downhill so badly in the last ten minutes that it's suddenly unsafe?"

Emmory laughed and Alba looked a little sheepish. I continued down the hallway back to the meeting room. It was empty, no signs of the chaos that had filled it earlier except for a few chairs still pushed away from the table.

I dropped into mine and swung a leg up over one of the

arms. "Alba, do we have footage of the room when the bomb went off?"

"Yes, ma'am."

"Get me a clip, starting thirty seconds before I entered and going until I left the room."

My *smati* pinged several minutes later and I queued up the playback. Taz was giving his passionate speech, but I muted the sound so it wouldn't distract me as the scene played out. Both *Upjas* and Taz jumped at the unexpected rumble, and so did the others around the table. Even I twitched, my head swinging toward Cas, looking for an explanation.

Something caught my eye and I started the playback over again.

"Emmory, look at this. What do you see?" I asked, throwing the file onto the screen embedded in the table in front of me.

My *Ekam* tilted his head to the side. "The *Upjas* were as surprised as everyone. Or they're very good at faking—" He broke off and reached out to tap the screen, sending the images back several seconds. "Matriarch Zellin, however, doesn't move at all. Even you flinched a little, Majesty."

"It shook the room, everyone should have reacted. She stops tapping her fingers just there." I froze the playback. "As if she were counting. But several hours earlier she was very vocal in her opposition to the *Upjas*."

"It makes a decent smokescreen."

"Shiva save me from political machinations, Emmory. Can't people just say what they mean?" I rubbed my face with both hands and then looked at him. "This is all your fault."

"You stayed, Majesty," he reminded me with a slight smile.

I would have stuck my tongue out at him, but Cas escorted Taz and the two young men into the room. All three dropped to their knees.

"Bugger me, get up. Groveling makes me uncomfortable. Sit down." I pointed at the row of chairs Emmory had pulled out on the other side of the table from me.

Taz winced when he sat, a hand going to his ribs.

I threw Cas a sharp look. "Cas, did I or did I not expressly say not to harm our guests?"

"You did, Majesty."

"I want to know who wasn't listening to me."

"I'm fine, Majesty. It's nothing."

"It is not 'nothing,' Tazerion. You are my guests and your safety is my responsibility."

"My apologies, Majesty," he replied, dipping his head.

"Shut up."

Garhi choked down a laugh while Salham just kept looking from Taz to me to Emmory and back again.

"So, Christoph is responsible for this, yes?" I asked, leaning back and tapping my heel against the chair. "He had to have known you were meeting with us."

"It wasn't exactly a secret," Taz said. "He must have hoped you'd take it badly and have us arrested."

"He's right about the first part," I muttered. "What do you think his plan would be if I actually did that?"

The silence stretched. Taz thought over my question for a while before answering. "He'd keep killing, Majesty. Try to make it look like it was the *Upjas* demanding our release. Abraham has left the capital. There's no one but me right now to speak for us."

I swore under my breath, but Taz continued.

"He'll likely keep at this even if you let us go. The man is insane. He wants you and every matriarch dead, and he wants the empire in ashes. He's not someone you can reason with or negotiate with. He won't stop until he's won this fight or he's dead."

"And even if we kill him, his followers will carry on. I know how these people work." I swung my foot to the floor with a thud. "So you're telling me there's nothing I can do."

"There is. You probably won't like it."

I arched an eyebrow and stared at Taz for a moment. "Everyone out."

The younger *Upjas* got to their feet, and my BodyGuards headed for the door. Taz didn't move. Emmory didn't move.

Life was back to normal apparently. I waited for the door to close before I gestured at Taz to continue.

"Let us go. Let us handle this."

It was my turn to stare at him with wide eyes. "You want me to authorize you for some kind of gang war in the streets?"

"I would hope it doesn't come to that. We'll do what we can to avoid bloodshed. There are more of us, Majesty, and we know Christoph better than your people."

Rubbing my hand over my face with a sigh, I looked up at the ceiling. The gray stones varied in color, making them easy to count from one tip of the arch to the next. I reached 103 on the halfway point before I shook my head.

"I can't, Taz. I can't ask you to take care of my problems for me."

"If you'll pardon my bluntness: You already have a war to fight, Hail." Taz glanced at Emmory, but my *Ekam* didn't comment on the familiarity. "It's going to take everything you have to get up to speed on the Saxons and keep the empire safe. I know Christoph. I know how he thinks." Taz got out of his chair. "*Ekam*, may I approach?"

Emmory raised an eyebrow at him but nodded, and Taz knelt, putting a hand over mine.

"Let me do this for you, for Indrana. We were a good team once."

"We were, weren't we?" I murmured. My thoughts were spinning in circles, but my hand turned itself over without command to link my fingers with his. "Please keep our people safe." I met his brown eyes, hoping my *"Please keep yourself safe"* was clear enough on my face.

"I will do whatever is needed, Majesty."

I cleared my throat, untangling my fingers from his and feeling suddenly awkward about the whole thing. "I want someone with you. Emmory, could we steal Captain Gill and her squad?"

"I'll check when she gets here, Majesty. I already called to see if Sergeant Terass was nearby."

I shook my head as Taz got to his feet. "That was kind of you, but she won't be able to help him. Taz doesn't respond to Farians. I'm surprised you didn't know that."

Humanity had started to believe we were truly alone in the universe when the Farians made contact. According to them there were more races out there in the vastness of space, but they didn't venture this far to the Milky Way's outer edges.

The Farians though were driven to explore. Their unique ability to heal or kill with a touch was the touchstone of their beliefs as well as a biological drive.

Humans, as it turned out, were perfect for a race that needed to heal. Our fragile bodies provided the outlet for energy that would otherwise burn a Farian up should they try to hoard it. However, one in every million humans didn't respond to the Farian touch, and Taz was one of them.

"It's all right," Taz said with a smile and a shrug that had him putting his hand on his side again. "I don't think they broke anything."

"Majesty, if you'll head back to your rooms with Cas I'll finish up here?" Emmory suggested as he opened the door.

I nodded and followed him through the doorway. Alba was standing in the hall with that look on her face. The one that I recognized meant she had something important to talk to me about. So rather than argue with Emmory—again—I gave the *Upjas* a final smile and headed off down the corridor.

"Majesty, I have a message from Ambassador Toropov requesting dinner this evening if it's convenient."

"Has he been under a rock all day? Tell him to pick a time when my people aren't being killed in the streets."

Alba blinked at my sharp tone but nodded. "Verbatim, Majesty, or should I soften it?"

"Verbatim, we'll see what he does with it." Jaden Toropov wasn't the sort of man to commit such an unbelievable faux pas, and I wondered just what he was up to. "Alba, let the networks know we'll be addressing our people this evening around 20:00. I think we'll do it from my office."

"Do you want me to start writing something, or would you prefer to do it yourself?"

"You can start it; I'll probably edit before I go on though." I stopped in the hallway and waited with Indula by my side while Cas and the others cleared my rooms. When it was safe we headed inside. "Cas, I want those guards who can't listen in here now."

"Yes, ma'am."

Alba moved to the couches, already composing a speech with her *smati*. Contrary to what I'd said, I probably wouldn't have to fiddle with it all that much. I flipped the news onto the far wall and stood with a hand over my mouth as the reports filtered in.

"How do I respond to this?" I whispered when Emmory joined me. "How can I possibly respond to this without sounding—" Words failed me and I waved a hand helplessly at the wall. "I've been here a month, Emmory. How can I lead them through this horror?"

"You can, Majesty," he said without looking away from the newscast. "Captain Gill is going to shadow Tazerion and report back about his plans. He agreed to wait to take any action until you were informed."

"I'm surprised you got him to agree to that."

Emmory shrugged. "I may not agree with him, and I certainly don't trust him, but he was right about knowing Christoph better than any of us."

"And he's got more people on the ground. How many places did they hit us?"

"They detonated explosives in four spots around the capital, including the one at the palace gates: two restaurants and one park."

"I want someone on Matriarch Zellin."

"It's already done, Majesty."

I paced, trying to keep the walls of my rooms from closing in on me as my brain spun for a way to cope with all the horror. The capital was still reeling from the explosion at Garuda Square, and now there was more death.

Had I brought this on my people? I shook my head before I'd even finished asking the question. Christoph and the others had been gunning for the throne before I got here. *Don't wallow in a bunch of useless self-pity, Hail, it won't accomplish anything.*

"Majesty." Cas came into the room with a man and woman in tow. "Matriarchs Desai and Hassan were very helpful. After a review of the footage it was determined these two were the ones who misheard your orders about proper treatment of our guests."

"Yes, my orders. Which were what, exactly, Cas?"

"Detain the *Upjas*, but don't harm them, Majesty."

"Don't. Harm. Them." I watched the pair flinch with each clipped word. "And yet my guests were harmed. Who has an explanation for me?"

"None, Majesty," the woman said, keeping her eyes on the floor. "We reacted rashly and we apologize."

"Apologies don't mend broken bones," I said. "I'll be drafting a letter of reprimand to put in your files. Be thankful you are not my Guards or you'd be out on your asses." I looked at Cas and jerked my head toward the door.

He led them out.

I crossed to where Alba was sitting and leaned against the table. "Okay, what have you got for me?"

"Take a look at this."

My *smati* pinged as Alba sent the draft over.

"I thought if we started with something soft and then raise the volume it would have more impact."

I nodded. "I like it. Move the second line here and add in 'the tears of the empire' to the bit before that."

"Yes," Alba said. "Are we still using *terrorist*?"

"Without hesitation," I replied.

# 9

We kept my address to the empire short and sweet. I managed not to snarl too much, even though my seething gut wanted to swear vengeance for those who'd died.

*You are no longer a gunrunner, Hail, and hasty words start wars.*

Wars were something I'd had too many of already. Taz had been right about that, and I was now grateful for his offer of assistance. We were only two days out from the bombings and already the *Upjas* had subdued two different bands of Christoph's terrorists. The fact that they'd turned them over to Captain Gill without any complaint had even impressed my *Ekam*—at least a little.

The next day I was sitting in my office with Caspel and Admiral Hassan, finally hearing some decent news about the 2nd Fleet problem. My office was shielded from listening devices, but we still had Emmory's jamming system on to be safe.

"There are twenty-eight ships under Admiral Shul's command." Admiral Hassan threw the descriptions up on the wall.

There were seven Nadi-class carriers, each capable of holding sixteen smaller Jal fighters. Two Asvin medical frigates. Ten Jarita-class battlecruisers with enough firepower to level a comparable force. And nine Sarama destroyers.

Caspel stood and tapped on the various names of the ships as he spoke. "According to my operative, eight of the battlecruisers, including Admiral Shul's flagship, one of the medical frigates, three of the craft carriers, and six of the destroyers, are crewed by officers who seem sympathetic to Christoph and his position. There's a chance of a mutiny on at least one of the other craft carriers, but my operative is attempting to contact the captain of that ship and let her know her XO is suspect."

Admiral Hassan nodded her dark head. "I know several of those captains and commanders personally, Majesty. They are loyal to you."

"I'm so tired of dancing around this issue with him." I tapped my fingers on my knee. "Let's get Shul on the line, Admiral. See what he has to say to me."

"Ma'am?"

"Call him, Inana. I want to see him lie to my face."

Caspel cleared his throat. "With apologies, Majesty, but I can't let you jeopardize my operation. If you tip him off too soon, before we have things in place, it could result in the loss of your supporters."

"Damn it, Caspel—"

"Excuse me, Your Majesty." Alba broke in, not quailing from the sharp look I sent her. "President Hudson of the Solarian Conglomerate is on the line for you."

"Took him long enough to get around to calling," I muttered, and Hassan choked on a laugh. Confronting Shul was going to have to wait. I looked at Hassan. "Notify who you can, as carefully as you can. Tell them to keep an eye on Shul and be prepared for the worst. I want you two to cook up a viable reason to recall 2nd Fleet home without tipping our hand."

"Yes, ma'am." Hassan snapped a sharp salute. I nodded at her, and she turned on her heel. Caspel followed her out, closing the door behind him.

"Throw the call up on the wall, Alba." I smoothed the wrinkles out of my shirt but stayed in my office chair. A quick glance over my shoulder confirmed that Emmory would be visible, standing in parade rest just behind my right shoulder. I rolled my neck, nodded at Alba, and pasted a smile on my face as she opened the connection.

"President Hudson."

The president of the SC Council was an older, distinguished-looking man with pale skin and silver hair. I caught the flicker of his eyes toward Emmory before he composed himself and smiled at me with the slightest tilt of his head. "Empress. It is a pleasure to speak with you even though the circumstances are so somber. On behalf of the Solarian Conglomerate, allow me to offer my condolences for the loss of your mother and the recent difficulties."

I wanted to laugh at the ridiculously careful phrasing, but instead I settled on a cool look. "Our thanks, President Hudson. It's been a troubling time for Indrana. The recent attacks both here at home and on other worlds of the empire is heartbreaking. It is a disappointment to us that the Saxon Alliance would violate the peace treaty that has stood for so long."

President Hudson didn't bat an eyelash, but I heard the gasps in the background. My people were silent and for that I was grateful.

"That is terrible news, Empress, though the accusations against the Saxons are unfounded. We haven't heard anything from the Solarian consulate on Major, and one would think had anything happened in violation of the treaty they would be the first to say something. I would caution you to think of your people in this time of grief. Hasty measures for revenge don't make for good business."

"And fomenting dissent in my empire doesn't make for keeping peace treaties, President." I crossed my arms over my chest and gave him the look that used to scare the pants off hardened gunrunners. It worked just as well on politicians, because bright spots of color appeared on President Hudson's cheeks and the conversation behind him grew in volume.

"Empress—"

"Let us be very clear here." I switched abruptly to the more formal royal *we*. "When we find the proof linking the Saxon Alliance to this plot, we will pass it along to you. But the Indranan Empire is no longer a member of the conglomerate and has not been for fifteen centuries. We do not need your approval when making decisions on matters that affect our people. We wish to continue our good relations with the Solarian Conglomerate, but we will not sacrifice lives or territory to maintain those relations.

"We appreciate your call, sir," I said with a sweet smile. "However, we have things that must be attended to and we're sure you do also. Have a nice day." I waved a hand at Alba, who cut the connection before President Hudson could come up with a reply.

Alba exhaled.

I glanced at her. "Too much?"

"No," she said, surprising me. "Though hopefully you didn't give him a heart attack."

"There are plenty more old men on that council to take his place." I rubbed at my neck and turned in my chair. "Emmory, thoughts?"

My *Ekam* raised an eyebrow at me and I rolled my eyes at the ceiling. It was apparently enough to prompt him as he moved back toward the door of my office. "It was harsh, Majesty, but well controlled. You'd do well to establish with them that you're not some blushing young thing who will be bullied."

I snorted. "I'm not sure anyone would mistake me for a 'blushing young thing,' Emmory."

"If they haven't read your file there's always a chance."

"Alba, I think my *Ekam* is teasing me."

"He may be delirious from lack of sleep, ma'am."

The banter helped relax the shards of tension lodged in my back, and I actually laughed. "It's his own damn fault for getting me into this mess. Alba, did we get a response from Ambassador Toropov?"

"Not as yet, ma'am."

"Interesting." I started to push out of my chair. "I've got a meeting with Alice in about an hour, don't I?"

"Yes, ma'am. Then an appearance at the arts center," Alba said.

"You're letting me keep that one?" I looked at Emmory in surprise.

"I figured you would fight to keep it, Majesty. Security will be tight, it's not too much extra trouble."

I couldn't speak past the lump in my throat. There was a memorial concert scheduled for the children and other victims of the Garuda Square bombing this evening. I had lobbied for it, had somehow talked Emmory into letting me go, and had been convinced that the newest wave of violence meant I was stuck in the palace.

Busying myself at my desk, I struggled for the words but

was saved by the ping of an incoming message. "It's Alice." I answered the call.

"Majesty."

I nodded. "Judging by the look on your face, we're going to need to reschedule our meeting?"

She nodded. "Something has come up, Majesty, I'm terribly sorry."

"Don't be." I waved a hand. "Usually I have to pass out at an important meeting to get some free time. Get with Alba and she'll reschedule you."

"Yes, Majesty."

I closed out the call and bounced out of my seat, drumming my hands on the desktop, unable to contain my delight. "A whole three hours to myself, it's unprecedented."

Alba cleared her throat. "I almost hate to say it, Majesty, but I just received a message from Ambassador Toropov. He says he is at your disposal whenever it is convenient."

"Bugger me," I muttered, falling back into my seat. "Don't you dare laugh, Emmory."

"I would never, Majesty."

"Liar. Alba, tell him to meet us in the library in twenty and order some food from the kitchen."

"Yes, ma'am."

I waited until she was out the door before I got up. "Emmory, I'm going to ask Trace for a meeting." If I'd learned anything over the last month it was that my *Ekam* hated surprises and if I wanted him to agree to things it worked in my favor to fill him in ahead of time.

Trace Gerison was the king of the Saxon Alliance. He'd inherited the position from his father, who'd been killed in a naval battle shortly after my father had been assassinated. For a while it looked like Indrana would take the upper hand in the war. But Trace, even at seventeen years old, was a far better strategist than my grieving mother.

"To what end, Majesty?" Emmory's question was cautious, his face guarded.

"To stop the war before it happens." There were times I felt like I was talking to my father instead of my BodyGuard. "You know we can't stand up to the Saxons for long in a straight fight." I leaned against the desk. "I've been told I'm a pretty good negotiator."

"What are you going to offer him?"

"Honestly? I have no idea, and while I'm sure I can make a final decision I'm not about to go up against the Matriarch Council on this. What I really want, Emmory, is to see his face, or more accurately to be in the same room with him. I want to be able to learn what I can from him before this thing implodes on us. At least then I'd have a halfway decent chance of beating him."

"I've underestimated you again, Majesty," Emmory said with a smile.

"I hope that's a compliment."

"It is." He waved a hand at the door, still smiling. "Let's go meet with Toropov."

I'd picked the library, which seemed to be fast becoming the new default place for informal meetings, since even I wasn't crazy enough to try to convince Emmory to let the Saxon ambassador into my rooms.

I curled up in the chair by the fire reading an old-fashioned book. *There are three ways in which a ruler can bring ruin upon her army.* I looked up from the ancient writings of Sun Tzu with a smile when Zin leaned down.

"Majesty, Ambassador Toropov is here to see you."

"Let him in." Closing the book, I put it aside as I stood. "Ambassador, thank you for coming to see me."

"Thank you, Majesty, for making the time. It's quite an honor and a pleasure to see you again." Toropov took my out-stretched hand in both of his scarred ones and squeezed gently. He was dressed in a deceptively casual outfit, but I caught the faint sheen on his shirt as he sat in the chair across from me. Only silk looked like that in firelight.

Which meant the shirt he was wearing cost almost as much as the book I'd just put down.

"Majesty?"

I blinked and laughed. "Sorry, Ambassador. I was ruminating on how easily fortunes change. I've had food prepared."

"Fortune is fickle." Toropov followed me to the table in the corner, nodding his thanks at Alba as she set a cup on the table. "Would you like to hear the story of how I got here?"

Picking up my cup of blue chai, I gave Toropov a nod. We ate and I listened as he spun a tale of a boy born to poverty who ended up in trouble and was given the choice between jail or service. He chose service and spent nearly forty years with the Saxon Marine Corps before retiring.

"Ten years ago, I was offered the chance by His Majesty to come here. I'm glad I took it. You have a fascinating empire, Majesty."

"Thank you."

Toropov leaned forward in his seat. "But you didn't agree to see me to listen to an old man ramble about his past. Especially since I'm sure your BodyGuards already knew everything I just told you."

I smiled at him over the rim of my cup. "True, but it was a good story nonetheless. I need to speak with Trace."

Toropov didn't bat an eyelash. "I can set up a com with him, Majesty, but you don't really need my assistance with that. Your chamberlain could have just…ah." He stopped and smiled. "That's not what you mean, is it?"

"I am willing to let him choose the meeting spot. I believe there is a list of neutral planets for just such a purpose."

The hesitation on Toropov's face was fleeting, gone so fast I thought I must have imagined it. "Does Your Majesty have a reason I can pass on to the king? It would help facilitate matters."

I held in my laughter at the ambassador's careful phrasing as I rose from my seat. "Let's call it a discussion of the issues that concern both our peoples."

"Very well, Your Majesty." He gave me a sharp nod and walked with me back to the fire. "I will see what I can do."

"That is all I can ask." I set my cup down and reached for my book.

Toropov smiled, canting his head to the side as he read the title. "It has been years since I read that, Majesty. Though it was a translation, not the original Chinese. I'm most impressed."

"I get through it," I replied with an answering smile. "It is not the same as Cheng, but there are quite a few similarities."

"Have a good afternoon, Majesty. I will send your chamberlain a message as soon as I have news."

I nodded my thanks and settled back in the big chair after Toropov excused himself. I'd probably just stirred up a hell of a hornet's nest, but if it worked out, it could stop this headlong slide into war.

And I had to stop the war. We would fight if we had to, but I knew Indrana wouldn't survive, not by herself.

I picked the book up again, returning to the page where I'd left off.

*There are three ways in which a ruler can bring ruin upon her army. The first is by commanding the army to advance or to retreat, being ignorant of the fact that it cannot obey.*

# 10

I took the handkerchief Alba handed me and wiped the tears from my face. I'd gone for so long without music from home, and now it surrounded me, carried on the high, clear notes of a young boy's voice. According to my chamberlain, the singer had lost a cousin in the recent bombings, yet he'd insisted on performing.

Now he sang a prayer to the gods more ancient than Indrana. A prayer that forgave the killers. A prayer that said good-bye to loved ones. It broke me open, broke open the whole audience. Only my BodyGuards had dry eyes.

The silence that settled on the audience lasted for several heartbeats before I broke it with the tapping of my left foot on the floor. It rippled out around me, filling the auditorium with the sound. The young man pressed his hands together and bowed low, his shoulders shaking with tears that were finally released.

I finished wiping my face and tucked the handkerchief into the deep green sleeve of my shirt as I stood. My BodyGuards formed up around us as we made our way out of the auditorium into the chaos of the waiting press.

"Your Majesty! Is it true you've come to an agreement with the *Upjas* to fight these recent attacks?"

"Majesty! We've heard reports Abraham Suda is no longer in charge of the *Upjas*. Is this why Tazerion Shivan was at the palace the other day?"

"Your Majesty, any plans to visit the wounded you've been chatting with on Hansi?"

"Your Majesty, Tazerion Shivan was once your mother's choice for your husband. Is there still a chance you'll consider him for the consort position even though he's the new leader of the *Upjas*?"

"Excuse me?" I whirled on the reporter who'd asked the question, and the woman backed away. The crush of her companions around her prevented her from gaining the distance she suddenly decided she wanted. "Who are you?"

"Eljia Yulin, Majesty, *Pashati Daily News*." She swallowed hard. "We were just curious about—"

"I heard the question the first time." I didn't bother to stop the snarl in the back of my throat even though more than a dozen cameras were sure to pick it up. "We just got done at a memorial concert, Ms. Yulin. A hundred and forty-three Indranans have been killed in the last few weeks and your first thought is gossip." I leaned in, surprised that Emmory didn't stop me. "Shame on you."

"Majesty, I—"

"Shame," I repeated, turning around and walking away. The other journalists melted from my BodyGuards' path in stunned silence.

"It's not a primary news source, ma'am," Alba said once we were back in the aircar. "She doesn't have palace access."

"Make sure it stays that way. If I see her again I promise it will result in a public relations nightmare."

"Yes, ma'am."

We rode back to the palace in silence. By now my people could read my moods well enough to know when to be quiet, and they left me alone to stew over the incident.

I was still angry the next morning. With some difficulty, I shoved it away before my scheduled call with Trace. I met Ambassador Toropov at the door of my office with a smile, but he raised an eyebrow at me.

"Is everything all right, Majesty?"

"Well enough." I was sure he'd seen the coverage; it had been all over the news this morning. Settling into my chair, I nodded at him to proceed and he threw the screen up onto the far wall.

I had seen my fair share of news reports about the king of the Saxon Alliance in my years away from home, but it was a testament to my self-control that my mouth didn't fall open when Trace appeared on the screen.

"Empress." He dipped his blond head, his smile reaching up into his eyes.

The last time I'd seen him in person, he'd been a gawky eleven-year-old. Now Trace Gerison was a tall, broad-shouldered man with short blond hair. I couldn't deny that he was attractive, but he wasn't my type. He was also, thankfully, married. So I wasn't going to have to answer any infuriating questions in that regard.

"It's good to see you."

"We've both come up in the world, haven't we, Haili?" Before I could reply, he continued. "I was sorry to hear about your family. We'd been concerned about the declining state of your mother's health for some time but never considered it could be something so horrible."

"I'm sure you didn't, Your Majesty," I murmured.

Trace blinked and started to protest, and then I watched as that all-too-familiar mask of leadership dropped onto his face. "I know there have been rumors, but I can assure you that Saxony was not involved in the recent events. I am committed to keeping the peace treaty between our people."

"As am I," I replied, even though I wasn't entirely sure how I was going to make it happen. There was a moment of tense silence as we stared at each other.

"Well." Trace cleared his throat. "Jaden said you wanted to talk about meeting. I have plans to look over the list of neutral planets with my head of security. As a gesture of good faith we'll pull three and you can go over them with your *Ekam* to choose the final spot?"

I nodded, unable to find any suitable reply among the mess in my head for several moments. "That's very generous of you."

He shrugged uncomfortably. "Saxony doesn't want a war. I figure you and I have seen enough death in our lifetimes, and we're not interested in starting something up so more young men and women will see the same horrors."

That was true enough at least, and I felt relatively certain he believed what he was saying. However, of the two of us I was also certain I was the only one who'd ever seen anything close to combat. It still didn't answer the question of Canafey, but I couldn't ask about it here. Not when he'd just offered to let me pick the meeting spot.

Instead I smiled. "Very kind of you, Trace. I appreciate it."

"We'll talk soon." Trace disconnected, leaving me staring at the blank spot on the wall.

Ambassador Toropov cleared his throat. "With my apologies, Majesty. His Majesty can be very abrupt at times; it was nothing personal."

I laughed and stood. "You seem to have forgotten I've dealt with far worse."

Toropov laughed himself and rose with a fluid bow. "I seem to have done just that, Majesty. I will pass along the list as soon as I receive it."

"A pleasure as always, Ambassador."

He nodded and left my office.

"Well, that was interesting," I said, tapping Zin on the shoulder. "It's been a long time since I've talked to Trace. We met briefly when I was seven. King Geri visited Mother the year before the war broke out. It was a last-ditch attempt to stop the growing tension. He was a cute kid, all gangly and awkward."

"He's grown up, ma'am," Zin said.

"Both of us have." I laughed again and then rubbed a hand over my face. "In very different ways."

"What I meant was he's confident, sure of his right to rule. It's an advantage. You're still—"

"Wondering if I belong here?" I waved a hand before he could apologize. "No, it's the truth."

"Majesty."

"Emmory." I turned to my *Ekam*. "I was wondering when you were going to speak up."

"King Trace kept looking to the left. My guess is at someone standing behind the recorder."

"Do you think he was being coached?"

Emmory tilted his head in thought. "That short an interaction, it was hard to tell. I'll know better when I see the people around him. I'd recommend caution here, Majesty."

"I'm in agreement with you." I replayed the conversation, this time catching the quick flick of Trace's eyes to the left of the camera. I wondered who he'd been watching and just what it meant.

\* \* \*

Matriarch Desai wasn't happy about my decision to include Taz in the morning briefings, but I insisted, mostly because it saved me from having to sit through the same information three times in a day.

She was coolly efficient as we moved through the details of the official negotiation process with the *Upjas*, and turned the floor over to Taz without protest.

"Your Majesty, we've made good progress cleaning up Christoph's cells. However, as Captain Gill has no doubt informed you, we've still been unable to locate Christoph himself."

"He's still on planet though?"

Taz nodded. "Still in the capital, we think, but he's constantly on the move and changing his face. Captain Gill has the legal body modification centers under close supervision, but there're a lot of chop shops out there."

"Keep after him. Make sure you get some sleep, Taz, you look tired."

A smile flickered to life, but Taz didn't call me on my hypocrisy in front of everyone. "Yes, Majesty."

"Your Majesty, are we getting some kind of verification for the information this rebel is presenting us?" Prime Minister Eha Phanin, by contrast, had been less than pleasant to Taz since he'd joined us.

"Captain Gill has been our liaison with the *Upjas* since this started."

"Captain Gill also has several family members who are sympathizers."

That was news to me, and I stopped myself from glancing at my *Ekam*. "Captain Gill is trusted by us," I said.

"I'm sure, Majesty. I'm just suggesting we cover all avenues rather than trusting a single source of information."

I stared at Phanin, but he didn't flinch. I didn't have a good reason to tell him no and we both knew it. "Fine. We will find a second source to verify, Eha. Will that satisfy you?"

The annoyed expression was only on his face for a second, but it was enough to make me triumphant. Phanin nodded. "Of course, Majesty. I am only concerned for the safety of the empire."

"As are we."

Clara cleared her throat. "Moving on to the next item on our list, Majesty, I have a list of potential suitors for you to interview. I'll pass the list on to Alba so she can get them slotted into your schedule."

Taz raised an eyebrow but wisely remained silent.

I looked away from him, feeling my cheeks heat. "Clara, now is not the time for this."

"You insisted he be here for the morning briefings, Majesty. Perhaps you should have looked at the topics beforehand?"

I couldn't punch her in the throat. I'd get in trouble. Folding my hands into my lap, I took a deep breath. "Matriarch Desai, I dislike being pushed and prodded. If you haven't figured it out, you soon will. The more you try to get me to make a decision, the more I will resist. Since I am the empress, there is very little you can do to actually force me. I will look at your list and fit this relatively minor issue into my schedule as it allows. This is the last I want to hear of it. Am I understood?" I stood and there was a lot of noise as everyone else in my office rushed to do the same.

"Yes, Majesty." Clara bowed, her eyes unrepentant.

"Have a good day, everyone." I reminded myself again that I couldn't punch her and left the room.

My BodyGuards were silent as we headed back to my rooms. I flipped the news onto the screen of the far wall as we walked through the door and unwound my gold sari, tossing it onto the back of the couch. I flopped down and took the cup of chai Stasia handed me.

"You can't punch Matriarch Desai," Emmory said.

"I know," I replied with a tight smile. "Doesn't mean I don't want to though."

Gita and Kisah settled into their spots by the door. Zin appeared to be having a silent conversation with Emmory as they both looked out the window at the bay. I drank my chai and picked at a stray thread on my cream-colored pants.

"More rumors continue to swirl about the empress's relationship with the *Upjas'* new leader, Tazerion Shivan. A source inside the palace confirms they've met in private several times and that Shivan is now part of Empress Hailimi's inner circle. He's attended several daily briefings and is no longer being subjected to searches when he enters the palace."

"We're still searching him, Majesty, that part isn't true."

"What do you mean 'that part'? None of it is true," I snarled in return.

"Of course, Majesty."

Before I could say anything, the bubbly newscaster continued. "There's been a great deal of speculation about the empress's necessary search for a Prince Consort. Is Tazerion the front-runner for the position? Our viewers weigh in on the issue."

The screen died as I abruptly cut the feed and got to my feet. "Source inside the palace?"

"There are a lot of people around you, Majesty," Emmory replied. "They do sign nondisclosure contracts when they come to work, but the press is offering a lot of money for information about the new empress. We can't follow them all to make sure they're not talking."

"Your Majesty could make worse alliances," Zin said with a shrug.

"Oh, could I?"

He either missed or ignored the sharpness in my voice. "He's not a noble, ma'am, but the Shivans are an old family who have been in favor of the throne for a long time. You were paired once. And it would cement an alliance with the *Upjas*."

I dropped to the couch and set my mug down before I threw it at Zin's head. My buried grief surged up my throat and choked me. Portis's face and his dying words rang in my head, clamoring for my attention.

"Has everyone forgotten that only a little over a month ago I woke up covered in blood next to Portis's body? Because *I* haven't." I slammed a hand down on the table, making everyone but Emmory jump. "I lost the only man I ever loved and you all just want to farm me back out with a smile on my face and my gods-damned legs spread.

"All for the good of the empire. Fuck you. I won't do it."

Gita gasped. Zin swallowed.

I stood up, my hands curling into fists. "I will not. Do you hear me? I will not get married. I loved him. Only him. I—" Tears clogged my throat and I pressed a hand to my mouth. The grief sliced through me so painfully bright and sharp I couldn't breathe.

"You three, out." Emmory's voice was soft.

As the door slid shut behind my BodyGuards, I sank back to the couch. My sobs rang in my ears. My breath was choppy, catching and wheezing as I fought for air. I folded over, my head on my knees, and cried until exhaustion set in.

Emmory's hand settled onto the back of my neck with gentleness I didn't realize he was capable of. "Get your breath, Majesty."

I dragged in a shaky breath and then another before I lifted my head. Emmory handed me a handkerchief and after I'd wiped my face and blew my nose, he handed me a glass.

"Find your center, Hail, or you're going to fly apart here and there's nothing I can do to save you."

"I don't know if I can," I whispered. "I thought—I fooled myself into thinking the grief was gone. I'm not over him. I don't know if I ever will be." I took the drink from Emmory and tossed it back.

"You don't have to be over him."

"Can't they just be happy with Alice? She's a better option than a newborn anyway."

He took the glass from me and rose to fill it again. I blew my nose a second time before I followed him.

"I can't do this, Emmy."

"I know, Majesty."

"No, I mean I physically can't have children." The story of the fight on Candless spilled out of me.

Emmory listened, handing me the drink midway through without comment. "I know."

"How can you know? Portis didn't tell anyone. There's no way you would have bothered with dragging me home if you'd known." I tossed back the drink. "Did you hear me? I can't have children. What's the point of protecting an empress who can't produce an heir?"

"I heard you, and I already knew."

I stared at him, the expression on my face one of abject shock. "How?"

Emmory smiled. "I'm not an idiot. I was standing right there when the technician did his scans. He may have been too distracted by you to flag it, but I saw the results." He took my empty glass and filled it a third time, but he didn't hand it to me, instead he drank it himself.

I gaped at him as my brain grappled for something, anything about this to make sense. "You knew all this time."

Emmory nodded.

"Why?"

Emmory raised an eyebrow at me. "Why what, Majesty?"

"Why are you here? Why did you stay? Why didn't my mother find out about it?" I waved my hand in the air. "I'm useless, Emmory."

"Your empress-mother didn't find out because I erased the results of the scan."

"Why would you—"

"Hail," Emmory said, giving me the Look. "Your value as the Empress of Indrana is more than your ability to bear children. The empire needs you. As you've been pointing out, the issue of who's taking over after you is the least of our worries right now. I can't afford to worry about dynasties when we don't know if Indrana will last out the year."

I stared at him for a good ten seconds before I snapped my mouth shut. Clearing my throat, I turned away so he wouldn't see the tears suddenly burning my eyes. "So, what do we do now?"

"I'd advise against making this information public," Emmory said, and I laughed.

"That would not go over well."

"Only you and I know. I haven't even told Zin. It's probably best to keep it that way until things calm down. You've already told Matriarch Desai to back off, and Alba will schedule or not based on your desires. She knows better than to let someone else influence her in that regard."

I turned back to look at him and shook my head. "I can't believe you're backing me on this."

"I have backed you from the beginning, Majesty."

"The beginning?" I raised an eyebrow at him.

Emmory gave me a half smile. "From the moment I swore my oath. Happy?"

"Less sad." I mustered up a smile of my own, looking at my tearstained face in the mirror above the fireplace. "Zin's going to want to apologize. Just tell him it's fine. I'm sorry for snapping at him."

"I will." Emmory headed for the door. "Get some rest."

I nodded but poured myself another drink in the glass Emmory had left sitting there and sipped at it as I stared out the window. The sun reflected off the dolphins playing in the water, casting a rainbow sheen upon their dark gray sides.

"Majesty? May I have a moment?"

Looking over my shoulder at Gita, I tipped my head toward the window. My BodyGuard joined me. Her curly black hair was pulled back into twists that were caught at the base of her skull. She didn't look at me, instead focusing her dark eyes on the ocean lapping at the edge of the beach.

"What's on your mind, Gita?"

"If you'll forgive my boldness, I have been there, ma'am. Blank with grief and then mad at the universe for reminding me how little we matter by continuing to move on when my world ended.

"Nothing I can say will help, but I wanted to let you know I am here if you want to talk about him."

"Who did you lose?"

"My husband, ma'am. He was killed—" Gita stopped and inhaled, clearly struggling. "It was an accident. Drunken kid in an aircar who didn't use the auto-drive. It was stupid and senseless and ten years ago, but I still wake up sobbing some nights because I miss him so much."

"I'm sorry."

Her laugh was tinged with grief. "Thank you, Majesty. That's not why I told you though. It never goes away. They leave us and we have to wake up every day after that without them."

"How do you do it?"

She shrugged. "Some days it's easy and you go about your day. Some days you're going to wake up cursing his name."

We fell into silence and I watched my BodyGuard chew on her lip as she wrestled with whatever she wanted to say next. Finally I laughed. "Just spit it out, Gita. I promise I won't fire you."

"Given your understandable reluctance to involve yourself with someone, perhaps Your Majesty should consider having a tubed-baby?"

I blinked at the suggestion. "It's not done, Gita."

"With your pardon, ma'am, nothing about your reign thus far has been anything close to conventional. Why start now?"

"Point," I replied with a quiet chuckle. "Wouldn't that turn everything upside down?" Gita didn't respond and while I wasn't sure even a tubed-baby would solve my problems, I did realize the importance of naming Alice as my heir.

I only hoped she would be able to hold the line should something happen to me.

## 11

"Your Majesty?" The captain in front of me cleared her throat. "I'm sorry, but have you been—"

"Listening? Yes." I tapped a hand on my desk and looked up at General Prajapati's lawyer. "The court convicted the general of conditional treason and several other lesser charges, but realistically the treason is the only one we're concerned about here. Despite this ruling and General Prajapati's own confession that she was involved with my late cousin's attempts to kill me, both you and the court seem to think that the throne should grant clemency." I shot a look at General Pai. The head of the tribunal was a short woman with close-cropped dark hair. "What that really means is no one wants to take responsibility for the actual sentencing and so you're tossing it in my lap."

"It is traditional—"

"Oh hush," I snapped at her. "You should know better by now than to say that to me."

The weeks had sped by, but thanks to Emmory's stubbornness my schedule remained as light as he could force Alba to make it. General Prajapati's trial had wrapped up three days ago, and since then there'd been nothing but endless back-and-forth from the army tribunal and the general's lawyer.

"How many people have you killed?"

General Prajapati blinked at me from where she stood by the door, her arms shackled behind her back and my BodyGuards flanking her. "Majesty?"

I grabbed a stack of photos off my desk and came around the edge of it, throwing them at her. They rained down, settling around her boots.

"I could give two shits about you trying to kill me, Maya. It's been attempted too many times over the years for me to worry about holding grudges over it. However, the people you backed killed children. Killed my sisters. My niece. My mother. They destroyed anyone in their way and so many who just had the bad luck to be in the wrong place at the wrong time." I leaned against my desk and crossed my arms. "I've killed people. I've never denied that. I've probably been indirectly responsible for the deaths of thousands. I've made my peace with it, just like I've made peace with the fact that as empress I'll do it all over again. The only difference between the two is it's supposedly legal now that I have a crown on my head.

"You told me that you did what you did for the good of the empire. I haven't yet heard an argument that proves to me that killing you isn't in the best interest of my empire."

"That's because there isn't one, Your Majesty."

Her lawyer swore under her breath at the general's quiet reply. Maya didn't notice it; she was still staring at the face of a three-year-old boy on the toe of her left boot.

"His name was Ronson," I said. "His mother told me he loved dogs and never stopped laughing."

Maya closed her eyes and swallowed. When she opened

them again, they were shiny with tears. "As I told the court, I wasn't aware of the plot against your family and thought it was awful circumstance and nothing more. I joined with Matriarch Khatri when you returned home because I couldn't see how allowing a criminal onto the throne was good for Indrana. I am still not convinced it is a good idea. You didn't seem interested in leaving quietly, so killing you was the most expedient solution. War with the Saxons is coming; Indrana can't afford to wait for you to prove yourself."

"I'm not interested in proving anything to you, General."

She raised her head, dark eyes meeting mine. "I know, Your Majesty. It is presumptuous of me to even think it."

I shoved away from my desk and got in her face. "You're Shiva-damned right it is! I should take my *Ekam*'s sidearm and drop you right here." I held my hand up and Emmory put his gun into my hand without question.

Several people shifted uneasily at that, but the general didn't move or look away.

"You're right, General. Indrana is about to go to war," I said. "I'm trying like hell to stop it, but even I might not be able to hold back the Saxons. The only thing keeping you alive is that I know our forces would suffer from the loss of your expertise. Think about that the next time you wonder about my commitment to this empire."

I handed Emmory his gun and walked back to my desk.

The stunned silence bounced around for several minutes before General Prajapati finally lost her composure. "You're not going to execute me?"

"I'm not even going to demote you," I replied. "You might, however, wish I had when we're done here." I waved a hand and the woman who'd been standing silently in the corner until now came forward. She was shorter than the general, with a shaved head and a nasty scar running from her left ear to her chin.

"This is Lou. She used to be ITS, now she's mine. She answers to me, no one else. You answer to her. If she thinks for a second you're plotting against me again she's got orders to put a blast through the back of your skull."

There were a few strangled gasps by those in the room who hadn't been privy to my plans before the meeting started. I lifted a hand and silence descended.

"Now, before the captain here has a stroke, you do have a choice. If you don't find this acceptable, I'll bust you back down to corporal and dishonorably discharge you. You will never again serve Indrana." I sat, folding my hands in my lap.

General Maya Prajapati's whole defense had been based off her insistence that she'd done what she thought was best for the empire. Now that defense was on the line more definitively than it had been the whole trial. Would she take the badge of shame—a keeper outside the chain of her command with orders to kill her at the slightest provocation—just so she could continue to serve Indrana? Or would she prove herself a liar?

"Your Majesty." Maya bowed low, an impressive feat given her shackled arms. "I will gladly accept Lou's presence for the chance to continue to serve Indrana, and I thank you for being so gracious in giving me a second chance."

I nodded in reply. "Zin, get her out of those cuffs. Admiral Hassan will brief you on your new assignment, General."

"Yes, Majesty," Prajapati said, bowing again as she rubbed at her wrists. She started to follow everyone else as they filed out of my office.

"General?"

114

She stopped and turned back to me. "Majesty?"

"Lou can take care of herself, but if anything happens to her I'll be very upset."

Lou grinned. General Prajapati nodded sharply and left the room.

"I really hope I don't regret that," I said to Emmory as I kicked a foot up onto the edge of my desk.

"I think it was the right choice, Majesty. Whatever her feelings for you, it appears she has Indrana's best interests at heart. Colonel Nyr will keep her in line regardless. Was there any particular reason you gave the general the impression that Lou had been kicked out of the ITS?"

I grinned. "Reputations are sometimes best when shrouded in mystery. It helps that most of Colonel Nyr's commendations are for classified missions and the general no longer has clearance for such things. If she thinks Lou is a criminal she might behave herself."

"Let's hope so."

"Don't be a pessimist, Emmy."

"That's what you pay me for, ma'am." Emmory tilted his head to the side as a call came in on his *smati*. "Captain Gill, what have you got?"

I was still laughing when my own *smati* chimed and I answered the incoming call from Taz. I dropped my foot to the floor at the sight of his bruised face.

"We've found Christoph, Majesty. He's cornered in the Hethan District." Gun blasts echoed behind him. "My men have got him trapped in a building and they're closing in. Captain Gill has called in reinforcements. As soon as they arrive we're going in after him."

"Take him alive if you can, Taz. I don't want him martyring himself."

Taz nodded once and cut the connection. I lunged out of my seat, but Gita and Zin were blocking the door.

"Majesty, what are you doing?" Emmory asked.

"I'm going down there."

"Sit down." I stared at him a moment before I sank back into my chair.

"Captain Gill is sending us a live feed," he said, throwing it up on the wall. The ITS captain was using her optic camera rather than the one in her hand, so we were watching the scene through her eyes. It was a little disorienting.

"We chased him into that building." Ilyia pointed a gloved hand to the abandoned and crumbling warehouse on the right. "Taz has men in the building sweeping it floor by floor, but they're meeting heavy resistance. Captain Hilts and her team are on the door. I've got the rest of my team and half of Taz's people surrounding the exits. We'll have him out one way or another, Majesty."

The screaming of sirens echoed through the air as several ITS vehicles arrived. Within moments they were on the ground and Captain Gill had briefed the new arrivals.

I caught a glimpse of Taz as Gill nodded his way and they headed across the trash-littered street at a low run. I sank lower in my seat, tangling my fingers together.

They hit the main entrance. Captain Hilts and her people moved swiftly through the still-smoking door. Ilyia and Taz were on their heels.

"Clear!" They swept one room after another, the radio chatter limited to short bursts of tactical.

"Captain, I'm seeing—"

"Wired! This whole place is wired!"

"How did we miss it?"

"Get out, get out now!"

The view blurred as Taz grabbed Captain Gill and shoved her down the stairs they'd just raced up. The camera abruptly cut out, leaving us in silence.

"What happened?" I stood up from my chair. "Emmory, where did the—"

My *Ekam* was staring at Zin, who wore a look of horror. Gita swore, a gasping curse that was as much prayer as any solider could manage.

"What happened?"

"The building exploded, Majesty."

"Taz." I pressed a hand to my mouth, the only thing I could do to hold back the scream building inside me. "Dark Mother, Emmory."

"Sit, Majesty." He pushed me back into my chair, his hand lingering on my shoulder. "Yes, Admiral? No, the empress is still in her office. We all are. We were watching via Captain Gill's cam when it went black."

I squeezed my eyes shut, hoping that it would keep the tears at bay, but they slipped out as the names of those I'd lost echoed in my ears. Now Taz, and Ilyia Gill, and Fasé were—

Emmory tightened his fingers on my shoulder when the sob escaped. "Yes, ma'am. Keep us posted. Majesty, Admiral Hassan has rescue craft inbound to the site to look for survivors. It's radio dark over there. We're not sure if there was a *smati* disrupter in the blast."

Or if everyone was dead. The unspoken words hung heavy in the air. I pushed out of my chair, turned the news on, and put it on the wall with a flick of my wrist. It wasn't great as intel went, but it was better than the voice in my own head repeating the names of the dead over and over again.

"An explosion rocked the abandoned Hethan District just a few moments ago. The area is cordoned off, but from what our reporters have learned there was some kind of military operation going on." The newscaster's face was appropriately solemn. "We're going to Talia on the scene now."

The camera cut to a pretty young woman with the smoking ruin of the building in the frame behind her. "Thank you, Kalini. I'm here just outside of the blast zone, which is as close to the destruction as the ITS troops on the scene will allow us. If you'll look up, that sound is several naval medical transports coming in for landings in that field to our left. I haven't been able to figure out who is in charge just yet to get more information on what caused the explosion and what the ITS troops were doing here in the first place."

I paced the confines of my office for close to an hour. Dread evolved into certainty as report after report on the survivors trickled in with no mention of Taz or Captain Gill. Fasé was unharmed; the Farian had been far enough away from the back side of the building when it blew that she'd been protected from the blast.

"They found them." Emmory grabbed for my arm, already moving toward the door. "Roger that, Admiral. We're en route, we'll meet you at the hospital."

"Are they alive?" I matched Emmory's stride, Alba hurrying behind us as Zin and Gita cleared the way. Teams Four and Six met us at the garage entrance.

"Captain Gill is hurt badly, but Fasé was with them when they dug her out and used what juice she had left to stabilize her." Emmory's mouth thinned, the way it always did when he had news he didn't want to tell me.

"Tazerion is—it's not good, ma'am. They're not sure if he's going to make it."

"Shiva. Tell them to hurry, Emmory." I sank back against the seat and knotted my hands in my lap.

## 12

The Royal Indranan Hospital was a scene of organized chaos that stilled only briefly when my grim-faced BodyGuards marched into the emergency area.

"Your Majesty." The bright-eyed young man at the desk leapt to his feet and bowed.

I was all too aware of the eyes on me and chose my next words with care. "We have come to see our people."

"Yes, Majesty. I'll—"

"I can take them back, Ishan." An older woman with steel-gray hair patted his shoulder and gave me a smile as she hit the button to open the doors. "Your Majesty, I am Head Nurse Oni Suggitt. I'm sure your *Ekam* would like to go ahead of us?"

Emmory passed instructions over the com. He didn't move from my side. Team Six moved through the doors, hands on their weapons. I stayed where I was until I felt Emmory's hand on the small of my back.

"Majesty." Fasé bowed. "They won't let me in to see Lieutenant Saito."

The ITS sergeant was dirty and disheveled but otherwise

appeared unharmed so I pulled her into a hug, trying not to squeeze her too tightly. "I am glad you are safe," I murmured as I released her.

"Dr. Flipsen is in the operating room with Tazerion Shivan," Oni said. "I'll let her know you are here, but it's hard to say how much longer she'll be in with him. Captain Gill is resting, as Sergeant Terass is supposed to be." The nurse gave the Farian a stern look that the red-haired woman acknowledged with a wan smile. "And she can't see Lieutenant Saito because they are prepping her for surgery in the hopes they can save her other leg, and you have exhausted yourself already, young lady." Oni stopped at a room and tapped lightly on the half-closed door.

"Come in."

"Stay down, Captain," I said as we came into the room.

"Majesty." Ilyia struggled to sit up anyway until Oni clucked at her and moved around the bed to set it in position. Captain Gill's face was bruised, a partially healed gash near her hairline evidence of Fasé's aid. "I am so sorry. It was a trap. The whole thing was a trap and we—I stepped right into it."

"You couldn't have known, Captain."

"How many did we lose?"

"Not right now." I shook my head. "We'll discuss it after you've healed. Taz is in surgery. Rest, Captain."

"Yes, ma'am," she replied, but we both knew she was lying.

We fell into an uneasy silence. Fasé dozed in a chair by the window. Emmory spoke quietly with Ilyia and I tried not to pace.

"Majesty, sit," Zin said quietly, pulling a chair in from the hallway. "They're going to be a while."

I drifted in and out of wakefulness as reports filtered in from Admiral Hassan and others. The building had been leveled by the blast and it would take them days to uncover all the bodies.

Or what was left of them.

"Empress Hailimi."

I sat upright in the chair, blinking at the woman standing above me.

"Your Majesty, I am Dr. Eleanor Flipsen." She held out a pale hand and smiled as she bowed.

"How is he?" I took it and stood.

"Still alive. He suffered massive internal injuries and a nasty concussion. We have repaired the worst of the damage, but it will be a day or two before I know for sure if he's out of danger." Her Indranan was heavily accented.

"You are not from here, Doctor."

Despite the exhaustion in her blue eyes, Eleanor smiled. "I am not, Majesty. Though I have lived here most of my life. My parents came here on missionary work from Sanctaria when I was ten, and I fell in love with your empire. I returned after I graduated from medical school."

"I am grateful that you did. Can I see him?"

"He's in post-op, Majesty. When he wakes." Her eyes unfocused as she checked her clock. "Shouldn't be much longer. Let me go check with the nurse."

I crossed to where Emmory was looking out the window. *"Dr. Flipsen is one of the best trauma surgeons in the empire, Majesty,"* he subvocalized over our private com.

*"Are you telling me not to worry?"*

I saw him smile out of the corner of my eye. *"I know you are worried, ma'am, and with good reason. They dropped a building on him. He's lucky to be alive."*

*"Have you gotten anything new from Admiral Hassan?"*

*"No. They found the rest of the ITS team who went in ahead of Captain Gill. No survivors."*

*"Christoph is lucky he's dead."*

*"What makes you say that, ma'am?"*

*"Because I'd kill him myself if he weren't."* I turned around as Dr. Flipsen came back in the room.

"He's awake, but still pretty groggy, Majesty. If you'll come with me?"

We headed down the hallway. Zin and Gita already stood outside the room Taz was in, and my other BodyGuards were spread out at either end of the corridor. Emmory gave the nurse and Dr. Flipsen a pointed look and then shut the door behind them when they left the room.

Taz's face was even more battered than it had been when he'd called me this morning, and his olive skin had a sickly yellow cast to it that turned my stomach.

Bolstered by the privacy, I couldn't stop myself from touching his face. "Hey, you."

Taz's eyelids fluttered up, closed again, and then snapped open liked a kicked-in door. Emmory was more prepared than I was and pressed him back against the bed, speaking low and quick in his ear.

"You're safe, Shivan. Safe. At the hospital."

"Tresk?" Taz's voice was rough. "Where am I? What happened?"

"Christoph dropped a building on your head." I curled my fingers around his bandaged hand. "You just got out of surgery, so try not to mess up Dr. Flipsen's handiwork."

Taz blinked at me, hearing the words but clearly not quite comprehending them. But his fingers closed around mine as he relaxed against the bed. "I don't—I remember waking up this morning and then nothing. Captain Gill and I were—" He tried to sit up again, glaring at Emmory when my *Ekam* pushed him down.

"Is Ilyia okay?"

122

"She's fine. Took a worse beating than you, but Sergeant Terass got to her in time and she doesn't have your issue with Farians."

Taz mustered up a smile, but it faded. "Who didn't make it?"

"Corporal Danse still hasn't been found. According to Captain Gill she was right next to the building when it blew. Lieutenant Saito is in surgery. They're trying to save her leg."

"What about Madu? And my people?"

"I don't have a count on the *Upjas*." I'd been more concerned about Taz and the ITS troops. Guilt swamped me and I had to look away. "Corporal Chaturvedi didn't make it."

Taz swore, the words cutting through the air. "Her birthday was tomorrow."

I glanced at the doorway as the sound of voices filtered into the room. "I'm so sorry, Taz. Captain Gill thinks that Christoph wanted to take out as many of you as he could when he detonated—"

Emmory stiffened at the escalating noise outside the room and we both went to see what the commotion was. A man was holding the hand of a young girl, pleading with Zin and Dr. Flipsen. I would have recognized him anywhere. The younger copy was behind me in the hospital bed.

"Easy," I murmured, putting a hand on Emmory's arm when he moved to stop me from leaving the room. "It's Taz's father."

"Your Majesty." Benton Shivan dropped to a knee. "I beg you to let me see my son."

"He is outcast. You don't deserve to see him." I arched an eyebrow. "Where's his mother?"

"She doesn't know we're here, Majesty. I snuck Ahlaya out of the house." Benton raised his eyes to mine. "I have regretted every moment since my wife banished him. When I heard the news I thought my chance to see him again had been lost forever."

I bit back the harsh words that leapt into my mouth. Standing up to Vama Shivan would have left him out in the street the same as his son.

"Your Majesty. Don't blame my father. He was only doing what Taz had asked when he left." Ahlaya watched me with dark eyes that were identical to her older brother's.

"Which was what?"

"To stay and take care of me."

The girl would have only been a baby when Taz was banished from his home. It didn't surprise me he would have felt responsible for his younger sister and asked his father to watch over her. I'd never cared for Vama Shivan and her unpredictable temper.

"You may go in. If he says you stay, you'll stay. If he says otherwise or you upset him, I'll have my BodyGuards throw you both out in front of the news cameras."

"Yes, Majesty." Ahlaya curtsied and slipped around me.

I didn't need to worry about her, as it turned out; Taz's face lit up and he held out his arms for his little sister. Ahlaya embraced him gently, resting her head on his chest and whispering something my ears couldn't catch.

Benton hung back by the door, uncertain or unwilling, I couldn't tell which until Taz raised his head and the utter shock at seeing his father crashed over his face. "Papa?"

"My son." There were tears in Benton's eyes.

I moved out of his way and quietly closed the door on my way out. "Let them stay," I said to Dr. Flipsen. "And if Vama Shivan shows up, don't let her in without contacting me first. I don't care what she threatens. I'm in charge, not her."

"Yes, Majesty."

"You will let me know about Lieutenant Saito as soon as she's out of surgery?"

"Of course, ma'am."

I held my hand out. "Thank you for everything, Doctor."

"Let's get back to the palace, Emmory. Tell Admiral Hassan to meet me there. I want a full report on her findings within the hour."

"As far as we can tell, Christoph had a central charge strapped to himself with several secondary incendiary charges scattered about for maximum damage. It's doubtful we'll find his body intact, but they're scouring the wreckage for DNA to confirm he died in the explosion." Admiral Hassan rotated the image in the air above the War Room table, highlighting the spots she was talking about as she pointed to them.

"How many casualties?"

"All ITS personnel have been accounted for. We lost seven. Captain Hilts and her team were wiped out and Corporals Chaturvedi and Danse were also killed. Thankfully the other two teams were far enough behind that they only suffered cuts and bruising from the debris. Of the *Upjas* who were present, we think at least a third of them died since they were already in the building when it blew. I suspect Christoph's people took them out as they came in to sweep the building. We're still working with Tazerion to get an accurate head count."

"The only bright spot, Majesty," Caspel said, pacing the length of the table with his hands clasped behind his back, "is that this seems to have broken Christoph's radical faction rather than energized them. We don't know how many men Christoph had in the building with him, but I'm not hearing any chatter. Anyone who survived has gone silent."

"High price to pay," I whispered, scrolling through the ITS files of the team who'd died.

"Without a doubt, Majesty," Caspel agreed. "A necessary evil. Those of us who make the decisions have to live with it."

"At least we're living." I turned from the row of dead faces. "Keep me updated about Christoph's body. I want to be sure this is over before we leave for the negotiations."

"Of course, Majesty."

I nodded, which was a mistake. The room spun around me. Caspel's eyes went wide with alarm and he caught me by the arm, but it wasn't enough to keep me from sliding to the floor.

"Majesty!"

"I'm all right." I closed my eyes, felt Emmory's gloved hand on the back of my neck. "Just got dizzy."

"You haven't eaten. Alba?"

"I've already got food headed for her rooms," Alba replied. "I assumed she'd head back there after we were done. I called Dr. Ganjen. He's coming this way."

Caspel and Admiral Hassan both quietly said their goodbyes and left the room.

"I'm fine. I just got dizzy." I tried to sit up, but Emmory shook his head. "Bugger me. Do I have to keep lying on the floor?"

"I don't like your vitals, Majesty. I'd rather wait for the doctor."

I blinked at his serious tone and pulled up my vitals with my own *smati*. Then I whistled low. "Oh, on second thought I'll stay right here. Why are those so bad, Emmory? I thought that enforced rest was supposed to help."

My tease fell flat. The truth was the new schedule had helped and I'd been sleeping better in the last week than since I hit planetside. In fact, other than being worried about the events of this morning I'd woken up feeling better than I had since the coup attempt.

"I don't know, Majesty. I'm running a scan now." Emmory took the blanket Zin produced and spread it out next to me.

I scooted onto it, closing my eyes and resting my head back against a second, rolled-up blanket.

The door opened and Dr. Ganjen rushed in. Emmory left me with Zin to speak quietly with the doctor.

"Hey, my blood pressure's out of the critical range." I grinned at Zin, who gave me a strained smile. "Oh relax, will you? If you stress out, it'll just make me stress out."

"You're not going to be able to do these negotiations, Majesty, not if your health doesn't improve."

I made a face at him. "My health is fine. I just got dizzy."

"You're a young woman, Majesty. With no health issues in your history. You shouldn't be getting dizzy spells." Zin moved out of the way as Dr. Ganjen knelt at my side with a smile.

"Majesty."

"Fancy meeting you here on the floor, Doctor."

Dr. Ganjen blinked at me, but smiled. "How are you feeling, Majesty?"

"Fine now. All my readings are back to normal. Can I sit up?"

"In a moment, Majesty. Let an old man feel useful?" Dr. Ganjen put his hand on my head and his eyes unfocused as he began running his own tests.

I waited as patiently as I could for what seemed like forever until the doctor nodded and Emmory helped me up off the floor.

"What's the verdict, Doc?"

"You are fine, Majesty."

I blinked. "That's it? I'm fine?"

Doctor Ganjen smiled and patted my hand. "You are exhausted, overworked, and stressed, Your Majesty. Not to mention still recovering from your Phrine usage, though I am very pleased just how well you've recovered. Other than that, there is nothing wrong with you."

"My *Ekam* would possibly disagree with you, Doctor. But thank you for coming. I promise to try to get more sleep."

The doctor smiled again at my lie and bowed.

Emmory wasn't smiling. "Majesty, why didn't your warnings go off?"

I looked at the ceiling and ran my tongue over my teeth before I answered. "I may have turned them off—"

Emmory gave me the Look.

"A while ago."

"Majesty," he sighed. "Turn them back on, please?"

It was my turn to sigh, but I did it. "Happy?"

"Not in the slightest."

"That makes two of us," I replied. "Now I think I can make it back to my rooms without falling over and since I'm pretty sure you've canceled all my appointments for today I'm going to lie on the couch until dinner."

"Alba ordered food for you. You'll eat first, Majesty."

"Fine." I sighed at him. "I'll eat and then lie around. Bully."

# 13

Emmory was once again ruthless with my schedule, and despite Alba's protests he cut out all but the most critical of appointments.

Which was how I found myself in Father Westinkar's study midmorning several days later sipping a glass of whiskcy. I pushed away from the table littered with empty dishes and wandered to the small window. The wide sill was the same gray stone that made up the rest of the room, and it was cold under my palms.

The day was gray, the sun struggling to cut through the heavy cloud cover and failing miserably. "Is this winter ever going to be over?"

"Nothing lasts forever, Majesty. Not the cold, not the heat."

"Nothing lasts," I murmured, still staring out the window. There was an ache in my chest I couldn't define.

"I would tell anyone else that the gods last." Father Westinkar smiled. "But I know that means very little to you, Majesty."

He was right, but I couldn't bring myself to say it out loud. I had some newfound faith. It just didn't include believing gods lasted forever. "Do you think I'm doing the right thing meeting Trace?"

He raised a gray eyebrow at me. "I am just a priest. My opinion on state matters is worth very little. However," he continued before I could finish my inhale and voice my protest, "Indrana needs peace. More war—especially one we are unlikely to win—does us no good."

"So in other words, what harm can it do?" I returned to the table and tossed back the last of my whiskey. "I could start a war, Father."

"You have been in war, Majesty, or something close to it. I can see it in your eyes. You would not throw your people needlessly into such horror."

"You have a lot of faith in me."

Father Westinkar laughed and spread his arms wide. "I am a priest, Majesty. Faith is something I have an overabundance of."

I hugged him and laughed, but it was strained enough that the priest held on for a second longer before he let me go.

"You are a good person, Your Majesty. Never doubt that, and never doubt your abilities."

I mustered up a smile as I stepped away. "Thank you for lunch, Father, and the conversation. I appreciate it."

"My door is always open, Majesty." He bowed low, exchanging a nod with Cas as he came up. My young *Dve* returned the nod and we headed back through the temple.

Emmory's new schedule may have given my chamberlain and my new heir heartburn. I, however, loved the fact that I could lie down for an hour before my meeting with Alice so that I wasn't all groggy and dimwitted.

It was necessary. My heir was quickly getting over her awe

of me and had started to voice her opinions during our regular get-togethers.

Most of the time she remembered I was empress.

"There are a few women obviously not qualified to be part of the negotiating team," I said, leaning back in my office chair and fiddling with the photograph of my father and his friends. "Matriarch Maxwell is too old for space travel."

"Don't let her hear you say that," Alice murmured with an amused look.

"Clara is also out of the question; we need her here, along with Zaran. I don't want to disrupt her work with the *Upjas*."

"You crossed Matriarch Zellin and Prajapati off the list?"

I nodded. "We're still not sure about Tare Zellin's involvement in the Christoph affair, and given her sister's poor judgment I'd rather not be on a ship with Matriarch Prajapati right this second even if she did publicly denounce Maya's actions." I studied the list for a long moment. "Do we think Matriarch Tobin is in good enough health to go?" Masami Tobin had a sharp mind despite her age, and I could see her laughing in the face of the Saxons and their male-dominated culture.

"According to her last physical, yes."

"Let's ask her then. I was thinking about asking Matriarch Naidu also. I thought the work would help take her mind off things."

Alice shook her head. "She is doing poorly, Majesty. I don't think she would be as focused as we would like."

"True." I set the frame back it in its spot. "What are your thoughts on Caterina Saito?"

Matriarch Saito was fourteen years older than me and had been quiet during all the debates on my legitimacy. Her family ran one of the largest private banks on Indrana.

"She and my mother were close, despite their age difference," Alice said. "Her husband died the year I was born. Mother used to say she never recovered from the loss, and threw herself into her work instead. She's smart, Majesty; I think she'd be a good choice."

I slid Caterina's name over to the other side of the screen and studied the remaining names. "I want Matriarch Vandi," I said, sliding the youngest member of the council over as well.

"She's very inexperienced, ma'am. Her mother only passed last year. I'm only five years older but I've been on the council for—"

"I want young. She'll bring a fresh eye to the whole thing." I smiled at Alice. "Times are changing, aren't they? Best if we use the ones who are more open to it."

"Is that why I'm not going with you?"

I blinked at her in surprise. "What?"

"I'm not going because I'm not open enough in my thinking. Too set in my ways even though I'm younger than you are."

"Are you putting your mother's words in my mouth?" I asked softly, and Alice flushed.

"I'm sorry, Majesty. I just—"

"You're not going with me because you're my heir, Alice," I replied, tapping a finger on the desktop. "Both of us off-planet at the same time is bad enough, but to have us in the same room on an unsecured planet with potential hostiles? If something went boom, where would that leave the empire?"

"Why do you assume something is going to explode?"

I shared a look with Emmory. "Because something always does. You should probably figure that out, Alice, before it catches you off guard."

She nodded. "Yes, ma'am. Matriarch Desai wanted to remind you that Prime Minister Phanin will be part of the delegation."

"More's the pity," I said. "We've still got a week though; maybe the prime minister will fall and break something in the shower."

"Majesty!"

I rolled my eyes at Alice. I'd been browbeaten and overruled about having Phanin as part of the delegation by practically everyone. In truth I wasn't all that surprised, as "I don't like his face" wasn't a good enough excuse to bar someone of Phanin's abilities and political clout from the negotiations.

I needed someone more experienced and he was the man for the job . . . no matter how much I disliked him.

"You dislike him because he's an ass." Taz shifted in his hospital bed, winced, and hissed at me when I moved to help him. "Leave off, Hail. I'm fine."

We were alone in the room, which was the only reason he could get away with both the irritable tone and using my name. Still, he smiled sheepishly when I raised an eyebrow at him.

"You still have that disapproving eyebrow. Can I blame that slip on the pain meds?"

"Nurse Suggitt says you've been refusing the meds the last few days, so I'd say you're better off blaming it on the lack of meds. Or being an idiot, take your pick." I stood. "Now, do you want me to help you or should I call Oni?"

Taz sighed. "You're as much of a bully as Nurse Suggitt is, Your Majesty. Don't call her. I really am fine and she'll fuss for a half hour if she comes in here, which means I lose my time with you."

He gave me such an earnest smile I sat back down. "I'm only going to be gone a week."

"The last time you left I didn't see you for twenty years."

I made a face at him. "Saying stuff like that is what leads to the gossip, you know."

Taz smiled. The bruising on his face was fading and his obvious cuts were healing. It was the internal injuries that kept him under Oni Suggitt's watchful eye.

He wasn't healing as fast as Dr. Flipsen had hoped, and the concussion had been brutal enough that Taz occasionally forgot where he was or how to do simple tasks like use a fork. He'd protested but she insisted on keeping him until he'd been at least a week without any episodes once his internal injuries were fully healed.

"What?" I finally asked when I couldn't take the silence any longer.

"I do still love you, Hail."

My heart twisted. "Taz, please don't."

"Hear me out? This needs to be said." He reached for my hand. "I always will, but I know things are different now. I can see the ghosts in your eyes.

"I'm grateful for the chance to get to know you again and hopefully forge a new friendship. I'm not going to push for more than you want to give. Let them gossip, you and I know the truth."

His gentle words eased one of the million knots that had taken up residence in my stomach, and I let slip a relieved laugh as I squeezed his hand.

"I am really glad you didn't die."

"Me, too." He grinned and released me. "All right, Your Majesty, enough sappy talk. Captain Gill said they found some bone fragments that were ID'd as Christoph's."

Nodding, I settled back in my chair after giving his hand one last squeeze. "They did. Ilyia seems fairly sure that's all we're going to find given the size of the explosion and the fact that he was right on top of it when it blew."

"Lucky we even found that much," Taz murmured. "When are you leaving?"

"Three days. I've instructed Alice to continue to come see you and keep you updated."

"Do you think she'll actually do it? I'm pretty sure she doesn't like me."

"She'll do it because I told her to." I smiled. "And you'll be surprised, I think. She may not support the *Upjas* movement as wholeheartedly as Zaran, but she's fair and she believes in what's best for Indrana."

"I promise I'll behave myself."

"I'll believe that when I see it."

"I am crushed you think so poorly of me," Taz said.

"Prove me wrong."

His amusement fled and he stuck a hand out at me. "I swear I will, Majesty. We want what's best for Indrana, no matter the cost."

I took his hand in mine. "So do I."

# 14

Good morning, Your Majesty." Phanin bowed low.

"Morning." I waited for him to come up before I smiled. "Would you care to join me on my walk?"

"With pleasure. One does get quite restless on board, *ayah*?" He fell into step with me, Zin trailing behind us.

Emmory had shifted the team assignments on board the *Para Sahi*. Even with the size of the massive ship, it was close enough quarters that trying to go anywhere with three Guards made the already claustrophobic space unbearable.

Besides, Captain Starzin had assured me her crew was loyal and since I trusted Zin's older sister, I was reasonably sure no one was going to try to kill me.

At least no one on board.

We'd jumped from ship to ship after leaving Pashati and boarding Admiral Hassan's command vessel, the *Vajra*, finally settling the whole delegation into the *Para Sahi*.

Phanin had suggested we break the delegation into separate ships, but that made it more challenging to organize meetings on the trip to Red Cliff.

I'd promised Alice I would try to get to know the prime minister better, and that meant being on the same ship with him.

"Did you sleep well?"

"Surprisingly yes, Majesty. I think I'm sleeping better here than at home." Phanin smiled. It transformed his severe face into something more pleasant. "Might have something to do with the fact that I'm not being bothered several times an hour."

I laughed. "It might."

I'd had the best sleep of my life the first night on board. I hadn't even realized how much I missed the gentle hum of a ship's systems until we were under way. My claustrophobia didn't extend to spaceships, not that the *Para Sahi* was in any way cramped. There were perks to being the empress—my cabin was massive.

"I have that list of requests you wanted, Majesty," Phanin said. "Shall I send it to you?"

"Yes, please." We were three days out from Red Cliff after this morning's float into warp. Even though this meeting was largely informal, I wanted a solid platform of issues to talk with Trace about.

Starting with Canafey.

According to Caspel, the situation was bad and moving steadily to worse. The only good news was his operative had retrieved Governor Ashwari, and they were going to meet us at Red Cliff.

It didn't answer the question of how I was going to retrieve the forty-seven brand-new ships from a shipyard near an occupied planet, but it meant I would be able to do it. We'd left the three ships that had escaped back at home where they'd be safe.

If Caspel's operative got the governor to us alive, or soon

enough after her death for us to retrieve the information from her *smati*.

I shuddered at the gruesome thought, and Phanin looked at me in concern.

"Always so chilly on board," I lied with a smile.

Only Emmory and I had been there for the final meeting with the GIS head before our departure. Caspel had asked that we keep the news about Governor Ashwari secret, and even though I was trying to improve my attitude around Phanin I had no trouble with the request. The fewer who knew about the governor and Caspel's operative, the safer the pair was.

We walked along in silence until we met Matriarch Masami Tobin and a guard coming in the opposite direction.

"Good morning, Your Majesty." The elderly matriarch greeted me with a smile and let go of her guard's arm to curtsy.

"Good morning. How did you sleep?"

"Horrible. Too noisy on board these things. Apparently the children had no trouble though; I'm certain they're still asleep."

The fiery older woman hadn't supported me in the beginning, but she'd come around eventually. Luckily for me her support of my cousin had been more logical and less emotional in nature. Despite her age, her mind was sharp, and she'd been my first choice to come along for the negotiations.

The "children" were the two other matriarchs, Sabeen Vandi and Caterina Saito, who rounded out my delegation and gave some balance to Tobin's acerbic personality. Matriarch Vandi was practically a child at only twenty-seven. Matriarch Saito was almost twice her age, but still far younger than Masami Tobin's eighty-seven years.

I hunted for a suitable reply, but thankfully the matriarch didn't need one as she turned her attention to Phanin.

"And a good morning to you, Prime Minister."

"Matriarch."

"I will leave you two here. I must head back to my quarters for a meeting with Alice over the com, and I'm sure that someone will insist I eat first."

"Eating doesn't sound like a bad idea," Phanin said. "Would you like to join me, Matriarch Tobin?"

I left them deciding if they were going to eat in the mess hall or in Masami's quarters and headed back down the hallway with Zin at my heels.

"Your meeting with Alice isn't for another hour, Majesty."

"Thanks for not saying that until we were around the corner." I smacked Zin on the arm. "I didn't fancy getting sucked into having breakfast with those two and I do have some things to read before that conference with Alice."

Three days later, I sat on the edge of my seat as one of the shuttles from the *Para Sahi* took us down to the surface of Red Cliff.

The tiny independent world was located some seventy-five hundred light-years from the Ashvin system and about twice that from Trace's home planet of Marklo. Designated as Tango on the Solarian Conglomerate's list of neutral planets, Red Cliff was available as a meeting site for occasions just like this.

For a price.

I didn't begrudge them that. It was one of the major means of income for this little blue jewel floating out here all alone. I'd gladly paid the fee, since I was the one who'd requested the meeting in the first place.

The fact that Trace had offered to pay half was kind of endearing, though it added a wild story to the rumors flying around that marriage to Trace's little brother was on the table as part of the negotiations.

It didn't help matters that Trace had been in discussion with my mother—before she started her slide into madness—about the possibility of a union between his youngest brother and Pace.

Now there was no one left except for me. However, I was seventeen years older than Prince Samuel and there was zero advantage to that sort of alliance—even if it were up for discussion.

I pushed aside the maudlin thoughts and stood as soon as the pilot gave the all clear. Shaking out the cream silk of my sari, I let Alba fuss for a moment with my hair. Stasia had done it up into a complicated braid and there was a spike with rare black Earth pearls hanging down it in a midnight cascade.

It was similar to the one I'd used to bust out of the room on the *Para Sahi* back when this all started. The synchronicity appealed to me and I'd let her put the fanciful thing in my hair.

"Majesty."

I nodded to Emmory's unasked question and followed him from the shuttle.

Trace waited inside the hangar a few meters from the shuttle, surrounded by his own bodyguards. A retinue as large as my own stood behind him.

A man with pale skin and jet-black hair smiled from the edge of the ramp.

"Your Imperial Majesty." He executed a bow with all the pomp of one used to the motion. "I am Executor Billings. Welcome to Red Cliff. We are most pleased by your choice of our planet. If there is anything you need at all, please don't hesitate to ask me. If you'll permit me, I will introduce you to the others who were invited."

"Thank you, Executor." I paused a moment under the pretense of letting Alba fix something on my dress so I could get a look at Trace through the filter of my BodyGuards.

He wore a shirt as blue as his eyes tucked smartly into a pair of black pants I was willing to bet were military issue. The boots were combat ready, and I felt a pang of envy because Stasia had insisted I wear something "proper" on my feet. My only victory had been that the shoes were heelless, but it appeared that might have been a miscalculation because it put me several centimeters below Trace in height.

At least he wasn't wearing his crown, and I felt relieved that my guess on that front had been correct.

"It's like two gangs of schoolyard bullies sizing each other up," I muttered to Emmory. "Come on. If I let this silence drag on any longer it's going to get awkward."

I crossed the space between us, stopping within arm's reach of Trace and giving him a quick nod. "Trace," I said before Billings could launch into his speech.

"Hailimi." Trace held out a hand and I took it. Covering it with his other one, he squeezed gently, still smiling. "It's good to see you again. Executor Billings, I do not wish to be rude, but I think we can take it from here."

"Of course." Like any good functionary, Billings knew exactly when to vanish.

Trace watched him go, then turned back to me. "If you'll allow me to present my fellow countrymen?"

At my nod the introductions started and voices filled the air as Indranans and Saxons said their hellos. After half an hour, Trace leaned in.

"I'll walk you to your quarters. Our bodyguards can follow and glare at each other behind our backs."

I only just managed not to laugh. Trace grinned, folding my hand over his forearm and gesturing toward the back of the hangar.

Our footsteps and voices echoed off the cavernous ceiling

until we reached the doors on the far side. They slid open and we crossed from the noise of the hangar into the relative silence of a well-lit corridor.

"You look good," Trace said as we turned a corner. "I wasn't sure about the hair, but it suits you."

"So does yours."

He grinned sheepishly. "It's expected. Truth be told, I'd grow it longer if I thought I could get away with it."

"What's the point of being king?"

He laughed. "It's a little easier for you to buck tradition I think, Haili. I've been doing this for a while. If I suddenly started acting weird I think Ivan there might have a heart attack."

"Not a heart attack, Majesty." The massive man to Trace's right had a voice like two battlecruisers colliding. "I would be concerned about the state of your mental health." His eyes were gray, harder than stone as they bored into mine with no deference whatsoever. "I remember you, Your Imperial Majesty."

I blinked at him in confusion for just a heartbeat before the memory came back. This time the laugh slipped free.

"She punched my charge in the stomach." Ivan spoke past both of us to Emmory.

"Knocked the wind out of me." There was a strange glee in Trace's announcement.

I shrugged at Emmory. "He tried to kiss me."

Trace was still chuckling. "I guess that answers the rumors about the wedding plans. My little brother wouldn't stand a chance against you, Haili."

I arched an eyebrow at the familiarity, and Trace misread it.

"I tease; I'm sorry. I know that's not why you asked me here." He sobered, waving his free hand in the air. "We'll have plenty of time to talk about affairs of state, and I don't want to squander the opportunity to catch up with you. Here are your quarters. I'm up the hallway. There's a lovely garden on the grounds and it's spring here, so all the trees are in bloom." He smiled, releasing my hand from his arm. "If your guards would like to check it over, I'd be grateful if you'd have dinner with me out there this evening."

"That would be nice." I returned the smile. "I'll let Emmory and Ivan hash out the details."

Trace gave me a sharp bow. "I will see you later then."

# 15

That went better than I expected," I announced as soon as Emmory let me into my quarters. Gita and Willimet were set up by the wide windows on the far side of the room, and Stasia greeted me with a smile and curtsy. They had come down to the planet with the advance team to secure our rooms. I'd been a bit surprised Emmory hadn't sent Zin down with them; instead he'd sent Indula.

"The weather is much nicer, Majesty; would you still like chai?" Stasia asked.

"If you brought it I may as well drink it," I said.

"Were you expecting them to take a shot at us, Majesty?" That question came from Zin.

I punched him in the arm. "Maybe just at you, because I can see the appeal. No, I was expecting cold, awkward formality." I frowned. "I wasn't expecting the humor, or the overly familiar tone."

Crossing the room, I rested my elbows on the windowsill and studied the city in the distance. I'd spent most of the trip here rehearsing what I was going to say to Trace, and now it seemed like formulaic garbage.

"What do you think?"

Emmory lifted a shoulder at my question. "He was polite, Majesty. Genuinely pleased to see you and more relaxed than he was on that call."

"Alba?"

"Same, Majesty. I saw no tension from the king or from his delegates."

Turning from the window, I looked across the room at Zin. "Zin, thoughts?"

"Their guards were also relaxed, I'd even go so far as to call it arrogance." The nodding of several heads around the room showed most everyone was in agreement with him.

"I would agree, Majesty," Alba spoke up. "It wasn't quite malice, but…" She frowned. "I can't find a word for it I like. Arrogance works as well as anything. Even when they didn't think we were looking, they're all so relaxed."

"Interesting. Gita?"

"Ma'am?" She jerked, dislodging the ornate vase between us. I caught it with my left hand.

Setting it back onto the lacquered pillar, I gave my Body-Guard a raised eyebrow. "Thoughts, Gita."

"I wasn't there, ma'am."

"We didn't see very many people, Majesty." Before I could say anything else, Indula cut in with a sideways look at his fellow BodyGuard. "His staff is efficient and tight-lipped. Stasia had more success, I think, probably because she's prettier than me."

My maid blushed and Indula grinned.

"Not much, Majesty, success that is."

Several people were unsuccessful at holding in their laughter.

"The king's valet is a dour old man who did little except tell me good morning. The younger boys were careful, but they let slip a few things—the king had a very loud argument with his mother just before he left."

"About?"

"I didn't get specifics. I'm not sure they knew, ma'am, but I'll see what else I can find out," Stasia replied. "And while the government may be denying it, even the Saxon people think that they have taken over Canafey."

"Do they now?" I shared a look with Emmory. "I wonder where they got that idea."

"Good question, Majesty."

I waved a hand. "Okay, everyone out. I need to get ready for this dinner. Gita, hang back a moment."

Everyone else filed out and Stasia disappeared into the bedroom. Gita dropped her chin to her chest.

"I'm sorry, Majesty."

"I depend on my people to see things I might miss. Next time I expect you to be paying better attention."

"Yes, ma'am." Gita bowed.

"Go on." I waited for her to leave before speaking to Emmory. "I want to trust him. But something is off; I can't explain it, I just feel it in my gut. The worrisome part is if the Saxons had anything to do with what happened at home, then did Trace know about it?"

"The best-case scenario here, Majesty, is that someone in his government is in control and he doesn't know about it. Worst case is he's actively involved."

"Pessimist."

"That's what you pay me for."

I rolled my eyes at him. "Go make sure the gardens aren't filled with people who want to kill me, *Ekam*. I'd like to enjoy my dinner."

"Of course, Majesty."

\*　　\*　　\*

I managed to get to the garden before Trace and Ivan. Even though Red Cliff's sun had set, the spring night was balmy and a pleasant change from Indrana's winter.

The garden itself was lovely. Our table had been set up in a little gazebo surrounded by some species of fruit tree in full bloom. The delicate petals were iridescent in the floating lights and their sweet smell reminded me of *modak*.

The treat had been a favorite of my little sister's and the thought of her clung to my heart, making it beat painfully for a few seconds before I shook the sadness loose. "Pace would have loved these trees, Emmory."

"So would my mother, Majesty." He reached up and touched a branch and the light danced through the flowers. "Anything shiny catches her eye." A smile flickered on his face. "That's how my father caught her attention—at least that's the story she likes to tell. He claims it was his intellect."

I laughed. "Pace would have loved you, too."

Emmory didn't respond, and the subtle shift of his shoulders welcomed our company. I pasted a smile that was mostly genuine on my face before I turned.

"Trace."

"Haili." Trace crossed the stone path with his hands held out as if we were old friends, moving with a jerky, barely contained energy that put me on edge. He took my hands and squeezed them, leaning in to press a kiss to my cheeks. "Nice outfit." He grinned and winked before he pulled away.

For dinner I'd chosen a pair of black pants and a Nehru jacket in emerald green. I'd worn the only sari Stasia had brought with us for that first meeting. Everything else was an assortment of my usual uniform-styled outfits and a few *salwar kameez*.

Trace was dressed in a spotless white shirt and gray trousers. He'd rolled the sleeves up and raised an eyebrow at my amused snort. "What?"

"Your butler fussed about that, didn't he?"

He grinned, the smile calling up the crow's-feet around his eyes. "Hubert was very put out. Bad enough I refused the jacket, the vest, and his god-awful choice of neckwear. The empress will think I am a total barbarian." He laughed. "You didn't have to argue with your staff at all, did you?"

"They learned quickly." I slipped my arm around his and headed deeper into the garden. "I'll give you some pointers."

Trace's laugh this time was tinged with sorrow. "In another life, maybe. It really would create far too much chaos if I started behaving like—"

His awkward pause was priceless and I couldn't resist the tease.

"Like a gunrunner?"

Trace went red all the way up to his hairline and covered his face with a hand. For a moment I felt slightly guilty, but his shoulders started to shake with suppressed laughter.

"Hailimi, Saxony is not ready for the likes of you."

"If it helps at all I'm sure Indrana wasn't either, but they're recovering." I glanced back over my shoulder. "It appears dinner is ready."

I let Trace push my chair in and settled back with a smile as a white-jacketed man wheeled a cart up to the table.

"They have some very nice wines here on Red Cliff," Trace said, studying the cart. "Unless you'd prefer whiskey?"

I kept my surprise hidden behind the smile. "Wine would be lovely. Thank you."

Trace poured two glasses. Emmory intercepted mine before he could hand it over and I gave a little shrug.

"My *Ekam* is twitchy about such things, if you'll forgive him."

"Ah, yes. Understandable. Proceed, *Ekam*, I wouldn't dream of interfering." He smiled and took his seat.

"It's clean, Majesty," Emmory said, handing Willimet the glass. She'd become my unofficial food taster for the trip and sipped it, wiped off the glass with a napkin, and returned it to Emmory.

I took it and raised it in Trace's direction. "To peace," I said.

"To peace, and to family," he replied.

I swallowed down the lump in my throat with a sip of wine and smiled to Emmory when he handed me the plate from the server. We settled into the meal, a lovely rice dish with chicken and spicy peppers that went well with the wine.

Trace had far more practice with small talk than I and kept me entertained with stories of his younger siblings' antics while we ate. He couldn't seem to stay still though, either tapping a hand on the table or his heel against the floor of the gazebo.

"It's a pity we can't just hash out the issues over dinner and wine, eh?"

Leaning back in my chair, I rolled my wine stem between my fingers and considered my reply. "It is a necessary evil, I think. With so many lives in the balance, it doesn't seem right for the two of us to make those decisions alone."

"You disappoint me, Haili. What I heard of your exploits while you were away from home seemed to indicate you'd take a more direct leadership role. What's the point of being ruler unless you rule your people?" he asked, and saluted me with his glass.

"Don't believe everything you hear," I replied with a smile and a tip of my own glass. "I think it's prudent to listen to older and wiser voices, especially on important issues. That's what a good leader does." Or any voices really; Hao hadn't let the age of the person speaking impact if he listened or not.

"True, I suppose." He waved a hand. "I hadn't thought of it that way."

I pushed aside my sudden annoyance, reminding myself that Trace's upbringing had been very different from mine. It shouldn't be a surprise he'd be convinced that his way was the best.

"Besides." I smiled. "There are so many issues to discuss we can't hope to cover them all by ourselves. Canafey itself is going to be quite the puzzle."

My heart sank when Trace looked to his left, ostensibly to set his glass back on the table, but he hesitated slightly as he let go of it. "Yes, nasty business. You have my military at your disposal, Haili, to help take care of the mercenaries responsible for this."

"That's so very kind of you." I set my own glass down, the taste of wine sour in my mouth. "I think we'll be able to handle it." I didn't quite bare my teeth at him as I stood. "If you'll forgive me, Trace, I think I'm going to retire. The wine appears to have left me with a disappointing headache."

He stood. "I'm sorry to hear that."

"Me, too. I expected more from it. Good night, Trace." With a nod I left the garden, Emmory trailing behind me.

*"He knows. Shiva damn it, Emmory."*

*"I'm sorry, Majesty. I know you wanted it to be otherwise."*

*"You know what the really worrisome part of that was?"* I didn't slow my stride as we turned the corner and headed into the living quarters. *"He offered me whiskey."*

*"I noticed."*

*"I haven't drunk it outside of my quarters since I've been back."*

*"And you didn't drink it before."*

I nodded. *"Portis drank it. I never cared for it. We never drank much in public anyway. Hao thought it was poor form to show your enemies your weaknesses—and he considers alcohol a weakness."*

I knew from the look on Emmory's face that he was recalling every time I'd had a drink and who had seen me do it, because I was doing the same thing. The list was small and I trusted almost every single person on it.

Which meant either someone in my inner circle had betrayed me, or Trace had somehow gotten an agent close enough to me to find out such a personal detail. I couldn't believe Hao would talk about me and Portis to someone he didn't know. None of the options were appealing. If Hao had turned on me, there was going to be a hell of a splashback from all the stories he could tell.

"I don't like this, Majesty."

I shoved the door of my quarters open. "I'm in agreement with you, Emmory."

"Good morning, Fasé, how are you?" The next morning dawned bright and warm, chasing away some of my unease about the previous night's dinner with Trace. The Farian stood by the door of my rooms talking to Stasia. Her team was in tatters from Christoph's suicide bomb, and Captain Gill was still healing, and so I'd asked specifically for her to join us for the negotiations.

"Well, Majesty. Thank you. Did you sleep well?"

"I did. Thank you. I heard Lieutenant Saito had a good day yesterday at therapy."

"She did, ma'am. Stood up on her own and took a few steps."

I nodded. Dr. Wendle had been able to save the lieutenant's other leg. Fasé and several other Farians had been able to heal the worst of her injuries, but learning to walk on her new prosthetic leg would take some time.

"Morning, Majesty." Alba came in, Cas and Emmory behind her. "Did you have a chance to look over the briefing I sent you?"

"I did. I had a question about the file from Colonel Hagen." Waving a hand at my Guards, I took Alba's arm and led her over to the far side of the room. "Did we get verification on those images?"

"Not yet, ma'am, the director is working on it. He said to pass it along to you, but that we definitely didn't want to say anything until he could get a third-party ID on the uniforms."

I nodded, tamping down my impatience. I knew he was right, but part of me wanted to march into the meeting this morning and throw the photos Colonel Hagen had taken during a running battle on Canafey Major onto the wall for all to see.

The Saxon features of the pale man with ice-blue eyes weren't the nail in the coffin, but the visible—if blurry—emblems for the Saxon Shock Corps were.

"Let Director Ganej know I concur with him, but he needs to hurry it up."

"Yes, ma'am." Alba nodded.

"Has anyone talked with the matriarchs this morning?" I asked, checking the time stamp on my *smati*. "They should have been here—"

The door opened and the three matriarchs as well as Phanin were ushered in. They curtsied and bowed.

"Good morning," I said, taking a seat in a stiff-backed gray chair away from the windows and brushing a piece of lint off my black pants. I could see Phanin's reflection in the toes of my boots as he took a seat.

"Morning, Majesty."

Saris rustled as Matriarch Tobin and the other two women settled into their chairs. Sabeen Vandi was wearing a light blue drape of shimmery fabric that complemented her curly red hair. Caterina Saito was dressed in a sari with a complicated black-and-white pattern, and her chin-length black hair was decidedly out of fashion. I liked the way it looked with her high cheekbones and was relieved not to be the only person in Indranan high society who didn't care about fashion trends.

Matriarch Tobin was wearing a deep red sari shot through with gold thread. It was a specific choice to play off my all-black outfit, and I appreciated the elderly matriarch's wily sense of style.

Rubbing my hands together, I looked at their expectant faces and took a deep breath. "All right, people, I want to set some ground rules for the negotiations today. First, nothing gets agreed to that doesn't have my seal of approval on it. I've made it very clear to the executor that whatever we discuss, I am the one and only voice for Indrana. I want you to continue to impress that upon anyone you speak with today.

"That isn't to say I won't listen and take into account your opinions. That's why you're here, after all." I smiled at Sabeen, hoping to ease the younger matriarch's worried frown. "I want honest input from you; don't hold back."

"Yes, Majesty." She dipped her head, the tension in her shoulders easing slightly.

"Secondly, no one is to mention Canafey."

"But, Majesty." Phanin shifted in his chair. "Isn't that—"

"No one, Phanin. We'll discuss it in due time, but not on the first day in the first hour of negotiations. Is that clear?"

"Of course, Majesty. What should we say then, if they bring it up?"

"That we're not prepared to talk about it at this time and change the subject to one of the other fifteen things on the list you gave me."

He gave a sharp nod, still unhappy about it, but he didn't say anything else in the following silence, so I turned my attention to Matriarch Saito.

"Caterina, I want you to get a good read on all the faces at the table. By the end of the day I expect a report back with some kind of baseline for facial expressions and what we can expect from our Saxon friends."

"Yes, ma'am."

"Right." I clapped my hands on my knees and pushed to my feet. "Let's go stop a war."

The others filed out. I grabbed Gita by the arm on my way past her.

"I want you to put your eyes on Trace and don't take them off. Record everything."

"Yes, ma'am." The unasked question was heavy in her voice.

"My gut isn't happy, Gita, and it's not because of my breakfast. I want you to watch him because I can't."

"I will, ma'am."

"Good." I squeezed her arm once and let go, heading out into the corridor with Emmory and Cas flanking me.

Negotiations are tedious, tense things, and that fact doesn't change if it's governments or gunrunners. The first hour of the proceedings was composed of Executor Billings making formal introductions. The second was the reading of the original peace treaty.

The room itself was cozy, designed to bleed the tension out of its occupants. The cream-colored walls were accented with a soft circular ochre pattern the same color as the comfortable leather chairs surrounding the wide, round table. There was a heavy buffet table on the far wall filled with snacks, tea, and coffee. Several pitchers of water were set out on the table itself and the rings of the massive tree trunk the table was made of reflected against the metal containers.

"Empress Hailimi," Executor Billings said as the time stamp on my *smati* flipped over to the third hour. "If you would care to proceed with Indrana's grievances?"

"Of course." I pushed my chair back and began to read from the list Phanin had provided me. I'd buried Canafey as the fourth item on the list and didn't pause at all as I moved on to number five. But still there was grumbling from the Saxons, and Trace clenched his jaw for a second.

"Thank you, Your Majesty," Executor Billings said when I'd finished and turned to Trace. "King Trace, do you have a response from the Saxon Kingdom?"

He stood and pressed his palms to the tabletop. "Nothing save to protest the vile and baseless accusations of Indrana. They have no proof of anything on this list." His voice was completely different from the previous night and he didn't look in my direction as he spoke.

The room exploded into shouting. Phanin and Matriarch Tobin both surged to their feet. Matriarch Vandi just stared with wide eyes, and I was pleased when she looked to me for guidance. I shook my head, reaching a hand out at the same time to keep Caterina in her seat.

*"Both of you sit down, now."* I issued the order over the com and Matriarch Tobin dropped into her seat. Phanin followed her half a second later.

"Silence!" Executor Billings's order filled the air.

Several people jerked, Trace included, and stared at the executor in astonishment. I'd expected such a reaction from the mild-mannered man. The Solarian negotiators prided themselves on their ability to navigate such difficult situations, and crowd control was at the top of the list. It was the reason the service was so successful, and so profitable.

"The next raised voice will be ejected from the proceedings— permanently. Am I understood?"

There was a chorus of murmured assents. Trace dropped into his chair with a surprising amount of sulk. I dipped my head to Billings and sat back down.

"Now as it turns out, Your Majesty," he said to Trace, "Her Imperial Majesty has provided proof for some of the grievances listed. Most of them are simple issues that will easily be taken care of should you be willing to listen to my suggestions. The matter of Canafey—"

"With apologies, Executor." I knew it was a risk to interrupt him, so I offered up a smile I hoped would deflect the bulk of his annoyance. "We are presently gathering our evidence for the issue of Canafey, if you would be so kind as to table it until the end?"

Billings narrowed his brown eyes at me for a fraction of a second before he smiled and nodded. "Of course, Your Majesty. You have forty-six hours to come up with proof or the grievance will be dropped from the list with prejudice."

"Agreeable. Thank you."

"I will lay out my suggestions for the other issues on Indrana's list." Billings cleared his throat and a list appeared on the blank wall behind him.

I poured myself a glass of water, handing it back to Emmory without comment. He scanned it and handed it to Willimet. She sipped from the glass, wiped the edge off, and handed it back with a nod.

I spotted Trace watching the whole exchange and saluted him before I took a drink. A very intriguing look that was part frustration, part calculation flickered through his eyes before he returned his attention to the executor.

We broke for lunch shortly after Billings wrapped up his suggestions. The three-hour gap was designed to give both parties a chance to look over and discuss all the options. Since Indrana had started the process, we didn't actually have anything to discuss until Trace and his people had decided to accept or counter the executor's suggestions.

Waking to the sound of shouting never bodes well, and I woke from my nap groggy and disoriented, which only made matters worse. *"Emmory, what's going on?"*

*"Phanin and Matriarch Saito are having a discussion, Majesty."*

I snorted. *"About what?"*

*"Item three, Majesty. Phanin thinks the monetary reparations that the Saxons are being asked to pay is too small. He wants to counter with an amount triple what Executor Billings suggested."*

My sigh floated up toward the ceiling and I rolled out of bed. Running my hands through my hair as I crossed the room, I pulled the door open and the shouting died immediately.

"Have I mentioned that being woken up like that is extremely annoying and tends to put me in a bad mood?"

"Apologies, Majesty." Caterina curtsied. Phanin turned from the window and gave me a short bow but didn't say anything. "I was trying to explain to the prime minister—"

"That we don't get to counter any of the suggestions made by Executor Billings. Correct, Caterina. We only get to do so if the Saxons don't accept the proposal." I smiled, then raised an eyebrow in Phanin's direction. "You know that, Eha. So I'm curious why you're even debating the issue with Matriarch Saito."

"I wasn't debating anything, Majesty. I was merely suggesting that the monetary amount will barely cover our economic losses caused by the Saxon Kingdom's interference in our shipping lanes."

I took a deep breath. "I think we're all aware of that. If the Saxons were willing to agree to any terms we threw at them we wouldn't be on the brink of war. Executor Billings's job is to come up with suggestions he thinks they might be more agreeable to."

"Yes, Majesty."

"Good. Might I suggest we stop going at each other? Presenting a united front against the Saxons is important."

"Of course, Majesty." Phanin bowed again. "Matriarch Saito, my apologies."

"Thank you, Eha. I am also sorry," she replied.

"Majesty, Executor Billings is at the door."

I shared a look with Emmory at Zin's announcement. My *Ekam* lifted a shoulder.

"Let him in, Zin," I said, brushing the wrinkles out of my shirt.

"Empress Hailimi." Billings bowed deeply.

"Executor. I wasn't expecting to see you for another hour."

"I know, Majesty. I heard from King Trace and thought I would come speak with you directly." He frowned and looked around the room. "May we speak privately?"

"Emmory, clear the room."

He did, settling in by the door after Alba closed it behind her. "Executor?"

Billings rubbed a hand over his chin. "I apologize for this, Majesty. It is most strange. I have been an executor for almost forty years and have never seen anything like this."

"They rejected all your proposals." I laughed when Billings blinked at me in confusion. "It was either that or they accepted them all, Executor, and since you look more frustrated than shocked—" I pointed at him. "Plus their behavior this morning didn't really indicate they were going to cooperate."

"I confess I'm at a loss, Majesty," he said. "I don't see much use in reconvening this afternoon. There will be nothing to talk about. If you will permit me to look at the situation again and rework my suggestions, we can meet in the morning to see if they are acceptable for Indrana and I'll present them to King Trace after."

"This is agreeable." I smiled and patted him on the shoulder. "I trust in your abilities, Executor. It's one of the reasons we chose Red Cliff for the negotiations."

"I appreciate your faith in me, Majesty. I will see you in the morning."

# 17

I muttered several curse words after Billings left the room. "I knew this was going to be a challenge, Emmory, but—"

"You expected them to be somewhat logical about it?" he asked, shaking his head. "The fact is, Majesty, they have the upper hand and they know it. They don't have to agree to anything."

"They can't want to go to war?"

"If they think they can win, the losses would be acceptable. The empire controls a lot of very profitable territory. Without it we would go under."

"Bugger me. I can't believe Trace would—" I paced to the window and back. "Have Gita come in. Go tell the others what happened. We'll all meet for dinner here and discuss our options. Tell Alba to call Alice and fill her in also. I'll want to talk with her after I'm done with Gita."

"Yes, ma'am." Emmory nodded sharply and left the room. Gita came in through the open door, closing it behind her.

"Majesty?"

I sat down and stared at my hands, trying to find a way through my agitation. Now my gut was screaming at me to get the hell out of there, but leaving the planet wasn't an option. Not unless I wanted to really mess things up.

"Gita, you've seen combat."

"Yes, ma'am."

"Sit down." I smiled. "The hovering makes me nervous. You ever get that feeling that things are about to go downhill fast?"

"We were running an op on the edge of the shipping lanes once against some smu—pirates, Majesty."

I snorted at her correction. "You can call them smugglers, Gita. I will not be offended."

"Yes, ma'am. We had everything planned out, everything set up perfectly. The intel had checked out, it was a source we used before. Still, I couldn't shake the feeling that things were going too well. I mentioned it to my CO."

"Did she listen?"

"She did, ma'am." Gita smiled. "We still got hit and hit hard by an ambush team warping in out of nowhere. But if we hadn't waited we would have been wiped out."

"Well, things are far from perfect here." I laughed, dragging a hand through my hair. "My problem is I haven't shaken the feeling of people trying to kill me, so I have no idea if my gut is accurate or not. What's your take?"

"King Trace is incapable of holding still. People like that make me nervous, ma'am. I don't want to make baseless accusations, but I've seen that behavior in too many junkies to ignore it. As far as negotiations went—his protest was too quick. He would have said what he did even if you'd listed out ten things you loved about the Saxon Kingdom."

"Funny." I laughed. Her sarcasm was enough to loosen the awful band of tension in my throat somewhat. "They rejected all of Executor Billings's proposals; that's almost unheard-of especially after so many years of peace."

"It would have been more understandable at the height of the hostilities."

"Precisely." I pursed my lips and tapped my fingers against them. "Go get Matriarch Saito. I want to hear her report on how everyone else was behaving."

"Yes, ma'am."

I stood to pace. The ping of an incoming call rang in my ear. "Admiral Hassan."

"Majesty. I'm relaying a message from Caspel. There will probably be some interference," she said. The screen split and the hawk-faced head of Galactic Imperial Security appeared in the second panel.

"Director Ganej."

"I got it, Majesty. Third-party validation from not only a journalist with Solarian Net News who covered the Indranan-Saxon war during the height of the fighting, but from an independent merchant vessel who was paid to transport Shock Corps troops from Marklo to Venvenzi Port."

Venvenzi Port was in the neutral zone between Saxony and Indrana, close enough to Canafey to be able to draw conclusions that would be damaging to Trace's claims of ignorance.

"It's about time something went right. Can we find someone at the port who will be able to speak to where the Shock Corps troops were headed after?"

Caspel grinned. "Already on it; there was a traffic controller at Venvenzi who can testify that their course didn't match the flight plans they filed. I'm sending you copies of the sworn statements I have so far as well as video testimony. Do you want me to include Executor Billings on the transmission?"

"No, I'll tell him myself. Thank you." I grinned back. "Have a drink tonight, Caspel. You earned it."

"That I did, but—" Caspel glanced over his shoulder with a

frown that quickly turned into an expression so cold it froze my skin. "Majesty, I'm hearing gunfire outside my offices. Where's your *Ekam*?"

"In the hallway, I assume," I said.

"I'm not sure what's going on. I recommend you get back onto the *Vajra* with Admiral Hassan now. I'll touch base with you as soon as I can."

"Gods go with you." My voice sounded strange in my ears. Caspel gave me a fleeting smile and disconnected.

"Majesty, I second Caspel's suggestion. We can better protect you—" Admiral Hassan broke off, her eyes flying wide. "Incoming. I've got multiple bogies of unknown origin coming out of warp. Majesty, you need to—"

I gasped when a laser blast that looked like it came from a Cheng-made StarFire 1011 slammed into the admiral from off-screen, knocking her from her chair. There were a few seconds of shouted chaos and then the screen went black.

"Oh, bugger." I stared, unbelieving, at the blank screen.

And then the building exploded around me.

Bugger me.

Everything hurt. I could feel my heart beating and hear it in my ears. The rapid *thump-thump-thump* drowned out everything around me and for a second I thought I was back on *Sophie*, locked in that nightmarish combat in the cargo bay.

"Dark Mother Destroyer—"

"Sitrep, now."

"Xi's dead. I can't reach anyone else from Team Five, sir."

"Must have hit us from orbit—"

"Where's the empress?"

"I've got vitals on her, she's still alive."

"I'm not reading any injuries on her." Emmory's voice

swirled out of the swearing and chaotic jumble of voices in the dust and smoke. *"Majesty, can you answer me?"* he said over the *smati* link.

Not *Sophie*. We were on Red Cliff and judging from the rubble pinning me in place someone had just brought the building down on us. I tried to speak, but something was digging into my ribs on the right and something heavy had my left arm pinned against my side. The breath had been knocked out of me and I couldn't get enough air to make any sound.

"Ma'am?" Stasia's hand closed on mine. "Cas, I found her!" Moments later my tiny maid wormed her way down into the pocket of rubble where I was trapped. "It's all right," she said. "Are you hurt?"

"Don't think so—" I forced the words out. "Can't breathe. Where's Emmory?" I was terrified to ask, sure that I'd imagined the bass of his voice in the jumble and in my head.

"I'm here, Majesty."

Relief rushed through me, hotter than plasma fire, when Stasia smiled. "He's banged up, but all right. So is Zin. I don't know about the others yet."

"Emmory, someone shot Admiral Hassan. I saw it before—"

"Copy that, ma'am," he replied. "Team Three, we have a Zulu situation. Repeat, SitZee in progress. Transport has been compromised.

"Lan, do you read me? Get your asses up to the bridge. You kill anyone who won't stand down in the empress's name. Is that understood?" The answer he got must have satisfied him, because he didn't say anything more.

"Let's get you out of here." Stasia turned, and fear gripped me when I realized she was going to squirm back out.

"Don't leave me."

"Stay with her, Stasia." Emmory's soothing voice rode down

and vanquished the crushing claustrophobia before it could take root and suffocate me. "Tell me what you can see."

While Stasia relayed the layout of my confinement, I focused on getting my left arm free. It cost me some skin, and I hissed a curse as I pulled my arm out.

Stasia loosened the rubble around my left leg enough for me to scoot out from under the chunk of ceiling that had nearly crushed me, and I scrambled up through the hole after her.

"It's all right, Majesty." Emmory cupped my cheek. "We'll get you out of this, I promise."

The familiar hissing whine of a Hessian 45 said otherwise, but before I could pinpoint the location, Emmory threw me to the side, covering me. I heard the discharge and the thud of a falling body.

"Emmory?" Zin called.

"Okay. We're okay. What the hell was that?" Emmory helped me to my feet.

In the slowly clearing smoke I saw Zin standing over the body of a Saxon guard. He rolled the man over with his foot, keeping his gun trained on him. "Dead," he said with a shake of his head. "He was about to shoot you in the back."

"That answers that question," Emmory muttered. "Come on, Majesty, we have to get out of here."

We crawled over the rubble and the next sight stole the breath from my lungs. "Oh gods." The exclamation slipped out and I pressed a hand to my mouth. Will was trapped under a concrete pillar from her chest down and it was clear the lower half of her body was mangled beyond repair. Cas was at her side, speaking to her, gently stroking her dark hair.

Ignoring Emmory's curse, I dashed across the space and dropped to a knee next to her. "Will, damn it."

She coughed, blood bubbling up from her mouth. It trickled

down the side of her face. "S'all right, ma'am. It was a good run. A great honor. Thank you—" She convulsed, spraying blood, and then went still.

Cas murmured something as he pressed her eyelids closed and then turned his face toward me. "Majesty, we need to go," he said, tears standing in his eyes.

I wiped my face, smearing blood and tears across it as I got to my feet.

"Emmory, I found Gita and Matriarch Saito. They lucked out and the room they dove into didn't get touched. I've also got us a way out." Kisah poked her head up over a pile of rubble to our right, breaking the stunned silence. "Oh, damn it, not Will," she muttered when she spotted her friend.

"Grieve later," Emmory said. "How do we get out of here?"

"This way, sir." Kisah blinked away her tears and pointed back over the pile.

We stumbled across the rubble, crawling at times, still choking on the dust until we emerged into a hallway that was still mostly intact.

Sunlight streaked across the debris-strewn floor from the bank of windows. I was still grappling with the idea that one of Trace's men really had taken a shot at Zin when I spotted the wreckage.

"Bugger me." The city I'd seen not moments before from my now-demolished room was nothing but a smoldering heap. "All those people, Emmory. The other matriarchs?"

"Nothing yet and I'm sorry, Majesty. But my priority is you, not them."

"Damn it, Emmory," I said even though I knew it was a futile protest. He gave me the Look until I nodded once, trying not to hate the coldness in his words. This is what they'd been tasked for and precisely what they were supposed to do.

167

"Gita, are either of you hurt?"

"We got lucky, Majesty." She shook her head. "The matriarch is in shock, ma'am, but she's uninjured." She was supporting Caterina by the arm and the woman's dazed look said it all.

I reached out and touched her face. "Caterina?"

The matriarch blinked. "Majesty?"

"You stay with Gita, do what she tells you."

"Yes, ma'am."

"Fix her sari into something she can run in."

"Indula and Tanish just checked in," Zin reported. "They've got Alba; she's got a broken arm, otherwise unharmed. Matriarch Tobin's guards report her quarters were untouched and Matriarch Vandi is with her. Phanin's are partially gone but he hasn't been located and I can't raise him or his guards."

"Tell Masami's guards to head for the Solarian military base. That's their safest option at this point. We're making for the shuttle bay. Once Lan and the rest of Team Four get the bridge locked down, we'll get the empress onto the *Vajra*." Emmory muttered, staring down at the map of the facility that Kisah was sharing on the floor. Cas and Iza had their guns out and were sweeping the hallway with wary eyes.

I hadn't missed the fact that Zin was between me and the window, or that my maid was at my back with a pair of dull-silver Glocks in her hands.

"Give," I said, and she passed one over to me with a smile.

"Let's see if this way is still clear." Emmory glanced up. "I'd rather get out of this building as soon as we can and circle around to the hangar to see if the shuttle is still intact than work our way through."

Kisah nodded and the map vanished. Cas and Iza started down the hallway at Emmory's signal, the rest of us following. We reached an exit and staggered out into the sun.

"Caspel said there was gunfire outside his office. I was talking to him just before the building came down."

Emmory swore. "Apologies, Majesty. I can only deal with one crisis at a time."

"I know. I don't want you asking me later why I didn't tell you." I grinned at him with a bravado that was only half-real.

"Majesty, can you run?"

I nodded at Emmory's question and sprinted across the ground after him.

I wasn't the only one whispering a prayer of thanks when we spotted the hangar still standing. Our joy was short-lived. As we came around the corner, the group of men inside the hangar turned on us with their guns drawn.

Skidding to a halt, I spotted Jul's bloody form on the floor at Trace's feet.

"You're alive." He laughed, the noise high-pitched and brittle. "By god, you really are damn near impossible to kill."

"Jul's dead, Majesty," Emmory murmured.

Trace stepped on my BodyGuard's back and spread his arms wide. "Can you believe this? I thought they were going to just blow your rooms, not bring the whole damn building down on our heads."

The words jumbled together in my head, all jostling for some kind of prominence. "You knew?"

Trace shrugged and fired at us. The blast slammed into Emmory, knocking him back into me. Instinct alone had me bringing my own gun up, but my shot was off. It cut harmlessly through the air and took a chunk out of the side of the building, showering Trace and his guards with bits of concrete.

I grabbed Emmory as we fell and fired again. This time my shot caught the man on Trace's left through the throat. He dropped, flailing and spitting blood. The others scattered as

Cas and Zin each killed two more, buying us enough time to drag Emmory to the dubious cover of a pile of cargo crates.

"Emmory, damn you. Don't die on me." There was blood, far too much blood on my hands. Portis's face flashed in my head, covered in blood as I begged him not to leave me. My knife slipped and slid as I tried to cut through Emmory's shirt and I swore again.

"Majesty, let me." Stasia took the knife, wiping it off on her pant leg and slicing through the black material. "I need something to stop this bleeding with."

"Here." Caterina shoved the end of her sari at my maid. The noblewoman seemed to have come out of her shock. "I have medical training. I can help you."

"Majesty." Emmory grabbed my arm before I could turn back to the fight. "You need to get out of here."

# 18

I'm not leaving you."

"Let me do my job, Majesty. Zin, take her and go."

"Let's go, Majesty." Zin reached for my elbow. His expression was hard, but it couldn't conceal the resigned pain in his eyes.

"No. Damn you, your job isn't just to die for me!" I slapped at his hand, leaning in close to Emmory's face. My voice trembled, but I ignored it. "I won't leave you here to die."

Either the fierce determination in my voice or the sudden influx of gunfire convinced them. Zin cursed and returned fire. I pushed away from Emmory, leaving Stasia and Caterina to do their work. "Find Fasé," I hissed. If the Farian had been killed in the explosion, I was going to lose not only my *Ekam*, but Zin also. The pain wrapping itself around my heart was like razor wire, but I fed it into my anger and it kept me upright.

"Trace, what in the holy fires of Naraka are you doing?" I shouted. My voice carried through the hangar and the gunfire halted.

"Haili." Trace's voice was singsong. "Come on out, I promise I won't shoot you."

Zin locked his hand on my arm as I started to rise. "Majesty, don't."

"He didn't miss me and hit Emmory by mistake. He was aiming for my *Ekam*," I snarled, a deep growl filled with pain that made Zin blink.

"What?"

"Trust me." I mustered up a smile and patted his cheek. "Keep trying to raise Fasé on the com. We need her." I'd seen the wound when Stasia cut away Emmory's shirt, and Caterina's inhale had confirmed my fears. I had to buy us some time.

I tucked my gun into the back of my pants and stood carefully. Trace was out in the open, but his men remained behind their cover.

"Haili, come on."

"You promised *you* wouldn't shoot me. What about your men?"

He threw his hands in the air with an exasperated laugh. "I promise my men won't shoot you either. I just want to talk."

I stepped around the cargo crates. "All right then, talk."

"This isn't personal, you realize that, right?" His grin was manic as he bounced from one foot to the other like a schoolboy.

"You shot my *Ekam*. That's extremely personal." I held up my hands and then wiped the blood and dust off on my pants.

"I wanted your attention." Trace dismissed my words with a raised shoulder and a wiggle of his head. "I mean, this whole war thing isn't personal, Haili. It started before you ever came home—you really shouldn't have come home. It's inevitable and I would have felt much better about it had it been your mother instead of you."

A cold lump settled into my chest as he babbled. "You? You murdered my sisters? You've been trying to kill me?"

"Oh no!" Trace took a step forward, a hand outstretched, and then thought better of it as Zin's weapon powered up in the stillness of the hangar. "No, that wasn't me. I didn't have anything to do with it. Phanin said your cousin went off the rails, she just completely lost it and thought she could rule Indrana. It put a kink in our plans, for sure. But we've worked around it."

"Our plans?" The lump grew, implanting shards of ice into my chest. "Phanin—"

"Is a smart man. Your empire is bleeding out much like your *Ekam*." There was such glee in Trace's voice that it took all my self-control not to grab my gun and shoot him right then. "My kingdom isn't doing all that great either, truth be told. The only way to save us both is to marry Indrana to us. Figuratively speaking, of course. I don't think—"

*"Majesty."* Cas's voice over the com link was steady in my head. *"Message from Lan: Admiral Hassan is critical but stable. Lieutenant Moran is tending to her now. They've put down the attempted mutiny on her ship, but those warp signatures were imperial forces arriving. It's Admiral Shul's fleet and he's coming up to Red Cliff fast."*

*"Tell her to run,"* I said.

*"Majesty, it's our only ride out of—"*

*"Now, Cas! Tell her to get the hell out of here, that's an order."*

*"Your Majesty,"* Indula chimed in over the link. *"We're with Fasé. We're on the other side of the hangar behind the Saxons. We've heard everything. What do you want us to do?"*

*"Zin, is Emmory—"* I couldn't say the word.

*"He's still alive, Majesty."*

*"Can we move him?"*

*"It doesn't look like we have a choice. What are you thinking?"*

*"Indula, is there anything to blow that shuttle with?"* I glanced

at Trace. He was still talking, unaware that I'd stopped listening as he paced back and forth, waving his hands in the air.

*"I'll find something, ma'am. Give me five minutes."*

I started the clock. *"On my signal, then. Circle around the hangar and meet us on the other side. Cas, get everyone ready to run."*

"—this was a foolish experiment to begin with, Haili. Women are too soft to rule. Phanin said your sister was so easily led, she would have walked Indrana straight into our arms without a fight."

"Why are you doing this? Billions of lives are at stake, Trace."

"We need the money." His eyes were glazed over with fevered dreams. "Your empire killed my father. Left my mother alone and grieving. I was just a kid, but I had to rule a kingdom in the daytime. Then at night I comforted my siblings as they cried themselves to sleep missing him. I like you, Haili, I always have. You should have gone back to gunrunning while you had the chance. The life expectancy is better there."

"Tough shit. I'm the empress now and you're just going to have to deal because I'm not going anywhere."

"I don't want to have to kill you, Haili."

"You leveled a building with me in it!"

Trace laughed. "Oh, true, I guess. But, really, I don't want to have to kill you. Just run. Take your people or leave them and get out of here."

"You should have been following things a little closer, Trace. I'm harder to kill than people think. And my empire has lasted for more than a thousand years. If you think you're actually going to tear it down, you're mad. All those people who live there are *my* people. I'm not leaving them behind."

Trace's eyes hardened into something unpleasant. "I will see Indrana destroyed for what you did to my family."

Indula said, *"We're good to go, Majesty."*

*"Everyone take cover,"* I said. *"Do it now, Indula."* Then, out loud to Trace, I said, "I could say the same to you. You killed my family, my friends, and you've put my empire in danger. You have no idea the wasps' nest you've stirred up, you stupid bastard. According to the reports I'm seeing, they're saying Saxony is responsible for the attack on Red Cliff."

"You bitch!" He sputtered at my insult, or at the news, it was hard to tell.

The shuttle exploded. All the air was sucked in and then flung outward along with flames and shrapnel. I was already running toward Trace and hit him in the chest as the fireball filled the hangar.

We hit the floor hard and slid across the hangar, slamming into the wall on the far side hard enough to knock the rest of the air from my lungs. I flopped around like a beached dolphin for a few stunned seconds until I got my knees under me.

Trace's eyes were wide as he gasped for breath. "My shuttle. You blew up my shuttle."

"That's on me, and so is this." I grinned unapologetically as I shot him in the knee.

He screamed in pain and thrashed underneath me.

I shoved my gun up under his chin and he went quiet except for the whimpering. "Be thankful I need you alive. That was for shooting my *Ekam*."

"Your Majesty." Ivan's voice, as hard as diamond plating and colder than space, cut through the air. I looked up to find him looming over me. "Put the gun down."

"Not happening." I shook my head. "And you know if you shoot me now it'll go straight through to him. So I'm out of here. If I so much as think you're going to fire on me anyway,

I'll squeeze the trigger. I can obliterate his head before you kill me." I rolled away from him, keeping my gun under Trace's chin and putting the king between me and his man.

"Put the gun down!" Cas said from behind me, but Ivan didn't move.

"I told you to run for it." I glared at my *Dve* over my shoulder.

"Sorry, ma'am. Not going to leave you here either." He grinned and dragged Trace upright as I got to my feet. "Saxon troops are incoming. We have to move."

"I know." I also knew my prisoner was just going to slow me down. So I shoved him at Ivan and grabbed Cas. "Run!"

We bolted around the wrecked cargo crates and out the hangar doors, leaving the shouting and cursing behind us.

"This way, ma'am." Cas took the lead, veering to the right. "They found us some ground transport. We'll head for the Solarian base."

"No." I shook my head as we reached the vehicles. "That's the first place they'll check. Message Matriarch Tobin's guards and tell them to get out of there. Tell them to get back to Indrana any way they can but to stay off the radar. Warn her about Phanin. I still don't understand what's going on, but we can't trust anyone right now."

Cas nodded, opening the door and ushering me inside before running around the front of the vehicle and getting into the driver's seat. I closed the door, squeezing Alba's outstretched hand. She had her broken arm bound against her side and the pain was etched on her face.

Fasé was bent over Emmory in the back, her hands red with his blood. Zin was next to her, his forehead pressed against Emmory's and his lips moving in a prayer or desperate pleading. Grief hung in the air like a fog.

My own grief squeezed my heart to the point of pain. I

couldn't even begin to fathom a world without Emmory. I didn't want to.

Fasé swooned and Indula caught her before she could fall onto Emmory. "He's stable, but there is a lot of damage. I will do more later when I have recovered," she managed to say before she passed out.

"Where are we going?"

"To my cousin, Majesty, she lives on Red Cliff," Alba said. "It was the major reason Emmory approved the planet."

Tears flooded my eyes and I wiped them away with the back of my hand. "He's very good at thinking ahead. What we need now though is a way off the planet. Admiral Hassan and the loyal ships should be long gone."

"I'm scanning the registers at the closest ports, Majesty." Alba's eyes were unfocused as she skimmed through the data.

"Send me the list when you have it. I might recognize something." I closed my eyes against the glare of the setting sun. Sleep snuck up on me in the inevitable adrenaline crash, and before I knew it the vehicle was slowing to a stop.

"Majesty." Cas shook me gently. "We're here."

A woman taller than Alba rushed out of the house, four young men on her heels. "How many wounded do you have?" The questions spilled out of her mouth even as she wrapped Alba in a fierce embrace.

"Emmory was shot, Leia, and Fasé is exhausted."

"Your arm is broken and you've all got some superficial wounds. Let's get inside. We'll want to get the vehicles out of sight. The boys will hide them."

"Majesty, this is my cousin, Leia."

The woman gave an awkward bow, still holding Alba close with one arm. "I wish this were under better circumstances, Your Imperial Majesty. Alba has spoken very highly of you."

"We're thankful for your help."

"Of course." She turned and propelled Alba toward the house.

I didn't complain when Cas wrapped an arm around my waist to hold me upright as we followed. We were out in the countryside, nothing but rolling hills and trees for as far as I could see in the growing dark. The house ahead was a sturdy, two-story structure with a sharply sloped roof.

He helped me into the house and lowered me to a chair in the living room. "Rest, Majesty."

"Coordinate with Indula for a list of our weapons and other supplies. We can't stay here long. Trace will have his people scouring the planet for us."

"I know, Majesty." A smile, so very much like Emmory's, flickered on his face.

"Sorry. I promise I'm not trying to tell you how to do your job."

"Except you are, Majesty."

My muttered response to that was short and pithy and made Cas's shoulders shake with repressed laughter. Others tried but failed to muffle their snickers, and I rolled my eyes at the ceiling with a smile. "Go on."

I settled into the chair as the activity buzzed around me. The local news was already covering the attack, but their information was garbled and useless at the moment. Indula had been right and there were reports that Red Cliff's planetary defense had recorded the Saxon ships' weapons powering up just before the facility was destroyed. I couldn't tap into any of the Indranan news outlets without access to the long-range transmitters on the naval ships.

Without a ship, we were cut off from Indrana.

"Majesty? Can you stand?" Stasia knelt by my chair. "We've

got a shower running and Fasé would like to make sure you're not injured."

"Everything hurts, but otherwise I'm fine." I pushed to my feet with a groan.

Fasé met me at the door of the bathroom. She was pale and shaking, leaning heavily on Zin. I shared a look with him.

"How is he?"

"There was a lot of damage, Majesty. I don't—" He swallowed and looked at the ceiling. "She thinks she's taken care of the worst of it and his vitals have stabilized. Now we just need time. His system should be able to keep him stable if we don't have to move him for a few hours. I don't know how he managed to stay alive long enough for Fasé to get to us."

I reached for his hand, squeezing it as I blinked back tears. "Because he's a stubborn bastard."

"Even with what she did, it's going to be touch-and-go. I'd feel better if we could get him to someplace with medical facilities." Zin choked back a laugh. "Fasé insisted on seeing you."

"There's nothing you can do except sleep," I told the Farian.

"I'm so sorry, ma'am. I wish I could do more. He'll need medical care, ma'am."

"It's not your fault." It was Trace's for shooting him in the first place. Anger rolled in my gut. "He's a Tracker, Fasé. He'll recover," I lied, mostly to convince myself. Emmory's healing systems were good, but Trace had nearly killed him and all the movement couldn't have improved matters. "We'll do what we can to help him until then. Go sleep."

"Yes, ma'am."

*"Zin,"* I subvocalized over our com link. *"You stay with Emmory. You make him fight to stay alive. That's an order. We've got everything else covered. Am I understood?"*

*"Yes, ma'am."*

*"And link me into his vitals; I want to know how he's really doing."*

Stasia took my clothing to see what she could salvage while I was in the shower. I scrubbed down, inspecting the various scrapes and bruises, as I ran through the list of ships in port. The water was glorious, but I knew I couldn't stay long. I stepped out and squeezed the water from my hair. As I moved on to drying off everything else, a name scrolled across my vision.

There, buried among the thousand names, was one I recognized. "Bugger me." I pulled up the details, praying for a miracle, and the manifest lodged with the port authority confirmed my suspicions.

"Cas!" I scrambled out of the room, yelling for him and Gita. They came running, along with Iza and Alba's cousin. I cinched my towel tight, rolling my eyes when Cas skidded to a halt and turned his back on me. "We're in a bit of an emergency here, Cas, suck it up. We need to go."

"We can't move *Ekam* Tresk, ma'am," Gita protested. "And Fasé is out cold."

"Not them, Gita, they'll stay here. The three of us need to go, right now. Iza, find Stasia, she took my clothes. I need something to wear and I needed it five minutes ago."

"Majesty, what is going on?" Cas's cheeks were pink and he was looking at the wall behind my head instead of at me, but he'd managed to inject a note of authority into his voice.

"Hao is here. We need to get to his ship before he takes off."

"All the ports are on lockdown."

"It won't matter to him. If anything it'll make him even itchier to get out of here. He's our ticket off Red Cliff unless we want to go out in the belly of a Saxon prison ship." It'd more likely be that they'd just bury us in shallow graves somewhere, but I didn't want to say that out loud.

AFTER THE CROWN

"Majesty, you have to come see this," Indula called.

There was a viewscreen on the wall of the living room. The volume was turned down, but I didn't need it to realize what was going on. Phanin stood on the bridge of a ship, his face grim. At the bottom of the screen the news of my death was blazoned in big black lettering.

## 19

It's the moons I remember most about that night—Red Cliff's twin spheres glowing in the black sky like a pair of half-shut eyes. I kept my gaze on them and my hands wrapped around the Glock I was carrying as Leia's aircar sped toward the landing field just outside Behanden.

The three of us in the car were all tense, adrenaline running high—no real surprise given it had been less than ten hours since Trace or Phanin, I still wasn't sure who was responsible, had leveled four city blocks on a Solarian neutral planet in an attempt to kill me and start a war.

They'd failed at half of it.

Now we were skulking through the darkness in a desperate bid to get off Red Cliff before Trace could do anything about the fact that I was still alive. My stomach was rolling. It was filled with anxiety for Emmory, whose vitals were even worse than I feared; worry for how I was going to get my people to safety; and anger that the only plan I could come up with was as dangerous as walking into a pit of venomous snakes.

And it was dangerous. Going to Po-Sin was a gamble, a calculated risk born of desperation.

Emmory was stabilized for now. My Tracker's augmented systems were hard at work on the damage from Trace's gun that Fasé hadn't had the energy left to fix, but he needed real medical care and time to heal.

And I needed allies, specifically allies who could get us off the planet.

Going to a hospital on Red Cliff wasn't an option, which meant we had to use my plan. The planet was swarming with Saxon troops, while my Durga-damned troops were back on Pashati, possibly embroiled in another damned coup attempt.

Eha Phanin.

That rat bastard. I almost cracked a tooth before I forced myself to relax my clenched jaw. The prime minister had orchestrated whatever plan he had going with an efficiency the gunrunner half of my brain admired.

The empress half of things was less than amused, and unfortunately for Phanin, my entire being was on board with the plan to rip his still-beating heart out of his chest.

According to his little speech for the news, Saxon agents within the capital had attacked and crippled the Indranan government at the same time they'd bombed Red Cliff and killed me. The matriarchs were scattered and Alice was missing, presumed dead because her home was a smoking pile of rubble.

I really hoped that was a lie as much as my death was.

I'd had to watch the replay twice because when I'd spotted the man standing next to Phanin, a red haze of fury blinded me.

Wilson.

The tall man stood with his hands clasped in front of him, a solemn expression on his face during Phanin's announcement. That blue-eyed bastard was responsible for the death of everyone in my family—my sisters, my niece, my mother and father.

That Durga-damned ghost had been working with Phanin this whole time.

And with Trace.

How many of my people had already perished in these madmen's desperate bid for power?

"Majesty." My *Dve*'s voice wafted from the front seat of the aircar like a curl of smoke drifting on a breeze. The single word, delivered in a tone both comforting and chastising, shook me out of my fury. Cas had stepped into Emmory's absence with far more certainty than I'd expected from someone so young, but I was grateful for his solid presence.

"I'm all right." I'm not sure why I bothered lying through my teeth. Maybe because while Emmory would have seen right through me and called me on it, Cas simply nodded.

I was presumed dead by most of the universe, about to meet up with a gunrunner pal who would hopefully take us off-planet instead of double-crossing me and turning me over to either the man who'd stolen my throne or the insane Saxon king.

Once we got off-planet my plan got even crazier: to take us straight into the dragon's lair and ask one of the deadliest Cheng gang lords in the galaxy to be my ally.

Despite my history with Hao, he was a gunrunner, and right now my head was worth a decent amount. Thanks to a private bounty issued by Po-Sin. I only knew about it because Hao had sent me a copy. If we boarded his ship, he'd have to take me to his uncle.

Or, Hao might decide to betray me and deliver us into Phanin's hands. I couldn't be sure that wasn't something my old mentor would consider.

I slid out of the car, Gita at my side. Cas came around the

other side and we all crouched in the shadows at the edge of the landing field.

Spotting Hao as he strode down the ramp of an unfamiliar ship, I elbowed Gita and jerked my head to the left. She nodded in acknowledgment and Cas took the point as our party moved across the open tarmac.

I whistled a complex tune. Hao froze, hand going to the gun on his hip when he saw us.

"Cheng Hao, it has been a long time."

"*Sha zhu*, a fortuitous meeting." Hao sketched a surprisingly elegant bow, keeping his eyes on mine the whole time.

I locked my hand onto Gita's arm when she flinched. "Nickname," I muttered, biting back a curse. "It's an old nickname."

Hao brushed his metallic-streaked hair out of his face, his gold eyes glittering with mirth. I swallowed down the second curse at my mistake. Now he knew that Gita spoke Cheng well enough to recognize slang when she heard it.

I kept my bow short, unable to show my former mentor the respect I normally would. "I request permission to board your ship and speak with you."

"You may come into the cargo bay." He turned his back on me and walked up the ramp. We followed, Cas whispering instructions to Gita as we went into the ship.

"How did you find me?" Hao leaned against the stairs, the picture of disinterest for anyone who couldn't recognize the line of tension in his neck and left hand as it hovered near his gun.

"The *Benson Porter*?" I laughed at him. "You're recycling old ship names. I need a lift off the planet, Hao."

"Force of habit. I figured anyone who knew the name didn't care about it any longer. Probably should have thought that through. Under what terms are we negotiating this ride?" Hao arched a copper eyebrow and a smile skittered over his thin mouth. "You'd like to bring armed men and women onto my ship. I'm not sure I'm comfortable with that."

"I have more people at a farmhouse outside of town. We need to get off Red Cliff. I won't leave any of them behind."

"And none of us will leave our weapons," Cas said. "You will be paid for your assistance, gunrunner, nothing more. As long as your people stay out of my way and away from the empress, no one will get hurt."

"Strong words for a child." Hao arched an eyebrow. "Where is your *Ekam*? Not dead, I hope."

"Cas." I put my hands up before Cas could spit a reply. "Let's keep this civil, shall we? I am sorry for his lack of manners, Hao. It has been—"

"A difficult situation." Hao gave me another bow. "The lack of manners is understandable and forgivable—this time. You didn't answer my question."

"Emmory was shot. He is not dead."

Hao smiled slowly. "I have forgotten how taciturn you can be when the mood suits you. How do I benefit from this assistance, *sha zhu*?"

"I can pay you."

"I do not need money. Sorry, but it is true. The Fates have been good to me lately." He shrugged. "I am not even sure a promise of a favor is worth anything, little sister, seeing as how you have lost your empire."

I snapped my arm up and Hao went cross-eyed from looking down his nose at the barrel of my Glock.

"Temporarily." I snarled the word, listening as the whine of guns being charged echoed around the bay. "It has been *temporarily* taken from me, Hao, and you have no idea the lengths I'm willing to go to get it back."

"And there at last is my deadly little sister. I thought she might have died, smothered under a layer of lace and palace protocol."

"I was trying to be polite. Now what will it be, Hao? Favor? Money? Or do I just shoot you and take your ship?"

"Temper."

"Sorry. I am a little pressed for time and every second we stand in the open is one less we have to get the rest of my people and get out of here."

"You don't say," Hao murmured. "They will be searching the smaller ports like this one once they get their heads out of their collective asses. I don't want to be here when that happens. It would lead to awkward questions."

"Make a decision then," I said, keeping my gun pointed at his head.

"Favor." He smiled slowly at Gita's hissing exhale. "I give you my word it will be nothing to jeopardize your honor or force you to put your empire in danger."

"Done. One last thing I need to know. Has anyone been around asking questions about me? Did you sell me out?"

Actual hurt flashed in Hao's eyes. "You are family. Even though I didn't know your true name, I know your true self. I would never betray you, Cressen, not for all the money in the universe."

"I'm sorry. I had to ask." I lowered my Glock and gave him a nod. "How much time do you think we have?"

"I would send for the others now. Judging from the chatter, they are working their way through the main ports. We are close enough that it won't take them all that long before someone thinks they should come out here for a look."

"Cas, call Zin. Tell him to get the others loaded, and double-time it."

187

He nodded sharply. I backed away from Hao and boosted myself up onto a cargo pallet. Hao barked a few orders in Cheng and the thumping of boots filled the air as his crew rushed off, presumably to get the ship ready for departure.

Hao didn't leave the cargo bay. He sauntered toward me, stopping when Gita stepped in his path. My BodyGuard was taller than the gunrunner, and she outmassed him. Still, his lazy grin was all too familiar as he looked her up and down.

"Gita, let him by."

"He's armed, Majesty."

"Hao, give her your gun."

Surprisingly, he complied and then joined me on the pallet.

"Is she available?"

I couldn't stop the laugh. "She would break you in half."

"It would be worth it." Hao ran his tongue over his teeth. "You have no idea how much flack I've taken for letting you ride with me, Cressen. A princess of the Indranan empire and a damned ITS trooper under my very nose." He rolled his eyes toward the ceiling. "I think the only reason Po-Sin didn't kill me is that he approved of you."

"I'd apologize, except I'm not sorry."

Hao flashed me a vicious grin I'd seen enough times to know I'd said the perfect thing. "I'm glad to hear it. I'd lose respect for you if you were. Why were you so far from home, little sister?"

I smiled. "It's a long story. If it helps your ego, I didn't know Portis was still ITS—or rather my new BodyGuard."

"What's the short version?"

"I needed out and you were in the right place at the right time."

"Ever my luck," he said.

We sat in silence. It was one of the things I'd always loved about Hao. He could sit for hours without so much as a word.

"Majesty, they have the wounded loaded up and are headed our way," Cas said.

"Thank you, Cas."

He nodded and headed toward the edge of the ramp to keep watch. Hao snorted and I elbowed him.

"Baby-faced children bowing and scraping to a former gun-runner. It's the end times."

"Don't tease him, Hao." I didn't attempt to keep the snap out of my voice. "He's doing his best."

Hao blinked. "I wasn't teasing him, *Your Imperial Majesty*." He gave a flourishing, mocking bow from his seat.

"Oh hush."

"He's got big shoes to fill from the sounds of it. You know you will lose two BodyGuards if your Emmory dies."

"I am fully aware, Hao."

He folded his hands together and shook them slightly. "Forgive me. It was not my intention to upset you."

Whatever I was going to reply with was lost when a pink-haired young man bolted down the stairs, skidding to a halt in front of Gita. He bowed. "Captain, we must go."

Hao jumped from the pallet and I scrambled off after him. "How long, Dailun?"

The kid shrugged a slender shoulder. "Five minutes, maybe."

"Get us ready. You leave on my word only."

Dailun nodded at Hao and took the stairs two at a time back up toward the bridge.

"Cas, what's their ETA?" I asked.

"Two minutes. Indula's flying."

"Tell him to floor it and to fly right up to the ship. Tell the others to be prepared to bail quick." I turned back around and pointed a finger at Cas. "And if anyone tries to say we should leave them I will personally kick their ass."

"Yes, ma'am."

"What kind of explosives do you have?"

Hao arched an eyebrow at me. "What are you thinking?"

"Buying them some time."

"*Sha zhu*, we were friends once. But even then I would have told you this—those are Saxon Shock Corps Marines incoming; five minutes and this ship is off the ground."

"Then you will leave me on the ground."

We stared at each other, the seconds ticking away with each beat of my heart. I wasn't going to beg or plead. The Hao I knew was a man of honor, and he'd already promised to take me off Red Cliff.

Still it seemed an eternity before he nodded, muttering a series of his favorite curses. "I have bottle rockets." He looked at Gita. "And I will need my weapon back, my dear."

Gita eyed him but handed him his gun.

"That'll do nicely." I clapped him on the shoulder. "It's just like old days."

"Right." Hao snorted. "Except if you get killed this one is going to take me apart in ways I'm certain I wouldn't enjoy."

"It's likely. However, I'm not planning on dying today." I dropped into a crouch and headed down the ramp. Scanning the landing field for targets, I selected what looked like a private short-range freight bus and lined up my shot as the headlights appeared in the distance. Behind us I heard the sound of a truck engine revving and tires screaming as they hit the pavement.

"Gita, go help them unload."

"No, ma'am." She shouldered a BR launcher with a shake of her head. "Cas said to stick with you. I'm sticking."

"We're going to have a talk about the chain of command when we get done here."

"He said you'd say that, ma'am, and technically he is my chain of command. So, either way, I'm still staying."

"Fine. See that stack of crates on the far side of the freighter? We're firing at those."

"Can I shoot the Saxon aircars?" Hao asked. "I don't want to get you into any political trouble—" He yelped, rubbing at his shin.

"I've already shot the king of the Saxons today, Hao. Don't think I won't shoot you, too."

"I was just asking."

"Shut up and fire."

The explosions rocked the darkness.

# 20

We booked it back to the ship before the pieces of the air-car and other assorted debris had fallen back to the landing field.

Indula and Zin carried Emmory up the ramp while Iza and Kisah rushed Caterina from the vehicle into the ship. Alba followed with Stasia, my maid supporting my chamberlain around her waist.

Tanish pulled Fasé, who was unconscious, from the back. He made it two steps before the blast streaked out of the darkness, slamming into his back.

"Bugger me." I tossed the BR launcher to Hao and sprinted toward them. Gita was on my heels. "Get him!" I shouted.

I scooped up Fasé, the Farian as light as a child, and dove behind the vehicle for cover as more gunfire tore through the night.

"He's dead." Gita punched the side of the vehicle with a vicious curse.

I squeezed my eyes shut for just a second and whispered a prayer for Tanish's family.

"Hao!"

"Yup!"

Thankfully, time apart hadn't dulled Hao's inexplicable ability to anticipate my needs.

"Need another round!" he shouted, and caught the bottle rocket someone threw back at him from inside the ship. In one smooth motion, the gunrunner reloaded, stood, and fired.

Heaving Fasé over my shoulder and hoping that Gita was following, I ran for the ship with everything I had.

I made it to the ramp before the stinging pain of a shot to my leg put me down on a knee. Fasé dropped to the ramp, her head hitting with a dull thud. Hao grabbed her, dragging her up into the ship.

I rolled off the ramp, firing my Glock, trying to buy Gita enough cover to get clear.

A silver-haired man marched through the flames toward the ship. I shot him in the left shoulder, and he jerked backward but kept coming.

"I'm out!"

Gita locked her fingers on my collar and hauled me onto the ramp as Hao laid down fire until the Saxon was forced to seek cover.

"Dailun, go go go!" Hao shouted over his com, and leaned back down, grabbing Gita's outstretched arm and pulling both of us into the ship as the ramp closed.

The ship jerked off the ground and banked sharply. I slid partway into the cargo bay before Hao managed to grab me more securely around the waist. "Everyone hang on to something," he shouted.

It is neither thrilling nor a rush to have your life in someone else's hands. Instead it's terrifying, leaving you feeling powerless and just a shade desperate.

So while Hao's pilot juked and dodged through what I

imagined was the defense grid's response to any ships leaving the planet, I started making a list of all the things I had to do.

"Let's get off this rock pile, first," Hao whispered in my ear. "Worry about what to do later."

"How did you—"

He laughed at my confusion. "I know that look, Cressen."

"My name's not Cressen."

"I know that, too. To be honest, I'm not sure I can call you Hail. It feels weird in my mouth."

And it would be a miracle to get him to use my title. I'd noticed the only time he'd used it so far it had been coated in sarcasm.

"I'm not sure any of my Guards will let you." I rolled my eyes. "Who'd you steal the ship from?"

"I bought it, *sha zhu*. As I said, life has been good to me lately."

Alarm bells in my head joined the ones ringing through the ship as Emmory's vitals went from bad to worse.

"No, bugger me. No."

More alarm bells joined the first set. "Let me go." I pinched Hao until he yelped and let me squirm from his grip. The sudden loss of an anchor sent me crashing into the bulkhead as the ship went sideways. I picked myself up and skidded across the cargo bay to where Emmory lay. "Hao, I need your medic!"

Emmory's heart was slowing. Whatever Fasé had done wasn't enough, or moving him had shaken something loose. My *smati* shrieked a warning about a collapsed lung, and his chest wasn't moving the way it should. The bandages Stasia and Caterina had wrapped at Leia's house were pristine, which meant he had to be bleeding internally.

"Don't, Emmory, please don't." I knew my plea went unheard. Just like it had when my father died.

The flatline tone sliced through my head.

"No!"

Zin's cry ripped through the cargo bay and my heart, an anguished scream of unimaginable loss. My own devastation was only a fraction of what Zin was feeling, and yet it destroyed me.

"Hail," Zin said, turning to me. The hopeless despair in his eyes was too much to bear. I slapped my hands on Emmory's chest, intent on trying to restart his heart.

Fasé lunged upright from where she'd been lying and shoved me to the side. The Farian was suddenly awake and moving with greater speed than any of us, muttering under her breath as she pressed both hands to Emmory's unmoving chest.

The flatline tone stopped, and a steady—if weak—heartbeat echoed in my head. Fasé went gray and collapsed onto Emmory, jerking everyone back into motion.

The ship leveled out. Hao rushed forward with Indula, my Guard gently moving Fasé to the side.

"She's still alive, Majesty," he said. "But her pulse is slow. I'm assuming that's not a good rhythm even for a Farian."

"Get her to medical—" I broke off. "Keep an eye on her, we need to get Emmory stabilized first."

"Henna, we have a medical emergency in the cargo bay. Coming your way." Hao's face was grim, but he effortlessly coordinated the chaos around him.

Zin pulled me to my feet as two other crew members rushed up with a stretcher. They loaded Emmory on. I grabbed Zin's hand and we leaned on each other as we made our way to medical.

I knew Hao's crew; once there would have been shouted greetings with backslaps, cheap shots, and crude jokes. Now there were only hesitant nods, sidelong glances at my Body-Guards, and so much awkwardness I wanted to scream.

I shoved the feeling back into the pit of my stomach, where it festered and burned, focusing instead on what Henna was saying.

"Bad, bad Cres—my apologies, Your Majesty." Henna and I had once been friends. Now the lanky one-eyed blonde wouldn't meet my eyes as she studied the scan above Emmory's chest. "Have to open him up. Alive, but still bleeding."

"No." Zin protested the news or the plan, I wasn't sure which.

"Zin, Henna knows what she's doing."

"Farian can't save." Henna looked over her shoulder where Indula laid Fasé's unconscious body on a bed. "Out of juice. Out of time. Get out."

"I won't leave him." Zin gritted the words as he sank to the floor. I dropped with him.

"Don't. Don't you dare," I said, cupping his face in my hands. "He's alive, Starzin, you have to hold on. For him. For me, please. Don't leave me here all alone."

Henna raised her eyebrow and turned the scan on Zin. "Dying, too. Sympathetic. Interesting."

I looked up. "They're Trackers, Henna. Bonded."

"Artery in bad shape. Lots of blood in chest, collapsed a lung. The other is on its way out. Have to save this one to save both," she said, referring to Emmory's lung or Zin—I wasn't entirely sure which. Henna dismissed Zin and turned back to Emmory. "Any of your people have medical training?"

"I've had some," Stasia said from behind me. "I'm the one who patched him up originally."

"Good. You help. The rest of you get out of here. Hao, others in cargo bay should live, but little girl's arm needs to be set." Henna's gray eye was unfocused and she gnawed on her thumb. Her genius mind was already spinning faster than a ship's warp drive.

Henna Brek had once been a brilliant surgeon with the roving Med-Fleet, but a hijacking and a three-year hostage situation resulted in the deaths of many of her co-workers, Henna's lost eye, and a large chunk of her sanity.

Unable to pass the psych profile for any of the major hospital corporations, she'd drifted like space rubble until she'd been caught in Hao's orbit.

Like so many of us. The misfits of the misfits. And Hao was the king.

I pressed my forehead to the window outside the medical bay.

"You're not staying here, Majesty. We need to look at your leg." Cas slipped an arm around my waist and tried to pull me away.

"I can't leave them."

"Yes, you can. Help your *Dve* out." Hao slid under my other arm. "The next door down is the secondary room, Caspian.

"I'm going to patch up her leg, BodyGuard, so don't shoot me." Hao boosted me onto the table and turned to the cupboards to rummage for supplies.

I reached out and threaded my fingers through Cas's. *"I'm okay. So is Emmory. Henna's one of the best out there."*

*"He died, ma'am."*

*"I know."* And Fasé brought him back to life. I couldn't believe what I'd seen, even though I'd been right next to her when it happened.

*"Majesty, those were Shock Corps troops down on that landing field."*

*"I know."*

*"What is going on?"*

*"That I don't know,"* I said over the com link. *"And we're blind until I can get ahold of Caspel or someone back on Pashati."*

"You two done talking about me?" Hao asked.

I smacked him. "The worlds don't revolve around you. Can I use your com relay?"

He finished wrapping the bandage around my leg. "You should get some rest. This just grazed you, but you're probably at the end of your rope, *sha zhu*."

"Messages first. Then I promise both of you I'll sleep." I slid off the bed, testing my leg before I put my full weight on it. There was pain, but the leg held instead of buckling, so I hobbled down the corridor after Hao.

"Dailun's about to send us into warp," he said, the warning just fast enough for me to brace myself.

The familiar disorientation washed over me and settled, and the eerie stillness of the bubble filled the ship.

"Your new pilot is better than Hoss."

That was saying something, considering that my former pilot had been a survivor of the Terran Wars and was awarded a Medal of Honor for his cover of the escape of several Solarian Conglomerate civilian ships during the mysterious Shen attack of Colony 17.

Then he'd been tossed out of Earth Conglomerate's Defense Force for one too many grandstanding buzzes past the council building.

I kind of missed Hoss. I didn't know what had happened to him. My still-hazy memory of the fight on *Sophie* was filled with some major holes on everything that didn't include Portis.

"We'll put you up in the secondary crew area. There's a lock on the door at the front of the corridor and a large sleeping area in the back." Hao continued down the corridor as the ship evened out into the smooth Alcubierre/White bubble of warp. "Whatever you need is yours, just ask."

"Thank you. I'll pay you for the supplies."

"It is a gift." He waved a hand.

"I will pay you."

"A gift," he repeated. "We are still friends, are we not?"

I studied him for a long moment before answering. For a large chunk of my life Hao had been father—older brother, he would say with a grin if I ever voiced the words out loud—friend, mentor, and protector. I'd once trusted this man with my life, trusted him as much as Portis.

I couldn't ignore the fact that he'd been here just when I happened to need him most. Whether it was providence or dangerous coincidence remained to be seen.

"We're friends," I replied finally with a smile. "And thank you."

"Dailun, give us the bridge for a few."

*"Hai."* The young man dipped his head and left us alone.

"Com, Hail," Hao said with an exaggerated bow and a look on his face that confirmed how odd my real name felt in his mouth. "I wouldn't stay on long. We're clear at the moment in warp, but they'll be tracking for us and I'd rather not make it easy for them to find our path. One hell-bent run for safety a day is my limit."

I nodded. "I'll keep it short."

Hao paused, but then left us alone without saying anything more. I connected my *smati* to the ship's computer and entered Caspel's private link.

"Majesty? You're alive."

"I am, and in better damn shape than you. What happened?"

Half of Caspel's face was bandaged, his left eye hidden beneath a swath of white. "It's a long story, ma'am, and I'm sure this line is no longer secure."

I gave him the quick and dirty version of events. "Is Alice alive? Tazerion? How many of the matriarchs?"

The view shifted and in the dim light of the room he was in I could make out Alice and Taz on the far side. He gestured them over.

"Majesty," Alice said, smiling in relief. "We are very glad you're not dead."

"That makes two of us. Are you unharmed?"

She nodded. "I was visiting Tazerion in the hospital with Captain Gill when the attack happened. They sent men looking for him, but Dr. Flipsen bought us enough time to escape." Alice swallowed. "They killed her, Majesty. Shot her right in front of the hospital for aiding traitors of the 'new Indrana.'"

I swore viciously.

Caspel returned his camera focus to his face. "I don't have many more answers for you, ma'am. I am truly sorry. The conspiracy went deeper than any of us imagined. I missed it. As of right now Phanin's troops have control of Pashati and the rest of the system, as well as twenty-eight other imperial planets we know of. They have at least half the matriarchs and their families in custody. No one has seen or heard from Matriarch Desai."

"Caterina is with us. I sent Masami and Sabeen to the Solarians, but then told them to run for it when we realized what was going on with Trace and Phanin. I don't know if they made it."

"Where are you now?"

"On a ship." I smiled. "No more than that. I'll check in again when we're somewhere safer. If you hear from Admiral Hassan, tell her to keep the fleet hidden and to wait for contact. I'll let her know where to meet me when it's safe."

"Yes, ma'am."

"Caspel, tell my people I'm alive. Tell them to hold on. We will not abandon them."

He nodded once and disconnected.

Hao was waiting with Dailun by the door when Cas pushed it open. "Let's get you settled." Hao gave me a cheerful grin. "Henna has good news. Your *Ekam* survived the surgery. She had to knock out his partner. Thinks he was feeling the surgery. Said it's the wildest thing she's ever seen.

"Dailun, drop us out of warp in ten. Then plot a course for home. If we're lucky, we'll get there before those Shock troops find us."

"Lucky?" I snorted. "I don't need to remind you that luck hasn't been in my pocket lately."

"You're still alive, *sha zhu*." Hao barked a laugh, ignoring Cas's growled warning and putting his hand on the back of my neck as we headed into the ship.

A warm comfort bloomed in my chest at the contact. Maybe I was a fool, but Hao's presence and heading back onto familiar territory made me feel better than I had since this whole nightmare had started.

The feeling faded as we passed by medical and I spotted Emmory and Zin lying side by side. I bit the inside of my cheek to keep from crying.

"Your rooms are through here." Hao stopped at the hatch and bowed. "I give you my word you are safe aboard my vessel, and if it will ease your *Dve*'s mind, I grant him full autonomy within your rooms. He has the authority to deal with anyone who breaches this entryway without express permission."

I managed a smile. "That will make him feel better, Hao. Thank you."

"Thank me when we get home in one piece. Dailun is an excellent pilot—"

"What happened to Gy?"

"Houken disease."

I winced. "That's genetic. I had no idea."

"Neither did I. He developed it far later than he should have and hid it for too long after. Henna did what she could to make him comfortable at the end. That was really all we could do."

"I'm sorry."

Hao moved out of reach before I could put my hand on his arm. "It is the nature of things. We lose what we love. Get yourself settled, *sha zhu*. I'll speak to you later if we make it out of this alive."

"I'm hearing that entirely too much lately," I muttered as I stepped over the threshold into our rooms. The others were already spread about the spacious quarters. Matriarch Saito and Iza were going through a pile of clothing and gear. Indula was next to them, weapons scattered around him.

Stasia was still in medical helping Henna set Alba's arm. I sent her a message to stay there for the night in case any of our people needed anything.

Now that some of the adrenaline had worn off, my injuries made themselves known. I dropped down into a chair in the common area with an undignified grunt.

"Majesty?" Kisah was on a knee by my side before I could inhale again.

"I'm all right. Just tired. How is everyone else?" I looked around the room. Seven BodyGuards—if Emmory and Zin survived the night; five if they didn't—plus my maid, my chamberlain, a matriarch, and Fasé. That was twelve strong, counting me, against Phanin's army and the Saxons.

I could only hope that the seven ships that had accompanied Admiral Hassan to Red Cliff were loyal and had escaped with her. Otherwise I was going to have to build my army from scratch, and I already knew from experience how damned difficult that could be.

"We're fine, Majesty." Kisah smiled, but I could see Willimet's death reflected in her eyes, and I pulled her into a hug.

"You are not fine. We are safe for the moment," I said. "Grieve for her." The young Guard's shoulders shook with sobs as I held her, and tears of my own for the loss of a friend slid down my face.

I released Kisah, and we both mustered smiles we weren't really feeling. "Is anyone else hurt?"

"We'll be all right, Majesty," Gita said. She'd stripped down to her tank top and pants and was busy trying to wash Tanish's blood from her uniform jacket. "A whole lot of bruises and the like, but they'll heal."

"I spoke with Caspel. Things are not going well back home." I relayed what little information I had to them from the conversation with the GIS director. "For those who didn't see it, we've likely got a Shock Corps team on our asses. We can outrun them for a while, but we'll have to deal with them eventually or the plan won't work."

"What plan is that, Majesty?" Cas asked.

"Getting back my throne."

"With all due respect, ma'am," Indula said from the floor. "That's an endgame, not a plan."

"Technicality," I replied, and he grinned. "And I'm working on it."

The first step had been to dispute Phanin's claims that I was dead. Doing that would hopefully light a spark in my people and at least provide Phanin with enough of a distraction to give me some time to make my move.

Only, Indula was right. Beyond getting my throne back I had no clue yet what that move might be.

"Hopefully it involves getting us more guns, because we're not knocking over a refuel port with this stash."

"It does." His words sparked a memory and I muttered a curse as I realized what had been nagging at the back of my brain since I talked to Caspel.

His operative and Governor Ashwari were supposed to meet us on Red Cliff. Now I needed those ships at Canafey more than ever. And I needed to know if the three back at home had also fallen to Phanin's forces. I made a note to ask Caspel about it the next time we talked.

"Majesty?"

I shook my head. "Sorry—just thought of something. Everyone get settled in. We may as well get some rest while we can."

My second-in-command BodyGuard had been taking lessons from Emmory on how to ignore my orders. Instead of crashing on a bunk, my *Dve* turned around and issued a few quick orders of his own to my BodyGuards.

I pushed out of the chair and headed for a bunk.

"Majesty." Cas cleared his throat.

"What?"

He gave a pointed look at a bunk on the other side of the room, far from the one near the door I'd been headed toward. I didn't have the energy to hassle him and changed course across the room. Stretching out on the bunk farthest from the door, I raised my head slightly. "Happy?"

"No, ma'am, but that's better."

## 21

I woke up in the dark, every muscle in my body screaming in furious dissent over the slightest movement. Someone had put a blanket over me and I pushed it aside as I rolled from the bunk. The even breathing of the others filled the room, not breaking rhythm as I made my way step by careful step to the door.

It slid open silently and I breathed a thank-you to Hao for keeping his ship in better than working order. The dim red light in the hallway washed nostalgia over me. In a world without sun, Hao's tactic of lighting the hallways with red at night was an easy fix to the problem of spaceborne insomnia. Red time was nighttime. The lighting had worked so well I instituted the use on my ship.

I spotted Zin, sitting near Emmory's bed in the dim light of the med bay. His hands were clasped together and pressed against his forehead as he whispered a fevered and relentless prayer over and over.

Closing my hand on his shoulder, I joined him in the old, familiar litany, and this time when we reached the end he stopped.

"Majesty, forgive me."

"What?"

Zin turned his tear-streaked face toward me. "I should have stayed with you. Not let my concern for Emmory take me from my duty."

"Shut your mouth." It came out louder than I'd intended, and I winced when Emmory shifted in his sleep. "Starzin Hafin, how can you even think I'd be angry at you?" I hissed, smacking him on the shoulder. "You were right where you needed to be. We had everything under control. I ordered you to stay with him."

"Emmory would have—"

"Been at your side or I'd have kicked his ass like I'm about to kick yours." I grabbed his face and jerked it close. "You listen to me and listen good. Don't you dare think I'd make either of you choose *me*. I know it's the way things might go down because of the truly messy situation we're in, but I would never demand it of you. I can take care of myself, Zin. Right now you take care of your husband, that's an order. Am I understood?"

He nodded. I kissed his forehead and then released him.

"Majesty?" Emmory's voice was heavy with whatever pain-killers Henna had shot him up with. He shifted, trying to open his eyes.

I leaned past Zin, wrapping my hand around Emmory's fingers and squeezing. "We're safe for the moment, Emmy. Go back to sleep."

"Hard to do with all the noise," he slurred, but he turned his head and his breathing evened back out.

"Where's Fasé and the others?"

"Next door," Zin said. "Henna didn't want her waking up and trying to heal Emmory again."

"Good thinking. I'm going to go check on them. Make sure you get some rest," I said to Zin.

"Back at you, Majesty. And go back to your rooms."

I grinned at him and headed for the door to the other room. It was easy to make out the silhouettes on the beds.

"Majesty?" Stasia's voice was thick with sleep.

I pressed her back down onto the bed she shared with Fasé. "Everything's fine. Go back to sleep."

My maid nodded and curled back around the Farian. Their breathing synced almost immediately and I watched with interest as the readings on Fasé's chart climbed.

Alba was out cold. Most likely because of the pain medication. She didn't have any of the accelerated healing my Body-Guards had, but the splint Henna had applied looked to be high-end Solarian-made and would do the job.

I turned and muffled a shriek at the sight of Hao standing in the doorway. His gold eyes glittered in the light. Flashing me a smile, he jerked his head toward the hallway and turned away.

"Come have a drink with me before your *Dve* wakes up and we both get in trouble."

I followed him down the hallway, hesitating at the doorway to his room. He rolled his eyes at me.

"I swear on the graves of my ancestors I will be the very soul of propriety." He shook a bottle at me, the clear alcohol sloshing against the sides.

I unlaced my boots and pulled them off, then crossed over the threshold and settled onto the blue cushions that surrounded the low wooden table.

Hao poured the liquor with a flourish, passed me a cup, and raised his. "To the Empire of Indrana and her empress, long may she reign."

Coming from anyone else it would have been pompous

sarcasm, but with Hao, he meant every word even if he still hadn't used my title. I saluted him back with my glass and downed the shot, sliding it back to him for the expected refill.

"And to Portis," Hao said, his voice solemn. "If we must go, there is no nobler way than to die for those we love."

I froze with the drink halfway to my mouth. "How do you know that?"

Hao smiled. It was surprisingly gentle and tinged with sadness. "He loved you, Hail, even before he got the courage to do something about it. I may not know exactly what happened, but I know he would have died to save you rather than let you come to harm."

I drank, letting the alcohol burn away my tears. Hao gave me the time I needed to compose myself but didn't fill the glasses again, and I gave him a curious look.

"I lied before. We are not going home. I must take you to my uncle, little sister." He looked at the tabletop. "I confess I do not want to, even though it would mean my dishonor and death. Were it just me, I would still consider it and likely be foolish enough to disobey because my debt to you is stronger than anything I owe Po-Sin."

"But your crew," I said.

"Yes, my crew. I cannot leave them to such a fate."

I reached across the table and threaded my fingers through his. "I was kind of counting on you taking me to Po-Sin, *gege*. Pour a third drink before you bring all the evil spirits down on our heads."

"You are a brat and I don't know why I ever allowed you on board my ship." Hao glared, pouring. "You could have told me that earlier."

"But then I wouldn't have gotten you to spill your guts to me." I took the glass. "To vengeance."

Hao raised his glass. "I have seen that look before. I would have pity for those you seek, but for the fact that they deserve whatever you have planned. May you find your revenge and may it taste sweet."

I tossed back my drink. Hao poured us another, but with the toasts done I could cradle it. We fell into a companionable silence, broken only by the occasional question or story as we filled each other in on the last few years apart.

"I had a cargo hold full of rugs for the SC." I tossed back the rest of my drink. "Would have made a fortune on it."

"What happened?"

"Emmory blew *Sophie* up."

Hao winced in sympathy and poured me another glass. "Let me tell you about the job we pulled on Primoria V a month ago. I'd gotten word that..."

Exhaustion and the alcohol took its toll and Hao's chuckle shook me out of my doze. He leaned down and plucked the half-finished glass from my hand. "Come on, little sister, let's put you back to bed."

"Majesty?"

I blinked at Cas and then at Hao, who'd backed up a step with his hands raised. "Hey, Cas. We were just catching up." I got to my feet without too much trouble and patted his cheek.

"You were drinking without someone to check it?"

I gave him a look. It was spoiled by the fact that I had to lean against the doorjamb to do it. "You sound like Emmory. Hao wouldn't hurt me."

"Take her to bed, Caspian. She is fine, you have my word."

Cas didn't reply to Hao. He just grabbed my boots and gave the gunrunner a sharp nod. I waved to him and headed back down the hallway.

"You can't wander off, ma'am. Not right now. If anything happened to you—"

"I'm perfectly safe here. Hao gave his word. And you weren't that worried, you didn't wake anyone else up," I said as I sank back down on my bunk.

"Go to sleep, Majesty."

"Yes, sir." I threw him a salute, rolled over, and let the liquor drag me down into a dreamless sleep.

I woke to the sounds of quiet conversation and the smell of food, at which point my stomach pointedly reminded me how long it had been since I'd eaten last.

"Morning, Majesty." Kisah handed me a plate as I rolled from the bed.

"Bless you."

She laughed. "Thank Captain Hao. I would have been happy with S-Rations."

"Me, too, but luckily for us he hates them." I grinned at her and took my plate over to a chair. "Where is everyone else?"

"Matriarch Saito is in the bathroom, cleaning up. We have some fresh clothes for you, ma'am. You can take a turn when she's finished. The others are in the medical bay for a briefing."

"Is Emmory awake?"

"He is, ma'am." Kisah held out a hand and I sat back down. "He asked me to make sure you ate first. They're just filling him in on everything that's happened."

"How is he?" I asked, shoveling food into my mouth.

"He's awake." Kisah grinned at my glare. "I'm sorry, Majesty. That's all I know. You'll have to talk to Zin and Henna about it after you've gotten cleaned up and she's looked at your leg."

"My leg is fine." I waved the spork in the air for emphasis, but my BodyGuard didn't even blink, so I went back to my food with a sigh.

"Good morning, Your Majesty." Caterina came into the room, dressed in a pair of dark brown pants and a lighter brown shirt a size too big for her.

"Matriarch Saito." I nodded, then snorted. "Caterina, let's drop the titles for the moment, shall we? Given the unusual situation, they feel very cumbersome."

"If you insist, ma'am. Kisah, I think you were right and we're going to want to take a few inches off these sleeves."

My BodyGuard laughed. "Yes, ma'am."

I finished off my food and headed for the bathroom, grabbing the stack of clothing Kisah pointed out by the doorway as I passed.

Unwrapping the bloodstained bandage from my leg, I studied the shallow furrow in my calf. It was already healing. Besides putting a new dressing on it, I doubted there was much more Henna could do for me that my own augmented systems weren't already doing.

I splashed water on my face, drying it off with the coarse towel, and bent over to run my fingers through the tangles of my curls. Cutting it would be the best option, but I couldn't bring myself to do it, even now when it was most practical. So instead I wove it into a loose braid.

Portis had loved my hair in all its ridiculous glory.

Stripping out of my blood-dappled clothing, I pulled on the clothes my Guards had gathered earlier. The pants were a little short, so I tucked them into my boots. Thankfully my new shirt fit. It was probably from Henna, judging by the strange, brightly colored characters cavorting across the front of it.

Kisha and Caterina were gone when I came back out into our quarters, but Indula waited in the hallway and he gave me a short bow.

"Ma'am."

"The shirt suits you," I said of his sleeveless green top, and he grinned in reply.

"Matriarch Saito said the same thing. She said it brightened my eyes. Whatever that means." He rolled his eyes. "It's clean and nonreflective. That's about all I need."

"How's Emmory?"

"He's better, ma'am. Awake and out of danger."

"None of us are out of danger."

"True." He shrugged and waved me through the door of the medical bay.

The conversation stopped as we came in the room, followed by a wave of "Your Majesty" and genuflections.

I rolled my eyes. "Can we table the pomp until later?"

"No, Majesty," Emmory said. "It's even more important to show respect to you now. You are the rightful Empress of Indrana."

"You look awful."

Emmory grinned because we both knew he was right and I was only changing the subject because I didn't have a good argument for him.

He did look awful though, propped up in the bed with a heavy layer of surgical heal-tape wrapped across his chest. The dark skin under his eyes was bruised to blue-black, and I noticed his left arm was close to his side.

The sound of Zin's keening in the cargo bay came back to life in my head and I crossed the room, wrapping my arms around my surprised *Ekam*.

"Don't ever do that to us again, do you hear me?"

# 22

Emmory patted me awkwardly on the back with his right hand. "Yes, Majesty," he lied.

I pulled away, wiping the tears from my eyes with the back of my hand. "Did Cas get you all caught up?" I asked once I trusted my voice again.

"He did, including how cooperative you've been."

"I think he's just mad because I didn't invite him to drink with Hao. We're headed to Shanghai Port, by the way. I need to meet with Po-Sin."

If anyone in the room had reservations about my announcement, they were waiting for Emmory before they expressed them. My *Ekam* studied me for a long moment and then surprised me with a nod.

"May I ask why, Majesty?"

"Hao kind of has to take us there or end up dead," I said with a grin and a shrug. "Po-Sin put a price on my head when he heard the news about who I was. I was planning on going to him anyway. We need help and he owes me a favor. If you've got a better plan I'd love to hear it, because right now this is all

I've got." I looked around the room. "I was supposed to meet with a GIS agent who was bringing Canafey's governor to me. She has the lock codes for the *Vajrayana* ships. We get those and we stand a fighting chance against whatever Phanin and the Saxons can bring to bear.

"Alice, Caspel, and Taz are heading up the resistance at home, but they'll need help. We need Po-Sin's network and permission to travel in his space. We need Hao's continued help, which he won't give without approval from his boss. And right now what we need most is time."

"Which we don't have." Emmory nodded, grimacing and resting his head back on the pillows.

"Everyone out," I ordered, and the others complied without comment. "We'll manage, Emmory." I put my hand on his.

He opened his eyes and smiled. "I trust you, Majesty. You're in your element. I told Cas to try to roll with the punches out there and not to interfere unless you were in actual danger."

I laughed, squeezing his hand. "You get better. I don't want to have to take my throne back without you."

"Yes, ma'am."

I turned to leave, but Emmory caught my arm before I could go. "Majesty, they say you shot the king."

"I did."

"Hail." His rare use of my name was filled with exasperation.

"He shot *you*," I said, waving a hand in the air. "So he's lucky I didn't kill him. I only shot him in the knee. He can be grateful I didn't aim higher."

Emmory chuckled, grimaced again at the pain, and let me go so he could press his hand to his chest. "Be careful with Po-Sin, Majesty. Don't trust him."

"I never have."

*  *  *

We weren't more than a few hours from Shanghai Port when we dropped out of the warp bubble back into normal space. I'd used my time on the ship to formulate several plans.

The first involved meeting Po-Sin at a rather seedy—even for this port—restaurant in H Section. If Po-Sin didn't agree to my terms, I'd have to move on to plan B.

Which was really going to piss off my Guards, and probably the enforcers at Shanghai, because the body count for plan B was a little high.

We disembarked the *Pentacost*, Dailun having removed the fake registry before we reached the port, with Hao in the lead and Dailun on his heels. Cas was at my side; Zin and Gita followed behind. I'd ordered everyone else to stay on board. Alba was up and moving around, but Fasé was still catatonic and sleep for Emmory was the best thing possible.

I spotted Nez as soon as I walked into Hotei's Cup. The runner for Po-Sin was tucked into the back corner watching everything with his beady black eyes.

I crossed the room in just a few strides, sacrificing stealth for expediency, and grabbed Nez by the upper arm before he could bolt.

"Don't run off." I hooked a chair with my foot, spinning it around. Dropping into it, I jerked him back into his own seat with enough force to rattle the empty glass on the table. "My friends don't like surprises, Nez. I'd keep both hands on the table and try not to twitch."

Cas cleared his throat. I took my eyes—but not my hand—off Nez, glancing up and around the bar.

"Mind your own business," I snapped, and everyone went back to what they were doing. I didn't miss the way the bartender's hand slid under the bar. "Zin, keep an eye on the door. We'll have company soon."

Nez had recovered from his shock some and beamed a smile at me through the greasy strands of black hair hanging in his thin face. "Cressen Stone, it's so great to see you!"

I tightened my hand on his arm until he winced in pain. "Drop the cheer, Nez. The whole fucking universe knows who I am by now. You're an idiot with poor personal hygiene, but you're not that stupid. I need to talk to Po-Sin."

I saw Hao tense out of the corner of my eye, and then the voice echoed through the bar.

"You could have just called, my dear."

Po-Sin stood silhouetted in the doorway—a tiny man flanked by his guards, two Amazon-sized women who were taller than Emmory. I let Nez go and he scrambled for the dubious safety of his boss.

I rose slowly to my feet, folded my hands together, and bowed while keeping my eyes locked on this powerful Cheng lord. "Forgive me for not allowing you enough time to plan a proper party, Grandfather. You look very well."

Po-Sin laughed, the sound surprisingly hearty for a man of his age. "You look even better. Being empress obviously agrees with you."

"I've come to collect a bounty."

Po-Sin raised one eyebrow and shook his head. "Sit down, Your Majesty. Tell your dogs to relax a bit, and we will talk."

"Back atcha," I countered, but I sank back into my chair and shot Cas a look.

He nodded imperceptibly and moved until he was at my right shoulder. Zin and Gita took their cue from him, keeping their hands well away from their weapons.

Po-Sin sat in the chair Nez had vacated, taking a moment to shake out his intricately embroidered robe so that it fell in graceful folds around his ankles. "Tea, Lily."

I swallowed back my laughter as one of the gigantic women headed for the bar. Po-Sin had a strange habit of renaming his bodyguards for flowers.

"What happened to Rose?" I asked.

"Killed by a clumsy assassin Fang sent after me."

"I'm sorry to hear that."

A smile quivered beneath Po-Sin's long beard. "You broke her nose once because she looked at you for too long."

"True." I wiggled a hand. "Fang's a waste of air though, and no one deserves to die from a clumsy attempt."

"Better her than me," Po-Sin replied, effortlessly reminding me that even though he looked like someone's gentle grandfather, he was a stone-cold killer.

Which meant I needed to cut to the chase. We were running out of time.

"You owe me a favor," I said.

"I owed a gunrunner named Cressen Stone a favor. I don't do business with governments."

I'd expected the reply; still a surge of disappointment filled me. Nothing about this was apparently going to be easy.

"Bugger me." My gun cleared its holster before I finished my sigh. Cas was a split second behind me on the draw, moving with a speed that would make Emmory proud.

There was a crash of porcelain on the floor as Lily dropped the tea and scrambled for her own weapon. Her counterpart had already drawn, as had several others in the bar.

Hao just dropped his head into his hand.

The rest of the patrons headed for the exit as if the room were filled with Hefistan Plague.

217

"Twice I've had your life in my hands. I gave it back to you once," I said. "Give me a reason to do it a second time."

Po-Sin wouldn't be the most feared Cheng gangster if the sight of a pissed-off woman with a gun could bring him to tears. He smiled at me, a slow, deadly thing that would have scared me if I'd had anything left to lose.

"Ah, there she is. My deepest apologies, Cressen. I did not recognize you at first. Of course I will honor my debt to you. What is it you need?"

"Permission to move through your territories unhindered. Allow Hao to take us from Shanghai to Guizhou and to continue with us if he so chooses. Protection from any Saxon Shock Corps or other mercenaries who may be hunting us. Medical care for my people free of charge and a promise of no less than ten of your best fighting vessels should I ask for them. Pay Hao for the bounty on my head and consider it done. And finally, no hard feelings for this little incident here."

Po-Sin studied me. "You ask a lot."

I bowed in my seat, keeping my eyes on his and my gun where it was. "Your life is worth much, Grandfather."

His mouth twitched and I knew I had him. Po-Sin should have known better than to negotiate with me out in the open like this where anyone could hear. If he refused, he rejected the honor I'd done by naming a price equal to his stature.

"All right, Your Majesty," Po-Sin agreed. "I will give you all you ask for. Any damage to my ships and crew will be paid for by you, and I will only provide free medical care for any injuries received thus far. Safe passage is guaranteed. There are no hard feelings and Hao gets the bounty. Does that satisfy my debt to you?"

"It does."

"Good." Po-Sin's eyes were black stones in his weathered

face. "Then I will suggest that the next time you point a gun at me, my dear, you pull the fucking trigger."

"Duly noted." I put my gun away with a smile.

"Now we'll eat something."

I didn't look back at Cas as a growl issued from behind me. "That would be lovely. Forgive my BodyGuards though, they're not accustomed to protocols out here. My *Dve* will mean no insult when he asks to scan my food."

"Perhaps you should explain it to him." Po-Sin was back to his grandfatherly smile. "Then he won't have to."

It wasn't a request, but this also wasn't a conversation I wanted Po-Sin overhearing. I gave him a little nod, got up out of my seat, and dragged Cas a few feet away.

"This is unwise."

"It's a test," I replied in an equally low voice. "He wouldn't dare poison me after publicly declaring us even. If I don't eat, or if you so much as shift a hand in the direction of the food, he'll take it as sign I don't trust him. All deals will be off. You hear me? Even our safe passage."

"I can't let you do this. Emmory would—"

"Want you to trust me. He said as much, didn't he? I know what I'm doing. I did business with these people for years and I know the rules that hold sway here. Damn it, Cas. Emmory trusts me, why can't you?"

It was a slap, petty and uncalled-for. I knew it as soon as the words left my mouth, but it was too late to call them back. Cas's face went blank.

"Fine, Majesty. Whatever you think is best."

It was the words I wanted, delivered in a tone that ripped my heart to shreds. I opened my mouth to say something, anything that might back us away from this, but no words came. So I closed my mouth, nodded, and headed back to the table.

Po-Sin watched us with a speculative gleam in his eyes, but I ignored him and grabbed the chopsticks from the hand of the server who approached the table.

It was obvious someone else's order had been co-opted for our dining pleasure. There was no other way the table could have been filled in the short time I was away.

We ate in silence. The food was delicious. And I'd learned a long time ago to enjoy a meal whenever I could.

"I used to regret my nephew stole you and that you'd never agree to work for me directly," Po-Sin said, patting at his mouth with a napkin. "Now I think it might have been for the best, my dear. Such trouble it would have caused."

I stood when he did, straightened my shoulders, and met Po-Sin's smile with one of my own. "You have no idea, Grandfather."

"May this agreement be profitable for us both. You have a hard fight ahead of you, Your Majesty. I hope you win." He smiled at me and gave a little bow I barely remembered to return before he headed for the door.

Dailun bowed low to Po-Sin and spoke a few hurried words that made both Hao and Po-Sin look back at me.

"Majesty, what did you do?" Zin muttered.

"Nothing." I hadn't said a single word to the pretty, cold-eyed pilot the whole time we were on board.

Whatever it was that they decided seemed to please Dailun at least, though Hao looked annoyed and Po-Sin actually seemed concerned. He glanced my way once more, nodded, and left the restaurant.

"That went better than I expected."

Hao grunted. "Go back to the ship. I need to get some supplies. We'll be on our way in an hour."

# 23

Guizhou was too close to waste energy on a warp bubble, even if it did mean a ninety-five-hour trip through space. It gave Emmory more time to heal, and at night while Zin was sleeping I helped Emmory walk around the ship.

Dailun watched from his seat as one night Emmory struggled up the stairs to the bridge. Hao's pilot had short, spiky hair that was dyed a brilliant pink. It shouldn't have worked, but somehow on him it did. If nothing else it said more clearly than words that he was a mean snake; otherwise he'd have ended up as some gangster's boy toy a long time ago.

"Do you mind if I use the com?" I asked after getting Emmory settled in a nearby chair.

"Go ahead." He hadn't said anything to me since that strange moment at Shanghai.

"You can stay." I waved him back down when he pushed out of his seat. Taking the chair next to him, I sent a message to Caspel.

"It's good to see your face, ma'am."

"Yours, too. The patch suits you. You found a Farian?"

Caspel's laugh was rusty. "Bina Neem is with the ITS. My

eye was too badly damaged to save, but she fixed the rest of it up quite nicely. I spoke with Admiral Hassan, ma'am. I'll send you encrypted contact information so you can speak with her directly."

"How are you all holding up?"

Caspel's smile was brief. "We're holding, ma'am. The generals have rallied what troops they can in your name. It'll be enough to take back the capital once we have air support."

"We're doing what we can." I nodded. "Have you heard from your operative? Were they on Red Cliff?"

"I haven't, ma'am." He frowned. "I don't know where they are."

That wasn't the news I wanted to hear. "We need to find them, Caspel."

"I know, Majesty. We'll work on it." Caspel rubbed his stubbled chin. "The 2nd Fleet arrived yesterday, ma'am. Phanin somehow secured the three *Vajrayana* ships, and Admiral Hassan ordered Home Fleet to abandon their posts when the initial attack happened and rendezvous with her. We thought it was better to regroup and come at them once we are at full strength."

I nodded. As much as I disliked the idea of leaving Pashati in the hands of Admiral Shul and Phanin, Caspel and Admiral Hassan were right. Every ship lost was one we wouldn't have in the end. And as powerful as those *Vajrayana* ships were, Phanin could easily handle anything we threw at him unless we got the other ships from Canafey.

"Majesty, where are you headed next?"

"We'll meet up with Admiral Hassan shortly," I replied, deliberately not answering the question. "We'll speak again soon."

"Yes, ma'am."

I disconnected and shared a look with Emmory before turning to Dailun. "So, is someone going to fill me in on that conversation in the restaurant?"

It was risky asking that question with only Emmory here. But Cas was nearby if I needed him, and Gita was keeping Hao busy so I could have this uninterrupted time with Dailun.

The young man hesitated. "It was something personal."

I crossed my arms, leaned back in my chair, and waited.

Dailun tried to outlast me, but up to this point only Emmory had ever managed it. The muttered curse in Cheng from the pilot made me grin.

"You are a patient one."

"When it suits me."

"I was not prepared to speak with you about this yet, but I also cannot lie to you. I asked my great-grandfather and Hao for permission to leave the clan."

I managed, barely, to keep my eyebrow from going any higher. Po-Sin had allowed one of his great-grandchildren to ride with Hao at such a young age?

Emmory hadn't moved and was still stretched out in the navigator's seat along the opposite wall. I knew he'd heard Dailun's comment. Moreover, he'd understood it since his Cheng was at least as good as mine was.

Dailun turned in his chair, pushed up the sleeves of his black shirt, and extended his arms toward me in a graceful, almost feminine gesture. The two lines of black calligraphy flared with light.

Now I could see, clear as day, the marks of Po-Sin's clan. But there was more than that.

"Svatir," I breathed. That explained why Po-Sin had allowed someone so young to ride with Hao. Dailun carried with him the knowledge of his race. Chronologically he was barely out of his teens, but he had lifetimes stored in his skull.

Emmory was up and out of his seat in an instant. I surged to my feet and caught him by the upper arm before he fell.

"First off, you're not in any shape to be moving like that. Second, just watch."

The light grew brighter, silver coating the black until Dailun's arms glowed. The air around us crackled with electricity. I could taste the ozone on my tongue.

"Majesty—" Emmory's voice was tight.

"It's all right, Emmory." I couldn't quite keep the awe out of my voice at what we were seeing.

The silver crawled up Dailun's arms, disappearing momentarily beneath his shirtsleeves before it appeared again on the skin of his neck. Dailun closed his eyes and shuddered delicately, and when he opened them again his black eyes were chased with silver—like the stars in the night sky.

Releasing the breath I'd been holding, I walked Emmory back to his seat before I spoke. *"Ah hala-locvaria."*

It was a Svatir blessing that roughly translated meant—*congratulations.*

"My mother was Svatir." Dailun's voice echoed a little with his transformation into what the Svatir considered adulthood. "Her dreaming came early and my translation was pushed back to my eighteenth year because of the mourning time." He held up his arms, now bare of any mark that claimed him as part of Po-Sin's family.

"Great-Grandfather has given me permission for the Traveling. I would now ask permission to travel with you for this journey." He dropped his head to wait for an answer, and I was glad for it because my chin had just fallen all the way to the floor.

"The Traveling?" Emmory hissed the question at me in the Old Tongue, a language Dailun would be unlikely to know.

"*Lu Xing*," I replied with a little shrug. "A rite of passage among those who are both Cheng and Svatir. Po-Sin has given his blessing for Dailun to separate from the family. He travels a different road than the one traditionally ascribed to him. If he finds something else he'd rather be doing, he's free to spend his life that way. If he chooses to return to the fold, he'll be welcomed with open arms." I blew out a breath and shoved both hands into my hair. "This is heavy-duty shit, Emmory."

"Can we trust him?"

"Yes," I replied, without hesitation. "He'd bring dishonor not only onto himself but the whole of his Svatir family and Cheng clan if he went into this with anything other than the purest of intentions. If he screwed me over, Po-Sin would come after him with a vengeance." A shudder crawled up my spine. "I don't even want to think what his other family would do to him."

"Do you have to say yes to him?"

"No," I admitted with a second shrug. "But I do think—"

"That we should take him with us." A brief smile flickered over Emmory's face at the shock that must have shown on mine. "I do trust your instincts, Majesty, despite questioning your methods on occasion."

Dailun was still standing with his head bowed, waiting patiently for a response.

There were a number of benefits to taking this kid on. If I said yes, the bond between us would be sacred. He'd pledge his oath to me with the same bone-deep loyalty as Emmory, and he'd be honor-bound to notify me when he chose to change the path of his travels.

We could use a pilot when we got to Guizhou. I could fly my ship, but it would be easier to have someone else do it. From what I'd seen so far, this kid was good—damn good.

It also wasn't going to hurt to add one more person I could trust onto my side of this game. Even if it meant Hao was going to kill me for stealing his pilot.

I put my hand on the back of his head. His hair was softer than I expected and my fingers sank down to his skull. The pink made my skin seem darker. Flexing my hand slightly, I sent a silent prayer upward that I wasn't messing this up.

I'd seen a *Lu Xing* ceremony only once before, but the words had stuck with me in their beautiful simplicity. Dailun seemed to trust I'd know the ritual, and I dragged in a deep breath.

"It is no small matter to walk the stars alone. Come, Seeker. Come and take my hand. I will walk with you."

Dailun didn't move a muscle, but I felt the tension bleed out of him in the space between one heartbeat and the next.

"Thank you, Sister, for taking this journey with me. Gladly would I have walked alone, more glad am I that I am allowed to walk in your glory."

I couldn't help myself and snorted with laughter. "I don't know about glory, but things will probably get pretty crazy around here."

Dailun's eyes sparkled with a mirth that surprised me when he lifted his head. "It will be a most worthy trip."

I choked back my laughter and gave him a little shove toward his seat. "Why don't you get us to Guizhou? I probably need to go apologize to Hao for stealing his pilot."

"*Hai, jiejie.* My cousin will forgive you, I am sure."

My laughter faded some when he returned to his seat and the enormity of what I'd done slammed into me. I'd just taken an eighteen-year-old Svatir-Cheng under my protection. The great-grandson of the most feared Cheng gang lord. A boy who'd probably killed more people in his short life than Emmory had in his whole career.

"Regrets?"

"Ten million," I replied without looking at Emmory. "This isn't one of them."

It was actually the truth.

We landed in Guizhou with no trouble and Hao took the news about Dailun with a shrug and a salute that bordered on rudeness on at least sixty different worlds. Otherwise, he was surprisingly sanguine about it, which troubled me.

Even with his bare arms proclaiming his separation from his families, Dailun was well liked in this outback station. We hired a shuttle pilot he promised I could trust—a mute girl named Shi who communicated in sign language—and were on our way within an hour of landing.

Guizhou was a barren planet, prone to vicious lightning storms, unexpected downpours, and long dry periods where the howling winds could rip meat off bone. The landscape was scarred with great plateaus and rabbit-warren canyons carved out by rivers that ran fast and high during the wet season but trickled down to almost nothing in the dry. There was little water above the canyons and even less vegetation.

Other than the people clustered around the station and a strange indigenous creature that some twisted person had named a Harvey, there was little life on the planet.

The Harveys looked like a disturbing cross between an Earth rabbit and the spiders from Jupiter IV.

For once the universe cut everyone a break and hadn't made these meter-across monsters carnivorous like the Jupiter spiders. Instead they were timid creatures that preferred to avoid any contact with the humans who did venture away from the station.

Of course, most people erred on the side of caution and

avoided wandering this far from civilization. It was one of the major reasons the ready-made cavern I'd won had been built here. Portis and I had both agreed this was the perfect spot for an emergency stash.

Memories slammed into me as the shuttle sped through the air and the brown rocks blurred beneath us. I dug my fingers into the seat under me and fought back against the past.

I didn't want to see Portis's laughing face. Didn't want to remember sneaking out here in the middle of the night. Didn't want to relive how he'd laid me down under triple full moons and made love to me.

All of that was gone and I wasn't ever getting it back.

I was tense and snappish by the time we touched down at the coordinates I'd given Dailun. The sun was high in the hazy purple sky and I shaded my eyes with one hand as I disembarked.

Everyone but Cas, Zin, and Dailun had stayed on board Hao's ship—despite Gita's protests and Emmory's disapproving looks. Emmory was in no shape to make the trip and Gita didn't know how to climb. Plus, I didn't need an audience for the trip down to my stash. It was bad enough that Hao knew what planet it was on.

Cas was a silent shadow at my back. He hadn't said much the past few hours, but the silence between us seemed to have settled back into some kind of comfortable rhythm after my fuckup in the restaurant.

There were conflicting reports about what had happened on Red Cliff, who was alive, and who was to blame.

The empire was worse. Phanin had been broadcasting all the way back to Pashati, and breaking some speed records to get home so fast. All the imperial stations were on lockdown, but Taz seemed to have a handle on the PR side of things and several *Upjas* stations were going full-tilt to contradict Phanin's claims.

"*Jiejie*, should I tell Shi to head back to port?" Dailun stayed well back as he asked the question. Emmory had apparently had a brief one-sided discussion with him before we left about trust and how close he was allowed to get to me.

"Just a moment," I murmured in reply. I closed my eyes to the sun and reached out with my *smati*.

"*Password, Captain?*" The computer's voice was as dry as the landscape around us. I responded with the complicated 218-digit code.

"*Verified. Your* smati *has been altered, Captain.*"

I breathed a grateful prayer for my last-second paranoia. "Yes, pursuant to Backup Plan IF. My *smati* was reconnected to the imperial network."

"*So noted. Please enter appropriate codes at entrance.*"

I nodded in reflex. The computer wasn't expecting a reply anyway, and it couldn't see me from where we were standing. Rolling my shoulders under the weight of my pack, I turned my back on the sun before opening my eyes again. "We're in business. Dailun, send your friend back with my thanks."

He bowed his head slightly and the ramp to the shuttle retracted. A few moments later, the four of us were alone on the windswept canyon edge.

"We go down," I said, and started down the steep path into the canyon. I heard Cas's hissed protest, but I was already out of his reach, and any interference on his part would have dislodged my grip. I was grateful for his impulse control. It was a hundred-meter tumble to the hard canyon floor if I lost my footing.

"Fan out and watch your step," he snapped at the others, and then I felt the impact of his feet ripple through the ground as he took off after me and allowed myself a grin.

The earth under my hands grew redder, coating my skin with a dull film as I worked my way down.

Memories continued to batter at me as I climbed, wearing down my resistance and the wall around my chaotic emotions. Thankfully I was far enough ahead of the others that my annoyed exhale as I shoved my thoughts aside went unheard.

Zin caught up with me when we reached the first plateau. I ducked under an outcropping that offered up meager shade and unstrapped my pack to get at my water.

"A little warning would have been nice," Zin said, settling down next to me. "Cas is wound tight enough to snap. How far do we have to go?"

"A ways." I shrugged and gestured vaguely with my bottle.

"Where's the route?" Zin asked.

"Down there." I grinned and pointed into the blackness over the side. "Come on, we've got to hurry. I'm not doing this trek in the dark, it's too dangerous."

Our descent to the plateau had taken more than three hours by my clock and the sun was already kissing the upper edge of the canyon wall. In another three standard hours it would be pitch-black in the canyon.

"Majesty, let me—"

"I know the way," I said, sliding over the edge before Cas could grab hold of me.

I dropped two meters, landing lightly on the balls of my feet, and blinked until my eyes adjusted to the sudden dimness.

"Just drop down," I called back up to the others, moving out of the way so they didn't land on me.

"Majesty, will you please—"

"I am not being deliberately difficult, I promise, Cas. Trying to describe the trail to someone else is impossible. I can walk the damn thing in my sleep. It's best if I go first."

I grabbed for the rocks to my right and swung out onto them, feeling the familiar little jolt in my stomach as I hung for just a moment over empty air. Then my feet found their purchase and I started working my way downward, trusting that the others could follow without instruction.

The change in terrain was almost instantaneous. The dust that plagued us aboveground was dampened by the moisture in the air. There were trees down here: scrubby, bushlike things that rose a few meters off the ground.

We climbed downward in silence for well over an hour, continuing a slow, even pace down a rocky trail that more often than not required clinging to rocks over open air.

It was quiet. The eerie echoing calls of the Harveys bounced back to us along the canyon walls, and the softer shushing of runoff still making its way underground layered itself over my breathing. Once we hit the main canyon, all that would change and the roar of the Guizhou River would drown out the sounds of everything else.

"We must have just missed the rains." I kept my voice low, but it still seemed unnaturally loud in the stillness. "I don't know if the lower path will be accessible or not." I swung my legs out over the edge of the cliff and boosted down onto the ledge below. The stillness and the climbing had eased my tension to the point where I felt almost giddy, almost back to my old self.

"Majesty, I have a rope." Zin started forward. "This would be easier—"

"There's no point in messing with it, a rope will just complicate things. I know what I'm doing." I grinned up at him just as the ledge came loose beneath me.

# 24

H ail!"

My grin vanished, replaced by panic. I grabbed at the rock face in a desperate search for handholds. There was a sharp stab of pain in my left hand as my nail ripped free and my swearing mingled with Zin's frantic curses.

I found a grip but it was precarious and left me stretched too far for a second move. The thirty-meter drop below wouldn't leave enough of me for a funeral.

Bugger me. It wouldn't hurt for more than a second, but I was going to make a mess when I hit. After all this, I was going to die on a gods-forsaken pile of Cheng rock betrayed by my own confidence.

"Hail, hang on."

I honestly wasn't sure what else Zin expected me to do, or for that matter, how long I could do it. Blood from my injured finger was eroding my grip by the second.

I jerked when Dailun's arm closed around my waist and I had to choke down a relieved sob.

"I've got you, Sister," he murmured in my ear. "It's all right."

I dragged in a breath, somehow managing to convince my

hands to let go of the rocks I'd been clinging to and grab onto Zin instead as Dailun supported me with a strength that was surprising.

Zin lowered us the rest of the way down, rappelling smoothly past jagged rock and the grasping limbs of trees growing out of the rock as Cas held the rope like an anchor.

We dropped to the canyon floor, where I barely resisted the urge to put my face in the dirt and kiss the ground. Here the dusty red gave way to green as life flourished out of the brutal sun and winds, soaking up all the moisture of the rains with greedy efficiency. Several Harveys scuttled back into their holes at our arrival.

I let go of Zin and stuck my throbbing index finger into my mouth. There was almost as much iron in the dirt as in my blood, and I turned my head to the side to spit it out.

"Are you trying to get yourself killed?" Zin grabbed me before I could move away, and I gasped when he pinned me back against the rocks.

"What?" I shoved at him, but he didn't budge.

He stuck his face too close to mine. He was angry. Really angry. My heart stuttered to a halt for a beat before it started again. I'd never seen this side of my normally calm and collected BodyGuard. Whatever iron-fisted control Zin had was slipping at an alarming rate.

"Do you want to die?"

I thought about taking a swing at him, decided against it, and exhaled a shuddering breath. "Zin, I—"

"Answer the question, Hail. Because I'm not going to let Cas and the others throw their lives away if you have a death wish. If you want to die there's nothing we can do to stop you and I'll be damned before I go through that again."

Shock again, this time at his casual use of my name three

times in as many minutes. Then the rest of it filtered into my head.

"You think I have a death wish?" The question came out a choked whisper, and the tears that followed were part grief, part hysterical laughter. "Half my empire is gunning for my head. I've made more enemies among the ass-side of society than I know what to do with, and you can bet Phanin will put *that* to good use if he has any sense. I don't need a death wish, Zin. I have a fucking WANTED notice tattooed on my forehead! Let me go." I shoved at him again, but he wasn't in the mood to let me get away.

"You can't keep doing this," he snarled. "People's lives are at stake. Your life. Emm—"

"I never asked for this! Shiva, Zin! Haven't you figured out that I'm not a pampered princess? I can take care of myself."

"I know you can. The question I'm asking is—do you want to?" He grabbed me by the shoulders, jerking me onto my toes. "I get that you never asked for this. I was there, remember? But you stayed and you promised. Are you going back on that? Because ever since Red Cliff you've done nothing but walk into situations like you're invincible. This recklessness has to stop. You keep waltzing into danger without waiting for us to go first and you're going to get killed.

"You're not a gunrunner anymore, Hail. You're the Empress of Indrana."

"I know very well what I am. The last woman standing." My voice shook, but I straightened my spine and stared him in the eye. "There's no one left but me. If I go down I leave Alice and all the rest of you to die. You think I'm so idiotic and reckless I don't feel the weight of that?"

I poked him in the chest, forcing him back a step. "I'm it, Zin. I don't have the luxury of rolling over and dying just because I lost everything I've *ever* cared about." He winced, but I refused to feel bad for the sharpness of my words. "I get to keep going. So guess what. I'm going to do it on my terms."

"Hail—"

"You're the one who said to me I could be both empress and gunrunner. Emmory trusts me, but the rest of you—" I spread my arms wide, looking at Cas over his shoulder. "It's like you think I'm no longer capable just because I put a fucking crown on my head. The weight of which did not scramble my brains, thank you very much."

The emotions still swirling through me demanded some kind of recognition, but I couldn't find the words for it. I couldn't find the words to express just how much it meant that Emmory had put his trust in me but everyone else seemed to think I was being reckless.

Zin opened his mouth to say something, but all that came out was a breath of air. His shoulders dropped fractionally and he nodded. "*Uie Maa*. You're right. I'm sorry. I am—we are all worried about you." His anger had dissolved and the concern in his voice settled into the cracks in my defenses, freezing and breaking them apart.

Cas looked wounded. "Majesty, I—"

"Don't." I pushed by Zin, grabbed my pack and started forward, then stopped abruptly and sighed. "I'm sorry, too." I was glad that the only other witnesses to this were the few Harveys poking their heads out of the trees.

"For what?"

"This." I waved a hand upward at the rocks. "I swear I wasn't trying to get myself killed. I just—it was easier for me to go first. I wasn't thinking. I'm back in a place I feel comfortable. I'm sorry to make things more difficult for you. I really don't mean to do it."

Zin looked ashamed; Cas shifted uncomfortably. Dailun watched us with an almost refreshing lack of concern for the drama playing out in front of him.

"Majesty." Cas went down on a knee and Zin followed him. "You are the shining stars in the blackness of space. The hope of the lost and forsaken. The spark that must not be extinguished. We are ever loyal to you."

I shared a resigned look with Dailun; the young pilot raised an eyebrow at me but he didn't say a word. I dropped my pack and pulled my BodyGuards into a hug, pressing my cheek first to Zin's and then to Cas's. "You are all the family I have left; I swear to you I will never thoughtlessly throw that away."

Their arms tightened around me and we sat that way for a few seconds before Dailun cleared his throat.

"Sister, we really should get moving."

I released my BodyGuards and wiped the tears from my face with the heels of my hands. "Are we good?" I asked, getting to my feet.

"Yes, ma'am," they both replied.

I picked up my pack and headed up the damp creek bed that would take us to the main canyon.

Dark shadows were crawling down the walls by the time we reached the mouth of the main canyon. The light retreated, leaving the damp walls an ominous shade of blood-red.

The roar of the river was so loud I could scarcely hear my own heartbeat, let alone Cas's shouted question.

Holding up a hand, I mouthed, *One minute*, then considered my options as I studied the reddish water rushing by less than five meters below us.

Our timing couldn't have been worse. It was the tail end of the rainy season and the Guizhou was still swollen, which meant the easier path to the cavern was underwater and would stay that way for at least another week.

We didn't have a week to waste.

I muttered a curse, looked over at Cas, and jerked my head back the way we'd come. He followed without question, mostly because asking me anything would have been a waste of time.

We cleared the bend and the noise level dropped, blocked out by the jutting rock and screen of trees clustered in the mouth of the side canyon.

"The lower path is blocked. I was afraid it might be, because of the rains, but I was hoping we'd get lucky and the river would still be low." I shoved my hand into my hair, wincing at the reminder of my injured finger. I leaned over and stuck my hand under a trickle of clear water. The blood stained the water, and I bit down on the inside of my cheek trying to keep the tears at bay.

"Take a seat," Zin said, slipping out of his pack. "I've got a medical kit."

I took off my own bag and dropped down onto it. "There's another route to the cavern, but it's dangerous enough in the daylight."

"So we'll camp here tonight," Cas said.

Zin crouched beside me, taking my hand and spraying the wound down with a disinfectant that stung enough to have me swearing.

"Bugger me, that hurts."

He just grinned at me and wrapped a seal-patch over my finger. "That will keep the dirt out. The nail will grow back."

"Yes, we'll camp here tonight. It's safer and there's no point in rushing. The other route will be slick from the rains and will take us the better part of the day to walk."

Zin finished with my hand and returned to his pack to pull out the tent. "You're sure the cavern isn't underwater?"

"The computer is still active, which is a good sign. There's always a chance that something has broken through in the last two years and flooded the chamber, but the entrance will be above water."

"Dailun, help me get some food put together," Cas said.

I tugged a collapsible lamp from my pack, shaking it out and tapping it twice until the glow spread out in a circle around us, chasing back the darkness.

We finished setting up camp and ate a tasteless meal. I realized my stomach didn't care about my tongue's input and wolfed the food down. Afterward, I rolled myself up in the thermal blanket and, pillowing my head on my pack, fell asleep almost instantly.

I woke out of the dream in a haze of confusion and lay there for a minute staring into the blackness before I figured out where I was.

Before everything came crashing down on me.

"Majesty?"

"I'm all right," I managed to whisper. "Just a dream." I struggled free of my blanket, putting a hand on Zin's shoulder before he could rise. "I'm fine. I need to pee and you're so not coming outside with me for that."

"Majesty."

I started to protest, then sighed as the whole argument we'd just had replayed in my brain. "Fires of Naraka. Fine, come on."

I thought I heard a rumbling chuckle as I stepped over him and out into the night.

It was cool, but easier to see outside the tent. The first of Guizhou's moons was high in the sky and I could see the edge of the second coming up over the rim of the canyon wall. The ghostly outline of Bai Gu—the massive gas giant neighbor—glowed against the dark sky.

I'd thought that sleep would have come hard, but the combination of the climb and the breakneck pace of the last few days had left me unconscious for close to six hours. I found an alcove and Zin thoughtfully stayed closer to the tent with his back turned until I finished.

Tucking my hands up into my sleeves, I wrapped my arms around my waist and picked my way back out to the main canyon through a combination of moonlight and memory. I sank down onto a rock near the edge and watched the faintly glowing water of the Guizhou tumble and swirl below. Zin sat next to me.

"Where's the light coming from?" he asked.

"There is a plant that grows near the river's edge. It soaks up sunlight during the day like a solar panel and then emits that pale blue light at night," I said. "When the rains come the fragile leaves are ripped free and sent spinning at the mercy of the water."

I snorted with suppressed laughter as the memory of a conversation drifted through my head. "Portis said something similar to me once. He'd said we were all just leaves in a river. Fighting the current wasn't just useless, it was impossible."

"That sounds like him."

"He was such a fanciful idiot." I let the tears fall. Zin wrapped an arm around my shoulders and I turned into his embrace. The sob startled me. It was drowned out by the rushing water, but I knew Zin could feel it jolt through my body and his arm tightened.

The dream that had woken me came back in a rush. The last trip out here with Portis had been routine. We'd left the crew in port and taken a shuttle out to the drop-off point. It had been the dry season, so the hike to the cavern was relatively easy.

We'd taken our time. It was a relief to be on land after more than eight months in space with little more than quick dock stops to relieve the boredom.

*"I love you."*

*I laughed and untangled myself from Portis, stretching with a sigh. "I noticed." The sun was warm on my bare skin.*

*He pushed himself up onto an elbow and slid his hands into my hair. "I'm serious, baby."*

*Frowning, I looked up into his green eyes. Worry lurked in their depths, partially hidden by a tenderness Portis only ever showed to me. "Is everything all right?"*

*"I just don't ever want you to doubt this. Doubt us. No matter what happens, promise me that, okay? Promise me you'll remember that I love you."*

*"You're making me nervous." I shifted, but Portis pinned me to the ground.*

*"Please, Cressen."*

*"Okay." I grabbed him by the head and pulled him down for a kiss. "There, I promise," I murmured against his mouth. "Happy?"*

*He sank down onto me, feathering kisses across my cheek and down into the curve of my neck. "Nothing could make me happier."*

Soul-crushing sadness collapsed down on me. There hadn't been time to think. Hadn't been any time to really let the reality settle into my brain. Portis was gone.

"Oh, Shiva. Forgive me." I wasn't sure who I was asking for forgiveness from—the gods or Portis. We sat there in the moonlight, tears spilling down my cheeks as I tried to come to grips with the gaping hole in my heart.

"There's nothing to forgive, Hail," Zin said, his voice cutting through the roar of the water. "Take a moment to grieve him. We're not going anywhere."

"I can't. I'm afraid I'll fall apart." Whatever I'd lost, I had an empire to think about, and falling apart from grief would have to wait. There wasn't time to grieve. Maybe there wouldn't be. Maybe I'd end up dead before this was all over and—

I didn't want to think about it. I didn't want to delve too deeply into the maybes and the possibility that this would end anywhere but with justice.

"I know how you feel." Pained humor rumbled in my ear. "But you gave me time when we didn't have any. Right now we have all the time in the world."

"I wish he were here," I whispered up at the stars. "Can you imagine the trouble we'd all get into?" I wiped the tears from my face with the heel of my hand and blew out a breath, finally feeling like I was ready to face whatever the universe wanted to throw at me since I woke on the floor of *Sophie's* cargo bay.

"It's terrifying to think of, Majesty." Zin helped me to my feet and we navigated back to the tent. Cas and Dailun pretended to be asleep as Zin and I settled back into our blankets.

"There's no point in trying to get an early start," I said, ignoring their ruse. "We'll want the sun up to dry some of the water off the path we have to take."

"Get some more sleep then, Majesty," Cas said. "There's no telling when we'll have another chance like this."

He was right. I reached out, curling my fingers around Zin's as I closed my eyes against the dark and let sleep drag me back down into the abyss.

# 25

I was alone in the tent the next time I woke. Daylight filtered through the fabric and I sat up, stretching my arms out in front of me with a yawn. I felt better, far better than I had in weeks.

Dragging my thermal blanket outside with me, I shook it out and then folded it neatly so I could stuff it back in my pack.

"Good morning." The greeting I called to Zin when he came into view died in my throat. "What?"

"Majesty." There was fury in his eyes and grief rolling off him in waves so strong I felt my own knees give a little.

"What is it?"

"Emmory just messaged me. Phanin has executed the matriarchs in his custody."

It was like a punch to the stomach. One hand flew to my mouth while I fumbled for purchase with the other on the nearby wall of the canyon. "Mother Destroyer. Their daughters?"

Zin shook his head. "Not yet."

"Do you have names?"

"Zellin, Acharya, Waybly, Surakesh, Naidu, and Maxwell."

My aunt, Leena's mother, Matriarch Maxwell. Oh, Shiva. I'd spent my childhood around those women. In some ways they were as much mothers to me as my own had been, and since my return I'd forged a new relationship with most of them.

"What about Leena? Taran?"

"No mention of them, Majesty. Let's hope they're safe."

"Zaran? The Matriarchs Hassan and Prajapati?"

"No word on them either, Majesty. Or if Clara Desai was among those killed, though I expect if she had been it would be in the news."

My anger rose up, burning the grief like a flash fire, and the next words out of my mouth were jagged-edged and sharp as broken glass. "Get packed up, we need to get moving. I'm not letting those monsters sit on my throne for *one second* longer than I must."

"Yes, Majesty."

We broke down the camp in silence, shouldered our packs, and headed toward the main canyon.

The trek was easier than I'd expected. My anger gave me a laserlike focus and I didn't slip once as we picked our way down the treacherous rocks to another side canyon closer to the raging river.

I slowed my pace, smiling in relief at the sight of the rock wall, streaked red by the setting sun, and reached out to the computer with my *smati*.

*"You can drop the camouflage, computer."*

"Holy—" Cas sucked in a surprised breath as the rock face before us wavered and vanished, revealing a pair of wide steel doors that stretched all the way up to the rim of the canyon. "You did not build this."

"Nope," I replied, starting forward again with a grin. "I won it."

"Excuse me?" Zin jerked around to stare at me. "How?"

"It's a very long story." I waved a hand in his direction and then slapped my palm down on the reader set just to the right of the door.

*"Welcome, Captain,"* the computer said, and a side door popped open in the rock to my right. It hadn't questioned my BodyGuards' presence at all, which was interesting.

Lights flipped on as we passed through the door into the cavern. The air was musty and a little damp, but a quick scan of things told me all was intact and dry as it could be. I raised my hands and spun in a little circle, facing the three men with a smile. "Welcome to my hideout."

My words echoed back to me, bouncing off the cavernous walls. I thought I saw a flicker of amusement fly across Zin's face, but he remained silent.

"Weaponry is over there. There's some on the ship but we might as well load what we can."

"Majesty," Cas replied with a quick nod and tapped Dailun on the shoulder. The young pilot dragged his eyes away from the ship and followed him.

I crooked a finger at Zin and headed for a room on the other side of the cavern. In reality it was nothing more than three walls of transparent aluminum set around a hollowed-out space in the cavern wall. Portis had built it when I couldn't set foot in the old, windowless room where the computer and other equipment had been kept. The walls had been too close, too solid, and triggered my claustrophobia so badly the first time I'd entered that the panic had stayed with me for the rest of the day.

I pressed a hand to the panel by the door, and it opened with a quiet *snick*, sliding aside. The air in here wasn't damp, it was dry and sterile-smelling. The rock wall and ceiling had been coated with the same transparent aluminum as the walls, creating a hermetically sealed environment that kept the hardware from dying on us.

The table in the center of the room lit up as the computer came all the way to life. I swiped my hand over it, glancing at the messages that had accumulated in my absence.

Most of them were job offers, and I caught myself reaching out to tap on one when Zin cleared his throat.

I glanced over my shoulder with a sheepish laugh. "Old habits die hard."

"Where did you get all this?"

"Here and there. The ship came with the hideout. I won them from a Xim-born cardplayer whose three-hand poker face wasn't nearly as good as he'd thought." I laughed. "I had a shit hand, too. He was an idiot.

"Portis and I took the little Saxon-made Cuttlefish out for a spin and a complete overhaul not eight standard months before all hell broke loose. Now I know why."

"What was the poker player's name?" Zin asked.

"Tob, maybe, or Bob. I don't remember, honestly." I raised an eyebrow at his frown. "Why do you ask?"

"We'd just like to know. He's a potential nuisance at the least, an enemy at the worst."

I stopped and grinned at him. "Are you keeping a list?" My grin faded when he didn't smile in return. "*Auho!* Seriously?"

"It's our job, Majesty."

"Bet you five credits that weasel is dead in a ditch somewhere, but his name's in the ship's official files as the former owner if you really need it."

A quiet chime dragged my attention back to the screen. Dropping my hand down on the screen froze the messages scrolling across, and I locked eyes on the notification bar at the top.

A new message, coded urgent, had just appeared.

"Are you kidding me?" I hesitated before tapping the message from Bakara Rai. There was a single line of text:

I HAVE A PRESENT FOR YOU, YOUR MAJESTY.

"Majesty, who is that?"

"I—" The ping of an incoming message from Hao cut me off.

*"Little sister, trouble is coming. Saxon ships are requesting permission to land in port."*

"Bugger me. We've got company." I was moving even before Hao finished talking. Swiping a hand over the screen of the table, I set the computer to download all my messages into my *smati* and shuddered a little when it complied. "Zin, we've got to move."

"Emmory just told me."

"Hao," I said out loud so I wouldn't have to repeat myself. "We've got a change of plans. We're not going back to Shanghai. Get out of there and head for Santa Pirata, we'll meet you there."

*"Sha zhu, that is unwise."*

"No time to debate it, go! We'll meet up outside the asteroid belt and I'll explain it all then." I gave Zin a shove. "Go help them finish loading, we have to move." My fingers flew over the tabletop. I transferred money from several accounts into something more accessible while we were on the run. I didn't like doing it, but I also didn't want the Saxons following a money trail back here and finding my hideout.

Zin closed a hand on my upper arm. "Move."

I'd learned a number of things over the past few hours, one of them being you didn't argue with Zin when he used that tone of voice. I did, however, grab a few things as he dragged me out of the room toward the ship.

I trailed a hand over the lettering on the side, letting a grin slip free when the reactive paint shifted to change the ship name to the false registry we'd logged her with. I'd fought with Portis over the name, but now I was glad I'd finally caved to his suggestion.

The result of the massive credit drop before we'd left the ship here was a sleek, well-armed vessel that was safely registered as a transport for a Solarian Conglomerate interest called InJex. The name on the registry, *Sakura*, was slightly more sedate than its real name—*War Bastard*.

Cas and Dailun had finished loading boxes and my new pilot slid into his seat with wide-eyed reverence.

"Try not to get us blown up your first time flying her," I said, and tapped out the code to open the bay doors. "Computer, prepare for departure. Code relock sequence on my authority."

"Pursuant to Plan *IF*?"

"Yes, please. And set the auto-destruct to go if anyone tries to tamper with you or the doors."

"Plan *IF*?" Zin asked, sounding surprisingly calm despite his white-knuckled grip on the instrument panel. "Do I dare ask, Majesty?"

I grinned at him and keyed up my *smati*. "Dailun, did Hao fill you in?"

*"Hai, jiejie."*

"I'm reading three Saxon vessels coming in to land at the port. Hao is probably waiting for them to get on the ground before he takes off." I buckled my belt, pleased when the others did the same without having to be told. "I'm fucked."

"Excuse me?" Zin blinked at me.

"Plan *IF*," I said. "*I-F* stands for *I'm fucked*."

"Because *WAF* just doesn't have the same ring," Cas muttered.

I couldn't stop the laughter that bubbled up out of me. "Precisely. I'm glad you're here, Cas. I don't know what I'd do without you."

"I wish I could say the same, Majesty."

"Spoilsport." But I returned my focus to the screen in front of me, watching the alarms for signs of the Saxon ships in port scanning in our direction. There weren't any, but I wasn't sure if that was a cause for celebration or a reason to worry.

"There goes Hao. They don't seem to be following him."

"We changed the registration tag on the ship in Shanghai," Dailun said, easing us out of the cavern entrance and watching as the doors closed behind us.

A warning bell sounded off to my right and I spat the curse out. "We're tagged. Go." I threw up a smokescreen of another ship registry as the Saxon radar pinged us. It was flimsy, but if they didn't get more than a glance we'd be okay.

Thanks to the fact that the Saxon ships had landed and Dailun's remarkable ability to leave the atmosphere of any planet faster than any pilot I'd ever seen, we made it into warp before the Saxons could get a bead on us again.

I input the coordinates into the computer for the asteroid belt that bordered the XgCD System.

"Sister." Dailun's quiet exhalation wasn't quite a protest, but it was enough to alert Zin, and I resisted the urge to reach over and cuff my newest charge for it. "We should not."

"We're going to Santa Pirata, Dailun."

"What's at Santa Pirata?" Zin asked.

"An old friend's place," I replied with a shrug.

"Bakara Rai is no one's friend."

That time I did cuff Dailun, hitting him just hard enough to make it sting.

He rubbed the back of his head with a stoic shrug. "Only the truth, *jiejie*. I would not see you have dealings with one such as him."

"We need information. He'll have it."

"Who is Bakara Rai?" Cas asked quietly.

I contemplated not answering, but Dailun would probably tell them everything anyway, so it was best if I chose how things were phrased. "He's an associate of mine. One who deals in information. Among other things."

Zin gave Dailun the Look, so perfectly copied from Emmory that I choked, and I swore the kid folded faster than a drunken Parisian with a handful of low cards.

"He is a gangster of the deadliest sort, honorable Body-Guard. An independent contractor. He deals in drugs, goods, people, information—whatever will make him a profit."

"Traitor," I muttered, attaching an endearment on the end so he knew I was joking.

"He hits harder than you, *jiejie*," Dailun replied without apology.

"No, he doesn't. Look," I continued before either Body-Guard could interrupt. "It's not the best of solutions, I'll admit. However I have two very good reasons for my decision. One is that Rai will have information that will be helpful. I'll have to pay him for it, but with him that's a guarantee it will be accurate."

"And two?"

"He said he had a present for me."

# 26

It was almost twenty-four hours in warp to the outer reaches of the galaxy. After I'd watched the footage of the matriarchs' executions, I spent a good chunk of that trying to catch up on my sleep.

The news reports were filled with the breaking story and it hadn't taken me long to find some less reputable sources who'd published the images released from Indrana.

Phanin had held a sham of a trial—in public, no less—implicating the matriarchs in collusion with the Saxons in the death of the empress. It was slick; I had to give him that. There was just enough truth woven into the lies and enough confusion as to what actually had happened to keep the situation from becoming immediately clear to outsiders.

The Saxons were, of course, denying everything. Phanin may have enlisted their aid in the first place, but now he was double-crossing them in a manner that would make a back-alley rat from Southern Amsterdam proud.

None of this had saved the matriarchs. They'd been marched, one after the other, to the front of the throne room, where Wilson had unceremoniously shot each woman in the head.

A few of the women had cried silent tears; the rest were stone-faced as they walked to their deaths. Matriarch Maxwell shouted, "Long live the empress. Long live Indrana!" before they silenced her.

I threw up twice watching it the first time but made myself watch it again. Then I drank myself to sleep. My dreams were chaotic, haunted by the faces of the matriarchs Phanin had killed.

I woke, gasping for air, as Cas cracked open the door of my room.

"Majesty?"

"I'm all right," I croaked, rolling out of the bunk and crawling for the sink in the corner. Cas helped me to my feet, holding me there as I threw up. He reached past me for the faucet.

"There's no water."

"There is, ma'am. We pumped some on board before we left."

"Bless you." I rinsed my mouth out, clinging to the edge of the sink until I was sure my legs would support me again.

"Occasionally I get things right."

"What are you talking about?" I turned, too quickly, and had to close my eyes as the room spun around me. "You're doing fine, Cas."

He helped me to the low bench on the other side of the room. "That's kind of you, Majesty. We both know the truth. I've been a poor replacement for Emmory."

I grabbed his arm and yanked him down. "Listen here. You're doing the best you can. I'm still alive, which means a lot. The fact that I'm feeling belligerent and uncooperative isn't a reflection of your abilities as a BodyGuard."

"Yes, ma'am."

"I'm serious." Taking him by the shoulders, I stared him in

the eye. "You're not Emmory, Caspian. I don't expect you to be. I expect you to be yourself."

He swallowed, nodding at me. "Yes, ma'am."

"Good." I released him with a smile.

"Dailun made some breakfast, ma'am. It's in the galley."

"Maybe later."

"You need to eat." He hauled me to my feet and led me to the door.

I heaved a sigh. "I am already regretting that pep talk."

"I know, ma'am, but thanks anyway."

According to the *War Bastard*'s computer we'd come out of warp an hour ago. In a move that was so close to something I'd have done it made me laugh out loud, Dailun had brought us out almost right on top of the asteroid belt. Most pilots floated from warp about five hours out from Midway. We were less than an hour from the way station.

The stronghold of Bakara Rai was a collection of three planets orbiting a red giant. It was close enough to the outer edges of the Orion-Cygnus Arm and far enough away from Earth that the authorities from the Solarian Conglomerate didn't bother much with Rai.

So long as he kept his piracy to a minimum.

From what I knew of the man he was more than happy to obey, when it suited him. When it didn't there were hundreds, if not thousands, of private contractors in his employ who would go after an SC merchant ship for the right cut of the profits.

Only one of the three planets orbiting the star known as XgCD was habitable. Aptly named Isla de la Vida, the Island of Life, it was used for growing what food the colony couldn't bring in via trade.

Isla de la Muerta was the planet closest to the star, one

that in another few million years would be swallowed by the expanding giant. It was, as the name suggested, uninhabitable, the surface a shifting mass of molten rock.

Santa Pirata floated in the middle—too close to XgCD for life to survive on the surface, but far enough away that the solar radiation couldn't penetrate the surface. It was there, in a vast network of underground cities, that the smuggler king Bakara Rai made his home.

First you had to make it past the asteroid belt surrounding the system. If you had an invitation from Rai it was an easy two-day journey through the heavily guarded artificial corridor.

If you didn't, you had to navigate the belt, a challenge that took longer—provided you didn't get smashed to pieces. Hao and I had both made the run. It was a rite of passage for anyone wanting to do business with Bakara Rai.

I finished my breakfast and cleaned up as best I could. We docked the ship and disembarked into the thriving port.

Dailun closed a hand on my forearm. "This way."

I kept my head down, hair covered by a hood, as we wove through the crowd. Zin and Cas's presence at my back was a welcome comfort. People melted out of our way, but it was hard to say if it was my pilot's easily recognizable hair or the grim-faced men behind me that caused their flight.

Whatever it was, we made it the length of the station and onto the *Pentacost* without incident. Hao was in the cargo bay, talking with Emmory.

"We're leaving your ship here," Hao said by way of greeting.

"Why?"

He laughed. "Because if we take yours, the chances that Rai will just blow us out of the sky are far greater, and if I'm going to die I'd rather it was in my ship."

253

"And if we take yours, Majesty, that cuts down on how many people we can take with us," Emmory said.

"You're not well enough to go with me anyway."

"I'll recover on the way out there. Between Henna's work and my systems, the worst of the damage that Fasé didn't heal is fixed," Emmory said. "The rest will be fine by the time we get there. You're not making the trip without me, Majesty."

"The *War Bastard* is smaller. It'll be easier to get through the asteroid belt. Hao—"

"I'm not going to tell him no, *sha zhu*. That's your job." Hao shook his head, his barely concealed grin making me want to punch him.

I looked at Henna for support. The doctor shrugged, waving a hand in the air. "He's better. Out of danger. He will heal."

"You're not helping."

"I'm coming with you, Majesty, like it or not."

"I don't like it," I hissed, and stomped up the stairs.

"Ma'am." Stasia handed me my old pants, cleaned and repaired along with a bright blue shirt that was blank on the front. She smiled and left me alone in our quarters. I finished changing and was folding my dirty clothes when Emmory came through the door.

He didn't say anything, just leaned against the wall with his arms crossed over his chest.

I mirrored his stance, jutting my chin out and wishing I didn't feel like I was in a standoff with my father.

"Majesty," Emmory said. "My place is at your side, until the end of it. I would go beyond that if I could figure out a way."

"I'm so tired of people dying for me." The façade cracked and the loss of everyone rolled through me. I saw the sympathetic grief surface on Emmory's face.

"I know. I'm sorry."

"He killed them, Emmy." I covered my face with my hands and sank down on the bunk. "How did I misjudge him so terribly? There was no expression on Phanin's face as they fell. Wilson—"

"Majesty." Emmory closed his hands, absent his normal gloves, around my wrists and gently pulled them from my face. "It is not your fault."

"Zin accused me of trying to kill myself. I'm not, I swear. I'm trying to hold it together, Emmory, I just don't know if I can. Everyone around me is dying. I can't keep you all safe. I should be able to keep you safe.

"I was trying to do the right thing. They suckered me into leaving the planet. And Trace? I haven't ever, *ever*, been that naïve about anything. I missed this huge thing right in front of me." I was angry, but not at my *Ekam*. "I left them there alone to die!"

*You almost died and left me here alone.*

I couldn't say the words out loud, but Emmory heard them anyway. Concern softened his face as he knelt in front of me and tugged me off the bunk into his arms. "I'm still here," he murmured, the words soft against my ear as he wrapped his arms around me.

"Why me? Why am I the one everyone is depending on? What fucking fluke of the universe put me, of all people, here?"

His arms tightened just like Zin's had that night in the canyon. "I don't know, Hail, but I'm grateful for it."

"You're crazy, you know that?" I pulled away with a laugh and shoved both hands through my hair.

"I am your *Ekam*, Majesty, it stands to reason." He offered me a hand as he stood up.

"Oh hush."

"Tell me about Bakara Rai."

"He's a dangerous man. Charming, unpredictable. He expects to get his own way, which isn't really surprising for someone running one of the largest smuggling rings in this sector of the galaxy. He's smart enough to stay in Po-Sin's good graces and to keep himself strong enough that Po-Sin isn't quite sure whether he could take him out."

"How much interaction did you have with him? Zin said you called him a friend."

I stared at the ceiling as I tried to figure out the best way to answer the question. "*Friend* is probably overstating it. We ran several jobs for him over the years, spent some time at Santa Pirata. I don't know him all that well. No one does, except maybe Johar."

Emmory arched an eyebrow at me and I shook my head.

"That's all you get, Emmy. Sorry."

"And we need to go see him why?"

"He said he had a present for me." I lifted my hands in the air. "And Rai isn't the sort of man you want to upset by not accepting his hospitality."

The trip through the asteroid belt was predictably tense. It took everything Hao and Dailun had to keep his ship—and us—in one piece during the five-day trip. They switched piloting duties like clockwork—one sleeping while the other flew. I filled in twice, but it was a struggle even for me to keep us from being crushed by the multitude of debris for those brief periods in an unfamiliar ship.

"Greetings, vessel *Pentacost*. You're a long way from home." The young woman at Port Control was pleasant enough with her wide gray eyes and easy smile, but the undercurrent of tension vibrated like a taut string.

"That we are," Dailun replied. He plastered a smile on his

face I was sure was deliberately strained. "My esteemed boss, Cheng Hao, would like to speak with Mr. Rai."

"I'll have someone meet you at G76. Don't disembark until they get there." The screen clicked off before Dailun could say anything in reply.

"We're going to have to move fast," I said, downing my tea in several gulps and wincing as the heat burned into my stomach. "Dai, I want you, Cas, and Hao to go see Rai."

Dailun nodded. *"Hai, jiejie."*

I suppressed the smile that threatened. Dailun's own grandfather was the most feared gang lord in the universe, and yet the disgust in his voice over Rai's profession was obvious.

"Hail, what am I supposed to tell him?" Hao asked.

"Make something up. Emmory, you and Zin are with me. I want everyone else to stay with the ship. We need to move, we'll want to be off the ship before Rai's goons show."

"Majesty."

Emmory was giving me the Look. I blinked at him. "What? Sorry—did you have a plan?"

"As a matter of fact, yes."

I grabbed him by the arm. "Mine's better. Come on."

# 27

Getting off the ship before security got to our dock proved frightfully easy. Emmory, Zin, and I slipped into the darkness on the far side just as four brown-clad men marched through the doors. Hao met them at the foot of the ramp with an innocent smile plastered on his face.

I couldn't hear what he was saying from our hiding place, but the subservient bowing from my new brother and Cas told me enough.

Our subterfuge was holding for the moment.

I tapped Emmory on the shoulder and jerked my head to the left. He frowned but nodded, and I led the way deeper into the shadows.

"This place smells like sulfur and crime," Zin whispered, and I had to choke down a laugh as we headed down an empty corridor.

Emmory punched him in the side. So at least my *Ekam* seemed to be feeling better, even if he wasn't back to a hundred percent.

Security in Rai's underground city was tighter than at the palace at home, but that didn't stop enterprising souls from selling schematics to the highest bidder.

I suspected it was part of Rai's larger plan, because often the schematics were sadly outdated. No one did that much redecorating without a very good reason.

The plans I had, however, were limited to two key areas. The outer ventilation shafts—which wouldn't have changed because they didn't pose any kind of security risk to the facility—and the location of Rai's private offices.

The second plans hadn't been purchased. There was no one stupid enough to cross Rai like that.

I'd drawn them from memory. One visit to Rai's offices followed by a week's stay on Santa Pirata, where I'd walked every single corridor in the place, had given me more than enough information to complete the map.

It was a simple matter to trace the route and follow the most logical course from the outer ventilation shafts to the interior ones and from there to Rai's office.

A simple matter of locking myself in a tube of plasteel barely wide enough for Emmory's shoulders.

"Majesty, we could—"

"I'm okay," I muttered, staring into the darkness of the ventilation shaft and trying not to throw up. "Besides, there's not really another choice." I forced a bright smile. "I'd better go—"

"I'll go first." Emmory cut me off. "Then you, Majesty. Here." He flipped on a light and clipped it to my collar. "Focus on where we need to go."

Emmory's quiet assumption that I could suck it up and do it on my own did more to shove aside my claustrophobia than any amount of coddling Portis would have engaged in. With a sharp nod, I exhaled and crawled into the vent after him. Zin followed us, dragging the cover back into place behind him.

I navigated us through the ventilation shafts with only one wrong turn and a near miss with a total breakdown. Trapped there with the dim light bouncing off the walls, I'd clutched at Emmory's ankle and fought with the hysteria clawing at my brain.

"Breathe through it, Majesty." Emmory's voice wafted like smoke, wrapping around me and easing some of the panic. "You're all right. Just breathe."

I dragged in a breath, letting Emmory's words lull me away from the sharp-edged sensation of the plasteel walls closing in on me, and released it. Fear rushed into the vacuum, but I pushed it out with another breath.

"Very good, Majesty." The approval from Emmory chased away the last vestiges of anxiety and a hiccuping laugh slipped free. "Now which way do we go?"

"Give me a second." We were at the juncture where my maps converged. Emmory had taken my guesswork over where to go next with surprising calm. Bringing up the maps in my head, I overlaid one on top of the other, looking through them at the options in front of us.

The fork on the left led nowhere, looping back in on itself and wandering off toward the general living quarters. The one on the right was equally useless. Eventually it dead-ended near the restaurant sector.

Of the three left, two led close to the area I thought was Rai's, but one of them—I tilted my head to the side and frowned.

"Emmory, look at this." I threw the whole mess to his *smati*. "Why does the path just in front of you break off three meters before hitting Rai's apartments? It just dead-ends into a wall."

"Because it's what we're looking for. Come on," he said almost as soon as the information hit his screens. "Trust me, Majesty," he chided when I protested. "I do know what I'm doing occasionally."

I didn't grant him a response, settling for a glare and a swallowed curse. Emmory didn't see it and I crawled after him when Zin carefully cleared his throat behind me.

*"Don't say a word."* The message from Emmory came across the com line and distracted me just enough I almost ran into him.

*"What is it?"* Zin and I asked the question simultaneously.

*"Observation room,"* Emmory replied. *"Two guards. Majesty. We've got enough space to turn around but there's no way for Zin to get in front of you; we'll have to do this quickly."*

I didn't bother telling him that I had no intention of staying behind anyway. *"What's the layout?"*

*"One by the door. One directly under the vent. I want you following right behind me when we exit and then try to stay out of the way. Zin, I'm going after the one by the door. If the other man is still conscious, you take care of him."*

*"Okay."*

The area we were in had widened just enough to let us flip around. I followed Emmory's lead and wiggled until I was also feet first. Emmory waited a beat while Zin adjusted, then gave us both a nod and kicked the vent cover off.

What he did was kick it free and drop from the ceiling, riding the cover to the ground like a plasma surfer from Ontario. The unfortunate guard beneath us played the role of the wave, and I landed to the left of his still form.

Emmory was headed across the room toward the second guard, who was fumbling for his communication link when I spotted the flaw in Emmory's plan.

There was a third man in the room, and no time to wait for Zin to get out of the vent. Time slowed as the wide-eyed young man went for the gun at his side. I vaulted the desk between us and snapped his head back with a spinning hook kick.

The guard's pretty blue eyes rolled back in his head, and he dropped to the ground. I landed lightly beside him and turned to find Emmory giving me the Look.

"What?" I hissed. "He was going to shoot you in the back."

"Zin—"

"Sorry. She beat me to him." Zin threw me a wink when Emmory looked away and mouthed, *Nice work*.

I stifled a giggle, earning a growl from Emmory, and headed for the bank of screens on the far wall. From the looks of it we hadn't set off any alarms and none of the guards had gotten distress calls off before being neutralized.

"They're all still alive," Zin announced. "I'll find something to tie them up with."

"Here," I said to Emmory, pointing at one of the screens.

A man with dark brown dreadlocks lounged on a low scarlet couch, his muscled arms spread out over the back. The casual pose was a ploy; even from here I could see the curious gleam in Bakara Rai's amber eyes as Hao and the others were ushered into the room.

"Can we get sound?"

I swiped a hand over the table in front of me, bringing up the control panel. A few commands later the entire wall was covered with the footage from the camera in Rai's private rooms, and conversation was as clear as if we were in the room with them.

"Such an honor to have one of Po-Sin's greatest generals come all the way out here to visit." Rai's voice was rough, a deep, shifting baritone that could go from seductive to deadly in the space between heartbeats. "I can't imagine what would require such an important man as a messenger and such secrecy that you didn't ask me for a pass at Midway. Even curiouser to bring the *Dve* of the currently deceased Empress of Indrana with you, Hao."

"He made Cas." I spat out a curse and grabbed for the gun on my hip.

"Easy, Majesty. Let's see what Hao does."

I stared at Emmory in shock, but his eyes were locked on the screen.

Hao folded his hands together, bowing low as he did so. When he came up, he extended his arms and pushed his sleeves up, revealing his uninked skin. "As you can see, Honored Rai, I am not currently in my uncle's employ. He has released me for a personal issue and Dailun for the Traveling."

"Clever," Emmory murmured.

"Did you really think he'd give us up?" I hissed.

"It's my job to be suspicious, Majesty. If it keeps you alive it's worth it."

"One of these days it's going to get you in trouble. Hao would be mortally offended if he knew what you just pulled, Emmory."

"I did not *pull* anything, Majesty. I merely took advantage of the situation to further prove his loyalty. It won't do any of them much good to go storming in anyway, so—" He gave a little shrug and looked back at the screen.

Rai was dressed in a red tank top and loose pants. The gray silken fabric was embroidered with thread as scarlet as the top. He wasn't obviously armed, but he didn't need to be. The hired muscle standing behind Dailun had shifted nervously at the mention of Po-Sin.

"Ah, yes, the Traveling." Rai eyed Dailun with a smile. "So you're bringing him here to do what? I don't do fosters, and some would say that coming to work for me is a bit of a step down for a Cheng—let alone the great-grandson of Po-Sin."

"He knows something's up," I said to Emmory. "He's just playing now. We might as well go out there."

Emmory didn't look happy about it, but he at least didn't argue with me. "Fine. You stay behind us, Majesty. Understood? If people start shooting, you jump back in here and get back to the ship."

I nodded, figuring it was a waste of time to tell him that Rai probably wouldn't shoot us. If he wanted us dead he'd just lock the doors and gas the room.

I'd seen that happen once before when some idiotic man thought he could strong-arm Rai.

Portis and I had been waiting for our own appointment, and I'm sure that letting us watch the whole scenario through the wide one-way mirror had been a deliberate show of power on his part.

Rai had sucked in the blue gas like he was smoking a vanity cigarette, while the other man choked and convulsed on the floor. Later he'd told me about the poison mod he'd had installed that filtered out all the known toxins in the universe.

The trouble with Rai was it could have all been a trick, an illusion to build up his power and feed the rumor mill that already circulated thousands of stories about him a day.

Or it could have been real.

Either way, after that incident I tended to stay as close to the door as possible when I visited.

The door to our hiding spot slid open, and I followed Emmory and Zin into the next room.

We were just in time to hear Dailun say, "My *jiejie* would like a word with you."

Rai's couch was facing the door we exited, with a long bank of windows behind him that looked down on the bustling gambling pit below. The door to the hallway was several meters away, guarded by two granite-faced men. Three more guards stood behind Hao and the others.

The floor under my feet was satin-wood, gleaming in the overhead lights. Several other couches were scattered throughout the room, and a table of polished steel nearby was so loaded with food it looked as though it would collapse any second.

"*Jiejie*, is it?" Rai rose from the couch in a fluid movement. "Now that, Dailun, *is* a step up." A sly smile spread over his face, and when he bowed, he kept his eyes locked on mine. "Empress Hailimi Mercedes Jaya Bristol, it is good to see you alive and well. I heard a horrible rumor you were dead, and it drove me to tears."

"I'm sure it did."

Emmory stood in Rai's way. Even barefoot, Rai was twenty or so centimeters taller than Emmory—not that it seemed to intimidate my *Ekam* at all.

Or me for that matter. I held my ground as Rai stepped around him.

"So sorry to hear of your boyfriend's passing also, though I confess I'm relieved the competition is gone. If your *Ekam* will forgive the impertinence, I'll greet you properly." He leaned down to kiss me.

The telltale whine of my Glock powering up filled the space between my lips and Rai's as I pressed the barrel to the underside of his chin.

"He won't and neither will I." I increased the pressure until Rai backed up a half step. "You will watch your tongue, Bakara Rai."

He tilted his head to the side, watching me with a tiny smile. "Or your BodyGuard will remove it?"

"Or *I* will." The tone in my voice was enough to make Rai's guards shift uneasily. Mine stayed still as stone.

"Such an interesting transformation," Rai remarked to Hao. "I'd always scoffed at the notion of royal blood, but she's proven me wrong. From gunrunner to empress and back again in just a matter of seconds. I'm honestly not sure who I like more."

"You don't want to cross either," Hao said, and Rai grinned.

"Portis was a hero and will be remembered as such." I returned the Glock to the small of my back.

"Yes, of course. I meant no disrespect to his memory." Rai snapped his fingers and a young woman in an outfit of gossamer threads the color of peaches glided over to him with two bowls of something blue and frothy. Rai took them and handed one in my direction. "Come sit down, Your Majesty. We will toast to the fallen. I promise it won't harm you, but I won't be offended if your *Ekam* insists on testing it first."

I let Emmory take the drink, picking the overstuffed red chair to the right of the couch Rai sat down on. It gave me a clear view of the door and the guards.

Rai raised it in my direction. "To Portis, so very noble even at the end."

I took my drink back from Emmory and tapped it to Rai's before taking a sip. A burst of tart lemon filled my mouth, and I leaned back in my chair with a smile. "That's very nice."

"I thought you'd like it." Rai slung his free arm over the back of the couch again and stretched out his long legs with a sigh. "So, as I said, I have a present for you, but that's not all." Rai grinned. "I have a surprise for you also—Johar is here. Do you want to see her?"

"I thought you banned her from Santa Pirata for life," I replied cautiously, using the pronoun Rai had chosen even though the last time I'd seen Johar she'd been male.

Rai gave a little shrug. "I changed my mind. It was a misunderstanding."

"She shot you."

Rai tipped his head in acknowledgment. "True. It was a misunderstanding. Come on, Hail. We'll miss it if we don't go now." He stood and offered me a hand.

"Majesty, a moment?"

I glanced over my shoulder at Emmory and then back at Rai, catching the amusement in his amber gaze.

"I'll just wait for you outside," he said, and headed for the door, leaving me alone with my three Guards, Hao, and Dailun.

"Is this safe?"

My eyes snapped wide and I laughed. "We're in a smuggler's hideout, Emmy. Safe is relative."

"I meant going into the arena, Majesty. Crowd control will be impossible. We should bring the others—"

"No, leave them on the ship for now. I'd rather not show our complete strength to Rai." I shrugged. "We'll be in Rai's box, not up next to some drunk bastard in the upper decks. That's safe enough as it goes."

"You'll be spotted," Zin said. "You're extremely recognizable, Majesty."

"I'm okay with that," I replied. "I like the idea of making Phanin out to be a liar every chance I have."

"This is dangerous, *jiejie*."

I rolled my eyes at Dailun's input. "No more so than anything else and you know it. Rai's a potential ally," I replied calmly. "I can't risk offending him or Johar. We might need them. And he's not going to tell me what my present is until he's damn good and ready, so we may as well play along." Even if the present wasn't anything planet-shattering, I would need Rai's help, for weapons at the very least, and mercenaries if things got bad.

Mother Destroyer, I hoped they didn't get that bad.

Emmory finally nodded. "All right, Majesty. If you think it's for the best."

I didn't, but it was the best we could do at the moment, and given what we were up against it would have to do.

# 28

The gleam of plasteel and dead gray concrete faded into the smooth black rock native to Santa Pirata as we left Rai's operational base and moved out into the public areas of the underground city.

I was burning with curiosity over Rai's casual remark about the present, but I wouldn't give him the satisfaction of asking. Harassing him about it would only make him clam up; that was just the way he was.

Emmory walked in front of us, having won the staredown with Rai's head of security after we'd left the room. Not all that big a surprise, considering my *Ekam* was on high alert. Still, Camon was a force to be reckoned with in his own right, and I could tell from the set of his beetled brows that he was unhappy about the arrangement.

The walls were so shiny our reflections followed us along like wandering ghosts. It was fitting. I could feel this weight between my shoulder blades, a frozen knife thrusting all the way through to my heart. And any one of the ghosts following me had the right to put it there. Never in all my life had I felt the weight of the dead as keenly as I had since fleeing Red Cliff.

Santa Pirata had once been packed with volcanoes that burned away the atmosphere and smothered any living things on the surface in a thick coating of ash a few million years ago.

The quick-cooling lava, a rock very similar to Earth obsidian, had been compressed with the ash, and the resulting substance could be powdered and smoked to produce one of the most powerful highs known to humankind.

I didn't understand the appeal. The thought of feeling like you wanted to crawl out of your own skin didn't sound like a good time to me.

Rai controlled the distribution with the same iron fist he used in all his business dealings, all too aware that the finite supply of Pirate Rock meant he needed to cash in on it while he still had the material.

Plus I figured he wasn't too keen on having to move his entire operation and gutting his underground empire just to make a profit. Though once the man figured out how to build a planet I'm sure he'd be all over it.

It was an instant death penalty to cut, scrape, or otherwise steal the rock—not only for the one doing the cutting but for anyone who saw the crime and didn't issue the punishment.

Privately, I thought it was a brilliant move on Rai's part. Forcing people to enact their own justice was really the only way to battle the endless temptation of having the rock right there for the taking.

Though I'm sure it helped that the ridiculously expensive cost of the drug meant it was out of the budget for most of the population of Santa Pirata. This was not AVI. This was a drug for the rich and powerful.

The noise level rose as we moved deeper into the public area, and I watched the set of Emmory's shoulders tense when people began to point and whisper to each other. "You have my word you are perfectly safe here," Rai murmured as we wove our way through the crowded bazaar.

I'd loved coming to the market the times we'd visited. Something about the crush of people ironically made it easier for me to relax about the idea of being underground. The first two times Portis hadn't even let me meet Rai, so I'd killed time at a little café, drinking chai and watching the crowds flow back and forth.

It was as diverse a group as you could get outside the Solarian Conglomerate, and certainly the more colorful elements of society were here. I chuckled as I watched a trio of young boys expertly lift a wallet from an unsuspecting man in a deep blue suit.

The eldest of the three threw a little salute Rai acknowledged with a nod. The thieves would transfer five percent of their score to Rai's accounts. That little cut kept them safe as long as they kept their pocketing to nonresidents and weren't clumsy enough to get caught.

"According to Emmory I'm never perfectly safe," I replied to Rai, grinning a little when the boy's gaze slid to me and he winked brazenly. He wasn't even half my age.

"He doesn't know you very well then."

I smothered a laugh, mostly to spare Emmory because I knew he was listening to our conversation. "Actually, he's fully aware of my abilities. I think that's what makes him nervous."

"He has my sympathies. I cannot think of a more demanding and less rewarding position."

"That would depend on your idea of rewarding, wouldn't it?" Emmory asked without looking back at us.

"I think you already know the answer to that one, *Ekam*."

Rai spread his arms wide and gave Emmory a smirking grin. "The gods were gracious enough to grant me this life. I would be remiss if I ignored their gifts."

Emmory ignored the comment and we passed out of the bazaar into a quieter tunnel of the same shiny black rock. The silence was only momentary; as we moved farther into it, a wave of noise rushed up and slapped me in the face.

It was the roar of the arena crowd, a sound that raised a spark of feeling out of the deadness in my chest. Portis wouldn't ever let me fight—for reasons I now understood. But I'd wanted to, wanted to so desperately we'd had some amazing rows about it over and over.

I couldn't explain the need if you'd put a gun to my head. Maybe it was the same driving force that fed my longing for the military service, something in my blood or in my very soul.

The crowd to my left broke slightly, revealing a familiar profile, and I veered abruptly with a curse.

"Majesty." Emmory caught me by the arm before I'd gotten two steps. The crowd shifted again, hiding away the angular golden face and unusual blue eyes of Bialriarn Malik, my mother's former *Ekam*.

"Did you see him?"

"See who?"

"Bial," I hissed. "Emmory, I saw—"

"Majesty," Emmory murmured, and I could hear the concern threaded into my title. "Even if you did, we can't go after him right now."

"Even if?" Only Rai's curious gaze kept me from shoving Emmory. Instead, I pulled the recording up in my *smati* and sectioned out the playback, sending it to Emmory with a raised eyebrow.

He muttered his own curse and looked at Zin, who nodded and melted into the crowd.

"Dailun, go with him," I said, and my new pilot followed Zin without question.

"Anything I can help with?" Rai asked.

"No," Emmory and I said simultaneously.

Rai watched us, a knowing look not quite hidden on his face, and gestured ahead of us. "Johar's match is about to start. I don't recommend being late; they do not usually last for very long."

As always, stepping into the arena took my breath away. It was designed to be glorious, after all: a monument, Rai said, to our darker natures, to the violence and bloody majesty of the human race. I'd thought it was pretentious the first time he'd said it, and told him so.

He'd merely smirked at me and led me into the arena without another word. It was the most effective move at that point and stopped my derisive commentary with stone-cold efficiency.

The arena at Santa Pirata, where people fought for pay, for punishment, for glory, was known across the stars.

My *smati* could give me the specs on the size of the place. But reciting how many meters deep and the number of seats was a poor replacement for the sheer immensity you experienced when walking into it. Tiers carved into the rock above us stretched on for what seemed like kilometers, leaving the action on the floor nearly invisible to the spectators above were it not for the viewscreens embedded into the walls and floating through the air.

We were on the bottom where the privileged sat, in a wide box filled with tables and comfortable chairs, close enough to see the blood spatter and smell the stink of the fighters' sweat.

I was ushered to a seat, Hao sitting down on one side. Emmory took a spot directly behind me while Cas assumed an easy stance by the door. Rai settled down on my left, speaking quietly to the young woman who'd appeared. She bobbed in acknowledgment of whatever orders he issued and vanished as quietly as she'd come.

"I trust you're hungry?" Rai asked. "Johar pitched a fit when she was told I wasn't in my seat yet." He rolled his eyes skyward. "So we've got a few more minutes. Once she calms down, the match should begin. I would—" He broke off, snapping a hand out so fast I couldn't stop myself from jumping.

Luckily for Rai, Emmory had better self-control.

Rai shot me an apologetic look and held up the camera that had just flown into our box. "Given the circumstances I am assuming you would rather your presence here be as low-key as possible? I had the bazaar cleared of news cameras before we came through. Shutting them down in here will be somewhat trickier to explain, but it is possible—"

"No, leave them on." I smiled.

"Majesty, they will know where we are," Emmory said.

"Point." I glanced at Rai.

"You will be safe here, you have my word on it."

"I have a message to send to my enemies and it may as well start now. Unless this is a fight you'd rather stay out of. If it is we'll go—" I started to get out of my chair and Rai stopped me with a hand on my forearm.

Emmory's snarl was practically silent, but Rai glanced upward anyway. I noticed he didn't remove his hand, so for the sake of my BodyGuard's blood pressure I moved it for him.

"I wouldn't cause any trouble for you, Rai."

"It is nothing we can't handle." He grinned at me. "Whatever your preference is, Your Majesty, is what I would be pleased to do."

"It's fine," I said. "Let them film." Leaning in, I gave Rai a smile. "If you touch me again though, Rai, they'll be filming Emmory wiping the floor with you. Is that understood?"

He blinked at me, and the laughter that rang into the air was genuinely delighted. "Completely, Your Majesty." He stood and executed a flourishing bow that rivaled anything I'd seen back home.

"Ladies and gentlemen, before the match today I have a special guest I would like to introduce to you all. She has something she would like to say." Rai's amplified voice rang through the arena. "I present to you Her Imperial Majesty, Empress Hailimi Mercedes Jaya Bristol."

You could have heard a rifle cartridge drop in the silence that followed. I shared a look with Emmory as I rose and stepped to Rai's side.

"My thanks," I said. "Citizens of Indrana, as you can see, I am alive despite Prime Minister Phanin's assertions to the contrary. Like so many before him, he has learned I am hard to kill." I offered up a mirthless smile. "He will soon learn the cost of that mistake.

"At a time when we most needed to be unified, Eha Phanin and his cronies have torn us apart. Proving beyond a shadow of a doubt they care not about you and they care not about Indrana. The Saxon Alliance may not have been responsible for the destruction at Red Cliff, but they are responsible for our recent troubles. I have the truth of that from their king's own mouth.

"Stand strong, my people. Stand firm against those who would put a bootheel to Indrana's neck. We will be home soon and justice will be done."

I nodded and the windows around the box went dark, cutting us off from the cameras, then shifting to a one-way view.

275

The crowd shook off their stunned silence and burst into cheers.

"Dramatic, determined, and a little scary," Rai said with a grin. "Nicely done, Your Majesty."

I sat back down and crossed a leg over the other. "I'm angry, Rai. I lost good people back on Red Cliff because these idiots want to play at owning an empire."

The announcer's call heralded the arrival of the combatants for the main match of the day. I leaned forward in my seat and got my first look at Johar.

Or rather, my first look at her in this form.

I'd already clued into the fact that she'd switched genders, thanks to Rai's not-so-subtle use of the pronoun.

For Johar, little things like gender weren't permanent. I didn't even know which way she'd been born to start with and I didn't really care. What I did know what she was a loyal friend when she chose to be, a fierce fighter whom I'd much rather have at my back than on it, and a hell of a tactician.

When the announcer roared her name, Johar strode out onto the black sand coating the floor of the arena. She was as tall as Rai, her lean limbs decorated with wide swaths of black, curling tattoos. Her hair was black also, but her skin was pale as snow.

The cheers of the crowd filled the air and I flicked my gaze to the screen nearby as a camera zoomed in for a close-up of Johar. Her eyes were the same as always—icy-blue. I swore they looked straight through me.

Then she smiled, a flashing grin that lit up her severe face, and her attention turned to her opponent.

Johar's opponent was taller and stronger than her, but it wouldn't matter in the end. She had speed and a willingness to beat the hulking man bloody.

They bowed toward Rai's box and then to each other. The gong sounded, tolling through the air, vibrating through my bones.

Johar moved in the space between the inhale and exhale of the crowd. Her left elbow slammed into the man's jaw with such force I could hear the impact in my seat. His head snapped back, exposing his throat.

"Oh well, this will be a short one," Rai snorted.

He was right. I didn't even see Johar's second punch, just the man sliding bonelessly to the sand.

The crowd lost their minds. Johar walked away from her win with little more than a wave of her hand, an almost lackadaisical recognition of their adoration.

"She's gotten better," I murmured to Rai.

"She said the other body was slowing her down," Rai murmured back. "I miss it a bit, but I can see her point." There was a note of pride in his voice I suspected he didn't let show very often.

Rai shook his head and snapped his fingers twice. The sounds of the arena vanished, filling the box with an expectant silence.

"So, the present first, I think. Then I'll let you rest a bit before dinner."

"You're enjoying this a little too much," I replied with a raised eyebrow.

"Please, it's not every day I get to reunite old friends. Especially when I think it was pure luck that brought these two here."

The doors slid open behind us and my mouth dropped open as Rai's guards escorted in a tall man with chestnut-colored hair. He was bruised and battered, his arms cuffed behind his back.

"Vasha?" I gasped as recognition blindsided me. I'd done a few runs with this gunrunner over the years, and we'd gotten on well—very well, actually.

Even bound as he was, Vasha's gray eyes burned with fury and he tried to protect the young girl at his side. "Rai, you mangy shitheel, when I get loose I'm going to rip out your spine in sections. You have no idea what you're interfering in."

"Rai, what the fuck is going on?" I asked. The only reason I could think Rai would consider Vasha a present was if he'd been involved in the coup. My hand went for my gun as I slid out of my seat and backed away from Rai. Emmory took his cue from me, and the room filled with uneasy tension as Cas and Hao stiffened and stepped to my sides without so much as a word.

Vasha's eyes snapped wide, and a tiny exhale of what could have been relief slipped from between his lips. "Thank Shiva and all the gods," he breathed. "Your Majesty, you're still alive."

Rai's chuckle was wicked and dragged my attention away from my old gunrunner pal. "Easy, Your Majesty, everything is fine. I'd rather people not start shooting in here, I just redecorated. First point of order, I'm not responsible for the damage there." He waved a hand at Vasha. "I believe that was some Saxon Shocker who hopefully looks worse than Vasha does. He's only in cuffs because he wouldn't calm down long enough to listen to what I had to say and I needed to be sure he was safe.

"It would have been embarrassing for him to try to kill you while you were under my protection."

"Your Imperial Majesty." The child at Vasha's side slipped around him and I realized she wasn't a child at all, but a very tiny woman. She dropped into an elegant curtsy despite her bloodstained pants and dirty shirt. "It is a very great pleasure to see you well."

"Who are you?" The question slipped out even as Rai muttered a curse.

"Go on, Jia. Ruin all my fun." Rai rose with a languid gesture. "Your Majesty, if I may introduce your loyal subject, the governor of Canafey Minor, Jia Li Ashwari."

# 29

I blinked, unsure if the words I'd just heard were real, but my *smati* confirmed it.

"Bugger me. Governor, I didn't think we'd be seeing each other anytime soon. You were supposed to meet us on Red Cliff."

"We were on our way when you were attacked and had to change plans," Jia replied, a smile curving her bruised face. "This was an unexpected destination, but fortuitous."

I glared at Rai. "If he's not a threat, why is he still cuffed?"

Rai snapped his fingers and his guards took the cuffs off Vasha. "Behave yourself, Vasha," he warned. "And don't be grumpy about the lockup. You know if you try to take my spine out it'll make Johar mad. I had to be sure you weren't trying to kill the empress here. That kind of publicity is hard on business."

Vasha shot Rai a look of pure contempt before dismissing him and settling those cool gray eyes on me. "Your Imperial Majesty." He dropped to a knee.

I groaned. "Oh, come on, Vasha." Ignoring Emmory's protest I moved forward and helped him to his feet, embracing him. The wince wasn't all from his injuries, and I rolled my eyes as he shifted away. "We used to be friends."

More than friends, actually, but I figured it was best to not embarrass the both of us by saying so out loud.

"You used to be a gunrunner, Your Majesty." His smile was fleeting and he glanced quickly over my shoulder at Rai. "We need to speak in private."

"I've had rooms prepared for you. Camon will show you the way," Rai spoke up. "If you could join us for dinner, Your Majesty, I know that Johar will appreciate it."

"Thank you. I will." I dipped my head at him; the movement felt oddly regal. "A physician for Vasha?"

"Has already been called. We don't have any Farians, for obvious reasons. He'll meet you at your rooms." Rai gave another flourishing bow. "Your Majesty."

We had a Farian, but she was still unconscious, a fact that grew more worrisome by the day.

"I'll see you at dinner, Rai," I said, when what I really wanted was to tell him to move his ass before I shot him. "Hao, go on back to the ship and get the others. Tell Stasia, Gita, and Indula to stay with Fasé."

Hao nodded sharply and left. No one else said a word as Camon led us back out of the arena and to the lavish set of rooms prepared for us. I waited in the hallway with Cas until Emmory gave the all clear.

The hardwood floors gleamed under the soft recessed lights. Couches of varying shades of gray dotted the front room, and the table by the wide fireplace was already filled with a dizzying array of treats. Most of the splendor was lost to the far wall and the beach scene projected on the viewscreens that stretched from floor to ceiling.

The moment the door closed behind us, I whirled on Vasha.

"What in the Mother's name is going on? Not that I don't like you, Vasha, but you're not really one for civic duty. How in the fires of Naraka did you end up with my governor? Caspel was sending an operative in after her."

"Your Majesty—" Jia started, but Emmory cut her off.

"Just a moment, please, before we get too deep into this conversation." He held up his hand as he and Cas moved through the rooms in a smoothly choreographed search for listening devices.

"Vasha, sit your ass down before you pass out," I snapped.

"I'm fine, Majesty." Shaking his head cost him his equilibrium, and Jia wasn't anywhere near strong enough to hold the big man upright.

Emmory moved before I could, glaring at me so fiercely I actually took a step back. He caught Vasha under the arms and dragged him over to the couch.

"Don't worry yourself, *Ekam*. I'm loyal to the empress." Vasha's voice was slurred with pain and he tipped his head back on the deep gray couch. "Even if I weren't, I'm in no shape to do her any harm. I've seen her fight. Just give me a moment. That Saxon shitheel got in a few good licks and I'm running on empty."

"He is loyal, Your Majesty," Jia murmured from my side. "Possibly more loyal than I am. He didn't even mention that he knew you." She moved over to sit next to Vasha, resting a hand on his knee.

Without opening his eyes, Vasha moved his own hand over to cover hers and I turned away with a smile. Whatever was going on there, it looked like my old gunrunning friend had finally found some happiness.

I just hoped it lasted.

"Majesty."

I raised an eyebrow at Emmory. "Clear?"

"As we can be," he replied with a shrug. "There are no obvious bugs, either audio or video, but that doesn't mean a whole lot. We're working with limited resources."

"And these two?" I wiggled my fingers in the direction of the couch.

"She is Governor Ashwari." Emmory gave a little nod. "That much I can verify. And the gunrunner is who he says he is—Vasha Ystrel, former imperial citizen, wanted for seven major offenses and a list of minor ones that would take me all day to recite."

"Bear in mind I was involved in some of those offenses, Emmy." I grinned at him. "Given what he's done for the governor I think we can make allowances."

"I try not to think about your past, Majesty. All my scans can do is confirm their identities, not their loyalties."

"Well, let's hear what he has to say then." As I moved around Emmory to take a seat on the couch opposite Vasha, it occurred to me that my BodyGuard was suffering. His faith in his judgment had been shaken just like mine had. We'd both tagged Phanin as nothing more than an unimportant politician, and now we were paying for it.

I filed that revelation away to deal with later. It wasn't something I could bring up in front of everyone anyway. I settled down onto the dusky gray couch opposite Vasha and Jia and rested my forearms on my knees as I studied both of them.

Jia met my eyes only briefly, looking down and away in a show of deference that I found slightly annoying. Vasha cracked one eye open and gave me a crooked grin.

"I can almost hear the wheels turning in your head, Cres—Your Majesty. That's going to be bloody hard to remember." He muttered the last bit to himself and flicked a glance at

Emmory. "Forgive me, *Ekam*, I'm not deliberately being rude. The empress and I were friends long before I realized who she was."

"Sorry about lying to you," I said.

"I'm afraid I wasn't entirely honest with you either, Majesty," Vasha continued. "My real name is Nakula Orleon. I'm with Galactic Imperial Security."

My *smati* confirmed his words as fast as Nakula spoke them. He dropped whatever screen had been in place, giving both me and my Guards a clear reading that verified his identity.

Rather than relax him, the revelation made Emmory tense. Jia froze when he jerked his weapon free, centering it on Vasha's chest. Cas followed his lead, stepping closer to my side.

"Easy," I murmured, putting a hand up.

"I'm the operative Director Ganej told you about. I was on Canafey for a job. He ordered me to rescue Jia from the Saxons. Which, as you can see, I did. I was trying to get her off the planet and head for Pashati, but the Saxons had a Shock team on our tail and nearly took her back."

"He came to rescue me a second time," Jia said.

I could have sworn Nakula's high cheekbones were stained with red. He slid forward on the edge of the couch. "I attempted to. Jia didn't really need saving. We escaped and I received word from the director to make for Red Cliff. When everything exploded there she pointed a gun at me and asked me who I was loyal to. I'll tell you the same thing I told her, Cres—"

He fumbled, clearing his throat of my old name as he awkwardly went to a knee in front of me. "Your Majesty. I am, as I always have been, a loyal servant of the throne of Indrana.

"Even more than that, I *know* you, Majesty. I know what

you're capable of, and there is no one else in this galaxy I would so willingly follow into battle. If you will allow it, I'd like the chance to help you retake your throne."

I was a bit shocked by the tears that sprang up in response to his declaration, and reached a hand out, sinking my fingers into his thick hair. "Your help is more than welcome," I whispered. "And your faith in me—I hope I can live up to it."

Nakula lifted his head when I removed my hand and smiled at me. "I am certain you will," he said.

The door chime announced Zin's return and saved me the embarrassment of scrambling for an answer. "Any luck?" I asked, meeting him at the door.

Zin shook his head. "Vanished like a ghost. Dailun wanted to look around more, so he took off on his own. If Bial's not off Santa Pirata already, we could ask Rai to—" He broke off when Emmory and I both shook our heads.

"I don't want to owe Rai any more favors than necessary. What do you think he was doing here?"

"I can't believe it was a coincidence," Emmory said. "As soon as I have access to a secure line I'm going to try to get in touch with Winston and see where she and Peche are."

The Trackers who'd been set on Bial's trail had lost it shortly before we left for Red Cliff. If they'd found it again, it was possible they were nearby.

"Let them know we're about to head out to meet with Admiral Hassan if you get in touch," I said with a nod. "I'm going to speak with Hao about using his contacts to keep an eye out for Bial also. They're a lot less noticeable than a pair of Trackers."

The door chimed again and Zin went to answer it, ushering the doctor inside and over to Nakula.

Hao returned at the same time with the others and greeted

the news about Nakula with a snort of disgust. "Is no one just a damn criminal anymore? If I end up paranoid from this whole thing it's your fault, *sha zhu*."

I stuck my tongue out at him and walked to the bank of viewscreens on the far side of the room. The turquoise-blue waters and palm trees were stunningly realistic. So much so, I almost smelled the salty air on my inhale.

"Majesty." Alba smiled, and I leaned in to hug her. "I am relieved you are all right."

"How's your arm?"

"Almost healed." She wiggled her fingers. "I am cleared to move around though, if you need me."

"I'm sure we can think of something for you to do."

"Your Majesty." Jia's lilting voice floated on the sounds of the surf. "I can confirm that the ships at the Canafey Major ship-yards were still intact as of a week ago."

"I can't believe the Saxons haven't destroyed them." I spun around and stared at her. She was standing next to Cas but was far enough away from me not to be a threat, her hands folded placidly in front of her.

The *Vajrayana* ships had better weapons systems, better Alcubierre/White Drives, and better technology. But locked down they were nothing but dead weight. The Saxons should have just blown them up and been done with it.

Jia smiled. "They are still hoping to get the lock codes from me. I would very much prefer to give the codes to you."

I held my hands out, the tiniest glimmer of a plan springing to life as Jia pressed her palms to mine and passed the coded information along our *smati* link. A look of relief flashed over Jia's pretty face.

"What else can you tell me?" I asked.

"Because the Saxons can't unlock the ships, they're attempting to reverse engineer some of the tech instead," Jia said. "I suspect the idea is that if they can get it to work they'll be able to use it for their own navy." She rubbed her hands together and looked over her shoulder at where Nakula sat with the doctor. "There is a Saxon Shock team after us, Majesty, lead by Captain Hume. He caught up to us at Midway. The only reason we escaped was that I surrendered us to the police there."

A delighted laugh escaped me, startling Jia. "And they took you to Rai once they figured out who you were. Good thinking."

"Hume is dangerous."

"We've got a Shock team of our own on our trail." I waved a hand in the air. "We'll deal with them. Cas, go tell Emmory I need to speak to him."

"Ma'am—"

"Cas, please. I could break her in half, and given everything they've been through to bring these codes to us I think it's safe to say they're on our side." I waved a hand at Jia, who bit her lip in a poor attempt to hide her smile. "Besides, Zin and Iza are two meters away. They'll come to my rescue if something happens in the ten seconds between here and there." I gave him a little shove. "Go."

"Majesty, what are we going to do now?" Jia asked.

I waved Kisah over. "You're going to go with Kisah and Alba here and get cleaned up. If I know Rai, and I do, there are clothes for you in the bathroom. Then we're going to have dinner and get a good night's sleep and worry about things in the morning."

"Thank you, Majesty. May I go see to Nakula first?"

She didn't hesitate or trip over his real name, and I held in the smile that desperately wanted to break free. "After, Jia. And thank you, for everything."

She dropped a curtsy, still a consummate politician even with the strange circumstances, and allowed Kisah to lead her away.

Jia and Caterina accompanied me to dinner along with Hao, Emmory, and all but two BodyGuards. I'd been right about the clothing for my governor, and Rai had also made sure the rest of us were dressed properly.

Johar babbled something unintelligible and launched herself into my arms before Emmory could stop her. I hugged her back, waving my *Ekam* off before he could do anything offensive—like touch her without her permission.

"You lied," she said, releasing me and shaking her head. "I am so very disappointed in you."

"It was a necessary evil. Forgive me?"

Johar smiled, her tattoos fading from red to a more soothing blue and then back to black. "Forgiven. I tease anyway. Lying is good for the soul. Bakara made dinner himself. He's very anxious about it."

"Johar, hush." Rai smiled when he said it and pulled a chair out at the head of the long table. "Your Majesty."

"He'll just stand behind me if you don't seat him next to me," I murmured as I took the chair.

Rai glowered at me, but gestured to the next one. *"Ekam?"* He seated the others, glowering again when Johar stole the seat on my other side with a beaming smile, and took the remaining seat.

He clapped, and servers paraded out with trays full of food. They were all well trained and stopped at Emmory's spot first, offering the food to him so he could serve it to me after checking it.

"To the Empress of Indrana." Rai raised his glass and the others echoed him.

We settled into the meal.

"Caterina, tell me about Indrana." Johar smiled across the table at the matriarch, who smiled back.

"What would you like to know?"

"Everything."

A steady stream of curious questions and observations issued around the table as we ate; after dessert was cleared away, I leaned back in my chair and toyed with the delicate teacup in front of me. "Rai, what's it going to cost me to get your help?"

He raised an eyebrow as the room fell silent. "That would depend on the kind of help you require, Your Majesty."

"I'm not entirely sure yet. What would the promise of help cost me?"

Rai mulled it over, lifting a shoulder, and then he named a figure that had everyone but me wincing. Even Johar rolled her eyes at the ceiling and smacked him in the back of the head.

"Rude."

"It's business, my darling," Rai replied.

"She's a friend."

"Cressen Stone was a friend, Jo. This is the Empress of Indrana."

"I am so tired of hearing that." I stared at him. "I'm the same damn person, Rai, and we both know it. So can we lay off the shitty excuses? If you don't want to help me, just say so."

He blinked at me and for a second I thought I'd gone too far and really offended him. But he folded his hands together and shook them in my direction. "You are right, Your Majesty. My apologies for my rudeness. I am, of course, willing to entertain requests from you. Obviously I have my business to consider, but I can make you a priority. Is that acceptable?"

"Quite." I sipped my chai. "I can tell you what I need right now. Information on a man named Wilson."

Rai wordlessly held his hand out and I took it, passing along what little information we had on the man to him.

"I'll see what I can do, Majesty."

"Thank you." I pushed my chair out and stood. "The meal was lovely. I hope you don't think it rude of me if we all retire?"

"Of course not, you must all be exhausted." Rai smiled. "Good night, Your Majesty. We will speak in the morning."

"Cressen, your empire is most fascinating. I may have to come visit." Johar looked across the table at Caterina with a smile. "I think it would be fun."

"You are welcome anytime," I replied, unable to stop the wide grin that spread across my face. My empire really was in for an awakening when I got home.

*"Majesty, Fasé is awake,"* Emmory said over the com.

"Iza, will you see Caterina back to our rooms? Hao, go with them."

"Where are you going?" he asked with a raised eyebrow.

I didn't answer and followed Emmory down the hallway with my other BodyGuards trailing behind.

"Majesty."

"Fasé." I sat down on the edge of the bed and reached for the Farian's hand. Her skin was so pale I could see the blue of her veins running through her fingers. "We're so glad you're awake."

A sad smile flickered over her face. "I wish I could say the same, ma'am."

"I know, Fasé. I'm sorry. I can't even begin to understand how you—"

"Please don't." She flinched. "Don't thank me, ma'am."

I shared a worried look with Emmory over her head, patted her hand awkwardly, and stood. "Get some rest, Sergeant."

Emmory took my place, Zin at his side. Stasia, Gita, and Henna followed me from the room. I waited for the door to close before I said, "Talk to me."

Henna shrugged. "Physically healthy, Cressen. I am not an expert on Farians."

"Something troubles her, ma'am," Stasia said with a glance back over her shoulder at the frail Farian on the bed. "I think she fears she's done something terrible by saving Emmory."

"There aren't any laws against it?" I wasn't overly familiar with the extensive religious dogma the Farians followed. Killing with their power was a death sentence, but I couldn't believe they would view giving life the same way.

"I don't know, ma'am." My maid shook her head. "All I know is she is not herself. I'd recommend we keep an eye on her."

"Done. You and Kisah stay here with her. Call us if you have concerns—no matter how small. Gita, I'd like you to come back with me."

"Yes, Majesty."

I mustered up a smile and touched Stasia's cheek. "Chin up, all will be well."

"Yes, ma'am."

In the other room, Emmory rose and pressed a kiss to Fasé's forehead. Zin followed suit and they met us out in the hallway. We were all silent as we left the bay and wound back through the corridors of Santa Pirata.

Dailun was waiting at the door of our quarters, leaning against the wall and flipping a credit chip over his knuckles. He pushed his hood back and bowed low, his eyes on mine. "He is good *jiejie*, like a *gui*. I gave his photo to several members of the thieves' co-op with instructions to notify me immediately if he is seen. I am assuming you want him alive?"

"Yes," I said. "Don't kill him, and tell them not to engage

him either. He's dangerous and I don't want those kids getting hurt."

Dailun flashed a grin that lit up his whole face. "You are softer than your reputation, Sister."

"Don't count on it. I want him alive so I can question him." I patted him on the shoulder. "Get some rest, Dai. I'll see you in the morning."

He nodded, flipped his hood back up, and headed down the hallway.

Emmory and the others had cleared the quarters and Hao stood as I came in the room.

"What did I miss?" he asked.

"I need a drink first," I said. "Then I'll catch you up and probably ask you for a favor."

Hao rolled his eyes at me. "You're lucky I like you, little sister."

"You're lucky Emmory likes you," I countered, and headed for the liquor cabinet.

"Everyone likes me." Hao stole the glass from my hand with a grin and drank from it before I could steal it back.

"Kalah didn't."

"She hated everyone, that doesn't count. Pour a drink and stop avoiding the topic. What's this favor you need?" He dropped into a chair and put his feet up on the table bolted to the middle of the floor. "I'm assuming it has something to do with your mother's *Ekam*?"

If Hao was trying to surprise me with how much he knew, he failed. Taking a drink from my glass, I let the whiskey burn on my tongue for a moment before I swallowed. "It might. I want to know where he's gone, Hao. I'm willing to pay—"

Hao cut me off with a wave of his hand. "I will put the word out. I'm assuming Dailun contacted the thieves planetside already?"

"He did. If I know Bial, he'll stay one step ahead of them. That is, if he's not already out of the system."

"He is if he doesn't want Rai cutting him up into pieces." Hao tipped his head sideways and studied me. "You didn't tell him?"

"He doesn't need to know." I shook my head. "This is my business. Besides, I didn't feel like owing him a favor."

"But I'm fine to owe favors to?" Hao's grin was just this side of wicked.

"I owe you a lot as it is." I didn't try to stop my answering smile. "One more isn't going to make much of a difference."

# 30

In the stronghold of a smuggler I slept through the night. No dreams. No waking up with my heart stuck in my throat. Just uninterrupted, blissful sleep.

Breakfast was a quiet affair with Alba, Jia, and Caterina. Gita stood by the door, arms crossed over her chest. My chamberlain, with her still-healing arm, had returned to running my time as though we were in the palace. I was grateful for it and for the fact that she was still with me.

"Supplies are sorted for the next leg of the journey, ma'am," Alba said, ticking off a box on the list the four of us were sharing over our *smatis*. "I let Hao coordinate most of it, but I was able to find a tea merchant in the marketplace who sells your favorite chai."

"Remind me to give you a raise when we get home," I said with a grin. "So what's the news on Matriarch Tobin?"

"After dinner last night, Nakula and I were able to get in touch with someone in his network," Jia replied. "According to them, the matriarchs made it safely off Red Cliff and rendez-voused with Admiral Hassan two days ago. The details of how are still a little fuzzy, but I figured since we were talking to the admiral later this morning we'd be able to ask them directly."

I exhaled and tapped my fist lightly on the tabletop. The safety of the other two matriarchs had been weighing on me since the moment we'd fled from Red Cliff. "I am glad we can let that worry go," I said.

"Yes, ma'am," Caterina agreed. "We received a message from Caspel that Matriarch Hassan and her children were able to make it to an *Upjas* safe house early this morning. With the exception of Matriarch Desai, all my fellow matriarchs are accounted for and safe or have gone to temple."

I touched my hand to my heart, lips, and forehead. The three women echoed the gesture and we sat in silence for a long moment.

I cleared my throat. "What's the news saying, Alba?"

"Once the initial shock of the attack on Red Cliff died out, the intergalactic stations aren't covering much of the situation on Indrana. I see scattered reports and some think pieces about what it means for stability in the region, but not much else. What I don't know is if that's because Phanin has the official news stations on lockdown or because no one is talking."

At least one of the royal stations had suffered "catastrophic equipment failure" and gone off the air permanently—which was to say Phanin had blown the building up when they refused to stop broadcasting a message of support for me.

"If the Solarians are interested they are keeping it very quiet at the moment."

"Oh, they're interested. Trust me." I pointed a finger at Caterina. "I want you to write three press releases for me. The first one detailing our outrage at the senseless violence inflicted on us and on a Solarian negotiation planet by the Saxon Alliance. The second one needs to condemn Eha Phanin's illegal takeover of the Indranan government and his barbaric murders of the members of the Matriarch Council."

Caterina nodded as she logged the information into her *smati*. "And the third?"

"You'll want to talk with Johar about this one; she can walk you through how to do it. I want a bounty on Phanin's head, for forty-five million. Alive is optional, his head is required."

Caterina paled. "Majesty, the empire cannot—"

"That's not for the empire. I'm paying the bounty out of my own pocket." I smiled slowly. "Use Cressen Stone on the notice if it helps ease your mind; for once we can get something out of the fact that I used to be another person."

"Yes, ma'am."

"Good." I tapped my knuckles on the tabletop again. "We're done here then. You can all go. I need to speak with Emmory, and then I believe Nakula and I have a call with Caspel. Jia, if you'll let him know to head this way?"

"I will, Majesty," she said with a smile.

The three women left me alone with my *Ekam*, and I got up to pace the floor as I debated how to broach the subject of the Canafey ships to him.

Why I even bothered I don't know, as my *Ekam* once again proved he could read me better than most.

"We'll go after the *Vajrayana* ships, Majesty?" Emmory sighed when I stared at him. "It's the best plan we could have. Phanin's got three already. I've been reading up on the specs for them. Even if only half are intact it will be enough to defeat 2nd Fleet and give the Saxons pause in their plans to go to war."

I laughed. "I owe you an apology, Emmy."

"For thinking I'm just another pretty face?" He grinned at me but then sobered. "It's going to be bloody, Majesty. The Saxons won't give up Canafey without a fight."

"That's all right. I'm kind of spoiling for a fight."

The door chimed and Emmory moved to let Nakula in as I

headed for the com and punched Caspel's contact information in. Nakula murmured a greeting as he sat next to me.

"Your Majesty." Caspel's one good eye flicked to my right where Nakula sat. "Good morning."

"Good morning, Caspel. I know who he is," I said with a smile and nod in Nakula's direction. "We have the lock codes. Governor Ashwari is safe. He did good, Director."

"I'm pleased to hear it."

"If we survive this I'm going to have to think of something suitably embarrassing to do as a thank-you—like knight him."

Nakula looked horrified, but Caspel laughed in delight. "It would be fitting, Your Majesty, I've been trying to promote him and bring him back to Pashati for years. Now that you have the codes, what is your plan?"

"I'm still working on that," I hedged, unwilling to say anything more about it over the channel, no matter how secure it was. "Any word on Clara?"

"Still no word on Matriarch Desai, Majesty. I am sorry."

"Find her, Caspel. Please." I rubbed a hand over my forehead. "What about Leena and Taran?"

"They came in about an hour ago with a squad of her mother's guards. Her sister managed to hide them before Phanin's men got there and they were able to escape. We're moving them to a safer location in the morning."

"Good. Thank you. Tell them—" I stopped and swallowed, unable to find the words.

"I will, Majesty," Caspel said.

We talked for several more minutes about the situation at home. Then Nakula excused himself and I turned back to Caspel.

"I need to speak with Bina if she's there."

"She is, ma'am. Hang on. I'll connect you."

The connection blacked out for a moment and then returned.

"Yes, Majesty?" Lieutenant Bina Neem had the same distinctive elfin features and red hair as Fasé, but she was older, and her hair was cut short, just above her pointed chin. "What can I do for you?"

"Lieutenant. We have one of your—" I broke off, at a loss as to what I was supposed to call Fasé. *People* sounded very rude and *countrywoman* wasn't quite right either. I cleared my throat. "Are you familiar with Sergeant Fasé Terass?"

"I am, ma'am. We're linked, distantly, but it's there." Bina frowned. "You are obviously concerned, Majesty. What it is?"

"She was unconscious for a while after Red Cliff. She woke last night, but her behavior is odd. I'm worried about her. We don't really know how to help."

"What happened?"

"Emmory had been shot. She was able to patch him together enough for us to move him, but then we had to move him again and... he died."

"You mean she kept him from dying?"

I remembered the flatline in my head and the scream that had issued from Zin and shook my head. "No. He was dead. He was gone. I was going to try to restart his heart, but she pushed me aside and—"

Bina's eyes went wide and I watched as her golden eyes flicked over my left shoulder where Emmory stood. "She brought him back," she whispered.

I didn't think it was possible for Farians to get paler, but the news somehow drained what little color there was out of Bina's face.

"We have some rudimentary medical facilities and she seems to be all right physically. She said she wasn't glad to be awake.

We'll be meeting with Admiral Hassan and there are Farians stationed on board the *Vajra*, I just—"

"She shouldn't have been able to bring him back." Bina interrupted me. The Farian looked around her, swallowed, and dropped her head. "Forgive me, Majesty. This is not common. I will contact the Farians with Admiral Hassan. You must not talk with Fasé about this. It will only make things worse. Wait until you get to the admiral for my kin to take over. There is nothing you can do to help her."

"She saved a life, Bina. I don't understand."

"It is forbidden." Bina's voice dropped even lower. "We do not kill. We do not give life. We heal. Only heal. We cannot bring back that which is dead. Most of us couldn't even if it wasn't forbidden. Fasé is in a crisis of faith, but more than her own troubles, there will be a reckoning. I do not know what they will do. They might take her home, they might extinguish her."

"What?"

"It is the law, Majesty. These are extenuating circumstances and Fasé is much loved, but I do not know what is going to happen." Tears appeared in Bina's eyes. "Please tell her I love her."

I nodded, my heart racing. "Tell the director I will speak with him later. And Bina, thank you."

"Keep her safe, Majesty. I know why she did it, but I wish she hadn't. It is a dangerous road to walk down even were it not a likely death sentence. Tasting that kind of power usually leads to madness. Tell my *ahblensha* I will pray she is strong enough to withstand." Bina made a mudra with her right hand and touched her ring finger to her temple.

I shared a look with Emmory before I rubbed my hand over my eyes. "Because we don't have enough problems," I muttered.

"We'll handle it, Majesty," Emmory said. "Will you be all right here for a while?"

"I'll be fine. I need to talk with Admiral Hassan, and Rai wanted to have lunch before we left. Go." I waved a hand at the door and turned back to the com link. I typed in the address Caspel had given me for Admiral Hassan and leaned back in my chair as I waited for a response.

"Breathe, Majesty," Gita said as she took Emmory's spot.

"Your Majesty." Admiral Hassan's face appeared on the screen. "You look exhausted."

"So do you, ma'am."

I laughed. "How are you holding up, Inana?"

"We're okay. Running low on supplies, ma'am, but spirits are good. We'll need to get somewhere safe to replenish water and food within the week."

"I can do better than that, I'll take you right to supplies. Send me your coordinates, encode them. We're leaving here in a few hours."

"Yes, ma'am. Admiral Shul brought most of 2nd Fleet to Pashati. I ordered the remainder of Home Fleet to run when he showed up." She shook her head. "I'm sorry, ma'am. It seemed the best solution. He had the *Vajrayana* ships locked up as soon as we left the system."

"Caspel told me. It was best. They could have made a stand, but they were outnumbered. I'd rather have the ships, Admiral. We'll get the planet back."

"Admiral Fon is in charge. She's headed our way, but they did take some damage in the escape."

"We'll deal with it as we need to. We can move personnel around once we're all together. I've got the lock codes for the *Vajrayana* ships, Admiral. Start picking crew members."

Hassan's eyes lit up. "Yes, ma'am."

"Inana, your mother and your sisters are safe. I don't know if Caspel had a chance to tell you."

300

Admiral Hassan's eyes filled with tears and she pressed two trembling fingers to her lips. "I am relieved to hear it, Majesty."

"I'm sending you a message for the ranking Farian with you. Lieutenant Bina Neem will be contacting them also, but I wanted them to hear it from me."

"Yes, ma'am." Curiosity was thick in Inana's voice, but I shook my head.

"I'll tell you more when I see you." I signed off and pushed out of my seat.

Brushing the wrinkles out of my blue shirt, I tipped my head at Cas as I crossed the room. "Let's go. I'd like to talk with Rai before lunch. Indula, you and Iza get us packed and let Emmory know you're headed back to the ship. Hao, Nakula, and Jia are with us."

We headed out from our quarters. The idea that had sprung to life with Jia's appearance grew with every second and every little piece that fell into place. I'd know better once we met up with the admiral and saw what kind of fleet she had, but for now I hoped we had a shot at securing the *Vajrayana* ships.

The door to the dining room slid open before Cas could move to clear the room and I nearly collided with the man exiting.

"I'm sor—" My apology died on my lips when I met the eyes of the silver-haired Saxon I'd shot back on Red Cliff.

He grabbed me by the hair, shoving me sideways into Cas and knocking my *Dve* into Nakula. I saw a flash of metal and just barely got my right arm up in time before the garrote closed around my neck.

Gita rushed at him, right into a kick that probably broke most of her ribs. She dropped to the floor with an awful sound. My attacker dragged me back into the room and the doors closed behind us.

301

"Let's have a private chat, Your Majesty." His voice was shards of glass driving through the air. He jerked his gun free and shot out the door panel.

I reached up with my free hand, digging my thumb into his shoulder where I hoped a gunshot wound was still healing. His wince of pain confirmed it and I used the distraction to slam us both into the wall. His Winchester 77 spun off across the polished floor. I spun in his grip and two quick punches to the kidney loosened his hold on the garrote but he nailed me with an elbow to the solar plexus and knocked all the air from my lungs.

He grabbed for the garrote, yanking it into the air, and I gagged as the heel of my hand got shoved into my throat. The wire cutting into my wrist was still better than the alternative, and adrenaline surged through me with the sharp stinging pain.

I kicked high, pleased at the wheezing exhale when my boot met some kind of soft target, and felt the garrote loosen. Kicking again, I managed to yank the wire off my head and sent it spinning after the gun.

*Go, baby, move in.* Portis's order echoed in my head.

I lunged. He was bent over, and I rammed my knee into his head with all the force I could muster, grabbing his head at the same time to steady him. His knees collapsed and he went down. I followed, punching him in the side of the head.

"Hail!" Several pairs of hands grabbed me from behind and dragged me away from the unconscious Saxon. "He's out." One of them grunted when I shoved an elbow into his gut, but held on. "You're okay. It's okay."

"Is she hurt?" Rai barely slowed to hear Hao's response as he bore down on the Saxon. "I am shamed. In my own home." He kicked the man twice and pulled a very nasty-looking knife from his belt.

"Don't kill him!"

Rai glared at my order, but stopped. "You have fifteen seconds, my dear."

"I need longer. He's Shock Corps. He'll have intelligence I need." I held up my hand, streaked with blood. "You owe me."

"Fine." Rai kicked the man again and walked away. "Johar, find out what mangy piss stain let this man ride on their ship through the belt, and I want to know why Port Authority didn't tag him the second he set foot on the dock."

I sagged in Hao's and Nakula's grip, and they lowered me the rest of the way to the floor as Emmory and Zin bolted through the pried-open doors.

"She's all right," Hao said to Emmory as my *Ekam* went down on a knee at my side.

I coughed. "Water."

Zin took a glass from Alba and passed it along to Emmory, who scanned it and handed it to me. I drank it all, coughed again, and grabbed for Hao as I sat upright.

"I'm all right," I said, my voice rasping in my abused throat. "Help me up."

I leaned on Emmory as we crossed back to where Rai was stripping my Saxon attacker of everything on his person.

"Is he clean?"

Rai nodded sharply. I looked over the pile of things he'd taken off the man as I mulled over my options.

Saxon Shock Corps Marines were well-trained, disciplined warriors. If we were going to have any shot at breaking him, it was going to be in the first few minutes of our encounter. If he had time to get his defenses in order, it was going to be easier to put a blast through his heart and recover what we could from his *smati*.

Then I spied it: a small gold locket buried among the weapons.

Reaching down, I pulled it loose and flipped it open to reveal a miniature digital of a little girl with jet-black hair.

I looked around. "We've got one shot at this. Everyone follow my lead—if you think you can't do that, get out."

There was a chorus of assents.

I leaned down and slapped the man until he opened his eyes. They were pretty, deep-blue eyes that darted around, not quite focusing properly.

"Wake up," I said, slapping him again.

He tried to scramble away, but the wall blocked his escape and the whining charge of his own Winchester filled the air. Rai was pointing it over my shoulder.

"Nowhere to run." Dropping into a crouch, I shook my head. "You should have brought your whole team."

"I thought I could handle it." He eyed me, wiping the blood from his face with the hem of his gray shirt. "I figured the stories about you were exaggerated."

I shrugged. "Oh, no. They're all true. What's your name?"

"Captain Earnest."

"You got a first name? Or am I really going to call you Earnest this whole time?"

He studied me carefully, eyes betraying his confusion. "Preston, ma'am."

The respect was good. The kid was younger than me, probably closer to Cas's age. The girl in the locket couldn't have been more than three or four, so I was guessing she was his younger sister, though his daughter was also a possibility.

"Good, Preston. That's good. How many other Shock teams did they send to kill me?"

He swallowed, looking from me to Rai to Emmory and back again before he shook his head.

I clicked my tongue. "Preston, we have a few problems here. The first and biggest is that you're in a roomful of people who aren't very happy with that useless sack of shit calling himself your king. See, he's involved himself with criminals who've killed a whole bunch of my people. Children. My family. My little sister died of ebolenza.

"Have you ever seen what that does to a person? You get a fever and chills, can't keep anything down so you throw up until you run out of stuff to throw up, but your body keeps trying anyway. Then your organs start to liquefy. You die—usually—from coughing your lungs out. Literally up and out of your mouth." I gestured with my hands. "Do you have children, Preston?"

He turned sheet-white but still didn't talk.

"Anyhow, that's how my sister died. The other one was blown up. So was my niece. And someone poisoned my mother. So you could guess I am very angry right now.

"Rai? He's angrier, because he said I was safe here, and then you tried to kill me. When he gets angry, that's when bad things start happening." I let the locket fall from my fingers and dangle in front of his face. He couldn't stop the look that flashed through his eyes.

"Rai's got contacts all over the galaxy. You have to ask yourself: If the criminals your king supported could infect a princess of Indrana with ebolenza right under the noses of her BodyGuards, how easy would it be for a man as powerful as Rai to infect the daughter of some random Saxon soldier?"

I handed Rai the locket without comment and watched Preston's eyes follow its path.

"Your other problem is, I have places to be, and not a lot of time to fuck around with you playing this closed-mouthed

305

game. Frankly, I'm kind of inclined to leave you here with Rai rather than mess with you myself. Especially if you're not going to cooperate."

"You can't do this. It's a violation of interstellar law. She's a child. I don't care what kind of stories they're telling about you, you wouldn't kill a child."

"Our kingdoms aren't at war, Preston," I reminded him with a gentle smile. "You're a criminal who tried to kill me, surrounded by a whole lot of other criminals who are far better at their jobs than you were. Did I mention that I'm angry?"

I got closer until his eyes filled my vision and I could smell the fear on him. "How. Many. Other. Teams?"

Preston looked at the wall and then back at me and I knew I had him. "Two more at Midway, plus the rest of my team."

"Who's in charge?"

"I was, but now Colonel Hume is."

Nakula, thankfully, kept his mouth shut though I swore I could feel him tense behind me.

"Ah, Colonel Hume. He was looking for my governor." I let the smile spread across my face and Preston swallowed again. "I found her first."

# 31

We left Preston under Zin's watchful eyes and moved into a room down the hallway so I could talk with the others in private.

"You're not going to let me cut little pieces off him, are you?" Rai asked.

I snorted and rolled my eyes at him. "Not unless he does something stupid."

"He already did that, Majesty, when he tried to kill you."

"Emmory, are you actually suggesting I let Rai cut him up?" He gave me the Look.

"I'm just asking, because I was bluffing about the whole infecting his daughter with that awful disease. Even with everything that's happened I've only added one name to the list of people I'd like to see die from it." I would be perfectly happy to sit and watch while Phanin coughed out his own lungs. Wilson I was going to kill with my own hands. "The deal is, he's more use to me alive than dead, especially if I can manage to convince him he's on the wrong side."

"What are you thinking?" Nakula asked.

I glanced at Hao and Rai. "I'm thinking we need to take those Saxon Shock vessels intact."

Nakula laughed, but it died out when he spotted the look on my face. "You're serious."

"Majesty, why?" Emmory asked, his tone more curious than dismissive.

"I'm working on a plan, and they'll be helpful. We don't have to have all three of them, but at least one will make things easier down the line."

Hao was grinning at me. "How do you want to play this, little sister?"

"I was thinking of something along the lines of the job we pulled on Tolen VIII?"

"Your Majesty, with all due respect, you are not going to play at anything." Emmory had that tight-set jaw that meant I wasn't going to be able to argue my way past his decision.

Honestly, I'd kind of expected it, and either Iza or Kisah could play my part in the subterfuge just as easily. I was also thinking ahead, and with deliberate precision filed this victory away to use later.

I nodded. "I know, I was speaking generally, Emmory. I wasn't planning on participating."

He eyed me suspiciously. I smiled back, keeping my heart-beat and breathing even to hide my lie. It wasn't really a lie anyway. I was okay with not taking the Saxon ships myself. What I was going to do was take back the *Vajrayana* ships, and I knew that would present an even bigger fight with my *Ekam*.

Rai ignored the tension as he thought over the problem with pursed lips. "Give Hao and me half an hour to plan things out, Hail. I've got a few tricks up my sleeve, and it is *my* port. I'd rather you not blow anything up."

"Of course." I caught Emmory and Nakula by the arms

before they could follow. "You're not going either, *Ekam*. I want you here."

*Where you're safe.*

"And you are not well enough," I said to Nakula when he tried to protest. "Go talk to Jia; I want a rundown of all the forces you know of in Canafey to present to Admiral Hassan when we meet up with the fleet."

He glared at me over his shoulder, muttering as he left, "This is why I became a spy in the first place."

"What are we going to do with Captain Earnest?" Emmory asked.

I sighed and dropped into a chair. "I don't want to kill him. Thoughts?"

"You're right about how much use he could be if we can turn him. Though explaining how he escaped will be tricky, especially if we end up killing everyone else."

"I don't expect them to surrender, if that's what you're asking." My smile was cold. "And I'm sure Nakula will be just fine with Colonel Hume finding his way to Valhalla before we head out."

"I'm going to let Zin work on him," Emmory said finally, smiling at my curious look. "You didn't think he was just going to sit there and watch the captain, did you? He's probably got the man's bank account numbers by now."

I couldn't stop the laughter even though it brought to light a new sore spot from the fight. Pressing my hand to my side, I shook my head. "That man terrifies me. What happened with Fasé?"

Emmory took the seat across from me. "Not much reaction, Majesty. Stasia said she's been a bit more active in the last ten hours or so, but she's still unresponsive. I'm going to sit with her when we get under way."

"Bina said not to talk to her about it."

"I know, ma'am, but she violated her beliefs to give me my life back. It's the least I can do."

"Fine, but I want you to speak with everyone who witnessed it, make sure they know not to talk with her about it. I'll speak with the Farians when we get on board."

"I don't want her to die for me," Emmory said quietly.

The rare vulnerability hit me right in the chest, and I reached out to thread my fingers through my *Ekam*'s. "Someone once told me we don't get a say in what other people choose to sacrifice for us. I don't want her to die either, and we'll do whatever we can to keep her alive. I can't violate our agreements with the Farians though, Emmory. I'll have to tell them, even if..." I trailed off, unable to even finish the sentence.

Emmory squeezed my hand and then let me go. "I know, ma'am."

We headed back to Midway aboard Hao's ship and a sleek little transport of Rai's that bore a suspicious resemblance to one of the Solarian military's newest fighter prototypes. Two days and six hours later, the acquisition of the Saxon ships went off without a hitch.

I listened to the whole thing over the com link. All three ships had been locked down to the port on Rai's order, and for further assurance he'd sent mechanics in at night to disable the ships.

To help secure Captain Earnest's assistance, we'd knocked his team out by shutting off the life support on their ship just enough to put them all out but not kill them. The other two Saxon vessels were supposed to go down the same way, but something had tipped off Colonel Hume, and the boarding parties met resistance.

Nakula fumed at my side the whole time. I'd repeatedly rejected his requests to join Hao. His injuries would have made him a liability. So we both listened as Hao laughed at Hume's demand that he fight him and instead killed the Saxon with a well-placed shot.

"Welcome to my life," I said, patting him on the arm and laughing when he glared at me.

"I'm not the empress."

I grinned. "No, but you're important, and more to the point you're still injured. Also, I like Jia, and I don't particularly want to see her crying because your stupid ass got killed on some revenge trip."

"I've never met anyone like her," Nakula murmured, glancing over his shoulder at the closed door that separated us from where Jia was hard at work detailing what she'd seen of the Saxon forces on Canafey Minor. "You should have seen her, Majesty—"

"Will you call me Hail? For Shiva's sake, it's just weird for that to come out of your mouth. At least do it in private, Nakula, for me?" I said before he could protest.

"Fine, Hail." He stuck his tongue out at me. "When I first rescued her, they'd been interrogating her for hours. She was beaten to shit. The first thing she said to me was I should take her head and dispose of it. Her voice was as calm as if she'd asked for a cup of tea." He closed his eyes as though he still couldn't believe it. "I dragged her through hell and back. Not a single complaint. She kicked my ass a few times when I even dared assume she wasn't capable."

"Not all us nobles are pampered and useless."

Nakula laughed, dragging both hands through his chestnut hair. When he looked up at me, his heart was in his eyes. "She's the world, Hail. My whole world. How do I even compete when we get home? She's a governor. I'm nothing. I don't even know who my mother was."

"You can start by not thinking of it as a competition, idiot." I punched him lightly in the chest. "You really think she gives two shits who your mother was? Don't put her on a fucking pedestal, Nakula. Treat her like a person. Pay attention to the way she looks at you and stop worrying so much about what you should do as far as Indranan society is concerned." I grinned at him. "I hear there's a new empress in town and things are changing."

"*Your Majesty,*" Indula said over the com link. "*The ships are secure. Rai says it'll be about an hour before they'll be ready for takeoff.*"

"*Good to hear. We're going to dock.*"

"*Yes, ma'am. Iza wants to know what to do with the prisoners?*"

"*Put them in lockdown. Separate them between the ships.*"

"*Acknowledged,*" Indula said, and the com clicked off.

"Dailun, come up to the bridge, please."

My newest recruit appeared a few minutes later. "*Hai, jiejie?*"

"Go get the *War Bastard* ready for departure. Take Nakula and Kisah with you. I'll send you coordinates when we get away from here."

Dailun nodded. Nakula got to his feet and smiled at me as he followed the kid to the door.

"You're a hell of an empress, Hail. Don't let anyone tell you differently."

I snorted with laughter and waved him out the door, but there was no denying the warmth in my chest at his words. It felt like I was—slowly—getting the hang of this.

I brought the ship into dock and spent a few minutes shutting her down. Satisfied, I got up and took the stairs two at a time to the lower level intent on going to the medical bay to check on Gita, who had suffered seven broken ribs from Captain Earnest's kick.

"You look like shit." I whistled at Hao, who was coming up from the cargo bay.

"I don't care what your *Ekam* says, next time you get to go," he teased. "I'm fine. Most of it isn't mine." He tossed me something covered in gore.

I bobbled the blood-covered device with a look of horror. "Bugger me. Hao, what the shit?"

"Hume's *zhù*. I figured you needed it. Now I need a shower while we're hooked up to Midway's water system."

I swallowed back the bile that threatened as I looked down at the *smati* hardware in my hand. "Take your time, Rai said it would be at least an hour to get crews together for those ships."

Hao nodded. "Then we're headed to meet up with your admiral. Do you have your plan together for retrieving these mystery ships of yours?"

"Still working on it. Why?"

"Been thinking about it myself, but I don't have all the details. If you're willing to share, you want to go over it once we're under way?"

"Sure." I edged by him. "Go clean up, you smell like a carrion house."

His laughter followed me down the hallway and I was smiling when I came through the med bay doors.

"Majesty," Henna said with a nervous little bow. "Your people get hurt a lot."

"Hazard of the job, I'm afraid." I handed her the hardware. "Will you clean that up as best as you can? Be careful. We need to see if we can get any information from it."

"Of course, Majesty."

313

I headed for the sink and vigorously washed my hands. "How are you, Gita?"

"Fine, Majesty." Her voice was breathy with pain and I rolled my eyes at her.

Henna was less silent with her disdain. "Not fine. She would have been better off getting kicked in the chest by a Hanover elephant. I'm still amazed none of those ribs punctured a lung."

"I don't need platitudes, Gita." The reprimand was gentle, but she still flushed and looked at the bedspread.

"I'm sorry I failed you."

I perched on the edge of the bed and rode the wave of pain I knew was going to come with my words. "You know, Jet said something similar to me, right after he'd saved me from being killed. All because I'd gotten shot in the process. That Saxon was waiting for me, and you were right where you needed to be—between me and him. Don't beat yourself up over the fact that he moved faster than you. Find a way to make sure it doesn't happen again."

"Yes, ma'am."

"Now rest. You're out of the lineup until we meet with Admiral Hassan and can get a Farian to heal you." I looked through the glass windows to where Emmory sat by Fasé's bed.

"Still not talking," Henna offered, anticipating my question. "Better though. Readings improved. Life coming back. Here's your brain chip." She handed me a little bag with the hardware inside.

"Emmory told me about your conversation with the Farian back home, ma'am," Gita said. "Is it really that bad?"

"It could be," I replied.

"What are you going to do, ma'am?"

"I don't know. It's out of my hands." I hated saying it, but it was the truth. I could object to a decision to end her life and plead Fasé's case with them, but the Farians were our allies and I couldn't risk that for just one woman. I gave Gita and Henna a final nod and crossed through into the other room. Alba got up from Emmory's side as I came in the room.

"Alba, I'll need you in a moment. I just wanted to check on Fasé." I rested a hand on Emmory's shoulder. He had his hands wrapped around hers, her pale fingers so tiny in his grip. I put my hand over the top, wishing I could just will her better.

"How did everything go?"

"You didn't listen in?" I asked, surprised.

Emmory shook his head. "I thought it would be better to be focused on her. There wasn't anything I could have done anyway."

"The ships are ours. Colonel Hume is dead, along with most of his team and all of the other team. They took Captain Earnest's team alive without firing a shot though, and Hao got this." I waved the bag and Emmory's eyebrows shot up.

"Is that—"

"Yeah. I'm not even going to ask him how he got it out."

"Give it to Zin. Hopefully he can retrieve something off it."

"I'll have him coordinate with Dailun. I sent Nakula and Kisah with him to get the *War Bastard* prepped for departure."

Emmory nodded. "Go find Zin now. I'll catch up with you in a little bit. The faster he gets into that, the better chance we have of not dying when we attempt this insanity."

# 32

We delayed our departure so Dailun could run back from the *War Bastard* and help Zin get the colonel's *smati* working. I paced in the background as they worked until Hao got in my way.

"Sit." He raised a copper eyebrow in perfect harmony with mine. "Your patience hasn't improved at all, *sha zhu*."

"Neither has your bossiness." But I dropped into a seat, crossing my arms over my chest and resisting the urge to tap my foot.

"See what you've gotten yourself into?" Hao said in Cheng to Dailun.

"I'm sure it will be okay, honored brother," Dailun replied with a laugh.

"I can understand you two."

"I should hope so. I'd be disappointed if your Cheng went to shit after only a few months of easy living."

"Oh hush. You call that easy living? People were trying to kill me."

"Such is life." Hao took the seat nearby. "Spill your plan, little sister. Let's see where it takes us."

"Right now the *Vajrayana* ships are dead weight. When the lockdown went into effect it shut down everything: navigation, engines, life support, gravity, the works."

"So why haven't the Saxons blown them up?"

I tapped a hand on the console. "According to Jia, it was because they still had her in custody and were trying to get the lock codes from her. I'd hazard a guess that now they're trying like mad to learn whatever they can from them even if they can't get the things to fly."

"There will be Indranan technicians as prisoners also," Hao said, and I nodded.

"I'm hoping they're keeping some of them in the shipyard and didn't send all of them down to the surface. If they're trying to reverse engineer anything they'd need some techs there. Cooperative or not, it wouldn't matter." I leaned back in my chair. "We'll need a few, I suspect. So breaking them out is the priority."

"So your plan is to fly in, take the shipyard, break the techs out of prison, get the ships, and take the system back?"

"It's a little more complicated than that, but essentially yes."

"Might I suggest something other than brute force? Since storming a Saxon-held shipyard is likely to get us all killed?"

"You're being awfully lippy today."

"Digging through someone's brains for a computer chip does that to me."

"*Yatta!*" Dailun thumped the console and grinned at Zin. "That should do it."

Code started crawling across the screen and Zin nodded in approval. "Looks like it did. Good job."

Dailun nodded, first to Zin and then in my direction, before he scrambled out of his seat and headed off the bridge.

"Rai." I keyed up the com link. "We're ready to go."

"*Haiya.* You have coordinates for me yet?"

"When we're far enough away from Midway that I can be sure no one's listening in."

Rai grumbled, but I held firm. We couldn't be certain that Captain Earnest had told us the truth and I wasn't taking any chances—beyond trusting Rai not to sell me out—about the location of Admiral Hassan's fleet.

"*Auho!*" Zin waved a hand in the air.

"Gotta go, Rai. I'll send the coordinates when we hit the rendezvous point." I hopped out of my chair and leaned over Zin's shoulder. Hao took the pilot chair and began running through the departure checklist.

"Colonel Hume was on Canafey Minor overseeing Governor Ashwari's interrogation. It's all here, ma'am. Their plans for the system, troop strength on the ground, and how many ships they sent to take the system." Zin began feeding me pieces of information via our *smati* link as fast as he could decode them. "It corroborates what Nakula and the governor have told us, but there's even more detail."

"They sent more troop carriers than actual destroyers." I muttered a curse. "Because they knew we'd pulled the 44th Fleet out of there. Phanin must have told them."

"That's good news for us though, Majesty. Easier to take the system back if there's only a handful of ships able to do battle."

"We're not taking the whole system back."

Zin frowned. "You didn't argue when Hao said it. Hang on." He grabbed me by the arm to steady me as the *Pentacost* lifted off from the dock.

I threw Hao a look, but the man just grinned. "No sense in just stealing a few ships, little sister. Not when you can take the whole system. You'll have your admiral's fleet plus fancy new ships. I just assumed you didn't want Saxons camping out in your backyard."

"Okay, fine. So what's your stealthy suggestion?"

"I'd think that if we brought them the Empress of Indrana they'd let us in with open arms."

Zin and I both stiffened.

Hao uncrossed his arms and looked at us. "Really?"

"Sorry—it's automatic. A lot of people have been trying to kill me lately."

He shook his head. "I am *hurt*. You are family."

I made a rude gesture at him. "I said I was sorry. Keep going. What's the plan?"

"Those Saxon ships are bound to have extra uniforms. We take those and march you to the detention center of the shipyard. Bust out the techs and take them back out with no one the wiser."

I exhaled, rubbing at my forehead. "I need the techs to work on the ships in dock. It would be easier for them to hack into them from the shipyard command center rather than an actual ship."

"How much easier?"

"They'd have heat, air, and gravity?"

Hao muttered a curse. "What precisely do you need them to do?"

"The *Vajrayana* are advanced ships with the capacity for self-sustained flight and preprogrammed maneuverability. They require far less womanpower than a normal ship. Theoretically we can slave them all under the control of one ship and order that one to warp from the system. The others will follow."

"I don't like that 'theoretically' bit you threw in there."

"Me neither, but it's the best we've got. They haven't been fully tested yet. Anyway, that will be easier to do from the command center than from the bridge of one of the ships."

"It's easy enough to modify the plan. We are still just going to take the whole system though, right?"

I couldn't really argue with him. Especially since I was more annoyed that all Hao had done was show me I was starting to think more like an empress than a gunrunner.

The bigger picture was that we win back the Canafey system, and now was as good a time as any. Plus, I didn't have a home base of my own, and Canafey would make the perfect spot.

"I would think warping out, getting people on those ships, and then warping back in with the *Vajrayana* fleet and all of Admiral Hassan's ships would be enough to subdue whatever forces the Saxons have at Canafey."

The biggest problem was getting from the detention center to the command center. "What if, when you take me into the detention center, I demand to see the commander of the shipyard? Chances on them complying with that?"

Zin thought it over. "Pretty good, I'd say, Majesty. Given your notoriety."

"The alternative is a shoot-out. But either way it's the best way into the command center without a lot of casualties." I made a face. "Zin, what about Captain Earnest?"

"What about him, ma'am?"

"This plan would go a lot smoother if we had him on our side. Can we convince him to walk us into a Saxon-controlled shipyard without betraying us to the guards?"

Zin shook his head. "I doubt it, Majesty. In all honesty, I don't think he'd do it. It's not that he's particularly loyal to Trace as his king. He's loyal to the idea of the alliance. His wife is from one of the Alliance worlds, not from Saxony proper."

"If we threaten his family?"

"His parents are dead. His wife and child are all he has left. We bought some goodwill not killing his team, but I don't think it's enough to get him to betray his kingdom."

"Realistically, what's waiting for him back home besides being shot as a traitor?"

Zin shook his head. "He hasn't given us anything of major value. And since he's the only ranking officer alive, he gets to tell the story of how we got the drop on the other Shock troops.

"Plus, technically he is a prisoner of war, ma'am. Official declaration of war or not, we were at war with the Saxons the moment Trace shot Emmory and tried to kill you."

I rubbed both hands over my face. "I want to talk with him."

"Of course, ma'am."

*"Majesty, Fasé is asking for you."* Emmory's voice sounded in my head.

"I need to go see Fasé," I said to Zin. "Stay here and keep working on that information. I want everything you can get out of Hume's *smati*. I'll message you before I go to see the captain."

"Hail, we're almost at the rendezvous point," Hao said.

I passed the coordinates for Admiral Hassan's location on to him via the *smati* link as I headed for the stairs. At the same time I started sending Alba the information I'd gotten from Zin and from Hao. I needed someone else to put the mass of details we'd just discussed into something legible for presenting to Admiral Hassan.

I was sure Emmory would balk at the idea of using me as bait anyway, despite the fact that one way or another I had to be in that shipyard.

"Majesty." Fasé lifted her head as I came in the room, but Emmory helped her sit up. Blue-purple bruises decorated the fragile skin beneath her golden eyes, and her fingers were knotted together.

"Fasé, you are looking well."

"Not well, Your Majesty, but I wanted to see you. Emmory told me you spoke with Bina and the others have been notified."

I sat on the bed. "How can we help?"

Her smile was wan. "You cannot, Majesty. I have violated the laws of my people. I have enjoyed your empire, but you cannot do anything to help me. Promise me."

"But you—"

"Good intent or not, Majesty. It is wrong to bring life from death. Only the gods have that kind of power. Only the immortal ones *should* have that kind of power. We are too weak for it. Even now I think of the feeling when I returned Emmory, and I—" She broke off and shuddered.

"Fasé." Emmory's voice was calm, and seemed to help her agitation. "That's enough for now. We'll talk about it later. Go back to sleep."

She lay back down and closed her eyes, and her breathing evened out almost immediately.

"Majesty, outside."

I followed Emmory into the hallway. "I see why Bina said not to talk with her about it. What do we do?"

He shook his head. "A crisis of faith isn't something that's easily solved, Majesty. No matter what we believe, Fasé believes she's done something unforgivable." He looked at the ceiling. "I will keep talking to her, but I fear there is not much we can do until the Farians get involved."

"Bugger me. See if you can get in touch with Captain Gill through Caspel. Maybe if we talk to her about this, she can do something?"

"I don't know that it will do any good, but I can try."

Emmory smiled slightly, but shook his head. "We can't force her to do anything. Your authority doesn't supersede her faith."

"I was afraid of that." I tapped him on the arm. "Zin cracked into Colonel Hume's *smati*. We've got the Saxon numbers at Canafey. And we've got a plan for taking back the system."

"The system?" Emmory raised an eyebrow. "I thought we were just going in after the ships?"

"The plan changed," I said with a grin. "Come on, I'll let Alba explain."

Emmory didn't take the news that I'd be going into Canafey as well as I'd hoped.

"Absolutely not. We get to the fleet and you're staying on Admiral Hassan's ship until this is over."

"Emmory, it's the best plan we've got. Their guards will be down thinking they've beaten us. Even if we can't convince Captain Earnest to help, we'll figure something else out to conceal the fact that the Saxons bringing us in as prisoners aren't Saxons at all."

"If you get killed, where does that leave us?"

"Alice is perfectly capable of leading an empire, possibly even better than I," I replied and threw my hands in the air. "I let you have the ships in Midway. That was an unnecessary risk. This one is *necessary*."

"I won't let you, Majesty."

"You can't stop me." I raised an eyebrow at him. "I have the lock codes."

You could have heard a shell drop in the room. In what under less stressful circumstances would have been comical, my BodyGuards looked at each other in silent question. Jia stared at me with a horrified expression over the com link. Only the gunrunners—both those in the room and those watching on screen—seemed unsurprised by my announcement.

Emmory visibly struggled to get his voice even before he looked past me at the image of Jia on one of the screens. "Governor, please tell me you kept a backup copy of the lock codes."

"I'm very sorry, *Ekam* Tresk. The codes are protected from copying. The whole file must be transferred."

The look Emmory shot me was deadly, but I answered it with a smile. "You need me. This is the best plan and you know it."

"Okay," Zin said, deliberately walking between us and breaking up the staring contest. "You win, Majesty. Let's hear the rest of the plan."

I watched through lowered lashes as Zin brought Captain Earnest into the *Pentacost*'s galley. The young Saxon's eyes flicked from me to Hao to Emmory and then back to me as he sat down at the table.

"Day of reckoning is at hand, I see," he said.

I ran a finger over the rim of my mug. "I like to think it's just a conversation, not anything quite so planet-shattering. Would you like something to drink?"

"No." His defenses were up, as expected, and rather than a frightened young man, a Shock Marine was staring back at me through those blue eyes. "Whatever you're going to ask me, whatever you want me to do, the answer is no."

"You don't even know the question."

"I don't have to. I'm not going to help you with anything else. I don't care what you do to me, ma'am."

"Honor and loyalty I get. However, spare me the macho bravado. Trust me, you would care, everyone does in the end," I replied, rolling my eyes. "I don't have time for it, Captain. I'm trying to save lives."

"Indy lives."

"Saxon lives," I countered, coolly, and watched his eyes narrow. "Do you really want Saxony to go to war with Indrana? Your home is right on the border, Captain; you don't think there's a damn good chance your wife and child would end up as casualties?

"I'm not threatening them," I said with a hand up before he could say anything. "I'm asking you to think about what happens when two giants fight. Do you really think they care about the ants that get trampled underfoot in the process?"

"I've already betrayed the Corps; you're asking me to betray my nation." He shook his head and looked at his hands. "I can't do it."

"I'm asking you to help me stop a war before it starts. How is that a betrayal?" The last few words were clipped as my temper struggled free.

*"Hail, take a step back,"* Hao said over our *smati* link. *"You won't get anywhere angry."*

*"I'm not getting anywhere period. Why am I doing this again?"*

*"Because you're stubborn?"*

I couldn't stop the snort of laughter, and Preston blinked at me as I pushed away from the table. "You're right," I said, not to him but to Hao. "Zin, take him back to his cell; we'll do this the hard way."

# 33

"Your Majesty." Admiral Hassan went to a knee, her command staff and the other sailors in the massive bay of the *Vajra* following suit.

"Inana, I am glad to see you well." I urged her to her feet and embraced her. "I have some prisoners for you and a few people who could use some assistance from a Farian."

"Of course, Majesty. Chief Warrant Officer Yash will take them into custody." Admiral Hassan snapped her fingers and a stocky woman with impressive biceps appeared at her side.

"Majesty." She bowed low.

"Zin will give you the details," I said with a smile and a nod.

"This is Lieutenant Hasai Moren," Inana said.

"Majesty." The slender young Farian held his hands out, his golden eyes warm. I took them and relief swept through me. "May you be well."

"Thank you." I swallowed back my fear. Despite Bina's warning, my gut was screaming at me about Fasé and I couldn't ignore it. "Are you the oldest Farian on board, Hasai? We need to speak about Fasé; I sent a message ahead."

"I am not. The others are on their way. I was told to instruct you to take my sister to your quarters and we will look at her there. The comfort of friends is best in times of crisis."

"She is your sister?"

He shrugged. "Of a sort. The distinction is too complex for your language."

"We will take her to our quarters if you will meet us there? I'd like to speak with you all privately before you see her."

"I will let the others know. Major Morri would like you to be reassured things are not always as bad as they seem. Do you have more injured?"

"Start with him." I grabbed Emmory by the collar and dragged him forward before he could protest. Hasai performed the same ritual and my *Ekam* lost his hunched-over posture. The lines of pain that had etched themselves into his face disappeared.

Fasé walked by her kinsman, leaning heavily on Stasia. Hasai only glanced her way with a gentle smile and then moved past to Alba so he could check her arm.

"Masami, Sabeen." I embraced Matriarch Tobin and then Vandi with genuine joy. "I am so very relieved to see you safe."

"Be relieved at this one's charms," the elderly matriarch replied, jerking a thumb in Sabeen's direction. "She's the one who talked an Indranan freighter captain into hiding us from the Saxons and getting us off the planet."

"He was going to do it anyway, but I may have promised him a government shipping contract as a reward, Majesty," Sabeen said, her cheeks flushing as she looked at the floor.

My surprised chuckles turned to laughter and the young matriarch blushed harder when I patted her on the back. "Well done. Get with Alba so she has the man's information. Once things have calmed down we'll get him on the payroll."

"Yes, ma'am."

"Admiral, allow me to introduce Cheng Hao, Johar, and Bakara Rai."

After much discussion we'd decided it was best if the bulk of Hao and Rai's people stayed with the ships, but I wanted these two with me for the discussion of our plan and there was no way Johar was staying behind.

Greetings were exchanged all around, with Johar holding Inana's hand a little too long. Rai elbowed her, and she rolled her eyes at him but released my admiral.

"If you'll follow me, I have guest quarters set up for all of you." Inana cleared her throat and started across the bay. "Everyone has instructions not to interfere with your Body-Guards or your other companions, and they are all authorized to wear weapons on board, though I'd ask if you wouldn't mind swapping them out for something slightly more friendly toward my ship."

I laughed. "Of course. We've had more than enough excitement lately and there's plenty more to come. I don't think we need to add explosive decompression to the list."

"No, we do not."

"Who was the traitor?"

Sadness swept over Admiral Hassan's face. "Cole. Commander Hamprasade," she clarified for the others. "My aide."

I muttered the curse. "I'm so sorry." I'd met the admiral's aide several times. Alba had worked with her closely and I glanced at my chamberlain with a sympathetic smile when she gasped.

"Me, too. I trusted her. Hell, I groomed her for the position. Phanin got someone on board down in engineering. Cole let him sweet-talk her into betraying the empire. Stupid idiot. Lantle shot her. We've got the man in the brig."

"Where are my BodyGuards?"

"In your quarters, Majesty. As soon as we got them set up, they insisted someone be on duty at all times. They've been running in shifts for several days now."

"They'll be happy for some relief then."

"I'd offer you food, Majesty—"

"Don't worry about it. We're headed for a place to restock. Pass these coordinates to your fleet."

I'd chosen this spot because it was just a short warp hop away from one of Po-Sin's resupply stations. I'd spent an hour on the com link haggling with him over the cost. Even Alba had been pleased with the results, though Matriarch Saito had gone paler than I thought possible as the cost went up.

"Yes, ma'am."

We came around the corner and I spotted Lantle at the door. The older man smiled, touching his hands to his heart and lips and forehead. "Your Majesty. It is a great relief to see you again."

I touched the back of his head, pulling him in and touching my forehead to his. "You as well. How are the other two?"

Elizah and Ikeki were both new guards, which was part of the reason they'd been on the ship and not on planet with us.

"They are sleeping, Majesty."

"Let them, and you go get some sleep as well." I looked over my shoulder at Emmory, who nodded.

"In a moment, Majesty."

Orders were issued in a flurry; Emmory stayed at my side as Kisah and Indula went into the quarters first. It all went like clockwork and I ignored Hao's amused smile as I headed into our new quarters.

"I'll let you get settled, Majesty," Admiral Hassan said. "If you'd like to com me when you're ready?"

"I will."

"You're relieved," Emmory said to Lan. "Good job, Lan." He held out his hand and the Guard took it with a smile.

"We've got quarters set up across the hall and just one door down," Lan said to Zin. "I can show you."

"Majesty, I'm going to take Fasé to lie down for a little while in the BodyGuard quarters," Stasia said, and I nodded.

"The lieutenant said it would help her to stay with us. Take Kisah with you." I didn't know how long it would be before Hasai brought the other Farians to see me. I hoped to have a little more time with Fasé to convince her things were going to be all right before we did.

"Is there anything to drink in here?" Johar flopped onto the couch, stretching her long legs out in front of her. "Would you believe those stupid Saxons didn't have any alcohol on their ships? How do people live like that?"

"We don't all have mechanical livers, my darling," Rai said, settling onto the couch next to her.

"Mechanical liver?"

"There was an accident," she said with a grin, and patted her torso. "This one works much better. Drinks, O imperial one."

Hao snorted with laughter. "You should keep her around, she'll make sure you stay humble."

"Rai would never let me."

"Rai's not the boss of me," Johar said.

"I'm not sure Indrana is ready for you until after this whole coup thing calms down." I blew her a kiss and went to investigate the bank of cabinets on the far wall. Three tries garnered me some glasses and a bottle of rather expensive Earth vodka.

Johar took them and poured out drinks. "The universe is a horrible place. I like seeing it treat my friends well. To the Empress of Indrana."

I laughed and tossed back the shot. "Don't break the furniture," I said as I handed Hao my glass for a refill. Taking it back, I headed for the bedroom. "Alba, I'm going to lie down; let me know when the Farians arrive. I'll—"

The door slid open and Cas scrambled through. "Majesty, it's Fasé."

"Bugger me." I set my drink down, sloshing liquid over the rim onto the table, and booked it out the door. Emmory was right behind me. "Where is she?"

"In the landing bay. I don't know how she got past me, ma'am. She took Kisah down at the door."

"She didn't..."

Cas shook his head. "No, she didn't kill her, just knocked her out. Stasia went after her."

"Majesty, what is going on?" Admiral Hassan met us in the hallway with Zin on her heels.

"Admiral, call your Farians to the main landing bay. Emmory, tell her."

Emmory's voice was clipped as he filled Hassan in on Fasé. I tuned him out, trying to calm the fear in my chest as we ran through the ship.

"Get all these people out," I said, pushing my way through the crowd that had gathered. Once the sailors realized it was me, the crowd parted.

Fasé stood at the far edge of the bay with a gun in her hand. My maid was several meters away, her hands up, and though I wasn't close enough to hear her words I knew she was pleading with Fasé.

Tears streaked down Fasé's face and her golden eyes darted wildly to me when I skidded to a stop. "Fasé, please put down the gun, we will fix this."

"There's nothing to fix, Majesty. I am unclean. I abandoned my faith, everything that matters. I am broken."

"Fasé, you saved two lives," Zin said from my side. "Please, there has to be some good in that. Your gods can't be so unforgiving they wouldn't see your intent behind your actions."

"I can feel it." Fasé slammed her fist against her chest. "You humans can't understand."

"Let me go." I slipped out of Zin's grasp. "Get everyone back. That's an order, Zin," I said when he didn't move, and the sharp crack of my voice shook Zin out of his shock.

"Fasé." Holding my hands up, I crossed the yawning space between us. I could feel Emmory staring at me from my right side, but he didn't move. There wasn't time. There wasn't any time to talk over a plan, and all I could do was hope that my *Ekam* had reached a point where he could at least guess my motives enough to play along. "You're right, I can't even begin to understand how you are feeling."

"Then don't stop me, ma'am." Tears spilled from her eyes, tracking down her face. "Let me end this awful nightmare."

"Don't you see that I can't?" I whispered, taking a step closer and reaching a hand out to her. "You are mine, Fasé. I won't abandon you, not when you need me the most. I can't understand your pain; I won't insult you by trying to pretend I can. All I can do is tell you to take a breath. Put down this decision, even if only for a moment. Let me carry it for you."

Fasé's empty hand fluttered upward, her fingers brushing mine. "Majesty, I—"

"Your Majesty, please step away, you are putting yourself in danger."

Fasé stiffened at the new voice and pressed the gun to her chin.

"Fasé, please, no," Stasia whimpered.

I swallowed my curse and glanced over my shoulder. Three Farians crossed the bay—Lieutenant Moren followed the two women. It was the older one who had spoken. Her red curls were streaked with white at the temples.

"Child, put down the gun," the woman said. "It does not have to be like this."

"I gave him life. I know I shouldn't have, but Zin..." Fasé looked in his direction. "I could feel his heart breaking and I just—"

"Child, you sinned. It is not—"

"The power." Fasé shook her head. "The awful rush of playing god. Ripping life from the hands of death. There is nothing left for me. I crossed the line that should never even be approached, and this is what is required of me."

Her finger tightened on the trigger.

"No." I grabbed her hand and watched her eyes go wide. The Farians behind me gasped.

"Majesty, no. Let me go."

"Why?"

Fasé shook her head. "If you're touching me when I— Majesty, please. It could kill you, too."

I tightened my hand around hers. "Then so be it, Fasé. You swore to me you wouldn't hurt me. Remember?" I stepped closer and pressed my forehead to hers. "Death you deal and death you shall become. You have dealt no death, Fasé, only life. So many lives. Emmory's life. Zin's life. Captain Gill. How many people have you saved over the years? All you do is give life—how is that wrong?

"Now it is my life in your hands, and on my honor, if you want to walk into the darkness, I will walk there with you."

No one breathed. I knew Emmory was close but not close enough to save me if Fasé pulled the trigger. I kept my eyes on hers, watched the pain slide through the golden depths and saw the decision in them before she even realized she'd made it.

"I am loyal to my gods and to you, Majesty. I will not harm you."

I caught her as she sagged against me and sank to the deck with her in my arms. Grabbing the gun as we dropped, I sent it sliding across the floor toward Emmory and then wrapped the sobbing Farian up against me. "It's all right. It's all right. We will get through this, I swear to you," I murmured.

Fasé went limp in my arms and I looked up into the furious gaze of the older Farian. Emmory stood behind her, his fury better concealed behind his carefully blank face.

"She could have killed you, Your Majesty," the woman said. My *smati* identified her as Major Dio Morri.

"The probability was better that she wanted to keep me safe more than she wanted to die." I didn't fight as the other two Farians lifted Fasé out of my arms. "Because she was dead set on dying until I made her add me into the choice." I got to my feet and stared her down. "The better question is, did I just save her for a worse fate?"

The question shocked the woman and she stared at me for a moment before she visibly composed herself and bowed. "My apologies, Majesty. This has been extremely upsetting for all of us. Forgive me for not being here sooner; I didn't understand the gravity of the situation and I should have told Hasai to bring Fasé straight to me. I did not think Fasé would take it so hard. He had just informed us you were here when the call came. Thank you for what you have done for her. I do not know what the future holds; that will be up to her and to the Pedalion to decide. However, you gave her the time and for that I am grateful."

"I would do the same for any of my people, Major."

"Of course." Dio bowed again. "I suspect your *Ekam* would like a word with you in private, Majesty. I will keep you updated on Fasé's condition."

"I appreciate it. If you'll allow it, I'd like Stasia to be able to go with you?"

Dio glanced over at where my maid stood, slightly supported by Zin, and nodded. "Of course, it may help." She gestured and walked from the docking bay with Stasia at her side.

I headed for the door, Emmory and Zin falling into place on either side without a word. I got the distinct impression of being marched back to my quarters like when we first met. No one said a word until we came through the door and Hao got up out of his seat.

"Is Fasé—"

"She's alive," I said, heading for the liquor cabinet.

"Should I go?" Hao looked between me and Emmory with a raised eyebrow.

"No, stay, you'll enjoy this." I poured a drink and dropped onto the couch. "Emmory's about to chew my ass."

Hao's eyebrow went higher.

"She grabbed a Farian with a death wish and practically dared her to kill them both."

"You what?"

"Oh, bugger me." I rolled my eyes at the ceiling and tossed back my drink. I'd heard that tone from Hao a few times over the years.

"Are you kidding me? What were you thinking?"

"That I didn't want Fasé to die," I snapped.

"You don't lead your people by throwing yourself recklessly into danger," Emmory said.

"Too right." Hao nodded in agreement. "I taught you better than that, *sha zhu*."

"Oh shut up, both of you." I got up for another drink and eyed Zin, who was leaning by the door with his arms crossed. He had been strangely silent while the other two shouted at me.

"You especially, Hao, pretending to be a criminal, but where do you think I learned the concept of never letting my people take the fall for me?" I waved my drink at him. "I never once saw you put yourself ahead of the crew. And you—"

"I haven't taught you anything, Majesty."

"Cowshit. You care about Fasé the same as I do. You always put others in front of yourself, Emmorlien Tresk, even when you don't have to."

My *Ekam* actually looked away and I could swear I'd embarrassed him. "Are you going to weigh in here?"

Zin raised a shoulder in a half shrug. "She did good." He shook his head and pinned his partner with a look. "Stop shouting at me, Emmory. You didn't want Fasé to die any more than I did, any more than she did. Hail did something about it, possibly the only thing that could have stopped a grief-stricken Farian from blowing her Shiva-damned brains out all over the docking bay.

"We're not loyal to the throne or to Indrana as much as we may try to pretend otherwise. None of us are. We're loyal to her." Zin jabbed a finger in my direction. "Because she's worth it. Because we know when it comes down to it she's just as willing to sacrifice herself for us as we are for her. Even this one," he said, pointing at Hao, "is here because of her; there's no other reason a member of Po-Sin's own family would be helping us."

Emmory closed his eyes. "Zin, she could have died," he whispered, his voice hoarse.

*"Hridayam."* Zin murmured the endearment, pushing away from the wall and grabbing Emmory by the back of the neck in a surprising display of affection. "So could we all. But Fasé is alive and so is our empress. I, for one, will take the wins where I can get them."

# 34

Zin's words hung around me long after my team had departed and left me to sleep. It had been desperation more than a concrete plan that had driven me to grab for Fasé, but I hadn't really considered that I'd been counting on her loyalty to save us both.

More than that, Zin's quiet certainty that not only he and Emmory, but Hao as well, were here purely out of loyalty to me and not because of some grander purpose was something that I couldn't quite wrap my head around.

That kept me up at night as we made the otherwise uneventful trip to the refueling depot. It was better than nightmares, even if it did result in me being right back to exhausted and unable to function. The resupply went off without a hitch, and later that evening I joined Admiral Hassan, the matriarchs, and several members of her crew for dinner.

We'd brought eight ships to Red Cliff for the negotiations, and all of them had made it out safely. Eight more had defected from 2nd Fleet when Admiral Shul arrived, and a dozen more from Home Fleet had arrived at the rendezvous point just before us.

We retired to her office to discuss the strategy for Canafey, joined by the matriarchs, Alba, Emmory, Nakula, Hao, Rai, and the admiral's staff.

"Thanks to the information the empress retrieved, we have a good idea of the number and types of ships the Saxons have at Canafey." Admiral Hassan tapped a few keys on her desktop, and an image of the Canafey system appeared. It zoomed in around Major, where the shipyard and my *Vajrayana* ships could be found.

"There are few to no vessels around Minor; all the fighting there has been on the ground. Even if there are ships in that vicinity, it would take them the better part of a day to make the trip in system." Hassan tapped another key, replacing the image with one of a ship. "The *Vajrayana* ships have a hive mind function that would enable us to warp them out of the Canafey system without having to put people physically on each ship."

"The problem is we have to either get someone on one of the ships to do this, or do it from the command center of the shipyard," I said, rolling my cup of chai between my palms. "We're hoping the Saxons will have some of the technicians who were working on the ships in the detention area of the shipyard so they have easy access to them. The alternative is they've sent them all down to the planet, which will make our lives extremely difficult."

"I'd bet good money they've got people in the shipyard, Majesty," Nakula said. "Colonel Hume made several comments about how they could get help elsewhere once they'd gotten the lock codes from Governor Ashwari."

"True." I nodded. "And Jia said she was sure they'd be trying to learn whatever they could. Which makes me think we'll be dealing with a bunch of engineers rather than Saxon Shockers." I pushed to my feet and leaned on the admiral's desk, setting the image back to Canafey. "We'll take two of the Saxon ships right into the shipyard. No one will question our presence. We grab a few techs from the detention center, head up to the command center, take over, get the ships linked up, and we all warp back out before anyone realizes what's happened."

"Majesty, how do the teams get past the security in the docking bay? Any kind of confrontation and the alarms will be raised." Admiral Zellin had shuttled over from the *Helena Bristol*. The slender officer didn't show any outward signs of grief over her sister's death, but I'd offered my quiet condolences when we met. We'd never found any proof that Matriarch Zellin was involved in the plot, but if she had been, her punishment had already been carried out.

"Well, we were hoping we could convince Captain Earnest to change sides, but that's not going to happen. So, Hao?" I gestured for him and he pushed himself away from the wall.

"I have several programs that provide excellent identity masking. It won't stand up against deep scans but should be enough to get us into the shipyard and past the guards in the detention center."

"Good." I nodded. "Once we're on the bridge, we'll have the technicians do their magic. The ships will warp out and we can leave in the chaos. No one is going to question three Saxon ships booking out of there when that's exactly what all the *Vajrayana* ships are going to be doing."

"That sounds like an excellent plan, Majesty." Admiral Hassan crossed her arms and raised an eyebrow. "You want to tell me why you think I'm going to let you do it?"

"Well, for starters because Saxon Shock troops bringing the Empress of Indrana back as a prisoner is going to open doors pretty damn fast." I grinned at her. "And I've got the lock codes. This doesn't happen without me."

Admiral Hassan looked at the ceiling and then at Emmory, who lifted his hands in surrender.

"I tried to tell her no, ma'am, but short of forcibly removing the codes from her *smati* there's no way to get them."

"I'm surprised you didn't hear the argument before we landed," I said. "Emmory was quite upset."

"Majesty—"

"We're not going over it again, Admiral. If Emmory couldn't convince me, I can promise you won't either. This is the option that gives us the best chance of doing this with no casualties. Anything else is going to end with more of my people dead, and I will not stand by while that happens. Am I clear?"

Inana eyed me for a long moment while the hammering of my heart filled my ears. Finally she nodded. "Perfectly, Majesty."

"Once we warp back here, we'll transfer personnel as quickly as we can. I'm assuming you'll come up with a plan for the actual assault on Canafey, Admiral, but things are obviously going to be much easier with at least half the Saxon ships away from the planet trying to figure out where the *Vajrayana* ships went."

"Admiral?" A woman sporting a pair of brand-new commander insignia cleared her throat and looked nervously around the room.

"Yes, Commander Zhen?"

"If we can get them to act in concert, why don't we just have them fire on the Saxon fleet?"

Admiral Hassan shook her head. "They're not autonomous, Petra. We could have them fire a salvo or two, but battles require split-second thinking and the ability to read a situation. The hive mind function was designed to help with coordinating warping into and out of battles as well as for maneuvers where the timing needs to be exact. It won't help us here." She smiled. "Good question though, keep them coming."

"We'll take the Saxon ships into Canafey," I said. "Emmory, Hao, and I will be prisoners on one with Cas, Indula, and three of your crew members, Admiral." We were short on people who could pass as Saxons, and so Emmory had agreed to pick from the admiral's crew to fill in the gaps. "Zin, Gita, Rai, and Johar will be on the other, with Kisah and Iza as well as three more of your crew."

"I can pull names for your *Ekam* to look over, though given our current predicament, we're reasonably sure everyone here is loyal." There were chuckles around the room.

"That'll work. Once we're in, Cas and the others will take us to the detention center, where I'll demand to speak with the commander of the station immediately. Cas and his team will escort us up there while the others stay behind and take over the detention area. Once we know they have things under control we'll make our move up on the command deck."

"With all due respect, Majesty," Admiral Zellin said. "There are a lot of things that can go wrong with this plan."

I grinned. It was sharp enough to have several of the staff shifting. "Tell me about it. Something similar worked for Hao and me back in ninety-eight. We'll sort through problems as they arise. It's all we can do. Unless someone's got a better plan."

Silence met my words.

It was a six-day journey from the refueling depot to a spot just out of range of Saxon scanners in Canafey. The arrival of ten ships from Po-Sin surprised me since I hadn't asked for them when we'd talked. Further investigation revealed that it was Hao and not Po-Sin who'd brought the mismatched fleet.

"Some people owed me favors and it seems a better idea to have as many ships as possible for this little adventure." Hao waved a hand at me. "Plus this way you've still got Po-Sin's promise in storage for when you really need it."

"What in the universe kind of favor could someone owe you that would convince them to bring that into a battle they're not a part of?" I waved a hand at the window where a gigantic if somewhat obsolete model Solarian dreadnought hung in the blackness of space.

"Trust me—you don't want to know. Honestly though, with Mel I'm not sure this isn't just an excuse to test out her guns. Usually no one messes with her."

"For good reason. Look at that thing."

"True enough. I got word on that favor you wanted," Hao said. "Your target somehow made it off Santa Pirata without being seen, but a dockworker on Midway spotted him boarding a ship headed for Undile. I have several contacts there; I've already let them know to be on the lookout for him." Hao tilted his head toward Emmory. "He knows about it."

"I let Winston know, Majesty," Emmory said. "If they can get ahead of him, they'll take Bial into custody."

"Will your contacts coordinate with Trackers?"

Hao shrugged. "Possibly. They're not nearly as official as some of your other people, so there's a good chance it won't spook anyone. I can't force them to cooperate though."

"I wouldn't expect it," I said. "If they will help, it's appreciated. Financially."

Hao grinned. "That will make a difference, Hail."

"Send Dailun, tell him to take one of the Saxon ships."

Hao raised an eyebrow but nodded and passed the instructions along to Dailun over the com. After he finished talking to

Dailun, he turned his back on the ships we were looking at up in the *Vajra*'s observation deck and studied me for a long time in silence.

"What?" I asked.

"How are you?"

"I'm fine. We're moving in the morning."

"You look like you haven't been sleeping."

My nightmares had come back with a vengeance last night, thanks to the anticipation of the fight for Canafey, but I wasn't about to tell Hao that. Or anyone else, for that matter. Emmory and the rest of my BodyGuards knew, of course. It was hard to hide that sort of thing from people who were wired into your health and well-being.

"I'm fine."

"Gita says you're having nightmares."

"Gita needs to shut her damn mouth."

Hao's mouth twitched and he failed to hold back the smile. "Your *Ekam* would say the same if I asked. He trusts me."

"Cowshit."

"I know you, Hail." Hao turned abruptly serious. "I watched the security feed of what happened in the docking bay. Zin was right. You saved her life. You won't always be successful. I know that feeling of being responsible for the welfare of everyone around you and just how much it hurts when you can't keep them safe."

I closed my eyes to hold the tears in.

"You've had a rough couple of months, *sha zhu*, and lost a lot of people you care about. Your *Ekam* is more forward than most of the men on your homeworld, but even he won't question your competence outright.

"I will. I need to know if you're okay to do this, or if you need to be honest with yourself and pass those lock codes over. We can come up with a new plan and I'd rather do it now than in a shipyard surrounded by Saxons."

"I should break your nose."

"But you didn't." He smiled. "That's a good sign. Temper is still under control."

*"There is a hollow place in my chest, filled with the screaming ghosts of the dead,"* I said in Cheng.

*"Ai,* little sister." Hao wrapped his arms around me. "Poetry from you is always painful to my ears."

I choked back a sob and clung to him. Once upon a time we'd been mentor and student. So much had changed since those days, but the man I'd relied on time and again to tell me the truth of things was still here. "I have lost so many good people."

"Any life worth living collects ghosts," Hao said. "The only certainty is we will join them someday."

"Do you remember what you said when I left?"

"I believe it was 'Don't fuck this up—you've got people's lives in your hands.'"

"This is far harder than being captain of my own ship," I whispered. "So many lives at stake, Hao, and I've barely been able to keep those closest to me safe."

"We can't keep people safe," he said, and pulled away. Taking me by the upper arms, he smiled. "You lead them, give them opportunities to make their lives better, but you let them live their own lives. Fasé would have chosen her death. You saved her from that, at least for the moment.

"However, you do no honor to the dead by trying to avoid making any choices of your own."

"I know." I leaned my forehead against his and sighed. "I'm exhausted."

"You need to sleep. Go on." He spun me around and gave me a gentle shove toward the stairs. "I'll talk to you later. I've got all the programs hammered out for our teams. I'd like you and Emmory to take a look at them."

I shot an amused look at Emmory as we headed down the stairs and into the hallway. "He always made me feel like a child who'd just been lectured by her father."

"He was in a sense, Majesty, a replacement father," Emmory said. "For a young woman grieving the loss of her own."

"A good one, though he'd deny it." I shoved a hand into my hair as we walked the quiet hallway. "I think I recall my father saying something very similar about loss to Mother after a battle."

Hao was right. I hated it. But I couldn't deny it. I packed away my fears and my grief for another day. Focusing on the plan to infiltrate the shipyard was where my head needed to be.

I went to sleep and wasn't bothered by a single dream. I slept like the dead and hated myself for it in the morning.

## 35

"Majesty, please stop pacing."

I paused in midstep aboard the bridge of the Saxon Shock vessel *Falki* and glared at Emmory. "It helps me stay calm."

"It makes the rest of us nervous."

I kicked the back of Hao's seat. "No one asked you. Cas, when we get to Canafey can you make sure they lock him in the tiniest cell they have?"

"Of course, Your Majesty."

"Power-hungry warlord." Hao grinned at me.

The banter helped calm my nerves more than the pacing. Hao and I used to drive Portis to distraction with our sniping just before missions. His infinite patience during stressful times was beyond annoying, and when we'd split from Hao I'd realized just how much I'd depended on my mentor to keep me grounded.

"Floating out of warp in ten seconds," Cas said.

I sat down between Emmory and Nakula and tried not to fidget as Cas counted down.

The disorientation had barely passed from the bridge when the cursing started.

"Holy Shiva!"

The dark gray ships of the Saxons were barely visible against the blackness of space, and I looked from the observation window to the screen in front of me, my stomach dropping into my toes as the numbers kept climbing.

"That is a damn sight more ships than we were expecting, Hail."

Nakula had come up out of his seat at the first exclamation and leaned over Cas's shoulder, studying the specifications scrolling across the screen. "Majesty, we've got a major problem. That's the entire Saxon 17th fleet out there. Fifty-seven ships."

"Turn us around and get us out of here, Cas," Emmory said. "Message Zin and tell him to do the same."

*Hai Ram.* I rubbed a hand over my face and got up out of my seat. "Everyone calm down." I leaned over Hao's shoulder to study the screen closer.

"I am calm, Majesty." Emmory followed me up. "We can't survive against an entire fleet."

"*We're* not taking on the fleet. We're going to the shipyards." I pointed at the station glowing in the black backdrop of the screen. "And when we get the *Vajrayana* ships, we'll be the ones with superior numbers and better ships. We won't get another chance at this."

The muscle in Emmory's jaw twitched. "Hail, this is too dangerous."

"We need those ships. Otherwise the ones in our little fleet aren't going to survive past the first battle."

"Emmory, I'm being hailed. We have about fifteen seconds to get out of here or commit to this." Cas's voice was strangely calm. "I'm with the empress. Let's do this."

*Dhatt,*" Emmory muttered. "Answer them, Cas. Hao, send

a tight beam message to Zin. Tell him to send the information back to Admiral Hassan. I want her to have some kind of warning, for all the good it'll do. We've got twenty minutes to get ready. Let's go." He grabbed me by the arm and practically dragged me down the stairs.

Indula met us in the bay, already dressed in one of the spare Saxon Shock Corps uniforms we'd salvaged from the ship's quarters. Standing with him were the three crew members from Admiral Hassan's ship, and I had to check my *smati* to remind myself of their names.

Lieutenant Bing was tall and black-haired, towering over her shorter, stockier companions. The two ensigns, Scholler and Roche, had obvious Saxon ancestry in their light complexions and angular faces.

"Lieutenant, get upstairs and take over for Cas," Emmory ordered. "You're staying with the ship. Don't let anyone on board except for us."

"Yes, sir." She saluted and took off.

Emmory looked back at me. "You ready?"

I nodded.

He pulled his punch, but stars still exploded behind my left eye, and I staggered back a step spitting curses into the air. As soon as the bells stopped ringing in my ears I returned the favor.

Emmory's head snapped back and he wiped the blood from his now-split lip on the sleeve of his white shirt, smearing it across the fabric and rubbing it in to make the injury look far worse than it was.

Hao came down into the bay. He already bore a long gash in his upper arm and stripped his shirt off as he crossed to us.

Of all Hao's tattoos, one had always stood out to me. A single white rose was etched over his heart, the petals falling across his chest. The significance of it was known only to him. He'd refused to tell me no matter how many times I'd asked.

Indula wrapped the cut on his arm and Hao pulled his shirt back on with a nod of thanks. He grabbed Nakula by the chin and sliced him across a cheekbone.

"Jia's going to kill you," Nakula said, pressing a hand to the cut and then flicking blood down the front of his shirt.

"Girls like scars."

Cas came down the stairs sporting a bruise on his right temple and dressed in the same uniform as Indula. "We're docking in ten," he said.

"Everyone better get their costumes on," Hao said. He touched the hands of the two blond Indranan men and I watched as my *smati* readings ceased to identify them as members of the Royal Navy.

"Corporals, you're in the back. Don't speak unless spoken to," Cas said, his identity now that of Captain Thomas Hebring from the Saxon Alliance. All trace of his Indranan accent was gone and I only just managed to keep from staring at him as he spoke in perfect Saxon.

I put my hands behind my back, and my heart jumped when Emmory closed the handcuffs around my wrists.

"Test the code, Majesty."

I sent it and the cuffs dropped off. Emmory caught them with a nod and put them back on me, squeezing my forearm gently as he moved away.

The minutes flew by, and the *Falki* shuddered as we docked at Darshan Station, the hub of the Canafey shipyards. Cas grabbed my upper arm. Weapons whined. And the ramp lowered to reveal a contingent of Saxon soldiers.

Cas and the others saluted sharply.

"Captain Hebring." The man at the front saluted back.

"Colonel Probst. Welcome to Darshan Station and may I be the first to congratulate you on your capture."

"Thank you, Colonel."

"We can take the prisoners from here, Captain. You and your men get some rest. I'm sure it's been a long trip."

"With all due respect, Colonel, they're our prisoners and they'll stay that way." There was a bite in Cas's voice I'd never heard before.

The colonel flushed, but the reputation of the Shock Corps held. Even though he outranked Cas in the broader Saxon military, the Corps was an entity unto itself, and unless someone from the Corps showed up who did outrank him, Cas was in charge.

"We'll escort you to the detention center at least," Colonel Probst said, trying to recover some semblance of authority in front of his men. "Desperate people can make stupid decisions, eh?" He grabbed my chin and tipped my head back, examining the bruise decorating my face.

I kicked him in the nuts and he dropped like a rock on a ten-G planet. The blow from the butt of a gun between my shoulder blades knocked the wind out of me and I went down.

The metal deck was cool under my cheek as the commotion raged above me. I heard Emmory swear and then the pained grunt as someone brought him up short.

"If all you're going to do is antagonize my prisoner," Cas said with a sigh from above me, "I think we can do without your help, Colonel. I had her calmed down before you went and fucked with her. Don't touch my prisoner." He jerked me back onto my feet and propelled me over the man still writhing on the floor.

We met up with Iza and Kisah masquerading as the other Saxon Shock team, and I exchanged a look with Zin, who was sporting an impressive black eye.

Our arrival had been announced to the detention center, but the notice hadn't seemed to help the poor sweating sergeant who had the misfortune of being on duty.

"Captain." He saluted, swallowing hard. "We're in the process of transferring some prisoners to make room for you."

"I want to speak with the idiot in charge," I said.

Cas backhanded me without even looking in my direction. I spat the blood at him and stared him in the eye when he shoved his gun up under my chin. The Saxon-made BrowningX vibrated as it powered up.

"You're not going to shoot me," I said with a sneer. "You and I both know it, so knock off the macho cowshit, Captain. I want to speak to someone in charge, and I swear to Shiva I will bring the weight of the intergalactic war tribunal down on your head if it doesn't happen in the next five minutes."

Cas sneered back, but he holstered his gun and turned to the sergeant. "Which way to the command deck?"

"Sir, you really should process them all first."

"She's not going to stop her bitching, Sergeant, and after a week of it, I'm really, really tired of hearing her voice. So you process the rest of this rabble. I'm taking Her *Majesty* to see someone who maybe can get her to shut up." He raised an eyebrow. "I trust you can handle it?"

"Of course, sir! Down the hallway, the first left you come to and at the end of the hall are the elevators. Take the elevator up to the top. I'll let them know you're coming."

"Good. Lieutenant Toss, and you two, with me. The rest of you stay here with the prisoners."

Cas marched me out the door, with Indula, Kisah, and Iza behind us. We piled into the lift, and after the doors closed I exhaled.

"That poor bastard is going to get eaten alive," I muttered

under my breath, and watched Cas bite his lip to keep from smiling.

*"We're not in the clear yet, Majesty,"* he said over the com link.

*"I have faith in you. Nice job back there, you were pretty scary."*

The lift came to a stop and the doors opened. "Move," Cas said, shoving me forward. We marched down the hall and through the doors onto the command deck.

Everyone turned to look, and the normal sounds of a command center died out. An older man with a hard-edged face got to his feet.

"Sir, Captain Hebring." Cas snapped a salute. "The prisoner requested a word."

"Your Imperial Majesty." The man etched a bow that was somehow elegantly sarcastic. "Allow me to introduce myself: Commander Gils Nilsen. Welcome to my station."

"It's my station, Commander," I said. "I want to register a formal protest over the treatment of myself and my people. According to the rules of the Extended Geneva Convention of 2767, all prisoners of war are to be treated—"

"Yes, yes, my dear, we're all very familiar with the EGC." Commander Nilsen waved a thin hand as he approached and gave me a sly smile. "I'm sure it'll all be sorted out in the end."

*"Cas, tell Emmory to move now."*

"I'm sure it will be," I said, unlocking my cuffs and catching the BrowningX from Cas. My four BodyGuards moved at the same time, their weapons snapping up and aimed around the room.

"Anyone who feels like dying today, feel free to stay where you are," I said, and pressed the barrel of my gun against Commander Nilsen's forehead. "If you'd like to live, get facedown on the floor."

All the Saxons dropped to the floor except for the commander, whose panicked look lasted right up until Indula clocked him in the back of the head with his rifle. He collapsed, and I stepped out of the way as he fell in a heap.

"Making friends, Majesty?" Emmory asked as he came out of the lift.

"Of course. What about you? How is the sergeant?"

"Locked in the cell with the other guards." He smiled and waved to three women. "I had Hassan's people stay back to guard the detention center and the path to the ships. These three volunteered to help with the computers on the *Vajrayana* ships."

"Your Majesty." The dark-haired woman of the group bowed low. "I am Senior Tech Ragini Triskan. These are Technicians Yama Hunkaar and Hasa Julsen."

"It's good to see all of you. Did they treat you all right?"

"Well enough, ma'am. Most of the officers were sent to the surface of Major. We were told to cooperate, which we've been doing. Being as unhelpful as we can, of course." She grinned.

"You smile a bit more than your father, Ragini," I said with a smile.

"My father?"

"Lieutenant General Aganey Triskan, yes? He's the newest member of my military council."

"Yes, ma'am." She smiled again. "What an honor for him. It's all he ever talked about when I was little."

"He has been very worried about you and your sister." I looked at Emmory, who held up a hand and wiggled it.

"We're fifteen minutes in, ma'am," he said. "Best get moving before someone notices we're here."

"We need to jam the signals. We've had some wire shorts lately, so that will buy us some time. They'll only get suspicious if it goes on for too long," Ragini said.

As my BodyGuards rounded up all the Saxon personnel on

the command deck and marched them back to the detention center, I settled into the chair next to Ragini.

"I want you to link all the ships together and set them to warp to these coordinates as soon as they're online. Program the engines to go to full stop after warp.

"We've got less than ten minutes from the time those ships go live to when someone out there notices," I said. "Let's do everything we can before we start engines."

"Yes, ma'am." Ragini nodded. "I'm in. Give me a second here, Majesty, and I'll make sure the network is secure. Okay, ma'am, you're clear."

I logged my *smati* into the network and uploaded the lock codes.

"Yama, Hasa, grab some terminals. I want one of you to start diagnostics and the other to start bringing shields up as quietly as you can."

The other two women found seats at another terminal and went to work, calling out back and forth to each other as they delved into the systems of the *Vajrayana* ships.

"All right, Majesty," Emmory appeared at my elbow. "You've done your bit, we're going back to the ship."

"Don't be pushy, Emmory. We're not leaving without everyone, and I need to figure out a way to program the station's defenses to give us a hand in this battle."

"What help do you need?" he asked.

"Get Hao. Once I'm in, you two start looking at firing solutions."

Emmory gave me the Look but whistled at Hao, who crossed the room with a curious expression.

"Station defenses. Make yourself useful," I said to him, and he grinned.

"Majesty, a moment?"

I looked back at Ragini.

"It looks like forty-five of the ships are in good enough shape to warp out. Two of them have been torn up in the Saxons' effort to figure out how they work." She tapped on the screen.

"Just those then, that's good enough."

"Life-support systems online. Bringing air levels up to requirements now," Yama reported.

"We'll be ready to bring the drives up in five minutes," Hasa said.

"We may not have five minutes," Emmory replied.

## 36

Bugger me, what?"

"Ensign Roche just notified me there's a contingent of Marines headed for the detention center. No alarms have gone up, so he's not sure what's going on, but it doesn't look good."

"Tell them to head for the ships, I don't want them getting trapped in there. We'll be right behind them. Ragini—"

"I heard, Majesty." Her fingers flew over the screen. "We've got to get enough air into those ships or they'll be useless."

I scanned the screen in front of me and then swore. "There was a check-in. Bugger me, Emmory, the detention center missed a check-in. Which means the command deck did, too."

"Ma'am, one of the ships is hailing us." Ragini swallowed. "It's the *Indomitable*, Fleet Marshal Kreskin's vessel."

"Cas? Why does that man have your last name?" I teased.

"Don't look at me, Majesty," he said with a grin. "Maybe an extremely distant relative, but that's about it. Kreskin isn't all that uncommon a surname."

I shared a look with Emmory, who lifted one shoulder the barest amount. "Put it through, Ragini."

A man with silver hair appeared on the screen at the front

of the command deck. His eyes were bright blue, the color of Pashati's sky on a clear summer day.

"Fleet Marshal Kreskin," I said.

"Empress Hailimi." The man inclined his head in a surprising show of respect. "I'm not sure what you're doing on the command deck of my station, but I'm going to have to ask you to surrender."

"And I'm afraid I must decline. This is my station, my ships, my system. If you'd like to surrender, I'd be more than happy to accept." I cut the sound off and turned my back on him.

"Yama, can you disable the network communications? I know we shut down the *smatis* for all the prisoners, but I want the whole station to go dark."

"Yes, ma'am."

"Do it as soon as I end this communication. Ragini—"

"Two minutes," she said before I could ask the question. "Hasa, will you grab that?"

"Got it. Ships have full life support. Just say the word and I'll send them out of here."

"Emmory, tell Lieutenant Bing to get her ass over to the other ship. Help them get everyone loaded, and then get the hell out of here when the *Vajrayana* ships warp out. We can fly ourselves. I don't want her hanging around waiting for us. If those Marines come after her, she won't stand a chance."

Emmory nodded, passing along the instructions. "They avoided the Marines, ma'am. They'll be ready to go in a minute. We've got incoming of our own."

I turned back around, hitting the open mic and smiling at the marshal.

"Your Majesty," he said with a frown. "You are outnumbered and alone and there is no way you can get enough of your people onto those ships before we blow them to pieces. And I

357

promise you, my orders are to blow them to pieces rather than surrender them back to Indrana."

I lifted a shoulder. "Alone, maybe. Outnumbered? I've been in worse. Where were we, Hao?"

"Pluto," he said.

"Too right." I grinned, pleased with the worried frown that knit itself into Kreskin's forehead. "So, forgive me for this, but I think I'll take my chances." I cut the link.

"Yama, now. How long until the Marines hit the detention center?" The alarm sounded and I rolled my eyes. "That answers that question. Rai, Johar! The door."

They nodded in concert and moved for the right side door. Zin and Indula were already headed for the door on the other side when the explosion rocked the command deck. Emmory shoved me behind the terminal, his hand on the back of my neck holding me down. Until he released me all I could do was listen to the sounds of gunfire and shouting.

"Clear, Majesty."

"Launch the ships, Ragini," I said as I got to my feet.

Forty-five ships pulled away from their docks in unison and disappeared, leaving nothing behind but the shimmering space of their warp bubbles. I could only imagine the panicked shouts aboard the *Indomitable*'s bridge.

"We've got more incoming," Zin announced. "I recommend a change of venue, Majesty."

"Hasa, how long will it take to get one of those two ships online? I don't need life support, just the engines."

"Not long, Majesty," she replied. "Especially if I don't have to do anything more than bring the engines up."

"Do that and then input this flight plan." I tapped the information into her console.

"Majesty?" She turned her wide dark eyes to mine and I smiled grimly.

"I know, it's awful, but we've got to buy some time." I crouched at her side and pressed a hand to the panel beneath her terminal. "As soon as you're done, let me know. Nakula, over here."

He darted over. The cut on his cheek had reopened and was bleeding again.

"You go first, I want these three after you." I looked up to find Ragini and Hao with their heads together. "Hao—"

Another tremor shook the station, followed by a string of epithets from Emmory so vile even I raised an eyebrow.

"They just blew up the *Falki*, ma'am."

"Did the others..."

Emmory nodded even though I couldn't finish the sentence. "They got out."

"But we're stuck here, with an entire fleet of pissed-off Saxons staring at us. Hey, Hao, what was that about having to come up with a new plan on a shipyard filled with Saxons?"

"I can't take you anywhere," he replied. "I said I didn't want to do it, Hail."

"Talk to the marshal. He's the one who blew up our ride."

"I can't believe Portis didn't shoot you two," Zin said before Hao could reply.

"He threatened that a lot." I grinned. "He knew better though."

"Majesty, I have that ship online," Hasa said.

"Do it. Then slag the shit out of your terminal."

She punched the button on her screen and we watched as a lone *Vajrayana* ship streaked away from the station. The target was the *Indomitable*, but another Saxon vessel intercepted V14 before it could complete its mission. It collided with the *Vajra-yana* ship and both vessels exploded in a searing ball of light.

The silence on the command deck lasted a full heartbeat before we jumped back into motion.

"Both exits are blocked with those pissed-off Saxons you were referring to, Majesty," Zin said. "We need a way out of here and fast."

"We've got one." I pointed to the bulkhead service hatch I'd opened. "Make those Saxons afraid to poke their heads out, Zin. We'll get everyone else into the tunnel." I pushed Kisah and Iza toward the opening.

"You two next," I said to Hao, and held up a hand before Ragini could protest. "I let you have one, that's all. Go on."

"Yes, ma'am." She bowed her head, clutching a data pad to her chest as she followed Hao into the tunnel.

Rai and Johar's door was still intact and they'd managed to drag a piece of a terminal in front of it. "That should hold for a bit," Johar said, firing her gun at the control panel in the wall.

"Good. What did you bring with you?" I smacked Rai when he gave me an innocent look. "I know you, you're lucky they didn't search us at the dock. What explosives have you got?"

Rai pulled a handful of what looked like plastic straws from his vest, and I whistled.

"Really?" I looked at Johar. "You let him carry suckers around? One punch from a guard and we all could have gone up."

"We figured out how to stabilize the mixture," she said with a shrug. "They're still a little twitchy, but it's better."

"All right, gimme." I took the handful of explosives. "Detonator?"

"I'll keep it."

"You'll give it to me, Rai, and get your ass in the tunnel. Everyone is leaving today. Nobody's dying."

"We're all dying, Majesty, it's just a question of when the candle gets snuffed out," he replied with a crooked smile, but gave me the detonator and herded Johar toward the exit.

I watched as the others ducked into the tunnel, until only Zin, Indula, Gita, Emmory, and I were left. I laid the suckers out along the window of the command deck and across both doorways.

"Indula, Gita, into the tunnel."

They glanced at Emmory but headed for the tunnel. Zin fired off several more shots and then followed. I dove in after him, Emmory on my heels as the shouting of the Saxons spilled into the room.

"Go!" I waved them ahead as Emmory pulled the bulkhead shut behind us, and I prayed it would hold as I hit the detonator.

The station shook as the suckers vaporized the window, the floors, and the Saxons who were unlucky enough to be on the deck.

We kept scrambling down the service tunnel, Zin in front and Emmory behind until we came to another open hatch and someone pulled Zin out.

Hao grabbed me, easily lifting me up, and set me next to Zin, reaching back in for Emmory.

"Where are we?"

"One level down from the command deck, ma'am," Ragini answered, tapping a few things into the data pad. "I've locked out the elevators. Hasa, did you get environmental control reestablished?"

"Yes, ma'am. We're good."

"We've still got them locked out, but they're trying to regain access," Yama said.

Ragini moved over to her and while the three techs conferred I waved the rest of my people over.

"We've got an hour, probably more, before Admiral Hassan can get personnel transferred and get those ships back up and running enough to start the assault. Nakula, you and Iza glue yourselves to Hasa and Yama. Keep them safe."

"Yes, ma'am." They both nodded.

"Thoughts, Emmory?"

My *Ekam* stopped scanning the corridor; Zin picked it up almost seamlessly without a word. "They could just blow the station." The floor under our feet shook as if to confirm his words. "I'm fairly sure King Trace and the others would like you dead, Majesty."

"So we need to get off here? How?" I tapped a finger on my lips as I ran through our options. "Ragini?"

"Yes, ma'am?"

"That other *Vajrayana* ship. It's no good for a fight, but how are the life support and the shields?"

She wiggled a hand. "Iffy, Majesty. But doable if we're not going far. I started up the air processors when your ship got torched." She smiled at me. "I've still got control of it and they haven't blown it up yet. They probably figure it's no good to us if we just left it there."

"We need to move," Zin said.

Flanked by Gita and Emmory, I followed the others down the corridor. Emmory's words about the Saxons blowing up the station rang in my ears.

Rai skidded to a stop at the same time, and narrowly missed being shot in the head. "Thirteen—" He peeked around the corner again and fired back. "Make that ten Marines camped out in the crossroads up ahead."

"Here," Ragini said, slapping her hand to a door panel. It

slid open and we rushed inside. "There's another service tunnel there." She pointed at the bulkhead on the far wall.

"I need to broadcast, Emmory. How much time do we have?"

"Now?" He looked around. "Five minutes, maybe. Less if they figure out which room we ducked into."

"They can't blow the station up if the news gets out," I said. "The Solarians would tear them apart for such a blatant violation."

"That will bring us a lot of comfort when we're little pieces of debris," Hao said.

"Politics," I replied. "They won't do it. They can't." The station shook again and Emmory grabbed me. "Plus if we're headed for the planet I want the people on Major to know we're here. It might give us the edge we need."

"Okay." Emmory nodded. "I need the communications back up to be able to broadcast it."

"No problem, sir," Yama said. "Just say the word."

"Get that bulkhead hatch open. Cas, I want you, Iza, and Kisah on the door. Get anything that's not too difficult to move in front of it."

Rai was already knocking a table loose from its floor mountings and with Johar's help they wrestled it across the room toward the door.

I ran my hands through my hair and straightened my stained top as best as I could. I gave Emmory a nod, cleared my throat, and waited for his signal.

"We're on, Majesty."

"Citizens of Indrana, people of Canafey. You may have heard that I died." I smiled. "It is obviously not the truth but a lie set forth by Prime Minister Phanin to take control of my empire. I am here on Darshan Station in the Canafey system, where we have successfully liberated the *Vajrayana* ships from the Saxons illegally occupying our territory.

"My citizens on the ground, rise up! Take back your homes, your cities, your planets. We are here to support you and to protect you. We ask only that you do the same for us. Spread this message.

"The Saxon Alliance has broken the treaty and Indrana is at war. Within and without, it makes no difference. We will prevail."

Emmory nodded. "Recorded and sending. I'm beaming a copy directly to the Solarian consulate on Major. Let's hope it does some good." He gave me a less-than-gentle shove toward the hatch. "Move, Majesty. We need to get out of here."

This time Emmory didn't let me make sure everyone else went first, and I dove into the tunnel after Nakula. We crawled through the maze for what seemed like an eternity but was only about ten minutes by the clock on my *smati*. I checked the countdown I'd started. We were still forty minutes or more from the arrival of Admiral Hassan's fleet and I didn't know how much longer the station defenses could hold up.

"Shields are down to sixty-seven percent, ma'am." As if she'd read my mind, Yama greeted me with the update when I boosted myself up out of the hatch.

"They're not even hammering at us with all their firepower," Nakula said. He put a hand on my arm and squeezed.

"Maybe the marshal is still hoping I'll surrender?" I tried for a reassuring smile and, judging by the look he gave me, failed.

"Ragini has the ship online. Life-support systems are holding steady, but she says there will be suits in the docking area we can grab on our way by just in case things go sideways."

"Where are we?" I held out a hand to Zin and hauled him from the hatch.

"Storage room, Majesty," Ragini answered. "About forty meters from where V23 is docked. The way is clear."

Hasa muttered a curse. "I'm about to get shut out of the communications system. When that happens they'll be able to pinpoint our location."

"We'd better move then." I turned back to the hatch to make sure everyone was through, but Ragini's sudden gasp stopped me.

"Holy Shiva!"

# 37

W hat?" Emmory and I demanded at the same moment.

"I'm showing warp signatures, ma'am—twenty-three of them, with more coming through." The grin spreading across her face told me what I needed to know.

"I didn't think Inana could get the ships up to speed that fast," I said, but Emmory was already shaking his head.

"She doesn't have the *Vajrayana* ships with her, ma'am. It's just her fleet."

"What is she doing? She's going to get herself killed. I told her to wait."

"I think she disobeyed you, Majesty." Emmory's voice didn't betray the slightest hint of amusement, but I shot him the Look anyway.

"All firing on the station has ceased, ma'am," Yama reported.

"We still need to move," Emmory said, taking me by the arm. "Hasa, are you locked out yet?"

"Not yet, sir."

"Can you hold them off until we get to the ship?"

"We've got them chasing their tails for about a minute, Emmory," Hao replied. "If we go now, we might make it."

Indula opened the door, checked the corridor, and stepped aside so Cas and Kisah and Johar could take point. We sprinted down the vacant dock, feet pounding on the metal surface, the sound echoing up and bouncing back at us off the walls.

A massive Saxon stepped out of a doorway. Johar didn't slow. She flew through the air, kicking the man in the chest and knocking him back a step.

He caught her fist before it could connect and twisted, sending Johar spinning toward the wall. She continued her roll, but he came after her like the interplanetary trains of the Kyoto system.

I couldn't stop the inhale when his massive foot narrowly missed her head. Rai chuckled and I punched him in the arm.

Johar rolled backward, her own foot shooting out and up into her opponent's chin. There wasn't enough power to knock him out, but it was enough to stun him and buy her the time to get on her feet again.

She didn't wait for him to finish shaking his head to clear it and moved in, landing several vicious punches to his solar plexus and right kidney before he backhanded her and sent her staggering back several paces.

With a roar, the man rushed at Johar. She pivoted out of the way, almost avoiding his gigantic paw, but he grabbed her and pulled her into a back-breaking hold.

"I don't have a shot," Emmory said.

"She's fine," Rai replied. "Give her a moment."

Johar grinned, blood streaming down her face from the cut above her right eye. She dropped to the deck, flipping him over her head and breaking his hold.

Johar lunged at the Saxon as he scrambled to his feet, punching him once in the head. As he turned to defend himself, she snapped a long leg out in a brutal kick that caught him right at the line of his jaw and his neck. Her opponent hit the floor hard, silence echoing at the sudden end to the fight.

Johar dusted off her hands and jerked her head. "Let's go."

Our trio of techs had the airlock open before the rest of us had reached the ship, and Hao shook his head at me before I could join them. "Let us go first," he said and closed the door.

"We've got to be on their scanners by now." I gripped my gun, my ears straining to hear the approaching sound of boots.

Rai put a hand on my shoulder and smiled. "Not quite yet. Johar and I had a little trick up our sleeves. I've never tried to mask so many people with this cloaking device, but it seems to be working so far."

The airlock cycled open again, and the rest of us piled in, except for Rai and Johar, who set about collecting environmental suits from the nearby lockers.

"The bridge?" I asked as soon as the airlock opened into V23.

"This way," Hao said, and I followed him down the corridor with Emmory and Gita on my heels.

The *Vajrayana* ships hadn't deviated from the basic design of the Indranan fleet, so we walked down corridors with the same rounded white walls and grated floor. But everywhere the half-finished—or half-torn-apart—state of the ship was evident.

Wires hung from the ceiling and large sections of the bulkhead were stripped away. When we got to the bridge most of the terminals were still covered in protective plastic, with a few recently opened. Ragini sat at one terminal, her fellow techs huddled around her.

"Shielding is up, Majesty," she said. "They don't know we're in here, at least according to the chatter I'm picking up."

"Admiral Hassan? And can I sync my *smati* with the computers?"

"She's holding her own, ma'am. They disabled several Saxon ships with their surprise arrival." Ragini's fingers flew over the terminal screen. "I'm working on the com systems now to see if we can get in touch with the *Vajra*."

Hasa peeled off from the group and with Indula's help removed the plastic sheeting from another terminal. A few minutes later, the positions of the various ships engaged in battle appeared in the air in front of us.

"We've got ten more signals coming in from Minor," she announced.

"Bugger me." I'd hoped that the ships from Minor would stay put, but it didn't look like that was going to be the case.

"Get me an ID on those," Hao said, and the gunrunner grinned when Hasa read one of them off. "Those are ours. I figured Mel would want to come in from the other direction." He looked at me. "If they can just get those damn ships up and running and back here, we'll be okay."

I couldn't dare let myself hope.

"Two squads of Marines are headed down the dock in our direction. There's no indication from the Saxon fleet that they know this ship is online, right?" Emmory leaned over Ragini's other side.

"None, sir."

I shared a look with Emmory as the rest of our group filed onto the bridge. Get moving or stay put? Neither option was great, but I'd never liked sitting still. "Ragini, how are the shields?"

"One hundred percent, ma'am."

"Do we have flight controls?"

"Yes, ma'am. And everything is automated, tied into the bridge computers. But if we take a hit and don't have someone down in engineering or wherever a problem may develop, we'll probably all die..." She offered an apologetic smile.

"It's a risk, but I'd rather get us out of this shipyard before someone realizes we're here and starts taking shots at us. Is this the right one, Ragini? Emmory, help me with this." At her nod I started pulling at the plastic on the terminal for the flight controls. Once we got it cleared off, I sat down.

"Majesty?"

"What?"

"Have you ever flown a capital ship?"

"No," I said. "I'm a very good pilot. How hard can it be?"

"Perhaps someone else should..." Emmory looked around the bridge.

Hao laughed and held his hands up. "She really is a better pilot than I am."

"Uncoupling from the dock," Yama said. "You're cleared to maneuver, Majesty."

"Hold on to something," I said, and hit the thrusters. V23 came loose from the dock as smoothly as an Indranan dolphin slicing through the water. The sleek ship responded instantly to the slightest correction and I felt the slight tug as the internal dampeners kicked on when we hit full drive power.

"I've got communications up, Majesty. You can sync up now."

I started the process as I punched in the coordinates for the nearest Indranan vessel. Emmory issued orders behind me, but I only paid partial attention as Nakula and three others left the bridge.

"Majesty, I've hailed the *Vajra*, and they're responding; should I put them through?"

"Yes."

Admiral Hassan's face appeared on the screen.

"Inana, what in the fires of Naraka do you think you're doing? Where are the *Vajrayana* ships?"

"We got your message about the 17th Fleet, and when you didn't return with the ships I figured something went wrong. I thought it was best to run some interference while they got the other ships up and running. What are you doing, ma'am? You're supposed to be on a ship back at the safety of the rendezvous point."

"We had some problems with our transportation. It blew up." I shrugged and grinned at her. "We're managing. This ship is pretty but her legs are short."

"I'm sending two ships your way to defend you. I want you to stay out of the battle, Majesty." Admiral Hassan gripped the arms of her chair as the *Vajra* shook and alarms started going off. "I'll see you after."

"You'd better," I said, and cut the link.

"Two ships headed our way, Majesty," Hasa said. "The *Moksha* and the *Devaki*; they're both Sarama-class ships. Looks like they've picked up some tagalongs."

"Can we fire the weapons on this bucket?"

"Not yet, ma'am," Emmory replied. "Nakula and Kisah are working on it."

I shot him a grateful smile. "Remind me to buy everyone a drink when this is over."

"Ma'am, the *Devaki* is hailing us."

"Put them on screen."

"Your Majesty, Captain Ellie Skel here. Admiral Hassan instructed us to cover you. Can you warp out?"

"I don't trust this thing to hold together, Captain. We've got everything else at our disposal though," I said after a glance in Yama's direction. The tech was shaking her head with a resigned look on her face. "We've got shields, and we're trying to get weapons back up. You've got company on your tail. Go take care of them, we'll hang back."

"Yes, ma'am." She gave me a sharp nod and the com link went back to the scanner overview.

"Ragini, link us in to the main command channel on Admiral Hassan's ship."

Status reports began to flow down the side of the main screen, and the verbal reports from the ships in the fleet filled the air. I kept one eye on the fight going on between the two battlecruisers and the five Saxon destroyers while I tried to take in the chaotic dogfight going on with the main group.

The countdown in the corner of my vision courtesy of my *smati* showed we still had seventeen minutes until the *Vajra-yana* ships would reemerge from warp. And that was if they didn't have any problems bringing the ships fully online.

"We're seeing heavy fire on the planet side."

"Shields down to seventy-three percent."

"This is the *Alix*, I've lost main firing controls."

"*Alix*, fall back to the *Devaki*'s position in the rear guard."

"Hull breach! Warp drive containment failing. Abandon ship!"

Light flared on the screen and I sucked in a breath as the *Alix* blew apart, the explosion engulfing several of the Saxon ships that were swarming it.

"Mother Destroyer," I whispered, pressing my hands to my lips, heart, and forehead.

A second flare of light, this one much closer, went off as the side of one of the Saxon destroyers vented flame into space.

"Shields down to twenty-two percent," the *Moksha* reported. "I've got a hull breach, sectors eighteen and nineteen."

"Do we have anything yet?"

*"Majesty."* Nakula's voice sounded in my ear as if he'd heard me. *"We have limited firing capabilities. Not sure for how long, so you might want to use them while you've got them."*

"Captain Skel, we have firing controls. Repeat, we have firing controls, how can we help?"

"Roger that, V23, could use your help putting down that wounded destroyer."

"Hao, pour everything we've got at that dying ship."

"Won't take that much," he replied, tapping the screen in front of him. "Firing plasma beam."

The improved firepower of the *Vajrayana* ships obliterated the destroyer, and Hao turned his attention to the other four without pausing. Molten iron, propelled to ninety-five percent of light speed, cut through their shields, destroying a second ship before the final two turned tail and ran.

"I like this ship," Hao said.

"You don't get to keep it." My laughter at his glare was cut short with Ragini's cry.

"Ma'am, Admiral Hassan's ship has been hit!"

The air rushed out of me, the crushing certainty of losing yet another person. "No..."

"Shields are down. I can't raise anyone on the bridge."

"Warp signals incoming."

I tensed, my timer still ticking away the minutes. We had more than ten left by my estimates.

Forty-five bolts of lightning dropped out of warp just behind the main fleet, opening fire with amazing precision right into the heart of the battle.

Several Saxon ships exploded, their light bright enough to be seen even without the scanners. Cheers and prayers echoed across the com lines for just a moment before returning to damage and casualty reports.

"Captain Skel, who's taken command of the fleet?"

"Admiral Zellin has, ma'am, aboard the *Helena*."

"Put me through to her."

The bridge of the *Helena Bristol* was filled with smoke. Admiral Zellin had a cut by her hairline that was bleeding badly, but her eyes were clear. "Majesty," she said, her exhale one of profound relief. "Fleet Marshal Kreskin just surrendered."

"Tell your ships to fall back; let the *Vajrayana* play cleanup. We'll meet you back at Darshan Station. I want a status report within the hour."

"Yes, ma'am."

"Find Inana, please."

"We'll do our best, ma'am. Admiral Fon is already on her way."

I rubbed my hand over my face with a muttered prayer for the crew of the *Vajra*. The loss of Admiral Hassan would hit us hard, not just emotionally but for the cause itself. She was our best strategist, the face of Home Fleet, and I—

*Stop thinking of her as dead. You don't know if she is, idiot.*

I let Hao take over for the flight back to the station and took the stairs up to the observational deck. Emmory was a silent ghost on my heels.

The damage to the station was mostly self-inflicted. Debris floated around the remains of the command center and on the bay where the *Falki* had been docked. I watched as several fast-moving shuttles docked at the shipyards and Royal Marines disembarked with guns at the ready.

Fleet Marshal Kreskin had given the surrender order, but we weren't taking any chances. I'd ordered my Marines to fire without hesitation on anyone who was stupid enough to have a weapon in their hands. Emmory wasn't about to let me set foot on the station again until he was sure things were safe. And I was done with my people dying.

It took the better part of an hour, during which time I listened to the reports coming in from Major. Riots had broken out shortly after my message reached the ground, and the remaining Indranan forces had staged an assault on the largest Saxon force near the capital city.

"Talked to Mel," Hao said, leaning on the ledge next to me and looking out at the ships swarming around the station. "She said there was only a small picket of four ships at Minor. They disabled them on their way through yesterday. I'd still send a small force over to be sure, but it sounds like Canafey is back in Indranan hands, little sister."

"I'm not sure the cost was worth it," I murmured. The casualty lists were scrolling on the side of my vision, a seemingly endless wave of dead and injured. There was still no word from the *Vajra*, though Admiral Fon had informed me she was docking with the ship and would report as soon as she knew what the situation was.

"It never is, Hail," Hao said, tilting his head to the side and studying me. "But it's sometimes necessary. You need those ships. This was just one battle in a war. One you handled beautifully."

I slid my eyes sideways at him, and he smiled.

"I'm serious, Hail. Portis would be proud. I'm just a gunrunner, but I'm proud of you."

"You're not *just* anything." I bumped him with my shoulder.

"This is important." He turned toward me and bowed with his eyes lowered to the floor. "You're going to be a hell of an empress, Your Majesty."

"I—you—" My choked reply was cut off by Ragini on the overhead com system.

"Your Majesty, Admiral Hassan is on-screen for you."

I took the stairs from the observation deck two at a time, my brain spinning over the fact that Hao had just called me *Majesty* with such respect and that Inana was alive. I slipped on the last stair and nearly landed on my ass, but Emmory caught me and set me back on my feet.

"Inana." The emotions that Hao had raised spilled over at the sight of Admiral Hassan's bruised face. "Thank Shiva for keeping you safe. I was—" I swallowed, exhaled. "I am so glad to see you."

"I am glad to see you, too, Your Majesty. I'm afraid your flagship has seen better days."

"We'll fix it." I gestured to my right. "We've got a shipyard that's not too bashed up."

Hassan smiled. "So I heard. Congratulations, Majesty."

"Thank *you*, Admiral. We couldn't have done it without you." I folded my hands together and pressed them to my forehead, then shook them at her. Hassan's cheeks went red as those on her ship and mine repeated the gesture of gratitude.

"Majesty," Emmory said. "Colonel Baleth says the station is cleared and safe for you to board."

"Good. Inana, I will see you in a little while?"

"Yes, ma'am."

"Admiral Fon?"

The older woman straightened her shoulders a fraction. "Yes, ma'am?"

"Could you send us a shuttle with someone who can fly this thing? I don't think either Hao or I are qualified to dock, and I really don't want to tear another hole in the station."

The laughter on her bridge was quickly snuffed out, but I grinned anyway.

"I'll pass the word along, ma'am. It'll just be a few minutes."

"No problem. We've got time." I settled into a seat. "At least for now," I said to myself as the screen went blank.

## 38

We set up a makeshift command center in a conference room two levels below the now-hollowed-out deck I'd blown up several hours before.

It was cramped, windowless, and packed with people, which didn't help my claustrophobia. I silently struggled to keep my breathing even and as slow as possible even while my heart rate was through the top of the station.

"Majesty, do we need to move somewhere else?" Emmory kept his voice low as he rested a hand on my back.

"This is the biggest spot on the station you can control," I said with a shake of my head. We could have done this meeting in the mess hall, but one look at all the exposed areas and I'd known my *Ekam* wouldn't have survived the meeting. He'd have died of a stroke before we were finished with introductions.

I'd tucked away any protests and let Emmory have his concern. We'd just won a massive victory, and I didn't want to ruin it by ending up dead.

What had seemed like a good idea was now looking more and more like something that was going to give me an aneurysm from the anxiety of it all before we were done.

I was thankful now that Rai and Johar had declined my invitation, and other than my BodyGuards, only Hao and Ragini had joined me for the meeting. That still left us with a roomful of five admirals, two Marine colonels, and more than a dozen assorted staff and junior officers.

Too many people. Too small a space. Not enough air.

My adrenaline rush had worn off an hour ago and now I was desperate for a drink, a meal, and somewhere to crash.

"Admiral, let's get started," I said, and the room dropped into silence.

"Of course, Your Majesty. If everyone will take a seat."

I stayed where I was by the wall. People moved for their chairs but no one sat.

"They're not going to sit until you do," Hao whispered.

"Oh, bugger me. Everyone sit down." My voice cracked through the room like a whip and several of the younger officers jumped, then dropped into their seats.

Admiral Hassan's smile peeked out from behind her hand. Lieutenant Moren had healed the worst of her injuries, but a mottled bruise still tracked its way across her face.

"I'd like to take a moment to thank all of you for this victory today and another to remember our fallen. They gave their lives for the shining star of Indrana, may it never be forgotten."

"May it never be forgotten."

The words echoed around my head and I fought the urge to bolt from the room.

"Admiral Hajuman, if you would give us the status report?"

"Yes, ma'am." Admiral Hajuman was a tiny woman with sharp, dark eyes who was unrelated to my BodyGuard Iza. "We lost five ships in the battle for Canafey: three battlecruisers and two destroyers. All six carriers are intact, though the *Vajra* suffered heavy damage and will likely be out of commission for some time. Eighteen Jal fighters were either destroyed or damaged, with half of the damaged ships repairable. None of the medical frigates suffered damage, and other than the one *Vajrayana* Her Majesty blew up, all those ships are in good condition."

"It wasn't in fighting shape anyway," I quipped, and the chuckles rolled around the room.

"Of course, ma'am. All ten of the ships Cheng Hao was kind enough to lend to the cause are also in good condition. We have twenty-eight captured Saxon vessels that are intact and another seven that will be demolished once we're done with them."

"How many prisoners?" I asked.

"Fifteen hundred sailors, ma'am. I don't know about the numbers on the ground." Admiral Hajuman looked to one of the Marines.

"We don't have them all yet, Majesty," Colonel Baleth replied. "I'd say upward of five thousand soldiers between both Major and Minor. They're still cleaning up. There are still some pockets of resistance, but the bulk of the forces surrendered."

The discussion shifted to the transportation of the prisoners to the planet's surface until we could decide what to do with them, and I made a mental note to send Captain Earnest and his team along. I settled in against the wall when Ragini took the floor; my senior tech was more than a little nervous as she explained the workings of the *Vajrayana* ships.

"That one is smart," Hao whispered in my ear. "Keep her around."

"Planning on it," I whispered back. "Rai said he and Johar are leaving soon. Are you..."

"I'm going to hang around for a while longer," Hao said. "I didn't have any jobs lined up and this is more fun, plus there's free food."

I choked on my laughter, earning a look from Admiral Hassan that made me feel like a schoolgirl again. Ignoring Hao's snickering next to me, I returned my attention to Ragini's presentation.

"There will be notes on this for anyone who is interested, and I can answer specific questions after the meeting." She wrapped up and sat back down with a relieved sigh when no one spoke up.

"We've got twenty of the three dozen ships in Home Fleet," Admiral Hassan said, bringing up a list on the screen. "Eight fled from 2nd Fleet when they entered the Red Cliff system and realized what was going on. Because of Prime Minister Phanin's claims, the other fleet commanders assumed the death of both myself and the empress. Her previous broadcasts and the one from today should change that, but I've already sent orders for them to stand their ground unless they are fired upon by their own people. We can't have them abandon their posts and risk the Saxons moving in until we know that we can keep our outer worlds safe. Intelligence suggests more than half the planets in the empire are under enemy control, but we have no official verification on that at this time."

"What's the situation on the ground at home?" Colonel Bristol was a distant cousin of mine, with dark brown eyes and the same wide jaw I remembered from my great-grandfather.

"We're unsure at the present time, beyond what you've all heard. Some of the matriarchs were murdered; the others are safe. Matriarch Clara Desai's whereabouts are still unknown. We've been in touch with both the head of Galactic Intelligence and Matriarch Alice Gohil and will hold a separate briefing for the situation at home.

"The fighting seems to dissipate the farther you go from Pashati, and most of Phanin's troops are limited to the Ashvin system, but we'll still have to move quickly to keep things from spreading. I'm already getting reports of fighting on other worlds, but as I said we don't have confirmation. As of right now he's got control of the Ashvin system and of Pashati especially, so that's our priority." Hassan shook her head. "The worst thing is we're fighting on two fronts and he knows it."

"And he's working with the Saxons," I said. "Or at least he was. Given Trace's mental state I'm not sure he can be counted on to hold up whatever his end of the bargain is, especially since it sounds like Phanin double-crossed him by blaming the Red Cliff attack on the Saxons." I crossed my arms over my chest and made a face. "Inana, bring up the map, will you?"

She switched the screen and I pushed away from the wall so I could look at it from a better angle.

"Ragini, how much of a tactical advantage do the *Vajrayana* ships give us over the Saxons?"

"Quite a bit, Majesty. The new ships are faster and have better shields, and as you saw, their firepower is far superior. Give us a month to train people on them and the Saxons will be hard-pressed to defend themselves."

"I don't know if we have a month, but that's something that needs to start now." I watched Admiral Fon nod and jot the comment down on her list. "What does the total number of ships look like?" I asked.

"They have ten more fleets—well, nine more now—than we do, Majesty," Admiral Zellin answered. "But fewer capital ships in total and they're spread pretty thin at the moment. That's just the Saxons, not their allies."

From what we could tell, both our allies and the Saxons' allies were staying out of it for the moment, but if things erupted into all-out war, a whole lot more people were going to join the fray.

"What are you thinking, ma'am?" Hassan asked.

"Insanity," I said with a grin. "I don't want to fight two wars at once, Inana. So what happens if I give Trace an ultimatum? He surrenders—" I jabbed a finger at Canafey and sliced it across the map to the Saxon home system. "Or I carve a swath through Saxony that will make the ancient march by the American general Sherman look like a stroll through the park." I tagged through each of the spots where the Saxons had ships as I said it.

There was a long silence.

Colonel Bristol cleared his throat. "With all due respect, ma'am, he'll call your bluff."

"Oh, it's not a bluff." I winked at him and he flushed bright red. "We're riding on a win, ladies and gentlemen. The momentum is ours. We've got the ships, we've got the advantage. Once we're done with the Saxons, we'll turn around and come home and if Phanin still thinks he can stand up to us after that"—I bared my teeth in a nasty smile—"he's welcome to try."

"Majesty, we've got Caspel and the others on the com link."

I shoved the last few bites of my breakfast into my mouth and grabbed my cup of chai, grateful that I'd had time to shower and dress before I ate. Someone had supplied me with a Navy uniform in my size and a plain black top with the twisted imperial emblem. I blended in with my BodyGuards as we all headed down the hallway to the office Admiral Hassan now occupied.

She stopped her conversation with the one-eyed GIS director as I came through the door and bowed with a smile. "Morning, Majesty."

"Inana. Caspel."

"Good morning, ma'am." He dipped his head. The camera pulled back a bit to reveal Taz and Alice.

"Majesty," the pair said in unison. Alice was leaning against Taz, his arm around her, and I stopped myself just in time before I raised an eyebrow.

All three looked tired.

"Majesty, I was just telling Admiral Hassan about the size of the force on Pashati and the rest of the Ashvin system. The good news is we've managed to consolidate a hold on the eastern side of the capital by the docks."

"And the bad?"

Caspel's smile was brief. "I'm not sure how long we can hold it without help, Majesty. We've heavily coded this com link, and I think we're safe enough for the moment. I'll send you more detailed files, and Admiral Hassan said she would have some information for me."

"Yes," I said, nodding. "We'll get it to you." I was already revising my plan. We couldn't leave Caspel and the others to be taken by Phanin's forces. At the very least it would result in Alice's death, as well as the deaths of the other matriarchs who'd found safety there.

"Who's in charge of Phanin's forces on the ground? Prajapati?"

"Surprising, I know, but no she's not." Caspel's smile was brief. "When I spoke to her last she was still on Basalt IV holding the planet for the throne. I advised her to stay put until orders came from you."

"Alba, make a note of that. It wouldn't hurt to swing through and pick her and her troops up before we go home."

"Phanin has put a former colonel named Regen in charge down here," Caspel said. "He was in prison, Majesty, until Phanin came back and released him."

I didn't have to ask what the man had been in jail for. I'd pulled his file when Caspel said his name. The rap sheet was filled with assaults, drinking, and misappropriation of imperial funds. The worst of the charges was the young ensign in his command that he'd beaten almost to death.

"Is he any good, or just a drunken brute?"

"He lacks tactical skill according to General Prajapati, but he's determined, Majesty. He'll hammer away at whatever is in front of him until it gives. Right now Captain Gill and some of the other ITS teams are making sure he can't focus on anything other than chasing them around the city.

"I don't know what his agreement with Phanin is, but I'm sure at least part of it involves a threat to put him right back where they found him if he doesn't succeed."

"That seems rather ill-planned for Phanin."

"Doesn't it though? I think he was forced to scramble for a replacement. From what I can figure out, General Mara was his first choice."

"What happened to him?"

"Your *Ekam* shot him in the throne room during the first coup attempt."

"Ah, bad luck for them," I said, and shrugged. "Speaking of Phanin, Caspel. How in the fuck did we miss him?"

The director rubbed a hand over his eyepatch. "I don't know, Majesty. He's good. The best I've been able to piece together, he's been plotting this for decades, somehow all under the radar and somehow without ever showing his hand to your cousin and nephew."

"I know how," I said, and spat the name between gritted teeth. "Wilson."

"Yes, our ghost man, damn him. Some days I think he's smarter than I am, Majesty. My apologies."

"Cowshit, Caspel. You're the smartest man I know."

"Yes, ma'am."

"What's the condition on the ground? Are my people happy about Phanin?" I was pleased the hesitation in my voice was so small no one except Emmory noticed it.

"No, Majesty. Not at all. They're scared, but also angry. What was grief over your announced death has become fury over Phanin's betrayal. They are determined to fight for you. It's one of the reasons Colonel Regen hasn't moved against us yet. He'd have to plow through civilians to do it.

"Now, I don't think he'd mind, but the Solarian embassy has been following the situation rather carefully, and Phanin is enough of a politician that he knows how badly it would go for him should he allow the slaughter. He's already taken a hit because of the matriarchs." Caspel raised an eyebrow. "And I hear tell there have been two attempts on his life so far. Something about a bounty on his detached head being offered by Cressen Stone?"

I gave the director my best innocent smile before I changed the subject. "What about the space above Indrana? We've got eight of 2nd Fleet's ships."

"You do, Majesty, but he recovered that number with the ships that defected from Home Fleet. Seven were destroyed in the fight before Admiral Smith retreated. Nine of them backed Admiral Shul in the fight, though I'm hearing from my operative that at least one ship and possibly as many as three are so badly damaged as to be out of commission."

"Your operative? They were supposed to get out, Caspel."

"I know, Majesty." Caspel's look was grim. "They deemed it of greater importance to stay, and while I am angry with them for not following orders, I can't deny the logic behind the decision."

"The information they've passed on has been invaluable.

We've been able to prepare for several air strikes because of it," Alice said.

Running my tongue over my teeth, I considered the next question before I voiced it. The moment it was out in the air I couldn't take it back, and as ruthless as it was I didn't see anyone in the room actually arguing with me about it.

Caspel waited patiently; the weight of his eye on me spoke to the possibility he'd already thought of what I was about to ask.

"Caspel, is your operative in a position to kill Admiral Shul?"

Admiral Hassan's intake of air was barely audible. Alice, true to her upbringing, gaped at me. Taz smiled, a slow feral thing that was a near mirror of Caspel's look.

"They can, Majesty, should we choose to go down that path." As reprimands went, it wasn't more than a slap and it rolled right off me. I'd put a bounty on Phanin because I wanted him to know I was coming. If someone got lucky, that was just a bonus. Admiral Shul wasn't getting the same warning. I wanted him to know who was responsible when he was choking on his own blood.

"We're already on that path. They started us down it in the first place. Tell your operative to be ready. When we show up, I want him dead."

"What about Phanin and Wilson, Majesty?"

Before I could answer, Admiral Hassan jerked and swore. "Majesty, there's another incoming com link from Pashati. It looks like it's coming from the palace."

"Keep Caspel up, I want him to see this. Can we do it so they can't see him?"

Inana nodded.

"Emmory, behind me. Everyone else out of the picture. I don't care what happens, keep your mouths shut." I checked my reflection in the mirror and then straightened my shirt before signaling to Hassan.

"Your Imperial Majesty, what a pleasure at last." The man on the screen sketched a bow that matched the mockery in his voice. Wilson was tall and broad-shouldered, his gray hair cut short and his piercing blue eyes set deep into his lined face.

"I'm afraid I don't know your name," I said.

Malice flickered in his eyes. "Of course you do. Wilson works as good as anything, and you know as well as I do, *Cressen Stone*, that the names we choose for ourselves are sometimes better than what we had before."

"Where's Phanin?"

"Busy." Wilson waved his right hand. "So much to do to run an empire. He's happy to do it, which is why I picked him in the first place. I don't have the time."

"What are you busy with?"

"Destroying your empire." Wilson dropped his voice into a conspiratorial whisper. "And before you threaten to run off and tell Phanin about it, he knows. The New Indranan Empire will look nothing like what you Bristol bitches have mangled for the last fifteen centuries."

*"Keep him talking, Majesty. His arrogance is getting the better of him,"* Emmory subvocalized over our private com link.

"What's your problem with my family, Wilson? Sounds personal."

"Oh, so very personal, Cressen. Personal enough to drive me to spend a fortune to wipe your family from existence. And I'm close." His smile was vicious. "So very close."

"You've been trying to kill me for a while now. Seems like I'm the *kabab mein haddi*."

"Yes, the bone in the meatball, so I've learned. At first it was extremely annoying, I confess. But now I've come to see this as a perfect culmination of years of work. I've expanded the scope of my plan, and all for you. I want you to watch everyone you've ever cared about die before I finally kill you. I like the poetry of it."

He jerked Clara into view of the camera and I heard the gasps from behind me that were quickly stifled, but I kept my own face like stone. She was disheveled and obviously injured, the left side of her face matted with blood.

"I'll find them all," Wilson snarled. "And one by one I'm going to put them down. You can't stop me. You can't save them."

Clara's eyes met mine and her pain-induced stupor vanished. She slammed her elbow into Wilson's gut, folding him over.

"Hail—" Whatever she shouted to me was muffled by the scuffling and ended with the awful sound of a gun being fired.

I forced myself not to turn away as Clara's body crumpled out of sight.

"I am going to kill you," I said, surprising myself with how calm my voice was. "I will have you on your knees begging for your life and it will be a pleasure to deny you any mercy."

Wilson smiled and wiggled bloody fingers at me. Then his screen went black.

I looked at Caspel's screen. Alice was weeping into Taz's shoulder, and he held her close with a hand in her black hair. Sorrow etched itself over Caspel's face and I bit down hard on my tongue to hold my own tears at bay.

"They're mine, Caspel. If someone has a shot, take it, but otherwise don't touch them."

"Yes, ma'am."

Taz looked up from Alice, his mouth tight with pain. "Hail, I'm—"

"Take care of her. Tell our people I'm coming home."

The story continues in . . .

***Book Three of the Indranan War***

Keep reading for a sneak peek!

# ACKNOWLEDGMENTS

I wrote *Behind the Throne* in three months and then refined the story over the course of six years with a hell of a lot of input and support from a ton of people. *After the Crown* came together in the same whirlwind three months but with a lot less time for additional fiddling.

That said, I am eternally grateful for the support of my family and friends during what was admittedly a stressful and chaotic time. Without you I couldn't have done this. "I love you" isn't a strong enough phrase to convey the depth of emotion I feel. Thanks for feeding me, for understanding when I turned down invitations because I had to write, for checking in, for forgiving my absence in both physical presence and emotional support.

To my little family—Don, Ben, and Dex. We've had a rough time of it; I hope we're through the worst of it and can sit in the sun for a while.

My critique partners kept up as best as they could with the breakneck pace. Many, many thanks to Lisa and Ana for your emotional support and insight. Thanks also to C.J. for all your love and for being there right when I needed you, I love you. You kept me afloat through a really dark time.

# ACKNOWLEDGMENTS

Andrew Zack is the best agent in the world. Thanks for handling all the "other stuff" so I could focus on writing.

Kelly O'Connor, Ellen Brady Wright, and Jenni Hill at Orbit books are a fantastic team, and I count myself lucky to have such amazing women in my corner.

I'd like to specifically thank Beena Gohil for beta reading and being a fan of this story from the beginning. She's responsible for a number of great things in this series; all the mistakes belong to me. And thanks to my good friend Abby for her advice on how to kill someone just enough while still keeping them slightly alive.

To the folks at Happy Cats Haven for allowing me to come and sit in a roomful of kittens during a truly awful time in my life. You helped soothe a grieving heart. Thank you. Also thanks for our new crew of cats. Please visit www.happycatshaven.org for more about this Colorado Springs no-kill shelter doing great work.

To the crew at Starbucks Southgate5802 for providing me with Saturday morning coffee; and especially to Lion & Christine for your tireless support and excitement for my work. You are great friends and I'm so blessed to have you in my life.

And finally to you, my readers and fans. I'm so glad you loved *BTT* as much as I did and that you wanted to read this one also.

# extras

# about the author

K. B. Wagers has a bachelor's degree in Russian studies, and her nonfiction writing has earned her two Air Force Space Command Media Contest awards. A native of Colorado, she lives at the base of the Rocky Mountains with her husband and son. In between books, she can be found lifting heavy things, running on trails, dancing to music, and scribbling on spare bits of paper.

Find out more about K. B. Wagers and other Orbit authors by registering online for the free monthly newsletter at www.orbitbooks.net.

if you enjoyed
AFTER THE CROWN

look out for

# THE INDRANAN WAR:
# BOOK THREE

also by

## K. B. Wagers

# 1

The impact of fist to bag echoed up through my arm, a rhythmic shock in time with the beating of my broken heart.

*One, one, two. Backhand, two, elbow.*

Sweat dripped into my eyes, burning. The sting wasn't enough to erase the image of Clara Desai's lifeless body sliding to the floor.

A matriarch of the empire. The head of the council; a woman who'd been there my whole life and had welcomed me back home without the slightest hesitation.

She was dead, slaughtered in front of my eyes by the same man who was responsible for the death of my whole family.

I snarled and slammed my fist into the bag again.

Wilson had engineered it all, from the assassination of my father more than twenty years ago to when he'd looked me in the eye and told me he wouldn't stop the killing until everyone I cared about was dead.

Then he'd killed Clara.

*One, one, two. Backhand, two, elbow. Elbow.* I grabbed

the bag and rammed my knee into it twice with a scream of rage, backing off only to wipe the sweat from my face before I surged forward again.

"How long has she been at that?" Zin's question floated through the air to my ears.

"About an hour," Cas replied.

"She looks ready to drop. Why haven't you stopped her?"

"Emmory wouldn't."

"Don't look at me," Indula said. "I don't want to get punched today."

"Her Majesty's care and feeding isn't my area," Hao replied, but the laughter in his voice was tinged with the slightest hint of concern.

He was right to be concerned. Clara's death had hit us all hard, drowning out our euphoria from our defeat of the Saxon forces at Canafey.

I spun, my bare heel slamming into the bag, and the men fell silent.

"Hail."

I swung at Zin, my fist coming around in what would have been a brutal haymaker had it connected. As per usual, my BodyGuard leaned out of the way of my punch with an exhale. He caught my wrist on its way past, guiding it past his expressionless face.

Fool that I was, I tried to hit him with my other hand as I sailed by, but Zin was already gone, his grip on my wrist a fading memory. I spun, fists raised.

"You know I'm not going to fight you again," he said. His voice was too gentle, teasing aside the anger in my gut to get at the pain underneath. "Stop."

I stared at him and sucked in a lungful of air before I replied, "I can't."

*If I stop I'll fall apart.*

A sad smile flickered over his face. "I know, ma'am. Keep moving. Don't stop. You'll break apart in front of everyone and be no use at all. I know. I did just that when you needed me most."

"Zin—"

He shook his head, and I swallowed back my words. I'd ordered him to stay with Emmory when my *Ekam* had been shot—killed, if we were being honest. Zin had done what I told him, but the cost to my BodyGuard's confidence was written all over his face.

I filed it away to bring up with Emmory later. We still had some downtime, and it was time best spent healing—for all of us.

"Majesty," Zin said, his voice more formal. "Your *Ekam* would like to see you."

I took the out he handed me along with the towel Hao passed over. I didn't have the energy to fight with my BodyGuard and we both knew it. Zin could take me down even at my best, anyway, and right now I was far from my best.

The others formed up around us and the two Royal Marines inside the door of the gym snapped to attention, opening the doors as we approached. The other three Marines were on guard outside the gym—all five hand-picked by Emmory—in the last week as supplemental BodyGuards.

My rock star status had gone through the roof since the battle of Canafey, and only someone truly insane would make an attempt on my life right now. That didn't stop my *Ekam* from being excessively paranoid.

Rumors swirled about my part in the fight for Canafey, despite my best attempts to downplay my involvement and turn the attention to Admiral Hassan and the real heroes of the fight. The "Gunrunner Empress" of Indrana was on everyone's lips, and, if Hao was to be believed, in everyone's hearts.

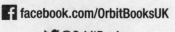